continued . . .

The Ghost Hunter Mystery Series

What's a Ghoul to Do?
Demons Are a Ghoul's Best Friend
Ghouls Just Haunt to Have Fun
Ghouls Gone Wild
Ghouls, Ghouls, Ghouls

The Psychic Eye Mystery Series

Abby Cooper, Psychic Eye
Better Read Than Dead
A Vision of Murder
Killer Insight
Crime Seen
Death Perception
Doom with a View
A Glimpse of Evil
Vision Impossible

GHOUL INTERRUPTED

A GHOST HUNTER MYSTERY

Victoria Laurie

AN OBSIDIAN MYSTERY

OBSIDIAN

Published by New American Library, a division of
Penguin Group (USA) Inc., 375 Hudson Street,
New York, New York 10014, USA
Penguin Group (Canada), 90 Eglinton Avenue East, Suite 700, Toronto,
Ontario M4P 2Y3, Canada (a division of Pearson Penguin Canada Inc.)
Penguin Books Ltd., 80 Strand, London WC2R 0RL, England
Penguin Ireland, 25 St. Stephen's Green, Dublin 2,
Ireland (a division of Penguin Books Ltd.)
Penguin Group (Australia), 250 Camberwell Road, Camberwell, Victoria 3124,
Australia (a division of Pearson Australia Group Pty. Ltd.)
Penguin Books India Pvt. Ltd., 11 Community Centre, Panchsheel Park,
New Delhi - 110 017, India
Penguin Group (NZ), 67 Apollo Drive, Rosedale, Auckland 0632,
New Zealand (a division of Pearson New Zealand Ltd.)
Penguin Books (South Africa) (Pty.) Ltd., 24 Sturdee Avenue,
Rosebank, Johannesburg 2196, South Africa

Penguin Books Ltd., Registered Offices:
80 Strand, London WC2R 0RL, England

First published by Obsidian, an imprint of New American Library,
a division of Penguin Group (USA) Inc.

First Printing, January 2012
10 9 8 7 6 5 4 3 2 1

Copyright © Victoria Laurie, 2012
All rights reserved

OBSIDIAN and logo are trademarks of Penguin Group (USA) Inc.

Printed in the United States of America

PUBLISHER'S NOTE
This is a work of fiction. Names, characters, places, and incidents either are the
product of the author's imagination or are used fictitiously, and any resemblance
to actual persons, living or dead, business establishments, events, or locales is
entirely coincidental.

The publisher does not have any control over and does not assume any re-
sponsibility for author or third-party Web sites or their content.

Acknowledgments

By my count this is my eighteenth book. Technically, it's the seventeenth to be published, but the eighteenth to be written. (Number seventeen—or eighteen depending on how you look at it—will be out in February.)

Anyway, the point is that I've written a buttload of books. Not as many as Barbara Cartland or Nora Roberts, mind you . . . but still, a buttload. Throughout most of them, I've acknowledged not only those people who've helped make that book a reality, but also those souls who've inspired characters and plots. To that end, I'm quite blessed. I'm surrounded by amazingly colorful people and I love showcasing them in fun ways—well, fun ways to me; maybe not always fun to them (just ask my sister . . . ahem!). Still, on the whole, they've all been incredibly good sports about it.

So while I list here the names of those wonderful folks who've assisted with the process of bringing Abby and M. J. to life, remember that many of them have often given more to the process than they bargained for!

To my amazing, dedicated, and incredibly supportive editor, Sandra Harding, who is just about the most gracious and talented woman I know: Thank you, Sandy, for all your time, effort, and insight. I absolutely adore both you and the opportunity to work with you.

Jim McCarthy, my agent, muse, and friend. True story about Jim: midway through this book I called him, complaining that I'd run out of new neuroses for Gilley. Without missing a beat he replied, "Did I ever tell you about the time I had a really bad headache on a plane and convinced myself that I was having a stroke, to the point that I spent most of the flight in the bathroom making sure I could raise and lower both eyebrows?" If you love Gilley like I do, then you may also have Jim McCarthy to thank.

Michele Alpern, my awesome and fantabulous copyeditor (who is probably right now itching to fix the word fantabulous!). Michele is so good that I refuse to be assigned to anyone else. I believe she walks on water.... Mostly, she just keeps me honest and makes sense of the prose. (Trust me, walking on water is less of a miracle!)

Clair Zion—my publisher extraordinaire! This woman is an absolute marvel, and I'm so grateful to huddle under her umbrella. Especially if it's an L. L. Bean umbrella. (Haha! Claire, that one's just for you!)

Kaitlyn Kennedy—my publicist and a veritable fountain of bubbly enthusiasm. You cannot talk to this talented young lady without feeling jazzed, energized, and enthused about getting the word out. Thanks, Kaitlyn. You've definitely made a difference!

Finally, a few personal mentions: My own Team Laurie, namely, Katie Coppedge and Hilary Laurie, who keep me firmly ensconced in a happy bubble of love and support, where I get to work without interruption. Thank you for creating such a secure and happy space for me. I love you both.

Also, some of my trusted inner circle should be noted here too: Nora, Bob, and Mike Brosseau; Karen Ditmars; Leanne Tierney; Neil and Kim Mahoney; Betty and Pippa Stocking; Shannon Anderson; Silas Hudson; Juan Tamayo; Ric Michael; Thomas Robinson; Jackie Barrett; Suzanne Parsons; Molly Boyle; and the woman who started it all, Martha Bushko. Love and special thanks to each and every one of you.

Chapter 1

I've always believed in ghosts. Actually, I had no choice in the matter. My childhood was full of encounters with disembodied voices, strange blue flashes, flickering shadows at the edge of my peripheral vision, and odd-looking orbs appearing right over my head.

And then, of course, my mother died and her ghost came to see me.

I was eleven going on twelve when her cancer finally won the war it'd waged so savagely against her. I knew the instant that she passed, even though every adult in my world had tried to shield me from the knowledge that it was coming. I remember playing with my new best friend, Gilley Gillespie, on the back porch of his house in beautiful Valdosta, Georgia. The memory of that day is as clear as if it happened yesterday.

Even back then his mother had indulged Gilley's

rather effeminate tastes. Gil had one of the best collections of Barbie and Ken dolls you've ever seen and we played with those dolls almost constantly.

In fact, on that beautiful early fall morning twenty-odd years ago, that's exactly what we were doing. While Gilley was setting Ken up on a blind date with G.I. Joe, I'd been happily working Barbie into a new pencil skirt, and just like that, I knew my mother was gone.

I remember dropping the Barbie and getting to my feet, the shock from the certainty of Mama's passing crushing something fragile inside of me. I couldn't breathe, couldn't move, and I certainly couldn't think past the terrible heartache building inside me.

My vision had clouded and stars had begun to dance in front of my eyes and I felt myself sway on wobbly knees. Somewhere nearby, I could sense that Gilley had noticed my strange posture and was calling my name, but I was unable to reply, or even acknowledge him. I felt like I was dying, and I didn't know how I would ever be able to live in a world without my mother. My only thought was to pray that she'd somehow find a way to stay with me.

And then, as if by some miracle, my silent prayer had been answered and my mother appeared standing in the doorway right in front of me.

"Breathe, Mary Jane," she'd said softly, coming quickly to my side. "It's okay, dumplin'. Just breathe."

I'd managed to take a very ragged breath, and with it my vision had cleared. I'd blinked and she hadn't vanished and that crushing heartache inside me eased. Maybe I'd gotten it wrong? Maybe she hadn't died after all?

"I have to go away for a spell, sweetheart," she'd said, that Southern lilt in her speech so sweet and caring.

"Mama?" I'd said as she'd knelt down in front of me and placed her warm hands on the sides of my cheeks.

"I'm so sorry I couldn't stay with you, Mary Jane," she'd whispered tenderly, bending in to kiss my forehead. And then she'd looked me right in the eyes and added, "I know what you can see, and I know what you can hear. I also know that your daddy and your nanny, Miss Tallulah, don't want to believe that you're a special gifted child, and not just imaginin' things. But you are special, dumplin'. I've known it from the day you were born. And during this whole time I been fightin' the cancer, I've known in my heart that if I couldn't beat it, then you'd still be able to hear me when I come round to visit with you.

"I'll never really leave you, puddin'," she'd assured me when I'd started to cry. "Anytime you need me, you just call out to your mama and I'll come, so don't be scared and don't be sad, you hear?"

I'd nodded with a loud sniffle, trying hard to be brave for her, and she'd let go of me and stood up. I'd noticed then how beautiful she'd looked. How radiant and gloriously healthy she'd seemed. Such a far cry from the bone-thin pale woman who'd occupied her bed for the last year.

A little gasp from behind me had told me that Gilley could see her too. She'd looked at him then, and she'd said, "Now, Gilley Gillespie, you don't be afraid neither. I need you to stay close to my Mary Jane, you hear? You be a good friend to her, 'cause I believe she'll be needin' a real good friend for a spell."

"Yes, ma'am," Gil had squeaked obediently.

And then my mother had looked one last time at me with such tenderness and love that I'd nearly shattered inside. She'd blown me a kiss, mouthed, "I love you," and then she'd vanished into thin air.

Gilley and I had never once spoken about that morning, and I carried the memory of it like a safely guarded secret. It was such a bittersweet memory that to tell anyone about it might forever taint it in some way, which is why I told no one, and I pushed it to the back of my thoughts to keep it safe and pure.

So, I couldn't imagine why, after all these years, I'd be dreaming about it on the eve of leaving Ireland for Dunkirk to film the next segment of our reality-TV show, *Ghoul Getters*, but here I was all grown up now having a dream about visiting that same porch back in Valdosta, which was once again scattered with Barbies, Ken dolls, and tiny clothes, and there was my mother, standing in the doorway, looking every bit as lovely as I remembered.

"Hello, Mary Jane," she said softly, almost shyly.

I blinked—just like when I was eleven. "Mama?"

My mother stepped forward, her smile filling up the room and my heart. "I've been watchin' you," she said, with a twinkle in her eye. "My, what a lovely lady you've turned into!"

I opened my mouth to speak, but the emotion of seeing her was too much and the words just wouldn't come.

Mama was kind enough to ignore that and simply stepped closer. Taking my hand, she said, "I am so proud of you, Mary Jane. You just light me up with how smart you are and how courageous you've become. Why, I remember when you were afraid of your own shadow!"

I swallowed hard and attempted a smile. In recent years I'd played on my natural psychic-medium talents, and become a credible ghostbuster. While working on the *Ghoul Getters* show, I'd faced and fought back against some of the most fearsome poltergeists you could ever imagine.

"Lord, Mary Jane!" my mother exclaimed knowingly. "I've watched you tackle murderous spirits, and vengeful witches, and now even a phantom!"

My chest filled with the pride and love from my mother. But just then her beaming face turned serious, and she seemed to hesitate—as if she was about to choose her next words carefully. "There is a mission about to be offered to you that I know you'll accept, honey child. One that involves the most horrendous evil imaginable."

I blinked again. Was she talking about the ghosts in the haunted village in Dunkirk—the next place on the *Ghoul Getters* agenda? "I've already read the literature," I said, trying to reassure her. "This time I'm going in prepared, and honestly, Mama, I don't think it's anything we can't handle."

My mother squeezed my hand, however, and sighed heavily. "Nothing can prepare you for this, Mary Jane. But I know better than to try and talk you out of it. Sam has come to me, you know."

I shook my head, utterly confused. Was she talking about the deceased grandfather of my fellow ghostbuster and current boyfriend, Heath? "You mean, Sam Whitefeather?"

My mother nodded. "He's tellin' me he's your new spirit guide."

I smiled. Sam had made himself noticeable to me shortly after I'd met his grandson, and since then he'd worked hard to keep me from getting too beat up during our ghost hunts.

"He needs your help," my mother continued. "He wants my blessin' before he asks you to help his people. I've seen how Sam's been lookin' out for you, and how he's even saved your life a time or two. For that, I'm truly grateful, but I just don't know that I can give my blessin' on this."

"Mama," I said, trying to sort through this cryptic bundle of information and decipher why my mother looked so uncharacteristically worried. "I don't understand. Are you telling me Sam won't be coming with us to Dunkirk?"

My mother didn't answer me. Instead she stroked my hair, stared deep into my eyes as if she was considering telling me more, and then abruptly looked over her shoulder. I followed her gaze and saw that Sam Whitefeather was now standing in the doorway. He seemed to be waiting for something like an invitation or permission to enter the room.

"May I, Maddie?" he asked, bowing formally to my mother.

Without answering him, my mother turned back to me and cupped my face in those familiar warm hands. "Stay safe, Mary Jane," she whispered, leaning in to kiss me on the forehead. "And under no circumstances are you to even *think* about joining me for a very, *very* long time, you hear?"

I nodded, still wondering what this was all about, but my mother turned then and moved away from me. "Mama, wait!" I called after her, but she simply walked over to Sam, placed a gentle hand on his arm, and said, "Protect her as much as possible or you'll have me to answer to, Samuel Whitefeather."

And then she was gone.

It was another moment before I could tear my eyes away from the place where she'd been standing to look directly into Sam Whitefeather's grim-looking face. "What's this all about?" I managed to ask.

Sam studied me for several moments, as if he was privately weighing whether or not to fill me in. "My grandson is about to receive a call. His uncle has been murdered."

I gasped. "Oh, no!"

Sam's shoulders sagged a little. "I didn't know until it was too late, M. J. The demon used dark magic to obscure itself from us, and by the time we understood that it was free, my son was dead."

My hand flew to my mouth. "Oh, Sam! I'm so, so sorry!"

Vaguely I remembered Heath talking at length about his three uncles, and I wondered which one of them had been murdered. I knew his favorite uncle was Milton, who'd been like a second father to Heath, and I held my breath hoping that it wasn't him.

"He's stuck," Sam said sadly, referring to the murdered man. "I've tried with our ancestors to reach out to him, but he's been through a terrible trauma and he's trapped now by his own fear."

I opened my mouth to assure him that Heath and I would certainly do what we could to help the poor man's soul cross over, but Sam held up his hand. "I know you're going to volunteer to do what you can," he said to me. "But I want you to know what you're getting into by volunteering."

"What am I getting into, Sam?"

My spirit guide sighed, as if the weight of the spirit world now rested on his shoulders. "There's a terrible evil afoot amongst my people. It'll kill again. And it'll keep killing until every last descendant from my tribe is wiped from your world."

"Sounds serious."

"It is."

"How do we stop it?"

"You must find the person who now controls it, and you must kill them."

I sucked in a breath. *What* had he just asked me to do? "You're joking!" And when Sam's serious expression didn't falter, I backed away from him. "Sam!" I said. "I can't *kill* someone! That's murder!"

"No, M. J., in this case it's definitely not murder. This demon can only be summoned by a willing and evil soul. Sending the person to jail won't stop the killings, and if you don't do as I say, then the demon will rise again and again until it kills all my children and grandchildren."

I was shaking my head vehemently. I wouldn't do it. Hell, I *couldn't* do it.

"And," Sam added, "once it's killed all of my family, it will come after you."

"Me?!" I squeaked. "Why *me*?!"

"Because I'm your spirit guide, and like it or not, M. J., you are now a member of my tribe."

Sam seemed to gather himself then and he began to move over to the doorway. "Tell my grandson what I've told you," he said over his shoulder. "He's about to have a terrible morning. Heath and his uncle Milton were very close. Heath won't be much help to you as you work to change your plans, but he must participate in bringing down the demon and the person who controls it."

My mouth fell open. Sam was assuming a lot right now, but my mind was so muddled with his statements and the visit from my mother that I was having a hard time coming up with a reply.

Sam paused then in the doorway and turned back to me. "The others may choose not to come along," he said. "But Gilley must accompany you. Your mother was right all those years ago when she left you in his care. He'll do what's necessary to help keep you safe. And so will I."

With that, Sam disappeared and I woke up to a ringing telephone.

Climbing out of my slumber with the dream still very much in my thoughts, I heard Heath's hand drop heavily on the phone and a moment later his throaty voice said, "Yeah?"

My eyes flew open and my heart began to hammer hard in my chest. Heath was lying on his side with his back to me. I sat up and leaned over him to try to get his attention. "Heath!" I whispered urgently, knowing what he was about to learn.

Heath's eyes were closed; he was clearly still half-asleep. "Ari?" Heath said, his eyes blinking a little. "Ari, is that you? Why're you crying?"

I squeezed his arm. "Please, honey! Give me the phone!" I didn't want him to hear the terrible news like this—half-asleep and jarred awake. I wanted him to have a minute to brace himself.

But it was too late. In the next moment I heard Heath suck in a breath and he sat up so fast that I was tossed to the side. "No!" he gasped into the phone. "Ari, there's got to be a mistake! Not Milton!"

I watched with pain in my heart as the caller repeated the information and Heath's handsome face seemed to crumple in on itself. His grief was quick and total.

I eased the phone out of his hand and spoke to the caller, but Ari—whoever that was—wasn't there. I could hear the phone being passed to someone else, a man who didn't identify himself but asked me who I was. I told him and then said that Heath couldn't talk right now, but that we'd call back soon for more details. After hanging up the phone, I just hugged Heath for a very long time. I know about losing a loved one better than most people my age, and I also know what a hug from someone you care about can do to ease the terrible grief.

Later, while Heath packed, I went in search of Gilley, our *Ghoul Getters* producer, and the rest of the crew, already bracing myself for the argument to follow. They wouldn't be happy that we'd have to put Dunkirk on hold, but I'd make sure they knew they had little choice in the matter. I was going with Heath to New Mexico to attend his uncle's funeral and figure out who or what had killed him. And if the other members of my special team wanted to tag along while we kicked some demon butt, all the better.

Heath, Gilley, and I landed at the tiny Santa Fe airport around midnight. I couldn't tell you the day; I'd lost all sense of time. I know only that when I looked at the clock on the airport wall and saw that both hands were pointing straight north, I felt a shiver of foreboding go through me.

Next to me, Gilley checked his pulse, then reached for my hand to lift it to his forehead. "Do I feel hot to you?"

In our struggle west to Santa Fe, we'd had the misfortune of spending forty-eight solid hours at Chicago

O'Hare, stranded by a snowstorm. As all the local hotels were booked to the rafters, Gilley had been sent out as a scout in the jam-packed terminal to find us a spot to settle down for the long wait until we could get a flight out. He'd come back triumphantly announcing that he'd found room for the three of us at the back of the terminal right next to four businessmen. I wondered what the catch was and soon discovered why there was available space in such a coveted section of the airport. The four businessmen were all sick with the flu and each of them was sneezing, coughing, wheezing, and hacking, creating a wide berth around them. Of course we discovered this only after we'd collapsed on the floor exhausted and spent, too tired to get up and look for something else. We kept as much distance from the men as we could, but I have to admit that it was like hanging out with four of the seven dwarfs, Hackey, Wheezy, Coughy, and Sneezy.

Gil, of course, had positioned himself as far away from the dwarfs as he could get—using me as a human shield—and oddly, Heath and I had suffered no ill effects, but Gil now had a headache and a slight temperature. "I'm sure you're fine," I told him. I'm a pretty good liar when I need to be.

"I don't feel warm?" he asked.

I eyed Gilley's pale face and the dark circles under his eyes. "You feel and look just fine."

Gil rubbed at his temples again. "Then this is bad," he whispered.

"What's bad?"

"A headache this killer isn't normal, M. J."

"You're probably just dehydrated."

"I had two bottles of water on the plane."

"Then it's probably exhaustion," I told him, willing

the baggage carousel to start moving so we could get our bags and be on our way.

"I slept at the airport and the last three hours of our flight," he said, more to himself than to me. I tensed. I had a feeling where this was headed. Sure enough, a moment later Gilley got right up into my personal space. "Do you think I'm having a stroke?"

I tried not to laugh. Really I did . . . but it was impossible not to. "Gil," I said once I'd gotten control of myself. "You're not having a stroke."

"How do *you* know?" he demanded, inching his face closer to me. He then raised one eyebrow, lowered it, and did the same with his other eyebrow. "Did both my eyebrows move?" he asked me. Before I could even answer, he gasped again, "Ohmigod! Is my speech slurred?"

"Gil," I said levelly.

He slapped his cheeks one at a time. "I think my face is going numb!"

"Gil," I repeated a little more firmly.

Gilley extended both arms and wiggled his fingers. "It's my right side!" he squeaked. "It's losing feeling!"

"Gil!"

Heath came up next to me after visiting the restroom, and Gilley nearly jumped him. Grabbing him by the lapels of his coat, he cried, "Heath! Heath!"

Heath pulled his head back and mimicked, "Gilley, Gilley."

"Brace yourself," I muttered.

Gil pulled Heath closer. "Is one side of my mouth sagging?"

Heath eyed me in a "What the . . . what?" kind of way.

"He thinks he's having a stroke," I said.

"My speech is slurred," Gilley told him. "And I can't

feel one side of my face! And my right eyebrow won't go up!"

"It's up now," Heath told him. "Both of 'em are up, actually."

Gilley's brow plummeted into a deep furrow. "Gah!" he spat, and stomped off to the restroom, likely to have a look in the mirror and see for himself.

"What was *that* about?" Heath asked while we watched Gilley's dash to the men's room. "Or don't I want to know?"

"He's got a headache," I said. Like that would explain everything.

"Ahhh," Heath said. "And he went with stroke over tumor?"

"Yeah, I know. It could've gone either way with him."

"Heath!" someone behind us called.

We turned to see a couple hurrying toward us. The woman was tall and lean with beautiful angular features. I knew right away she and Heath were related, especially when she launched herself into his arms and hugged him fiercely.

I stood there awkwardly with the man who'd accompanied her—he was also tall, with dark hair, black eyes, and a warm smile. He was dressed in surgical scrubs and a thick sheepskin coat. "Hi," he said, extending his hand to me. "I'm Brody Perez."

I returned his smile and extended my own hand. "M. J. Holliday."

Heath and the woman stepped back from each other and I was touched to see both of them crying a little. "It's been too long!" she said to him, still holding his hand tightly.

Heath turned to me. "Em," he said, using his new

nickname for me. "This is Arianna Perez. My cousin, but really more like my sister."

Arianna let go of Heath's hand and stepped forward to greet me with a hug. "I've heard *so* much about you, M. J.!" she gushed. "And I'm so glad to finally meet you!"

I'm not really a hugger, and I'd heard almost nothing about Arianna other than she was the one who'd broken the news about Milton to Heath. Still, I went with it, patting her on the back and saying something like, "Yes, but what a shame we had to meet under such sad circumstances."

She stepped away from me and nodded somberly, wiping at another tear. Just then Gilley joined our little group. "What'd I miss?" he asked.

"Gilley," Heath said, "meet Ari and Brody Perez. My cousins."

Gilley shook Ari's hand first, and when he swiveled to take Brody's, he must have caught sight of the surgical scrubs. "Are you a doctor?" he asked abruptly.

I barely held in a groan. "Here we go," I muttered to Heath.

Brody chuckled. "I am. I work at Santa Fe Indian Hospital."

Gilley sagged against him dramatically. "Oh, thank you, Baby Jesus!" he said. "Dr. Brody, I'm having a stroke."

Positioning myself behind Gilley, I shook my head vigorously to gain Brody's attention, then made swirling motions with my finger near my ear.

Poor Brody looked like a deer caught in headlights. "Uh . . . ," he said.

"No, *really*, Doctor," Gilley insisted. "I am. My speech is slurred and I think my right side is going numb."

"Your speech is slurred?" Brody asked, looking from Gilley to me (still shaking my head and making the "He's crazy!" sign), then back to Gil again.

"Yes, my speech is slurred!" Gilley said, like it was obvious. "Can't you tell?"

"No."

"Well, I have a headache too," Gil said, like that was *the* defining symptom for a stroke.

Brody appeared to be a nice guy, because he put on his serious face and said, "What other symptoms are you having?"

Gilley rattled off about twenty, including the foot cramp he'd gotten that morning.

Brody said, "Well, you do look a little pale to me."

Gilley turned to glare pointedly at me, before returning his attention back to the good doctor.

"I have a good test for patients who think they might be having a stroke, though," he said.

"A CT scan?" Gil asked hopefully.

I shook my head vigorously behind Gilley's back again.

"Uh . . . no," Brody said. "It's more like, can you smile and say your name at the same time?"

"Of course I can."

The corners of Brody's mouth quirked. "No, I mean, can you do that for me right now?"

I couldn't see Gil, but I knew he was flashing his pearly whites in a tight smile as he said, "Gilley Gilleshpie."

Brody pointed at him. "Well, Gilley Gilleshpie, I feel confident that you're not having a stroke."

"Gillespie," Gil corrected.

"What's that?"

"My last name. It's Gillespie, not Gilleshpie."

"Okay, then," Brody said, and I could tell he was quickly tiring of my neurotic best friend.

Blissfully, at that moment the baggage carousel began to turn. We got our bags and gear and wearily headed for the exit.

Looking around the largely empty terminal, Ari asked Heath, "Aren't there more of you?"

"Our producer and the rest of the TV crew had to fly back to L.A. to iron out some contract stuff now that we're switching networks," Heath explained.

"And they didn't want to come to a funeral," Gilley muttered under his breath so that only I could hear. I was about to elbow him, but the poor guy really did look pale. I knew he was likely coming down with the same flu that had plagued the dwarfs in Chicago.

A bit later when we were all piled in Brody's roomy SUV, Ari turned in her seat to peer at us and asked, "Where to?"

I looked at Heath expectantly. "Aren't we staying at your place?"

Even in the dim light I could see him redden. "It's being remodeled. My cousin's been working on it while I've been away, and he sent me a text right before we boarded that it isn't ready yet."

"Which is Ray's way of saying he hasn't touched it since you left," Ari quipped.

Heath's eyes darted to her. "You've seen it?"

Ari nodded. "He's taken it down to the studs, Heath, but he's done nothing else."

Heath's mouth pressed into a thin line. "That idiot," he grumbled.

"I told you not to hire him," Ari said.

"He's family," Heath told her. "I had to hire him."

"Yeah, well, your poor mom hasn't had a space to call her own since October."

"I thought your mom had her own place?" I said.

Heath rubbed his eyes tiredly. "She sold it and we thought it would only take a month or two for Ray to finish. She's been staying in Phoenix with my stepdad's sister."

I thought it odd that none of the Whitefeathers had offered Heath's mom a place to stay, but I had an inkling that Heath's family had quite a few lines of contention within it, so I didn't ask. Heath would probably tell me when he was ready.

"Is there a hotel or something close by?" Gil asked. I knew he just wanted to get somewhere so that he could lie down.

I fished around in my purse and came up with some headache medicine for him along with the last of my bottled water. "Take two," I instructed.

"I guess we could stay anywhere close," Heath said while I tended to Gil. "There's that Holiday Inn on Cerrillos, right?"

"Holiday Inn it is," Brody said, placing the car in drive.

"When's the funeral?" Gilley asked abruptly, handing me back the empty water bottle.

"The day after tomorrow, Gil," Heath said. Clearing his throat uncomfortably, he added, "But it's for tribal members only."

Gilley's eyes widened and he opened his mouth to say something (probably something inappropriate), so I quickly said, "Of course, Heath. We understand. Don't we, Gil?"

Gil's eyes glared at me, but his mouth formed a toothy smile. "Gilley Gilleshpie," he said softly.

I focused back on Heath and took his hand. "Will that give your mom enough time to get here?"

Heath nodded. "She's still trying to find a cheap fare, but, yeah, come hell or high water, she'll be here."

Out of the corner of my eye, I caught Ari and her husband exchanging a look.

"What?" Heath asked, obviously catching it too.

Ari tucked a long lock behind her ear. "My dad doesn't want your mom to come," she said meekly.

Heath reflexively tightened his grip on my hand and I winced. "I expected as much from Uncle Vernon. What does Rex say?" he asked.

Ari lifted her eyes then and smiled. "He says my dad's a mule and of course both you and your mom should be there."

The tension of Heath's hand around mine lessened. "Oh, we'll be there," he said stubbornly.

Ari's smile widened. "*We* want you there. And my dad's only got one vote. Aunt Bev's is the important vote and she definitely wants you and Aunt Serena there. I think if your mom just shows up, no one in the tribe is gonna complain. I mean, it's her brother after all."

Heath nodded, but there was still a stiff set to his shoulders. I didn't know what had happened within the Whitefeather family to cause such a rift, and I didn't really feel it was my place to ask about it. I wanted to give Heath time to tell me for himself. And I also knew that tonight was not the time to talk about such things. We needed to get some shut-eye before we all fell over from exhaustion.

At that moment Ari's cell phone chirped. I tried not

to listen as she took the call, but the rest of the car was quiet and there was no avoiding it.

"Hi, Ma," she said. "Yeah. We just picked him up. We're taking him to the Holiday Inn for the night so that he and his friends can get some sleep. What's that?"

I turned my head and looked out the window. The terrain was very dark, not even a hint of moonlight to give any description to the land we traveled past.

"No . . . ," I heard Arianna say. "When was the last time Molly heard from her?"

Heath took my hand again and brought it to his lips. "I'm glad you're here," he said.

I leaned in and gave him a quick kiss. "Me too."

"Has anyone called her work?" Arianna said.

My attention swiveled to the front of the car. Something seemed off.

"Maybe she stopped off for a drink or something and she can't hear her phone in the bar," Arianna said next.

I nudged my chin in her direction. "What's up?" I mouthed.

Heath turned his head and focused on his cousin. "Ari?" he whispered, and she looked over her shoulder at him. "Something wrong?"

She held up a finger and said, "Yeah, okay, Ma. Let me know when you hear from her, okay?"

"What's up?" Brody asked the moment she'd tucked her cell away.

"Beverly isn't home yet and Molly's worried."

Heath leaned over and whispered, "Bev's Milton's ex-wife, but the two were talking about reconciling right before Milton died. Molly is their daughter."

"Ah," I said.

Brody put on his turn signal and the bright lights of

the Holiday Inn lit up the car's interior with an unflattering glow. I could only imagine how fetching I must be in the harsh light after three straight days of traveling, airports, and only about seven hours' sleep total.

Brody helped us with our bags, and while Heath hugged and said good night to his cousin and her husband, I got us two rooms and a wake-up call for ten. It was now much closer to one a.m. than midnight and I was very much looking forward to those nine hours of sleep.

After collecting our key cards, I waited for Heath, waved to Ari and Brody, and tried to keep Gilley conscious long enough to see him to his room. That last task was a lot harder than you might think.

Finally, about fifteen minutes later, Heath and I were able to crawl under the sheets and sink into a wonderful slumber. I had no idea that it would be the last truly peaceful night's sleep I'd get for the next several days.

Chapter 2

The wake-up call came way too early for me. I crept my way out of the deep sleep I was in and reached out to knock the handle off the phone. "Shuddup!" I moaned, rolling over and pushing my face back into the pillow.

My body was still exhausted. My mind was still fried. And my mood was still grumpy. Fat load of good those nine hours had been.

I felt Heath roll over and lay his chest on my back, squishing me a little in the process, but I wasn't about to complain. I liked his weight on my back. "Morning," he said.

"Mmmf," I replied.

"I better hit the shower."

"Mmmf," I agreed.

Heath sighed. I could just feel the *thump*, *thump*,

thump of his heart drumming a beat against my back. "Feel like joining me?" he asked.

"Mmmf," I said wearily.

Heath chuckled. "I didn't think so. I'll be out in a few. You get a little extra sleep."

With that, he kissed my shoulder and I felt his weight lift off, leaving me cold without him. I sighed and tried to get a little more sleep, but Heath's phone rang and it startled me. In the bathroom I could also hear the water being turned on, and I decided not to call out to Heath. He deserved to take his shower in peace. I waited through all four rings for the call to go to voice mail, then sighed again and tried to will myself back to sleep.

Heath's phone gave off a loud chime and I opened one eye moodily. Voice mail.

Closing that eye, I thought sleepy, happy thoughts and just as I was starting to sink back into slumber again, there were three firm knocks on the door. My eyes flew open. "You gotta be kidding me," I grumbled. Sitting up on the bed, I called, "Who is it?"

"The clerk from the front desk, Ms. Holliday," said a male voice. "Your telephone is sending out a busy signal. Are you all right?"

I stared at the door incredulously. Was he serious? "I'm fine," I said tersely.

I could hear the guy clear his throat. "Yes, well, there's someone in the lobby wishing to speak with a Heath Whitefeather, and she believes he's staying with you in your room."

I scratched my head. Who? What? Huh? With a groan I got out of bed and said, "Hold on," then grabbed my sweatshirt and jeans. Tugging them on quickly, I trudged to the door to peek through the peephole. Some guy with salt-and-pepper hair was standing there all fidgety. I cracked the door open a smidge. "Say what, now?"

"Sorry to disturb you," he began, "But there's a woman in the lobby who says she's Mr. Whitefeather's cousin, and that she needs to speak to him right away. There's been a death in the family, ma'am."

I blinked and tried to focus on him. "Yeah," I said. "Their uncle was killed a few days ago."

It was the clerk's turn to look confused. "Oh," he said. "No, she said that her aunt died last night."

That got my attention. I opened the door wide and grilled the clerk. "What's this woman's name again?"

He looked down at a note he'd written to himself. "Arianna Whitefeather, ma'am."

That fit. "She said that Heath's aunt was dead?"

"Yes."

"You're sure she said *aunt* and not *uncle*?"

"Yes."

Behind me I heard the shower shut off and Heath began whistling. I swore softly. This was bad. Really, really bad.

"I'm sorry, ma'am," the clerk said, pulling my attention back, "but what should I tell the woman in the lobby?"

"Send her up to the room, please," I said, already turning to shut the door.

"Yes ma'am, I'll send her—" That's as far as he got before the door shut in his face. I'd have to apologize later.

I walked quickly to the bathroom and knocked softly. "Heath?"

He opened the door to reveal his naked glorious self, his shoulder-length wet hair slicked back away from his face, his toned shoulders and chest still dripping with water. "Change your mind?" he asked me, wrapping his arms around my waist playfully. "Because I can get back in, you know."

I opened my mouth to speak, but no words came out. I just stood there trying to tell him the terrible news, not knowing how to phrase it to soften the blow. "Oh, Heath," I said at last.

By now he knew something was up. "What's happened?" he asked, but I could only shake my head, at a loss for what to say. But Heath wasn't letting up. Cupping my face with his hands, he said, "M. J., whatever it is, just tell me."

I swallowed. "Your cousin's here."

"Which one?"

"Ari."

Heath leaned out of the bathroom and looked into the room. "Where?"

"In the lobby, but she's on her way up."

Heath blinked and his expression became playful again. "Aw, M. J., don't sweat it. She knows we're sleeping together."

I put my hands on his chest and looked him right in the eye. "It's your aunt," I said. "Ari's here to tell you about your aunt."

"Which aunt?"

It was my turn to blink. I had no idea. "I don't know, but, Heath, something bad has happened again and you need to brace yourself."

Just then there was an urgent knock on the door. Heath's head snapped in that direction and he hesitated ever so slightly before he let go of me and moved to answer it. Before he got there, he at least had the presence of mind to grab his jeans and put them on quickly.

I stood where I was in the doorway of the bathroom, wondering if I should stay or go. One look at Ari's face as she came into the room told me I should probably stay.

The poor woman was a wreck. She was sobbing, nearly in hysterics and gasping for breath. "I was on my way over to pick you up," she said, her voice thick and liquid, "when Brody called me and . . . Oh, Heath!"

"Who is it?" he asked, and I had to marvel at how calm and composed he seemed. "Ari, just tell me what's happened and who it is."

His cousin took a few more gulping breaths. "They came to tell Brody first," she began. "Bev didn't come home last night, and this morning Molly called me crazy with worry, so I got the word out and they found Bev's SUV about a mile away from the Pueblo on one of the back roads near the burial grounds. She was probably going to look at the grave site for Milton. . . ." Ari's voice trailed off here as she let out great gulping sobs before she could regain control again. "They said her SUV ran off the road and hit a tree. She didn't make it."

Heath staggered back and if I hadn't been behind him to catch him by the waist and prop him up, I think he might have fallen to the floor. He wrapped an arm around my shoulder and I squeezed him tight. It was a long time before anyone was able to speak.

"Who are 'they'?" Heath finally asked Ari.

"What?"

"You said 'they' said her car ran off the road and hit a tree. Who found her?"

"Pena and Cruz."

I didn't know who Pena and Cruz were, but Heath seemed to. He nodded, then let go of me and moved to wrap Ari in his arms, hugging her tightly while she cried and cried. Looking over his shoulder at me, his eyes revealed just how devastated he was. I knew that Ari had been like Heath's sister, and Milton had been something of a surrogate father to him. I thought that maybe Milton's ex-wife might still be considered his aunt, even though Milton and Bev had been technically divorced.

After a bit he stepped back from his cousin and said, "Let me throw on some clothes and we'll go." He then grabbed some folded jeans and a sweater from his suitcase and ducked back into the bathroom. I fished around in my own luggage for my last pair of clean jeans and a turtleneck sweater, and changed in front of Ari without worrying about modesty.

For her part, Ari just sat in a chair and stared numbly down at the floor. I really wished I could say something to take away even a bit of the pain, but nothing came to mind, so I just let her be.

Heath came out just as I was shrugging into my jacket and wordlessly we headed out of the room.

Once we were in the parking lot, I sent a text to Gilley that Heath and I had to take care of something and we'd be back soon. He'd need to sit tight until then.

When we got to Ari's car, Heath held his hand out for her keys. I was relieved; she was in no condition to drive. I hopped into the back of her small sedan and we were soon off again.

In the daylight, I had the opportunity to take in the passing landscape. I'd never been to the Southwest, and was surprised at the incredible beauty of Santa Fe. Vast expanses of relatively flat land fanned out from the highway, corralled by a huge purple mountain range in the distance. Grass was sparse, and most of the homes we passed looked like those adobe mud structures the Southwest is famous for.

It was all a far cry from the cottage feel of New England or the plantation classical-Greek-inspired architecture of my hometown of Valdosta, Georgia.

The three of us drove in silence, and the drive was fairly long. We made our way west along a well-paved highway, then north for a bit to a smaller two-lane road, and the scenery just got more breathtaking with every passing mile.

Finally, Heath turned down a road with a signpost at the entrance that read ZANTO PUEBLO. I had a moment to reflect that years ago the sign probably would have read ZANTO RESERVATION, and I was glad we'd come a little further in our sensitivity toward American Indians.

The road we turned onto was lined with windblown scrub and it inclined up slightly at first before reaching a much higher grade. We drove up into the heart of a small mountain, and I peeked over the side to see the edge falling away. After about ten more minutes we leveled out again, and Heath turned at a crossroads lined on all four sides with more of those adobe-styled homes and drove straight for an official-looking building with a sign indicating the Pueblo sheriff's office. He parked and turned to look back at me. "Will you stay here while Ari and I go in and figure out what's going on?"

I was surprised that I wasn't included, but I certainly wasn't going to protest. "Sure," I said.

"Thanks," Heath told me. "And please, don't get out of the car until I get back. I'll leave the heat on for you in case you get cold."

"Um . . . okay." I could feel my cheeks flush, because it felt like I was being treated like a little kid. I tried to push it off as Heath's anxiety after hearing about his aunt's death, but it still stung a little.

I watched while he and Ari headed inside and maybe I muttered something immature about being left behind, but whatever.

To distract myself, I reached for my cell and thought I'd call Gil to let him know what was going on, but his phone went straight to voice mail and the message said that his mailbox was full. "Crap," I said, tucking my cell away.

I eyed the area around the building. There didn't seem to be anyone about. Smoke from a nearby home curled out of a chimney, and behind one of the other homes a dog barked, but the small-looking village was eerily void of human activity.

I'm not sure if it was how still the place was or something else that gave me the creeps, but after a few minutes of sitting in the car alone with nothing to do, I noticed a definite shift in the atmosphere and I felt the hairs on the back of my neck rise and goose pimples form along my arms.

There was also the feeling of being watched— something I'm used to after several years in the ghost-busting business, but whoever was laying eyes on me now wasn't friendly. The palpable anger and menace floated around me like a foul breeze.

Working hard not to react, I kept my sixth sense alert, and focused on taking even breaths while remaining calm. I knew that I would only be feeling this way if whatever was lurking nearby was from the spirit realm, and negative forces can feed on your fear. It can give them a boost in energy and power, so whenever you encounter something creepy or scary, it is *very* important not to give in to your own fears. Just breathe through it the best you can.

I was so focused on my breathing that I didn't immediately hear the approach of a car until it pulled up next to me. With a jolt I looked up and realized it was a sheriff's vehicle with two passengers. The uniformed man in the driver's seat was closer to me and he got stiffly out of the car, his face a mixture of anger and something else I couldn't quite understand. What was even more odd was that his partner got out wearing the identical expression. Anger and something else. If I didn't know better, I'd have guessed it was fear.

The driver looked at the car I was in and I could tell he recognized it. Then he spotted me and his posture stiffened. I smiled and waved, but his brow lowered even more. He turned and said something I didn't catch to his partner, and they moved on inside.

"Friendly," I muttered when they went through the doors.

I sat back against the upholstery and twiddled my thumbs for several more minutes, wondering what was happening inside, when a tow truck rumbled up on the other side of me. Hitched to the back was a minivan with a smashed-in front end that gave me the shivers when I took in the damage.

The tow truck driver didn't seem to notice that I was inside Arianna's car, so I watched him surreptitiously. He got out and went into the station too, but when he got to the door, he did pause and look over his shoulder. What was strange was that he didn't look at me—he seemed to look at the vehicle he was towing, and I swore he gave an involuntary shudder before he turned again and headed inside.

I swiveled my head to peer again at the minivan hitched to the back of his truck. It was an older model that had definitely seen better days. The front of it was completely crumpled in—it was obvious it'd hit something big—probably a tree.

Immediately I knew that this must've been the vehicle Heath's aunt was driving when she went off the road. I had this compelling urge to get out of the car and take a look at the driver's side, but Heath had given me those explicit instructions about staying put, and I'd promised, so I didn't give in to the impulse.

But then I had an idea and glanced at the keys dangling from the ignition. Without dwelling on it, I wriggled my way into the driver's seat and put the car in reverse. Turning the wheel, I cruised over toward the parking slot next to the tow truck and crept along the side of the minivan, looking out the window at it to see what I could see.

My breath caught in my throat when I got to the driver's-side door. The front of the car was definitely a wreck, but what struck me most about the sight was the three long claw marks distinctly gouged into the metal from the edge of the driver's-side door all the way along to the middle of the minivan.

Now, I know you're thinking that those could have been scratches from a tree branch, but I knew different. I'd seen those exact same markings before on another ghostbust I'd done in San Francisco, and I knew they were the distinctive sign of a demon at work. By the thickness of each mark and the depth of its indentation, I was wagering this thing was a big demon. BIG.

And then I got that feeling again ... that creepy, something's-watching-you feeling, and the hair on the back of my neck rose and goose pimples formed along my arms and I started to shiver a little.

I swallowed hard and eyed the area. I couldn't tell from which direction the feeling was coming; it seemed to be everywhere. "Something wicked this way comes," I whispered to myself.

Then I backed out of the slot again and moved Ari's car back to its original space. After placing it in park, I shimmied my way over into the backseat again and waited nervously for Heath and his cousin. I also tried to cool my temper because my irritation over being made to wait in the car was really starting to cloud my judgment. I had to remember that Heath had just learned he now had two deaths in his family, so I couldn't allow myself to get all pissy about being made to wait in the car.

Still, it took another ten minutes for Heath and Ari to emerge. I was so relieved to see them, because that sinister feeling hadn't left and I knew I was still being watched. What surprised me was when I was watching Heath walk toward the car, holding his weeping cousin close around her shoulders, I saw his head snap up. I *knew* he'd just caught a whiff of the same foul energy swirling around the area.

His gaze went immediately to me, the concern evident in his eyes, and I forgave him immediately. I knew he must have had his reasons for keeping me behind and I was just glad he was back.

Heath quickened his step and moved his cousin to the passenger door, gently but firmly putting her inside before he closed the door and swept his eyes all around the group of nearby homes.

He then moved to the driver's-side door and before getting in, he looked at me again through the glass. I made a motion with two of my fingers, pointing them to my eyes and then pointing them out in a sweeping motion to let him know I felt it too.

Heath's lips pressed together and he got in the car without a word and backed out of the slot. "You okay?" he asked me when he'd turned the car around.

"I am now," I told him, deciding to wait until we were alone together to tell him about the demon marks on Beverly's minivan. That was something I definitely didn't want Ari to overhear—especially in her emotional state.

Heath's cousin sat huddled in her seat, her periodic sniffling letting me know that she was still crying. Heath drove along the sparsely populated road to the end, where a group of five houses were arranged in a sort of U. "Where's Brody?" Heath asked Ari, pulling into the drive of one of the houses at the top of the U.

"He's trying to get someone to cover his shift at the hospital," she told him. "He promised he'd be home soon."

Heath swiveled in the seat and seemed to consider me. "Em," he said, his voice low and quiet. "I'm sorry for leaving you in the car back there, but outsiders aren't welcome on the Pueblo without invitation, and they're not allowed inside one of our public buildings unless that invitation is by an elder. I wasn't thinking when I let you come along, and I couldn't let you come out of the car without causing you and me a lot of grief."

"Oh," I said, quite surprised. I'd never even thought his reasons were related to my possible trespass. "I'm sorry, Heath. If I'd have known, I would have stayed back at the hotel and waited for you."

Heath shook his head and I could see he was beating himself up a little. "It's not your fault," he said. "It's mine. Anyway, you're here now, and it'll take too long to drive you back. I've got a lot of family stuff to deal with, and I don't think my aunts and uncles are going to be too happy that I've brought a stranger into the mix on a day like today. I'm going to bring you in there and tell them you're here with me, and they'll probably let you stay. . . ."

Probably?

"But when you come in, don't be surprised if they're not exactly welcoming. Please don't react. Just stay as quiet as you can and don't say anything or call attention to yourself."

Arianna turned to me. "I'll stay right next to you," she assured me, and I was flooded with gratitude.

"Thank you, Ari," I said.

We got out of the car and Heath took my hand on one side and Ari came around to my other and looped her arm through mine. I felt a mixture of emotions— nerves, anxious hesitation, and warmth for both Heath and Ari, but especially for her because I knew how bad she was hurting and yet she still found a way to take care of me—a relative stranger.

We approached the house and the door opened even before we got to it. In the doorway was a large man, tall and barrel-chested with long gray hair and a wide flat nose. His gaze was sharp as an eagle's and as he leveled it at me, I would have withered under it had I not been propped up between Heath and Ari.

"Nephew," the older man said. His voice was deep and commanding and there was neither warmth nor coldness in the way he said the word.

"Uncle Vernon," Heath replied, oddly reflecting back

the same tone. If I didn't know better, I'd have guessed that Heath's feelings for this uncle were somewhat ambivalent.

"Who's this?" Vernon asked.

"M. J. Holliday," Heath told him. "She's with me."

Vernon stood blocking the doorway for a beat, and Heath didn't waver in his march toward the door. I seriously thought we were going to plow right into the old man, but at the last second Vernon backed his way inside and allowed us to pass.

As we walked by, I noticed two things: one, that Vernon seemed to snicker at us when we went past, and two, that Ari pointedly avoided looking at him altogether. I knew she was Heath's cousin, but at that moment I was so nervous I couldn't remember which of Heath's aunts or uncles she was directly related to.

The house smelled fragrant and earthy. Sage burned somewhere mixed with incense. I could hear the crackling of a fire too, and the gentle weeping of women and comforting words in a tongue I didn't recognize.

Ari let go of my arm so that we could all fit into the narrow hallway, but Heath continued to grip my hand firmly.

He led me straight through to the living room, where about two dozen people were all crammed into the space, including one terribly distraught young woman I'd put no older than nineteen. She wailed one word over and over, and there was a question mark at the end of the word. I didn't speak Pueblo, but I knew what she was saying nonetheless. "Why? *Why*?"

Two women tended to her. One held her and patted her back; another gently wiped away her tears. I had to blink a lot to hold back my own emotion.

"Heath!" I heard from across the room. A young man probably fourteen or fifteen jumped up from his seat at the hearth and dashed forward to hug my sweetheart.

Heath let go of my hand to catch and hug the young man back, and as all the eyes in the room turned first to Heath and then slowly over to me, I felt like I'd been cut adrift from my life raft.

"Hey, Eli," Heath said warmly. "How's it hanging?"

"I saw your show!" Eli said, stepping back to look up at him with pride. "It was awesome!"

I blinked. I wasn't aware that our show had aired yet, but then I remembered that *Haunted Possessions*, the first show Heath and I had done together, had been released the month before. That must have been what Eli was referring to.

"Did you?" Heath asked, and even though I could tell he tried to smile at the younger man, there was a stiff set to his shoulders, which let me know he was very distracted by all the tragedy his family had recently suffered.

Eli apparently wasn't as affected as the adults gathered around. "Maybe you could take me with you when you go on your next ghost hunt?"

"Eli!" Vernon barked, and the boy jumped. When he had his attention, Vernon growled, "This isn't the time or the place."

"Sorry, Uncle Vern," Eli said, and moved quickly back to the hearth.

I felt a slight pulling sensation on my energy and the image of Sam Whitefeather filled my mind. And then, something a bit extraordinary happened; I could literally see him across the room with his arms folded across his chest and a disapproving look on his face. He hadn't liked how Vernon had snapped at his grandson.

"Who's this?" a woman near Eli asked, and although her tone wasn't overtly rude, I could tell she didn't approve of my presence.

"This is M. J. Holliday, Grace," Heath said simply. "She's my girlfriend."

Every eye in the room turned to Heath and me. Most of them didn't look at all pleased to see a stranger at the gathering. Arianna took my arm again in a silent show of support. "We just came from the sheriff's station," she said. "Pena and Cruz had Bev's minivan towed and they're investigating the crash."

The eyes in the room shifted uneasily from me to Ari. "What did they tell you?" a man who looked very much like Sam asked. As if on cue I saw Sam's spirit glide over to stand next to the man.

Heath and Ari hesitated before answering him; instead they looked pointedly at the distraught woman sandwiched between two others. That had to be Molly, Beverly's daughter, I thought.

The two women tending Molly read between the lines and gently eased the poor girl to her feet and coaxed her down a hallway, probably toward one of the bedrooms. When she was well out of earshot, Heath said, "The skid marks show that Bev might have tried to avoid something in the road—probably a coyote—and she lost control of the truck before skidding into a tree."

"Where'd they find her?" Vernon asked.

"On the back road leading to the burial grounds," Heath said. "Ari thinks she was going to check out the spot Uncle Rex picked out for Milton."

The man next to the spirit of Sam Whitefeather nodded. "I told her where I planned to put his ashes yesterday morning," he said.

Ari leaned in to whisper in my ear. "Uncle Rex is responsible for burial placements."

"Where'd they take Beverly's body?" Rex asked next.

"They've sent her to the Jimez Pueblo," Ari said. "The same place they sent Milton for the autopsy."

There was a rustling in the room that I didn't quite understand. It appeared the Whitefeathers didn't quite approve of their dead being sent to another Pueblo for autopsy.

"That coroner's too damn slow," Heath's uncle Vernon barked. "He held on to Milton too long before he sent him back to us!"

Ari must have taken Vernon's displeasure personally, because she snapped back, "Take it up with Pena and Cruz, then, Dad!"

He scowled at her and Ari seemed to lose her nerve, because she shifted slightly back a step, using me to block Vernon's reproachful glare.

I wanted to say something, but remembered that I was an outsider here, and Heath had warned me not to.

Rex spoke next. "We'll have to postpone the ceremony for Milton," he said. "We'll wait for them to release Bev and perform both ceremonies together."

"You want to wait another four or five days to bury our brother?" Vernon practically growled.

Next to Rex I saw Sam's spirit move even closer to him, and he placed his hands on his son, as if he was giving him the strength to stand up to his brother. In my mind I heard Sam say, *It's what Milton would want.* A second later I heard nearly those same words come out of Rex's mouth. "It's what Milton would have wanted, Vern. He would've wanted to be buried with Beverly."

But Vernon was unmoved. "They weren't even still

married!" he snapped. Every time he spoke, I noticed, the whole room tensed. Apparently, Vernon wasn't so much loved and respected as feared.

Still, Rex stood his ground, likely because his father's spirit was giving him strength. "You know they planned to marry again in the springtime, brother," he said calmly. "No. It's my job to say when and where, and I say we wait for Bev and lay them to rest together."

Vernon swore under his breath and stalked out of the room. He didn't seem to like it when he didn't get his way.

At that moment Sam stepped away from Rex, shaking his head at the sight of his retreating son before looking pointedly at me. He then moved his arms in an odd way, as if he were shaping an hourglass, and in front of my eyes a large clay pot appeared. Beautifully crafted, it was painted black except for a large white feather on the side.

I didn't know what the pot was supposed to symbolize, but when I looked at Sam's face, it appeared very sad indeed. I had this feeling like I needed to ask Heath about it, but not here and not now.

Heath took me around to his relatives and introduced me. Most of them forced a smile and welcomed me, and I expressed my condolences for their loss, but I could feel the tension in the room with me there, and really I just wanted to go.

When we got to Rex, the older man nodded at me, but didn't take my extended hand. I tried not to take offense, but it was hard. "Your mom coming?" Rex asked Heath.

"Yes," Heath said tightly, clearly irritated that his uncle had just snubbed me.

Rex sighed. "Vernon's going to give her some flak."

"She's expecting it."

"I'll do my best to stand up for her," Rex added.

Heath met his uncle's steely eyes and his expression softened. "Thank you, Uncle. She could really use it."

Rex nodded, then turned away. I bit my tongue and followed Heath back to the other side of the room, where he waved to all his relatives and hugged Ari again. Holding up her keys, he asked, "Can you take me to get my car?"

"Take mine for today," she said wearily. "You two can bring it back when you get yours out of the garage."

Heath kissed her on the cheek, then took me by the hand and we left.

When we got outside, Heath walked me right to the passenger door and opened it for me. I got inside, and he leaned in a little. "I'm really sorry my family was so rude," he said, moving his finger along my brow to sweep a lock of hair out of my eyes. "They're set in their ways and they don't like outsiders."

"I understand," I told him, hoping he believed me. The truth was that the encounter had thrown me a little. It'd been uncomfortable and stressful, and I just wanted to get out of there.

Heath sighed and kissed me before stepping back to close my door and get in on the driver's side. We pulled out of the Pueblo and headed off.

As we drove, I waited for Heath to say something, but he didn't. He just drove silently, and I could feel the waves of grief and anger rolling off him. I knew he had to be at the end of his rope, what with the death of his favorite uncle and an aunt he clearly loved, not to mention the less-than-welcoming feeling his family had given me, and to top it all off, his mother was coming back into town and apparently wasn't welcome at her own brother's funeral.

I knew all this, and common sense suggested that I should have left Heath alone. He'd talk to me when he was ready, but maybe I was a little short on my supply of common sense that day. "Wanna talk about it?" I asked, just as Heath pulled over onto the shoulder of the road.

Heath sighed, and then the stiff posture he'd been holding while he drove sort of crumpled, and he rested his forehead on the steering wheel and pounded the top of the dash with his fist.

I waited a beat before reciting one of my favorite quotes. "Family," I said. "It's why God gave us friends."

It took a minute but Heath started to chuckle. He then lifted his head and regarded me. "I'm really, really sorry," he said.

"For what?"

"For dragging you into the middle of this nightmare. I should've told you to go hang out in L.A. or Boston. Not pulled you into all this crap."

My brow lifted. "What?" I said with a half smile. "This? *This* is all you Whitefeathers got? Please, sugar. My family makes your family look like the Waltons."

"Somehow I doubt that," he said, leaning over to rest his head on my shoulder.

I patted his hair. "Don't sweat it, honey. I can take it."

He chuckled again. "Oh, I *know* you can take it. I'm just not sure *I* can."

I kissed the top of his head. "Can I ask you something?"

"How'd I turn out so normal coming from that?"

I laughed. "No. Your grandfather showed up when we were at the house—"

"My grandfather?" he interrupted, sitting up to look at me. "Sam was there?"

I nodded. "You didn't feel him?"

Heath stared at the gearshift. "No. But that could've been because I was too focused on not telling my uncle Vern to shove it."

I ran my hand through his silky black hair. "I have the distinct feeling that Sam's very glad you held back."

Heath grunted. "So what's your question?"

"Sam showed me this pot."

"A pot?"

"Yeah," I said, trying to think how to describe it.

"What kind of pot?"

"It was sort of round and it was painted black, but on the side was this white feather. I had the feeling I needed to ask you about it, but not in front of your family."

Heath blew out a breath. "You aren't kidding about not mentioning that, Em," he said. "He was showing you our family's urn."

"An urn?"

Heath nodded, but his eyes were far away. "It was in my family for generations," he explained. "Each time a Whitefeather died and was cremated, a small portion of their ashes went into the urn."

That surprised me. "Why?"

"Well, it has a lot to do with our belief that we're looked after by our ancestors. It's why our lands and our burial grounds are so sacred. Our ancestors, we believe, are very powerful spirits and having their ashes collectively together in one spot allows us to call on them for help in times of trouble."

I remembered something then. "You said 'was.' "

"Huh?"

"You said this urn 'was' in your family. It isn't with you guys anymore?"

"Depends on who you ask," Heath said, and I noticed the bitter tone in his voice right away.

"So if I ask you, what's the answer?"

"Well, that's the irony. I don't know. But it's the one thing my grandfather asked of me on his deathbed. Something I haven't been able to do for him, which is no wonder that he's bringing it up to you now."

"I'm lost," I said. "Can we start from the beginning again?"

Heath sighed and it sounded like there was a lot of dirty laundry in that sigh. "The urn went missing right around the time my mom left the Pueblo. Vernon's convinced that my mom took it. Rex too, I think. But Milton, he always suspected it was someone else. Someone outside the family, who might've been jealous of us and our success and status within the tribe. He thought the person who took it wanted to deprive us of the benefit of our ancestors."

I waited a beat before I asked, "But your mom didn't take the urn, did she?"

Heath looked at me sideways. "No," he said. "At least, I'm ninety-nine point nine nine nine percent sure she didn't."

"Why not a hundred?"

Heath shrugged. "Who else could it have been? It disappeared the exact same weekend she left the Pueblo and she was the last person to see it. Hell, she was even in charge of it."

I waved at him. "Hi, yeah, I'm lost again."

"My mom was a master potter," he said. "That's what our tribe is known for, actually. We're famous for our pottery and special kiln techniques. Specifically that black-on-black glaze we give our pottery. Our Pueblo has produced quite a few stars in the Native Indian art world, and my mom was one of them."

"Really?" I asked. "I had no idea."

"Yeah, well, she hasn't thrown anything new since my stepdad died. She says it makes her too sad. But it put a little extra food on the table for a lot of years, and she was able to save a little for my college fund too."

"So, she was the last person to see the family urn?" I asked, getting back to the point of the story.

"Yep. She was repairing a crack in the side. According to her, she fixed the crack and left it on a shelf in the tribe's workshop. That night she left the Pueblo for good. The next morning, the urn was gone."

I thought about that for a bit. "Then, really, anyone could've taken it," I said.

Heath pulled his hair away from his face, reaching into his pocket for a rubber band to secure it with. "Yeah. But no one's ponied up to take the blame for, like, twenty-five years, Em. And lots of Whitefeathers have died since then. Their ashes haven't been able to join their ancestors, which means they're left to face the spirit world alone."

My brow furrowed. "But you know that's not true, right? I mean, Sam's made it across okay, and he personally told me that he's met up with your ancestors."

"Oh, I know that's how it works," he assured me. "But try to convince my family of that and they'll call you a liar right to your face. It's what they believe, and nothing I say is going to change their minds. Especially since most of them believe it was my mom who took the urn in the first place."

"But what possible reason could she have for depriving your family of the urn?"

Heath leaned forward and started the car again. "That's a whole other story," he told me. "And one I'll tell you later. Right now, I just want to get back to the hotel and lie down for a while."

It was then that I remembered the talon marks I'd seen on the side of Beverly's car. "Heath," I said, "there's something you should know about your aunt's accident." I then explained to him what I'd seen on the side of her car. "I didn't mention it when you came out of the station because I didn't want to say anything in front of Ari, and I don't know for an actual fact that they're really demon marks. I mean, in theory I suppose they could've been gouges from the tree she hit, but the pattern is way too similar to that demon we encountered in San Francisco. I really think we should check it out."

Heath's face was hard like granite, and without a word he put the car into drive and pulled back out onto the road. At first I thought he might be mad at me for telling him, but he reached for my hand again and gave it a gentle squeeze.

We wound our way through a variety of roads until we crept onto one that, I was guessing, didn't see much traffic. There was nothing as far as the eye could see but scrub and low mountains. We drove for about five minutes when Heath slowed down, and leaned forward, letting go of my hand to focus on the road ahead. "What'cha looking for?" I asked him.

He stopped the car and pointed out the windshield. "Those."

Heath put the car into park and got out, and I followed suit, joining him at the site of a set of skid marks that began near the yellow dividing line and ended at the trunk of a tree that'd been nearly broken in half.

My breath caught, especially when I remembered poor Beverly's car. We walked beside the marks, softly and reverently as if following a funeral procession, until we both stood under the boughs of the lone tree.

Heath's face was pinched and clouded with emotion. I moved closer to him and wrapped my arms around his waist. "I'm so, so sorry about your aunt and uncle."

He hugged me and said, "Would you reach out to Aunt Bev and see if she's here, Em?"

"You think she's grounded?"

He shrugged. "You know how it is with car accidents. Lots of 'em end up stuck at the scene."

I stepped back from him and took a deep breath, opening up my senses, looking for her spirit in the ether. I bumped into nothing but the emotion still lingering in the area, and I let myself follow the thread.

I moved back along the skid marks to their point of origin and then even a few steps farther along the road to spread my hands out, literally feeling the air as I went. "What is it?" Heath asked, coming to my side.

"She was really scared," I said. "Like ... terrified scared, and the weird thing is that she was terrified some feet before the skid marks start."

Heath studied me. "What else are you getting?"

My eyes fell on the tree and I lowered my hands to walk back over to it, sensing the waves of terrified energy running like rain down around me as I went, and when I got to the tree, the terror just ... stopped. "She was killed instantly," I said, my hand going to my neck. "Her neck snapped."

Heath was still studying me. "That's what Pena said."

I moved around the tree then, because something was still tugging at me. When I got to the back of it, I gasped.

"What is it?"

"Take a look at this," I said.

Heath hurried to my side of the tree. There, he ran his fingers along three distinctive talon marks carved deep into the wood. "Son of a bitch!" he whispered.

"Son of a bitch" was right.

Chapter 3

Heath and I stood there for several minutes just staring at the evidence of a demon on the loose, both of us muted by the sudden gravity of the situation.

"This is bad," Heath said at last.

"Really bad," I agreed.

Heath looked at me. "My grandfather told you about this thing, right?"

I started to nod, but my phone rang and I held up a finger to check the display. It was Gilley. I figured I better answer it, but I was annoyed that he'd called right in the middle of a heavy discussion. "Yeah?" I asked.

"Well, good morning to you too," he said. His voice was thick and froggy and I knew he wasn't feeling well. Still, what Heath and I were dealing with was much more important. "I'm a little busy, Gil. Can I call you back later?"

"How much later?"

"I don't know. Half hour, maybe?"

"That's fine," he said, coughing into the phone. "Assuming I'm still alive." And then he muttered something that I could have sworn sounded like "Gilley Gilleshpie."

"Are you running a fever?" I asked.

"Probably," he said, coughing again wetly. "I'm delirious, so you might not want to take my word for it."

I pinched the bridge of my nose. Gilley could be a handful. "Okay," I told him. "Heath and I are wrapping up and we'll be back soon."

"How soon?"

I sighed heavily and glanced at my watch. "I don't know. . . . Soon, Gil. I promise."

Gilley coughed a third time. "Okay, I'll call the ambulance. Maybe they'll get here faster."

With that, he hung up, and I pulled the phone away from my ear to glare at it.

"Gil?" Heath asked.

"Yep."

"I gather he needs us?"

"He's sick. Probably the flu."

Heath put his hands on his hips and eyed the road sullenly. "He was the one who picked that spot next to those sick guys at O'Hare."

"I know, I know," I agreed, feeling like I was being torn in two directions. "But when he gets sick, he gets really sick, so maybe we should just go check on him?"

"Yeah, okay," Heath said. "I have to call my mom anyway."

"Isn't she flying here today?" I asked as we walked to the car.

Heath nodded. "She doesn't leave Phoenix till ten p.m., though. Her flight should be in by midnight."

I got in the car and asked, "Why so late?"

"It was the cheapest fare she could find."

Heath started the car and took one last look at the skid marks and the tree before pulling onto the road again. "We'll need to talk about this, Em," he said. "If some demon is really out there killing my family, we're gonna have to shut it down."

"That's what your grandfather said," I reminded him.

Heath's eyes cut to me. "Bev wasn't out there?" he asked belatedly.

I shook my head. "Not that I could sense. I think she's made it across, but I can't feel her there either, which isn't unusual. You know how they all need a little adjustment period."

Heath grunted. "Especially when they've been in an accident," he said. "Jesus, how big would a demon have to be to make talon marks like *that*?" he asked, shaking his head like he could hardly believe it.

I eyed Heath carefully. There were dark circles under his eyes and his features looked pale and drawn, not to mention seriously stressed-out. I thought it was probably a good thing we were heading back to the hotel. I could check on Gil, and maybe convince Heath to rest. The emotional and physical toll on him the past few days looked like it was killing him.

I found Gil in his room, spread-eagle on the top of his comforter with a wet cloth on his forehead and a surgical mask covering half his face.

"Attractive," I said, nodding to the cleaning woman on her way out of Gil's room. (She seemed like she'd been looking for a reason to leave quickly.)

"I'm dying," Gilley moaned.

I softened and came over to sit next to him. It was then that I saw the litter of candy wrappers and empty potato chip bags on his nightstand. Apparently, the cleaning woman had missed those. Or she just didn't want to get that close to patient zero. "You're not dying," I said, lifting the washcloth and feeling his forehead. It was a little warm, but not as bad as the night before. "And your fever's beginning to break."

"I still have a headache," Gil moaned. "Gilley Gilleshpie."

"I see the headache hasn't dampened your appetite," I said, picking up the clutter on his nightstand.

"Feed a fever," he told me.

"I believe that's feed a cold, starve a fever."

"There's no way I'm going down hungry," he told me, following that with a small fit of coughing.

I threw out the trash, heated up some water from the coffeepot, and poured him a cup of Theraflu. He took it and lifted the mask to slurp it down. While he drank, I eyed him worriedly. He finished the medicine and handed me back the cup, then settled his mask back in place and lay back on the pillows. I couldn't tell if it was just the mask, or that Gil was developing a lung infection, but his breathing was definitely starting to sound like Darth Vader.

"Nice mask," I said, after rinsing out his cup.

Gil rolled his eyes lazily to me. "Thanks."

"Where'd you get it?" I didn't think the hotel gift shop was the source.

"There's a Korean couple staying next door," he said. "I rode the elevator down with them and they gave it to me. They said I look like I have SARS."

I wondered how quickly they'd also put one on themselves. "You don't have SARS," I said.

"How do you know?"

"You have the flu. That's it. Just the plain old flu."

"How do you know?" Gil pressed.

"Because Heath and I both got our flu shots before we all left for Europe and you said—what again?"

Gil narrowed his eyes at me, and said nothing. Not even "Gilley Gilleshpie," so I answered the question for him. "You said that you didn't need the flu shot because you never get sick."

"The flu shot doesn't protect against SARS, M. J.," he grumbled.

"Exactly my point, Gil. If those businessmen at O'Hare had really been infected with SARS, we all would have gotten sick, but only *you* caught a bug, which means only *you* caught *the flu*."

"Shuddup," he snapped grumpily, rolling over so his back was to me.

I suddenly felt bad. "Hey," I said after a few long seconds of stony silence. "I'm sorry, Gil. I didn't mean to be a pain. It's just been a long couple of days. Can I get you anything?"

"A new body," he said, rolling back over to lie on his back again. "This one aches all over. And if you find a new body, make sure it's got really good pecs."

I grinned and moved to his side again. Taking up the washcloth from the nightstand, I wrung it out under cool water from the faucet and came back to put it on his head again. "I'll come back in a little while and check on you," I told him, but Gil was already asleep.

As I was leaving, Gil's phone gave a chirp. I didn't want it to wake him up, so I moved over to turn his phone on silent when I caught the text on the screen. It was from Gopher, our producer.

Network approved salaries. Tell M. J. and Heath that your paychecks have all been wired out. Still working on production funding. More later.

I breathed a huge sigh of relief, grateful for the news. Our funding had been pulled weeks before in Ireland, and since then, we'd had to float mostly on our savings. And the airfare to New Mexico from Ireland had put a serious dent in those, so this was really welcome news.

I clicked Gil's phone to silent and left it on the bureau, but wrote him a note and set it on his nightstand.

We've been paid, it read. Then I left him alone and went to find Heath.

Heath was on the phone with his mom when I got back to our room, and the joy of discovering that we'd finally been paid plummeted when I saw his face. "Yeah, okay," he was saying, waving me over to sit next to him. "There's no rush, Ma. If the airlines are willing to let you change your flight without a penalty, and you want to stay there tonight with Aunt Evelyn because you're too upset to fly, then do it. And I'd tell you to do it even if there was a penalty. You take all the time you need, okay?"

I waited patiently through the rest of the call, and bit my lip when I heard through the receiver that Heath's mother was crying. Finally he gave his good-byes and clicked off.

He then, quite unexpectedly, reached out and hugged me to him, holding me tightly without saying a word. I was a little taken aback, but I recovered and squeezed back. "It'll be okay," I told him, not really knowing what else to say. It's ironic, isn't it? My business is all about death, but when personally faced with it, I never know what to say.

The rest of the night and most of the rest of the following day I did nothing but play nursemaid to Gil and comfort Heath, bouncing back and forth between the two hotel rooms like a Ping-Pong ball, and tending to them in much the same way, making sure they ate a little, drank a little, and rested.

During a brief one-hour period in the middle of the afternoon, both of them were asleep, and I took the opportunity to head out for a run, my first real exercise in well over a week.

It felt good and terrible all at the same time, but I kept at it for all five miles. When I got back, I found Gil awake and alert and looking much better, thank God. He was busy typing on his laptop, but still asked me to fluff his pillows and get him a soda. Apparently he took the maid part of nursemaid seriously. When I arrived back with his soda and one for me, he turned the screen to me and said, "I just ordered that!"

I popped the top of my Fresca and squinted at the screen. "An iPad?"

Gil nodded. "Best tablet on the market," he said, turning the laptop back around.

"Honey," I said soberly, mopping at the sweat on my brow, "you just got paid. Do you really think it's smart to spend it so quickly?"

"I got a good deal," he said without looking up. There was a *ding*, which came from his computer, alerting him he had mail, and it must have been good news the way his face burst into a sly smile when he read it.

"What?" I asked. I knew that face. It meant trouble.

"Nothing," he said a little too quickly.

"Gilley Morehouse Gillespie," I said evenly. "Tell me what."

But Gil is nothing if not stubborn. Snapping the lid of the laptop closed, he merely widened his smile and said, "It's a surprise. You'll find out in a day or two."

"Great," I said woodenly. "We all know how I *love* surprises."

Gil didn't say another word. Instead, he leaned back against the pillows and said, "I'm hungry. Can we go for something to eat?"

I got up and headed to the door. "Let me shower and check in with Heath. I'll call you when we're ready."

"Gilley Gilleshpie," I heard as I exited the door.

Half an hour later we were sitting in a café scarfing down some fantastic fajitas. Well, Gilley and I were scarfing. Heath? Not so much. He mostly pushed his food around on his plate and looked sad.

I swallowed the bite I'd just taken and felt terrible for him. "I'm so sorry," I said, squeezing his knee.

"Mwf moo," Gil said. Gil will talk through anything. Fajita, doughnut, muffin, pancakes . . . food is no impediment to his verbal expression.

"Gil's sorry too," I said, and saw a tiny quirk at the edge of Heath's mouth.

"Thanks, guys," he said.

Gil seemed to think of something then, and he took another huge bite, cocked his head to the side, and said, "Runeral wooday?"

I froze. Oh, God! Had I forgotten to tell Gil about Heath's aunt? Yes. Yes I had. "Uh, Gil," I said. "Sorry to fill you in so late, but Heath's aunt was killed in a car accident yesterday morning. The funeral for his uncle has been postponed until the family can make arrangements to have them buried together."

Gil's eyes bulged.

I nodded. "I know. It's awful."

Gil flailed his arms around in some sort of air origami pattern.

"Yes, he's taking it hard," I said.

"Gahkwrk!" Gil said, shaking his head.

I interpreted for Heath. "He wants to know if you'll be okay and he's here for you."

Heath, however, was staring hard at Gilley. "Actually . . . ," he said, dropping his fork and pushing back from the table before hurrying around me to stand behind Gil.

I watched as he grabbed Gilley around the middle and pulled him up so violently that he lifted Gil right out of his chair. "What're you doing?" I cried. "Heath! Put him down!"

In the next second there was a strangled sound from Gil; then Heath swung him around again, thrusting his fists into Gilley's middle. I was so stunned that I didn't realize what was happening until a small wad of food flew out of Gil's mouth and onto the floor.

Gil took a huge ragged breath. "Thank you, Baby Jesus!" he gasped, holding his throat. Heath let him go and Gil sank to his knees. "Gilley Gilleshpie. Gilley Gilleshpie. Gilley Gilleshpie!"

Heath bent down and lifted Gil up gently from under his shoulders; then he eased him back over to his chair. Meanwhile a manager had come running over to us and most of the patrons were staring. "Is everything all right?" the manager asked.

"Yes," I said quickly, placing a hand on Gil's arm to make sure he was okay.

"I almost died!" Gilley shrieked, then smiled tightly at the manager and said, "Gilley Gilleshpie."

The poor man visibly paled.

"He's fine," I said evenly, shooting Gil a warning look.

But Gil was having none of it. "That fajita almost *killed* me!"

Heath calmly took his seat again. "But it didn't," he said. "Gil, you're fine."

"No I'm not!" he snapped. "First I had a stroke on the plane, then I caught SARS, and just now I almost died eating the house special!"

"I'm so sorry!" the manager said. "Please, let me take care of your check. And if there's anything else I can bring you, please let me know."

Gil's eyebrows rose.

Uh-oh, I thought.

"Well, in that case," Gilley said, "I'll need to see the menu again."

For the next hour, Gilley ate his way through most of the menu, completely over his near-death experience(s). At least for the moment.

I, on the other hand, was still really shaken. How had I misinterpreted Gilley's choking for conversation? "Hey," said Heath when he caught me staring as Gilley ate each bite. I felt his hand on my arm. "You okay?"

I turned to him. "I should be asking you that."

Heath smiled, but it didn't reach his eyes. "I have to call my mom again," he said. "I need to check on her and see if she's okay. When she's upset, she sometimes forgets to take her medicine."

Heath's mother wasn't in great health. She had a

heart condition and diabetes and her doctor had advised her not to stress herself out.

I rubbed Heath's back. I had no idea what to tell him to make it better and it was killing me.

We left the restaurant and Gilley nearly needed to be carried to the car, he was so full. Behind his back, Heath and I left enough cash behind to more than cover the bill and we drove back to the hotel in silence.

Gil went back to his room for a nap, and I followed Heath out to the courtyard, where he called his mom. It was a tough conversation and he looked very upset after he'd hung up.

"Feel like talking about it?" I asked.

Heath sighed heavily and stared at the ground. "My family always makes things ten times harder than they need to be," he said. "I mean, it's bad enough that we lost Uncle Milton and Aunt Bev, but I know the flak my mom's gonna take when she shows up at their funerals, and it's killing me that they all know she's in bad health and they're still holding a grudge."

"A grudge?" I asked. "For what, Heath?"

But he shook his head. "It's a long story, Em."

"I've got time."

Heath sighed again. "Yeah, well, I appreciate that, but I'm not up to telling it."

I couldn't keep the hurt out of my voice when I said, "Oh, okay."

Heath lifted his eyes to my face then, and I could see the pained look there. "Aw, man!" he said. "I'm sorry, Em. It's just that my mom and I left the Pueblo a long time ago, and most of the rest of my family have never gotten over it. My granddad, and Uncle Milton and Aunt Bev, and Ari of course, are the only ones who never made me feel like an outsider. Everybody else resented the fact that I was a Whitefeather living off tribal lands. It's like, because I'm loyal to my mom, the tribe doesn't consider me an actual member and it hurts sometimes, you know?"

I wrapped my arms around him. "I'm so sorry, honey," I told him. I realized I'd been saying that a lot lately.

We sat there for a while, but I could still feel the intense sadness filling Heath's heart. Eventually he kissed the top of my head, saying, "Think I'll go upstairs and get some sleep." Then he hugged me tight one last time before moving off.

I could tell he wanted to be alone, but it still stung a little to be pushed away.

Gil found me about an hour and a half later still sitting in the courtyard. "You're a gloomy Gus these days," he said, coughing into his hand before sitting next to me on the bench.

I sighed. "What else would I be? My boyfriend's just lost two of his closest relatives, his mom's sick, and most of his family hates me."

"Oh, come on," Gil said. "I'm sure they don't hate you."

I told him what'd happened at Ari's house and about how just by being there I was guilty of trespass. "Ah," he said when I was finished. "Allow me to retract my previous statement. They obviously hate you."

I cut him a look. "Gee, *thanks*, Gil."

"What do you want me to say, M. J.? You know I'm not good at this sentimental stuff."

I pulled my legs up and hugged my knees. "I wish Teeks were here."

What I felt I really needed was the support of my best

girlfriend, Karen O'Neil. Karen lived in Boston (Gil and I lived there too) and she was currently looking after the pug I'd adopted from Scotland. Karen is also one of those breathtakingly beautiful women who just wakes up looking perfect. If she weren't so great and such an amazing friend, I'd probably hate her. Anyway, Karen is such a knockout that Gilley had been the one to first nickname her TKO, or Teeko for short. What can I say? The nickname stuck.

"Yeah," Gil said with a knowing smile. "If only Teeks were here."

There was something he was hiding from me, but just as I was about to press him on it, he coughed again. I listened hard for the telltale wet sound that indicated an infection was setting in, but he seemed to be recovering from his bout with the flu very well. "Maybe you should call her?" Gil said after a minute, and again that knowing smile returned.

But to my surprise, at the mention of calling Teeks, my eyes watered. I was starting to feel off-balance emotionally. So much had happened in the last few months and through all of it I'd just kept going. I hadn't paused long enough to stop and consider what I might be going through. "Naw," I said, wiping my eyes and sniffling. "She's got her own stuff to deal with. She doesn't need me to dump on her."

Gilley bumped my shoulder with his. "You know what, M. J.? Sometimes you're an idiot."

That got me to smile a little. "I'll call her later, after I get Heath through the next few days."

"Do you guys have any leads on this demon thing that might've murdered Milton?" Gil asked, blowing his nose loudly into a tissue.

I shook my head. "Heath's been calling members of his family to talk to them about the possibility that both Milton and his ex-wife were killed by something otherworldly, but according to the Pueblo coroner, Milton died of wounds consistent with a mountain lion attack, so no one's buying our alternate theory."

"A mountain lion?" Gil asked.

"Yep. Can you believe it?"

Gil eyed me soberly. "Only *we* would think it might've been a demon, M. J. Seriously, can you blame these people for wanting to believe it was some kind of wild animal?"

"Yeah, well, they've been no help to us in trying to figure out what this demon is or where it comes from or why it might be attacking the Whitefeathers."

"And we need to know that because ... ?"

"For a bunch of reasons, Gil. For starters, we need to know what we're up against, and Sam hinted to me in that first dream about Milton that there was a person who's involved with or possessed by this demon. A human that's no longer human, I guess."

"Are you *really* going to kill this person?" Gil asked me, just as I was having the same thought.

"No!" I said, more to convince myself than to convince Gil, I think. "There's got to be a way to deal with the demon without any further bloodshed."

"What's Heath say about it?"

"We haven't talked much about that part," I said, rubbing my temples, suddenly so homesick I wanted to cry.

"Why not?" Gil pressed.

"If you haven't already noticed, Heath's in pretty bad shape emotionally and I think it's best not to push him right now."

"But he knows what Sam told you, doesn't he? He knows that Sam said you'd have to kill the guy who controls the demon, right?"

"Of course Heath knows," I said defensively. That wasn't exactly the truth. I was sleep deprived, jet-lagged, and feeling somewhat lost emotionally: Thinking about how to tell Heath *that* had felt like too big of a challenge to take on right now.

"So if I ask him about it . . ."

"Don't you dare," I warned him.

"Yeah, that's what I thought," he said.

Gil sighed and got up.

"Where're you going?" I asked him.

"To send a text. And fix this for you."

I snorted derisively. "You can't fix this, Gil."

"No," he agreed. "But maybe I can fix you." And off he went to send his little text.

Normally I'd have been worried, but I wasn't feeling myself, so I just let him go without asking what he meant.

The next morning, just as I was starting to come out of a fitful sleep, there was a soft knock on our door. My eyes flew open and I looked at the clock. It was eight a.m.

The knock sounded again, no louder than the last time but with a few more raps.

I glanced at Heath. He was facing away from me, but he appeared to be sleeping. I eased out of bed and hurried to the door, peeking through the peephole first to see who it was. "No freaking way!" I gasped, then pulled on the handle.

When it opened, there stood five feet five inches of blond gorgeousness. *"Teeko!"* I cried, and threw my arms around my very best girlfriend.

In her usual calm style she laughed and wrapped one arm around me to pat me gently on the back. "Hey, girl," she said. "How you been?"

A lump formed in my throat, and it was several seconds before I could speak. "Okay," I said, squeezing her tighter.

"Really?" she asked. "I heard you weren't doing so well."

I backed up and noticed that she was also carrying a wriggling little black pug in her arms who was anxiously trying to lick the air between us. "Wendell!" I said, taking him from Teeko. "He's grown!"

"He's getting a little chubby," she admitted.

I cuddled the pup. "So's Gilley," I told her. Then I realized that she had come here from Boston, probably at Gil's request. "He e-mailed you and told you to come, didn't he?"

But Teeks just shook her head and beamed her beautiful smile at me. "No," she said. "I was already planning on coming here. John and I bought a house near the slopes three months ago and I came to make sure that the decorator's finished and all the art we purchased got hung in the right places."

I shook my head. "Wait . . . what? You guys bought a house here?"

"It's a lodge, really," she said, waving her hand as if it were nothing. Since she was engaged to one of the wealthiest men in America, the "lodge" was bound to be something more like an "estate."

"We bought it to have a place close to the Santa Fe art scene and the slopes," Teeks said. "The art here is amazing, M. J. We'll have to go into town and I'll show you around some of the galleries."

"Okay, so how did you know I was *here* in Santa Fe specifically?" I'd sent Teeks an e-mail telling her only that Heath's uncle had died and I was traveling to New Mexico to attend the funeral, but I hadn't mentioned anything about where we'd be staying...mostly because I hadn't known until the night we landed.

"Oh, *that* Gilley told me," Teeko admitted. "I e-mailed him to ask him where you guys were in New Mexico, because I wanted to see you, and if we were going to be in the same state, I really couldn't pass up the opportunity. He let me know you three were here, and that you really needed some one-on-one girl time, and he and I planned this big surprise!"

I hugged her again. "Well, color me surprised!"

"Hello," Heath said from behind me. "Please, come in and make yourself comfortable while I sit here awkwardly half naked."

I felt my cheeks redden and Teeks giggled. "Hi, Heath. Nice to see you again."

I whipped around and held up Wendell. "She brought the puppy, Heath!"

"I can see that," he said. "Now, how about everybody turn around while I put some pants on, okay?"

Teeks and I laughed and turned our backs to him. "God, I'm glad you're here," I admitted.

"I heard you guys had a rough time in Ireland," she said. "And my condolences, Heath, on the death of your uncle. I'm so sorry."

"Thank you," he said, and we heard a zipper close. "You guys can turn around now."

"I have another surprise for you two," she sang. "But first you and Heath need to pack your things and meet me in the lobby."

I cocked my head. "What've you done?"

She smiled wickedly and took Wendell back. "Just get dressed, get packed, and get downstairs, okay?"

With that, she turned away and walked elegantly back down the hallway. I heard her phone ring and when she answered it, she said, "Yes, Gil. I'm really here. I flew in on John's jet. Now pack your stuff and meet us in the lobby."

Heath was slow to get moving. He seemed to be far away and I knew he was hurting, so I didn't push him to hurry and I did my best to quell the excitement at seeing my friend. I just moved with steady progress to get us both packed and ready to go.

We met Teeks in the lobby and a man in a chauffeur's uniform tipped his hat at us when we arrived. We followed Teeko out to a stretch limo, and I thought Gilley was going to bust at the seams, he was so excited. "Gilley Gilleshpie," I heard him whisper when he saw the limo. If anything could send that boy into a stroke, it was the idea of being wrapped in luxury.

The trip was a good ride—maybe forty minutes—and the whole way Teeks refused to tell us where we were going. The only one who didn't seem to be enjoying the ride was Heath. He sat in gloomy silence and forced a smile any time one of us directed a comment his way.

Teeko asked him about his mother (apparently Gil had filled her in), and Heath confessed that she wasn't well but doing her best.

My gal pal looked genuinely concerned and I could have hugged her for that. The limo drove through a rather flat section of town, then up into the hills. The scenery was breathtaking and we all chatted noisily, Gilley and I talking over each other trying to catch Teeko up.

Finally the limo pulled into a cul-de-sac and there sat a gorgeous modern-looking structure made mostly of glass and wood. I got out and my jaw dropped. The house was an architectural marvel. "You like?" Teeks asked, coming to stand next to me while I ogled the outside.

"Uh . . . ," I said, totally at a loss for words.

"Can we live here?" Gilley asked, and I didn't think he was kidding.

But Teeks laughed. "Of course!" she sang, then moved to the door. "This is the lodge I was telling you about. When I heard you three were staying in a hotel because Heath's house wasn't finished, I thought that I'd invite you to stay here as long as you like!"

Teeks then inserted her key and the oversized wood door slid open easily. Gil and I stepped through and came up short, our jaws gaping. The front hall was big enough to fit my whole condo inside. "Holy freakballs!" Gil said, staring up at the twenty-foot ceilings.

And then, I heard it and I felt my heart thud hard in my chest. A low, lone whistle echoed out from somewhere deeper inside the home. I looked at Teeko, and her smile was ear to ear. "Go on," she said. "He's been waiting."

I dashed inside and followed the sound of a second whistle, past the kitchen to the massive living area, which was floor-to-ceiling glass.

There, against the French doors leading out to a huge deck, was a birdcage, and inside was my very own feathered gray friend.

"Hey, baby!" Doc said, fluffing his feathers and flapping his wings when he saw me. "How you doin'?"

"Doc!" I cried, running to his cage. It'd been months

since the last time I'd seen the beloved pet parrot I'd owned since just after my mother died.

I reached into his cage and he stepped immediately onto my fingers. When I had him out and held him at eye level, he said, "What's new, Magoo?"

"Doc!" I heard Gilley say behind me.

Doc fluttered his wings and made kissing sounds. "Gimme kisses?" he asked.

I held Doc close under my chin and cuddled with him, crying a little. I'd missed my little guy so much it hurt.

"Can I hold him?" Gil asked shyly. Gil loved Doc almost as much as I did.

I swiveled Doc around and he stepped onto Gilley's outstretched fingers. I turned then to Teeko, who'd come in with Heath. "Thank you," I said, my voice cracking.

She nodded. "I think Mama Dell and the Captain needed a break."

I winced. Mama Dell was our dear friend, and she and her husband—known only as "the Captain"—had generously offered to watch Doc while I was away in Europe. "I owe her huge," I said.

"Aw, don't sweat it," Teeks said with a wave of her hand. "I think she loves Doc to pieces. Which is the problem. I think the Captain was getting a little jealous."

There was a flutter, and then I felt Doc land delicately on my shoulder. "Oooo," he cooed, nudging my cheek with his beak. "Kisses?"

I gave him a peck on the beak and reached up to wiggle his tail feathers. "Missed you," I said to him.

"Captain!" Doc said in a perfect imitation of Mama Dell's voice. "Coffee's on!"

We all laughed. Well, all of us except for Heath. He'd

taken a seat at the bar and was talking on his phone to either Pena or Cruz about the investigation into Milton's death. By the sound of it, there wasn't anything new to report. Heath let them know we had new digs and where to find us if something came up that he needed to know. He then hung up his cell, tossing it aside and putting his head in his hands like he was simply weary of it all.

I swiveled Doc around so that he could see Heath. At some point I'd have to introduce my new boyfriend to my bird, which was likely to be problematic, because, according to Doc, I'm his, and only his. My last boyfriend had developed the habit of ducking every time he heard the flapping of wings. Doc's an ace dive-bomber.

My birdie seemed to notice the new person in the room, and just before I had the thought to stop him, he zipped off my shoulder, aiming straight for Heath. I nearly shouted a warning, but just as I opened my mouth, I watched Heath look up and calmly hold out two of his fingers. Doc landed gracefully on them and clucked his tongue a few times. Heath pulled him in for a closer look and my parrot dipped his beak and cooed.

"No . . . way!" Gil whispered.

"Has he ever done that before?" Teeks asked.

"Flown to a stranger and played nice?" I said. "Uh . . . no."

"He's sweet," Heath said, looking up at us while he stroked Doc's head.

Just then Heath's cell phone chirped and I moved quickly to retrieve my bird. For whatever reason, Doc hates phones and he'll bite me if I ever try to talk on the phone while holding him.

Luckily, I got to the bird before Heath picked up the line. "Hey, Mom," he said, and walked out of the room to get some privacy. I watched him leave, feeling anxious about all he had to deal with. I moved back to Doc's cage and set him on the play stand on top.

With a big smile I turned back to Teeko and gave her an impromptu hug. "You went to a lot of trouble for us," I said, squeezing her tight.

"Least I could do once I found out you guys were stateside."

"Is John flying in?" I asked.

Teeks smiled. "No. He's got some big deal he's settling and can't get away."

That figured. John was a workhorse.

Heath came back into the room looking like he'd been kicked in the gut. I knew immediately that he was super worried about his mom. "You okay?" I asked.

"Yeah," he said, taking a seat at the bar again. "She's really stressed-out. She knows she needs to be here, but she hates flying and she's upset enough as it is. I'm thinking about flying to Phoenix and bringing her back so she doesn't have to fly alone."

I moved over to sit next to Heath and Gilley, and Teeko came with me. We all huddled around him not knowing what to do or say.

"If I can find a flight that doesn't cost an arm and a leg," he said, pulling out his cell again to flip through the screens, "then I should be able to head there and back sometime today or tomorrow."

Teeko put her slender fingers on Heath's wrist. "Allow me," she said.

He looked at her blankly. "Allow you to what?"

"Let me send you to pick up your mother," she told him.

"You want to drive the limo all the way to Phoenix and back?" he asked.

Teeks smiled. "No, Heath. You can take John's plane out to Phoenix and pick up your mother."

"You'd *do* that?" he asked incredulously.

Teeks looked at me and winked. "Of course," she said. "M. J. cares a lot about you, and anyone M. J. cares about is like family to me."

"Thank you," I said, and the words simply didn't convey all the gratitude I felt.

Teeks took up her coat from the couch where she'd laid it, and Wendell trotted after her. I suddenly realized that the little pug had been following her every move with his big bulging eyes since we all got into the limo. "He's really bonded with you," I told her.

Teeks looked down and blushed. "I may have been spoiling him," she said, picking Wendell up and cuddling him.

"Teeks?"

"Yeah?"

"You should keep him."

Behind Teeko Gilley raised his eyebrows. I ignored him.

"You mean it?" she asked, and the look on her face told me how happy I'd just made her.

I laughed. "Yes," I said. "You've been so great about watching him, and looking out for me, Doc, Gil, and Heath. It's the least I can do."

Teeko hugged Wendell. "Thank you, M. J.," she said. "I'll take the best care of him."

Of that, I had no doubt.

Chapter 4

Heath's mother was a welcome surprise. She arrived around eight o'clock that night wearing a colorful print dress and layers of turquoise and crystal jewelry. Her hair was very long, braided all the way down to the middle of her back, and she was much shorter than her son.

She was also pleasantly round, with plump cheeks and eyes as dark as onyx. When she walked in, the air in the room where we were watching TV seemed to brighten, and I liked her immediately. "Hello!" she said merrily when she saw us gathered around the television. Heath came in behind her, carting her luggage and looking a thousand times better than the last time I'd seen him. He set her bags down next to the bar and swept his mother up in a hug, like he hadn't gotten enough of those in yet.

Gilley began waving his hands in front of his eyes, but a few tears leaked out anyway. The big softy.

Once Heath let go of his mom, he was quick to introduce us. "Ma, these are my fellow ghostbusters. Guys, this is my mom, Serena Lujan."

Gilley got right up off the couch and threw his arms around Heath's mother. "Welcome!" he said.

She laughed in surprise. "Oh!" she said. "Thank you, sweetie."

He stepped back and held her at arm's length. "Please," he said with a big wide grin. "Call me Gilley. Gilley Gilleshpie."

"Gilleshpie?" she repeated.

"Gillespie," I corrected, stepping forward to offer her my hand and introduce myself. "And I'm M. J. Holliday, and this is my girlfriend Karen O'Neil. It was her plane you flew in on from Phoenix."

Mrs. Lujan took my hand and pulled me in for a hug. "M. J.!" she said. "Heath has told me all about you!"

I could feel my insides tighten as I wondered what specifically he'd said about me. She must have sensed my reaction, because she pulled back, placed a hand on my shoulder, and said, "All good things—don't worry."

I let out a breath. "Phew!" I said with a laugh.

She then turned to Teeko. "Thank you so much, Miss O'Neil. You have no idea how grateful I am that you sent a plane to pick me up! I've never flown on such a beautiful thing! I felt like the Queen of England!"

Teeko blushed too and told Mrs. Lujan that it was her pleasure and to please call her Karen or Teeko like the rest of us.

"Are you hungry, Mrs. Lujan?" Gil asked, and I wondered if he was just looking for an excuse to eat again. He then sneezed so hard and so loud it echoed off the walls. "Thanks," he said when we all chimed in with a "Bless you!"

Heath's mother shook her head. "No, Gilley, thank you. I'm not hungry and please call me Serena." I watched her take Heath's hand in both of hers and she looked deep into his eyes. "You look exhausted."

"It's been a rough couple of days, Ma."

She nodded knowingly. "You should turn in."

Heath glanced at the clock on the kitchen stove. "It's only eight thirty."

"Eight thirty New Mexico time. What time does it feel like to you?" Heath didn't answer her, so she looked round to me. "M. J.?"

"It feels like four in the morning," I admitted. Heath cut me a look. "Sorry, sweetie. But it does. I'm still crazy jet-lagged."

Serena gave a few pats to Heath's hand. "You two, turn in, and that's an order. Gilley, you look like you're coming down with something."

"I had a stroke on the plane from O'Hare, and then I caught SARS and then I nearly choked to death on a fajita," he explained casually. "Gilley Gilleshpie."

I shook my head quickly. "What he means is that he had a headache on the plane from O'Hare, and then he came down with the flu, but that last part's true."

Mrs. Lujan took all of that in stride. "Well, it sounds like you're not quite over your bout with the flu," she said warmly. "I make the world's best hot toddy, Gilley. It'll cure what ails you."

Gil gazed at her as if she were his fairy godmother.

"Okay!" he said, ignoring the frown I gave him. The poor woman just got in from Phoenix, for cripe's sake.

Still, as I looked at Gil, I couldn't help but notice that he did seem a little pale and his brow was a bit moist. I moved over to cover his forehead with my hand. "Your fever's back."

"SARS is hard to kick," he said.

Mrs. Lujan winked at me while she rolled up her sleeves and moved into the kitchen. "Don't worry. He'll get a good night's sleep after he's had one of my remedies." Then she turned to Teeko, who'd been observing all of this quietly in the corner. "Karen, I'll need some rum and brandy—any chance you've got that stocked?"

Teeks pointed to the liquor cabinet next to the bar. "You should find everything you need in there, Mrs. Lujan."

We didn't all quite turn in right away. Instead we stayed up till about ten, sipping the hot toddies and getting to know Mrs. Lujan. I found her delightful and wonderfully kind—a far cry from her brothers. I could now see why she'd left the Pueblo. Her personality didn't seem to fit in with any of the other Whitefeathers I'd met—besides Heath, Ari, and her husband, of course. But then, maybe I was being judgmental. I'd been introduced to everyone on a terrible day. Maybe they hadn't been prepared for my arrival and were feeling a little defensive. I decided to reserve judgment for the time being.

When the clock struck ten, Mrs. Lujan clapped her hands and took up all our mugs. Gil's head was drooping on his neck—he'd had three helpings of hot toddy and he was a little tipsy. "Gillshie Gillshepy," he said into his empty cup.

Okay, so he was well past tipsy and more like drunk.

"Come on," I coaxed, helping support him as he hopped (fell) off the barstool. I got him to the room Karen had assigned him and managed to get Gil out of his shoes and his sweater before he simply plopped back on the pillows and began to snore. I covered him with the bedspread and left it at that.

Heath had wheeled Doc's cage down the hall and into our room, and was covering him up with an afghan just as I came in the door. "I didn't want him to get lonely out in that big room," he explained. I couldn't help but think he was such a good guy for taking care of my bird.

Truth be told, I would have likely jumped him right there to show him my appreciation, but two things stopped me: First, his mom was in the room right next door, and second, *his mom* was in the room *right next door*.

No way was I going to do anything more than shake his hand that night. Which was likely for the best, because we were both weary down to the marrow. In fact I think we were asleep almost as soon as our heads hit the pillows.

I was deep in my slumber when a tremendous *WHUMP* hit the side of the house.

The noise sounded something like a giant sack of flour hitting the structure. It rattled the windows and shook the walls. Heath and I sat bolt upright and looked around with large eyes and racing hearts. "What the freak was that?" I asked him. That's also when I heard Doc growling with fear from inside his cage.

Heath flew out of bed and moved to the window. Before he could peek through the blinds, however, there was a series of intense knocks on our door. "Guys?" I heard Teeko whisper through the wood. "Are you two okay?"

I hurried to the door and opened it to let her in. "We're fine. Did you hear that?"

Teeks came into the room, but before she could even answer, Gilley raced straight by us and launched himself like a high-diver onto the bed, burying his head under the covers. "There's something outside!" he shrieked. "Gilley Gilleshpie! Gilley Gilleshpie!"

Doc growled again and I turned on a lamp, hurrying to his cage to peek under the afghan. All his feathers were ruffled and his puffed-up form stared at me with big round eyes. "It's okay, birdie," I said to him. "It's nothing. Probably just the wind." Doc didn't look like he believed me.

"Gilley, did you see it?" I heard Teeks ask, while goose pimples rose on my arms and the hair on the back of my neck stood up on end.

Gil buried himself deeper under the comforter. "It walked past my window!"

I pulled the afghan back over Doc's cage and turned around. Teeks was trembling and pale, Heath seemed rattled, and Gilley's quivering form let me know exactly how he felt.

And then . . . we heard something else.

There was a slow grating sound unlike anything I'd ever heard before. It started at the corner of our room and seemed to pull itself along the outside wall. I felt the blood drain from my face and realized I was holding my breath until it stopped.

No one moved a muscle, and looking around at my

friends, I could tell I wasn't the only one who'd stopped breathing.

We waited in the stillness for something else to happen. It didn't take long. Perhaps ten seconds passed; then some sort of growl reverberated from outside, but it wasn't a growl like Doc's or anything I had ever heard in my life. This was very deep and guttural. If I had to compare it to anything, I'd say that it sounded like something right out of *Jurassic Park*. Whatever it was, it certainly didn't sound like a bear or a mountain lion—it sounded much bigger and ten times as deadly.

My eyes locked with Heath's. *"What the . . . ?!"* I mouthed, and he shook his head.

Karen edged closer to me and she was trembling head to toe. She gripped my arm so tightly it hurt, but I wasn't about to pull away. A second *WHUMP* rattled the house, followed by another series of drag marks along the wood, and all the while the growling never ceased.

Until abruptly . . . it did, and I think that was scariest of all.

We waited for about two more minutes in total silence, nobody moved a muscle, and I only took two deep breaths during that whole time. Finally Heath whispered, "My mom!" and ran out of the room.

Teeko and I raced after him, clutching each other like frightened little girls. Heath stopped in front of his mother's room and knocked twice. "Mom!" he whispered urgently.

There was no reply.

Heath knocked again, this time a little louder and more urgently. "Mother!"

Still no reply.

Heath's hand went to the door handle and he tried the knob. It wouldn't turn. "It's locked," he muttered, then knocked again and yelled, *"Mom!"* much louder this time.

But no one answered.

Beside me I heard Teeko suck in a breath and her hand flew to her mouth. "Oh, God!" she said. "What if it got to her?!"

Heath looked at Teeko, then eyed the door pointedly. She nodded and said, "Break it down!"

He backed up, raised his leg, and kicked at it violently. There was a splintering noise, but the door held. *"Mom!"* Heath yelled, this time at the top of his lungs, before he raised his leg again and thrust his heel forward with all his might.

The door smashed inward and all I heard was a scream before Heath flew past the shattered door. Karen was frozen in terror, and she was still gripping my arm so tightly I had to pry her hand off so that I could run into the room after Heath. A light flicked on and I blinked in the sudden glare. Heath had his mother already wrapped in his arms and she was quivering in fear beside her bed. "What's happening?" she demanded when everyone poured into her room.

Behind me we all heard, *"Ahhhhhhhhhhhhhhhhh-hhh!"* and Gilley came streaming into the room so fast he was a blur. He leaped onto the bed again, grabbing Mrs. Lujan's pillows and using them like a shield. *"How could you leave me alone?"* he shrieked, his voice hitting that awful howler monkey octave.

"Dude!" Heath commanded. "Pipe down!"

"Heath!" his mother said, trying to pull out of the smothering hold he had her in. "What's going on and what have you done to my door?"

"You wouldn't answer," he told her. "I had to kick it in."

"Did you try *knocking*?" she scolded.

I could feel Teeko's eyes turn to me. "We did knock, Mrs. Lujan!" I said quickly. "Several times."

Mrs. Lujan's hand moved to her head, as if to smooth out her hair. "Well, I didn't hear you," she said, looking back at the door, then to the clock on the nightstand. "It's three in the morning!" she exclaimed. "Why on earth did you need to knock on my door at three in the morning?!"

Beside her Gilley whimpered.

"And what's the matter with Gilley?" she asked. Then she squinted at each of us carefully. "What's the matter with all of you?"

"Something's out there," Teeko whispered.

Serena blinked. "What?"

I shook my head. "We have no idea. But whatever it is, it's big and it hit the side of the house so hard the walls shook."

Mrs. Lujan's eyes widened and she looked at her son as if to ask if that was really true. "I've never heard anything like it, Ma," he said. "It sounded like a dragon was outside our bedroom window."

"Oh, my," said Mrs. Lujan, her brow now creased with worry. "Should we go outside and have a look?"

"No!" we all said at the same time. Gilley squirmed back on the bed and held tightly to the pillows.

"Maybe we should look out from the living room,"

Mrs. Lujan suggested next. "There are wall-to-wall windows in there and we might see what's banging around outside."

I gulped. "I'm not sure I *want* to see it," I told her honestly. As a ghost hunter, I'm not easily scared, but something big, bad, and terrible had just paid us a visit, and I was in no hurry to get an up-close and personal introduction.

Heath, however, seemed to take stock of all the scared female energy in the room—including Gilley's—and he must have decided to be the brave soldier among us, because he said, "I'll go. You guys stay here."

I shook my head. "Don't."

He came over to me and gave me a quick peck. "I'm just gonna take a peek," he promised. "Whatever's out there is probably gone by now anyway."

He moved toward the door, pushing a piece of wood that had come loose from the door out of the way, and I knew I couldn't let him go alone.

"Wait," I called when he'd gotten as far as the hallway. "I'm coming with you."

"M. J.!" Teeko whispered. "Don't go!"

"I'll be okay," I promised, moving after Heath and adding with far more confidence than I felt, "We'll be right back."

I edged out into the hallway, hurrying to catch up to Heath, who paused only long enough to let me get to his side. Neither of us reached for the light switches in the hallway, finding our way by the light coming from the half-moon outside.

When we made it to the end of the hallway, Heath took my hand firmly in his. I tried to stop shaking, but that familiar eerie feeling creeping along my back had returned. Something wicked was out and about and neither of us wanted to risk having it spot us.

Heath motioned with his head to the left side of the wall, just in front of the living room. I moved silently with him and we each ducked down a little and edged our heads around the corner.

Outside we could see the trees whipping about. I realized I could also hear the wind howling with short but powerful gusts.

Heath and I listened intently. I couldn't hear the growl from before and was grateful for that at least. Heath squinted at the back deck; I could swear something caught his attention. Wordlessly he pointed to the far right corner of the deck, and as I peered into the dimness, I saw what he was pointing at. The wicker patio furniture had been torn and ripped and sliced into a mess of foam, shredded cloth, and splintered wood.

"What the *hell* happened to the deck furniture?" I whispered.

Heath was shaking his head. He didn't know either. He then lifted my chin and said very softly, "I'm going to go to the windows and get a closer look. You stay here."

My eyes flew back to the wall of windows. They seemed so fragile suddenly, especially given the condition of the patio furniture. "I'm coming with you," I whispered.

"No!" he insisted. "Stay here." Before I knew it, he'd let go of my chin, dropped low, and begun darting across the living room.

There was no way I was letting him venture out there alone. Ignoring his command, I scuttled along the floor after him, and when I came up next to him, he frowned but didn't protest further. We got to the couch and crouched down behind it; then slowly we both eased our heads up over the top and looked through the glass.

The first thing I saw was movement at the edge of the lawn, just before the tree line.

Something big . . . and I do mean BIG . . . was pushing its way across the lawn. The movement was subtle for something so huge, and if I had to describe it, I would say that whatever it was didn't so much walk as . . . slither.

I heard Heath take in a breath at the same time I did. He'd seen it too. And I had the most terrible feeling that whatever that thing was, it was backing up to look at the house and figure out the best angle to come crashing through the windows.

At that moment we both heard sirens. The huge monster out on the lawn stopped moving, as if it was listening too. The sirens drew closer and I prayed that by some miracle they were coming here.

My prayers were answered as the seconds ticked by and the sirens got closer and closer until finally the red and blue glow of strobe lights bounced off the hallway leading to the front door.

I looked one last time out at the lawn, and caught the monster disappearing into the trees. Then, there was a series of hard knocks on the door and Heath and I raced to answer it.

Karen came down the hallway clutching her cell phone and we met at the door together. "I called the police," she admitted.

"Thank God you did!" I said, opening the door for the officers.

There were two patrolmen there, and I couldn't help but think how ill equipped they were to handle whatever that thing had been out on the lawn. "We got a report of a possible break-in?" one of them said.

Teeko pointed to the back of the house. "There's something out there!" she said, still shivering in fear.

"Some*thing*?" the officer repeated.

Teeks nodded.

The two men exchanged a look and asked to come inside. We stepped back and Heath led them to the back of the house, flipping on the outside lights and unlocking the back door.

I followed the officers out onto the deck, Heath sticking close to my side, and we watched the beam from their flashlights as they trained it on the long trail of three talon marks that started at one end of the house and went all the way along to the other.

One of the officers whistled. The other looked around nervously. "Did you catch sight of this . . . er . . . this intruder?" asked the nervous one.

Heath and I exchanged a look. What were we going to tell them? "Not really," I said. "But whatever did this was big."

The nervous officer looked to his partner. "We got any reports of bears in the area? Specifically, a three-toed bear?"

"Nope," said his partner, moving over to the ruined patio furniture. "We'll put in a report tonight and alert the rangers that they may want to come out and take a look," he said.

I could have told him not to bother, but the men were already moving back inside.

Fifteen minutes later they'd gotten all of our information, assured us that the "bear" was probably gone for the night, and left.

The minute they got in their car, Teeks turned on every single indoor and outdoor light she could find. "Do you think they're right?" she asked me, eyeing the patio furniture nervously. "Do you really think it was only a bear?"

Before either of us could answer her, someone right behind us asked, "What did you see?" We both jumped and let out a small yelp.

"It's only me!" said Mrs. Lujan.

"Ma!" Heath chided, then lowered his voice to a whisper. "Don't do that!"

She sat on the couch and took in the damage outside. "Tell me what you saw," she insisted.

"Something big," I said.

"Very big," said Heath.

"Very, *very* big," I added.

"Yes, yes," she said impatiently. "I get it. The thing was enormous. What did it look like?"

I opened my mouth, but words failed me at first. Heath stared at me blankly—he didn't know how to describe it either. "It looked . . . ," I began, ". . . like a dragon."

Heath nodded. "Yeah," he said. "Like an evil dragon."

Mrs. Lujan's face paled. "It looked like a *dragon*?" she repeated.

I nodded. "It was like a demon dragon. Absolutely hands down the scariest thing I've ever seen!" And that was saying a lot coming from me.

"How tall?" Mrs. Lujan asked, and there was an urgent note to her voice.

Heath and I looked at each other. "Eight or nine feet tall. It's hard to tell until the sun comes up and we can see how far away the trees are."

"What color was it?" Mrs. Lujan asked next.

"Black," I told her. "But it sort of shimmered too.

There was this glimmer from the moonlight off its body." And then I realized what I was saying—that I'd just seen a giant dragon move into the trees—and I wanted to laugh.

But then I remembered the patio furniture and all the humor left me. Mrs. Lujan stood up and offered her hand to Teeko. I noticed that her lips were pressed hard together and she seemed to avoid our eyes. "You three should go back to bed," she said.

I was stunned by her suggestion. Heath must have felt the same way. "You're kidding," he told his mother. "You want us to go back to bed after seeing *that*?"

"Yes," she said bluntly. "We can't do anything about it now, and we'll have a lot to talk about in the morning."

"But what if it comes back?" I argued.

"It won't," she said as if she were certain. "It's gone for tonight."

Heath shook his head. "How can you know that, Mom?"

"Because I know more than you," she said, wrapping her arm around Teeks and moving with her down the hall to the bedrooms. "Get some sleep or just rest if you can't. We'll talk more in the morning." With that, Mrs. Lujan let go of Teeks, went into her bedroom, and ordered both her and Gilley to go back to bed too.

Gilley came out into the hallway clutching his pillow; then he latched on to Teeko like a joey koala bear. He and Karen looked at us as if they couldn't believe what Mrs. Lujan had just said. "Ma might be right," Heath said. "Whatever that thing was, it's probably moved on for the night."

My heart rate was starting to come down and I could feel the exhaustion seep back into my frame. I didn't know why, but I thought I agreed with Mrs. Lujan and Heath—whatever that demon was, it probably wouldn't come back again tonight. "We might as well turn in and at least try to get some sleep," I told them.

Gilley and Teeko looked at each other. "Can I sleep with you?" Gilley asked. That made me smile. Gilley. Asking to sleep with a girl. That was a first.

"Sure," she said, a bit of relief in her voice.

When those two had gone back to bed, Heath and I checked on Doc, who seemed fine and drowsy himself, and then we turned in. Well, I turned in. Heath stood by the window looking out for a long time after I managed to nod off.

The next morning I fought to stay asleep for as long as I could, but eventually the rich smell of waffles pulled me out of my slumber. With a tired sigh I opened one eye and gave in to the urge to inhale deeply.

"That smells like heaven," I mumbled.

Heath rolled over and wound his arms around me. "Ma's cooking breakfast," he said. "And I can tell you from experience, she cooks a mean breakfast."

I yawned. "Did you get any sleep after we came back here?"

"A little."

I felt something nudge my backside. "Well, good morning!" I said with a smile.

Heath chuckled. "Care to work up an appetite?"

I rolled my eyes. "With your mother here? Oh, I think not, honey."

"I can be quiet," he said, nibbling on my neck and nudging me again.

"No," I told him firmly, and got out of bed. There was no way I was risking her hearing *that*.

We made it out to the kitchen to find Mrs. Lujan busy cooking up a storm. We also found Teeko standing with a mug of steaming coffee, staring blankly at what was left of the patio furniture. I moved over to her and in the daylight could hardly believe the sight.

The patio furniture was hardly recognizable as anything but kindling. "It's pretty bad, isn't it?" I said when I sidled up next to her. She offered me her mug and I took a sip, relishing the delicious taste.

"I'm heading back to Boston this morning," Teeks said softly, never taking her eyes off the furniture.

"Okay," I said, my heart heavy because I missed her so much and had thought we might get a chance to hang out together like the old days.

Turning to me, she suddenly said, "Come back with me, M. J.!"

That surprised me. "Teeks," I said, "I can't leave Heath right now. Both his aunt and uncle have died." I didn't say what else I was thinking, that whatever demon had visited us last night—and I was now convinced it was a demon—would also need to be dealt with. But Teeks didn't need to know that, because all she'd do was worry. It was best to keep her in the dark.

She eyed me soberly and glanced quickly at the kitchen to make sure that Heath and his mother were out of earshot. "According to Gilley," she said very quietly, "Heath's uncle died under very mysterious circumstances. He said that Mr. Whitefeather was attacked by something that ripped him to pieces." Teeks then turned her head and looked pointedly back outside at the ruins of the patio furniture. So much for keeping her in the dark.

"Listen," I said gently, handing her back her mug of coffee. "Under normal circumstances I'd head back with you in a heartbeat. But Heath needs me and, in particular, my ghostbusting talents. I'm not going to leave him to deal with this alone."

"But I thought you two just started dating?" she said, her voice rising like a question.

"Yeah," I told her, "we haven't been together that long. But if the tables were turned, I know he wouldn't run off and leave me at the first sign of trouble."

"You really like this guy?" she asked.

I didn't answer her right away. Instead I took some time to think of Heath and all he was beginning to mean to me. "Yeah, Teeks. I *really* like this guy."

My friend bit her lip, and I could tell she was thinking about saying something else to me, but was hesitant.

"What?" I asked her.

"If I knew something about Steven, would you want to hear it?"

My brow rose. *That* wasn't what I thought she was going to say. Steven was my ex-boyfriend. We'd split about a month ago, after several weeks of being separated and finding that distance did not make our hearts grow fonder. "If you knew something about Steven, like what?"

"Something that might or might not upset you?"

I knew right away what she must be talking about. "Is he seeing someone?"

Teeks nodded. "I bumped into him," she said. "He

was in Cambridge at this restaurant that John likes and he had a girl with him. She wasn't nearly as pretty as you."

I gave her a sly smile. Good girlfriends were supposed to say stuff like that.

"Ah," I said, trying to get a handle on how I felt about the news that Steven had moved on. "Well . . . he's free to go out with whomever he likes. We're not seeing each other anymore." And then, I realized that I really meant what I'd just said. I still thought fondly of Steven—I always would—but Heath understood me in ways that Steven never could. Heath and I got along really well together, both on-screen and off, and above all, I trusted him. Trust is hard for me, and I wasn't sure that I'd ever really trusted Steven. Maybe it was the fact that he was a doctor and women were constantly throwing themselves at him. Maybe it was the differences in our cultures—he was from Argentina. Maybe it was just that we wanted different things in life. Deep down I knew Steven wanted a stay-at-home wife and tons of kids, and that was something that was never going to be a part of my future.

So after a minute I focused again on Teeks, only to find her staring at me with a knowing grin. "You really are over him, aren't you?"

"I really am."

"Waffles are ready!" Mrs. Lujan called, and we both jumped; then we both laughed and headed over to the table.

From the hallway Gilley came rushing in, still clutching a pillow. "Did someone say waffles?"

"On the table," Mrs. Lujan told him.

Gil set his pillow on the couch, which was when he

caught sight of what was left of the patio furniture. He made a small squeaking sound and I hurried over to him. "Don't look," I told him. "It's better if you don't stare at it."

Gil made another squeaking noise and moved with me to the table. When everyone was seated, Mrs. Lujan doled out the fresh waffles and said, "Did you manage to get back to sleep?"

I nodded along with Gil, but Teeks shook her head. "I couldn't," she said with a shudder, hugging her coffee mug.

"You're going back to Boston, then?" Mrs. Lujan asked, and I wondered if Teeks had already told her.

One look at Karen's surprised face told me different. "Yes," she said. "I was going to stay a few days, but whatever that thing was last night really freaked me out. I don't even know how to explain it to John."

"So we'll pack after breakfast and get out of your hair," I said.

Teeks was quick to hold up her hand. "Oh, no, M. J.! I didn't mean for you guys to leave too. You stay here as long as you like. Really. It's fine."

Next to me Heath shifted uncomfortably and Gilley's big eyes flew to the windows. "I liked our hotel," he whispered, and when Karen's expression turned to hurt, he was quick to explain. "No offense, Teeks, but if that thing did *that* to your patio furniture, I don't think those windows are gonna stop it."

She nodded like she understood fully. "Exactly what I was thinking, Gil."

Gilley then turned to me and said, "Maybe I should go back to Boston with Teeko?"

I nearly choked on my waffle. "You won't stay?"

Heath looked down at his plate, clearly disappointed and maybe also a little hurt.

"Do you two really need me?" Gilley asked. "I mean, I'll stay if you really want me to, but I might just be in the way here."

I swallowed hard. Dammit. Why did Gilley have to leave the decision up to me? "If you want to go, go," Heath said softly. Then he added, "Seriously, dude. This is my problem, right? It's my aunt and uncle who died. I should be the one to handle it."

I moved my hand to rub his shoulder, then glared hard at Gil. He scowled at me and shoved a piece of his waffle around his plate, but finally he sighed dramatically and said, "I'll stay."

Heath picked his chin up. "It's really okay, Gilley. If you're too freaked-out, then go back to Boston. I won't hold it against you. Hell, I can't even say I'd stay if I were in your shoes."

I leaned back in my chair so Heath couldn't see the look I was giving Gilley, which basically said, "Don't. You. Dare. Leave."

Gil's scowl deepened. "I'll stay," he muttered. "Really, I want to."

For the record, no one believed that last part, but I had to give Gil credit for saying it.

"Can we talk about the elephant in the room at least?" I said.

"Which one?" Gil muttered.

I ignored him and said, "Mrs. Lujan, you seemed to recognize our description of whatever that thing was last night. Can you tell us why it rang a bell for you?"

Heath's mother took a sip of her orange juice before

answering me. "It was something my father said," she explained. "He came to me in my dream last night."

I blinked. I didn't quite know what to say to that. "Really?"

"Yes," she said, her eyes glistening with the memory. "He hasn't come to see me in a very long time. But I understand he visits with you quite a lot," she added, looking pointedly at me.

I smiled. "I think it's because he believes I need looking after," I told her.

She laughed. "Oh, I think it's because he genuinely adores you." I blushed but she continued. "Anyway, it was such a powerful encounter with him last night that I believe it's the reason I didn't hear you all knocking on my door. I remember being so excited to see him after all these years and wanting to take in every word he said to me when *bam*! The door crashed open and I woke up."

Heath grimaced. "Sorry, again, Ma. I was worried about you."

Mrs. Lujan smiled and gave a pat to his arm. "It's not me you need to apologize to," she said. "Poor Karen here has to explain the damage to her fiancé. Am I right?"

Teeks waved her hand like it was nothing. "I'll have a handyman come by this afternoon. He can haul away the patio furniture and repair the door in no time. John never has to know."

I wanted to ask Mrs. Lujan what Sam had said, but I didn't want to be rude.

"What'd Sam say?" Gilley asked.

"You know my father too?" Mrs. Lujan asked him, her own face now surprised.

Gil glanced quickly at me. "Uh, no," he said. "But

M. J. talks about him all the time. He's helped us a lot on our ghostbusts."

Mrs. Lujan beamed. "That's Sam Whitefeather for you," she said proudly. "He told me that he's made M. J. an honorary member of the tribe and he's now watching over her as her spirit guide."

"I'm very grateful to have Sam's spiritual assistance," I told her, and that was the truth.

"What else did he say, Mom?" Heath asked.

"He said that he's very concerned about this demon that's come for the Whitefeathers," she told him. "He didn't want me to come back for the funerals, you know. I think that's why I got so worked up about flying here. I think Dad was trying to make me feel like it was a bad idea, but when you said you were coming to get me on a private plane, I couldn't say no."

Karen looked downright guilty. "I'm so sorry," she said. "I had no idea you weren't supposed to be here."

Mrs. Lujan shook her head vigorously. "Oh, stop," she said, attempting a smile. "It's not your fault, dear. You were so kind to offer! And how was I to know that a demon would come here last night?"

"Maybe you should go back to Phoenix?" Heath said, worry lining his forehead.

"I'm not going anywhere," she told him. "Now that I'm here, I'm going to help you three figure out why a demon is targeting our family."

"Did Sam tell you anything about its history or who might have summoned it?" I asked, determined to get to the bottom of things as soon as possible. In order to deal with this thing, we had to know its origins.

Mrs. Lujan nodded. "He said that it was very old, dating back to before the first of our ancestors, which makes it very dangerous and very powerful. He said that I held the key to what it was, but just as he was getting ready to tell me more, you all came into my room. After the police left, I tried getting back to sleep, hoping Dad would come to me again, but I tossed and turned the whole rest of the night, and never really managed it."

"Did Sam mention anything else about the demon before we woke you?" I pressed, thinking any detail left out might be the one clue we needed to figure this out.

Mrs. Lujan rubbed her arm absently. "I think he mentioned something about the histories," she said. "But I can't be sure."

"The histories?" I repeated. "What're the histories?"

Heath answered. "About fifty years ago when younger members of our tribe began to leave the Pueblos in earnest, each tribal council began to take the oral histories of each Pueblo and write them down in both English and Zuni so that, should those tribal members return, they'd always have a reference of their heritage. Each history is housed in a private library on each Pueblo."

"What's Zuni?" Teeks asked.

"It's the language of our particular tribe."

"Do you speak it?" I asked him.

Heath said something in reply that sounded almost like a mixture of Arabic and Spanish. It was beautiful and melodic. "What'd you say?" Gilley wanted to know.

Heath smiled. "I said, 'Yes, I speak the language of my people, the great tribe of the Zanto.'"

"Who's Zanto?" Gil pressed.

"We are Zanto," Mrs. Lujan said, pointing to herself and Heath.

Gil pointed to himself and me. "We are Valdosta." I slapped him on the arm. "Ow!"

"Behave," I scolded.

He scowled at me and looked at Teeko. "Is there still room on that plane, Teeks?"

She laughed. "Oh, no, buddy. If I take you back, M. J.'ll kill me. You're stuck here."

Gilley frowned and excused himself to go sulk somewhere. Meanwhile I asked Mrs. Lujan some more about the Zanto Pueblo histories. "Can we get a look at these histories and see if there's something about this demon in them?"

Heath and his mother traded an uncomfortable look. "I'll ask my brothers," she said after a bit of a pause.

"You have to ask permission to read the history of your own people?" I asked. I didn't get the sudden shift in energy at the table.

"My mother isn't welcome at the Pueblo," Heath said softly. "It's a long story, but suffice it to say that my uncle Rex is in charge of the library where the histories are kept, and if she asks, he might—and I do mean *might*—let her look through them."

"Ah," I said. I realized that I probably shouldn't probe too much deeper about that sore subject.

Teeks folded her napkin and picked up her plate. "I'd better pack," she said, excusing herself from the table.

That left just the three of us, and I thought that maybe Heath could use some time alone with his mom. I glanced at the clock. Doc would be anxious to come out of his cage anyway. I'd checked under his blanket right before heading to breakfast and he'd appeared calm and sleepy. "I better see about Doc," I told them, and started to push my own chair back when Heath laid a hand on my arm and pulled me forward to kiss me.

"Thanks," he said.

I felt my cheeks redden at the PDA in front of his mom. "For what?"

"For everything, but especially for not packing and getting on that flight with Teeko."

Okay, screw the embarrassment. I leaned in and kissed him back.

Later, after the handyman came and fixed the door to Mrs. Lujan's room, we saw Teeko and Wendell off. "Are you sure you don't want me to take Doc?" she asked, giving me a big hug next to the limo.

I was truly conflicted about whether to send my bird back with Karen or keep him here with me. I didn't yet know exactly what that thing was that had come prowling around the house, but I knew it was trouble. Still, I'd missed my bird so much that I just couldn't bear to part with him yet. If things got really dicey, I decided, I could find a local bird vet or aviary to house him for a few days. "Thanks," I told her. "But I think I want to keep him close for as long as I can."

Teeks patted me on the back and then stepped away to hold my shoulders at arm's length. "Are you sure you won't stay here?" she asked. "I mean, you don't know for sure the demon will come back here, right?"

"Which is exactly why we should go," I said. "The uncertainty is what'll keep us up at night. Plus, with those big picture windows, it's way too dangerous. We'd be too exposed. I think we'll find a hotel somewhere close to downtown with lots of traffic and people to play it safe."

"Okay," Teeks said. "But you guys don't have to leave right away. Just lock up anytime and throw the key under the mat, okay?"

"You got it, gal pal," I said, squeezing her hand. Heath

and I had already discussed it, and we'd decided to do some investigating while there was still an abundance of daylight out, then go for an early dinner and come back here to pack up before dusk.

Teeks leaned in and kissed me on the cheek, whispering, "Stay safe, you hear?"

I nodded vigorously, and then I watched her get in the limo and waited until it'd driven out of sight before going back inside, all the while knowing I'd miss her something fierce.

Around two o'clock the driver came back and took us over to get Heath's car out of a garage on the south end of town. I wasn't surprised to find that he drove an immaculately clean Dodge Durango polished to a shiny, silver sheen. We all piled in and Gil asked, "Where to now?"

"Now we go find some answers," Mrs. Lujan said.

I could feel her nervous energy all the way in the backseat. "Where do you want to start, Ma?" Heath asked.

"Your uncle Milton's cabin," she told him. "The scene of the first crime."

Heath started up the car and we pulled out of the garage. He drove in silence and not ten minutes into the trip I felt Gil's head hit my shoulder. That boy can fall asleep at the drop of a hat—or a nice cruise in a car.

Heath wound his way northwest, and we made our way back toward the Pueblo, but took a detour just before we got to the entrance, hanging a right instead of a left onto a narrow road that wound its way up into the foothills. Just when I was starting to nod off myself from the warmth of the car and the lull of the engine, Heath slowed and made a left-hand turn onto a hidden dirt road. "This is tucked away," I muttered as the SUV bounced and jostled its way along the uneven terrain.

Beside me, Gilley snorted and woke up. "Are we there yet?" he asked, rubbing his eyes.

"Almost," said Mrs. Lujan. "Milton kept a hunting lodge in these hills and it's at the end of this road."

Heath had to slow way down because the road became even more difficult to navigate. It was littered with potholes and large rocks. After a bit we were all bracing ourselves against the sides of the Durango to keep from bouncing around in our seats.

Finally we came around a large bend and there was a small but well-built cabin littered with debris and broken glass. Something caught my eye even before Heath put the car into park. I felt a wave of shivers creep up my spine.

Just below the window were three long grooves that looked like talon marks, just like we'd seen in the tree Beverly had hit, and along the back of Teeko's lodge.

We got out silently and I could see the effect of the condition of the cabin on both Heath's face and his mother's. They wore identical expressions of horror and shock. I'm sure I wore it as well.

The four of us stood by the Durango for a moment, and to a person we closed the doors quietly, almost as if we didn't want to disturb the scene with an obtrusive noise. I moved quickly to Heath's side and took his hand. He jerked a little when I touched him, as if he hadn't been aware of anything except his uncle's ruined cabin.

Mrs. Lujan approached the entrance first. She walked carefully around the bits of glass and splintered wood. The door was open and as I squinted into the interior, I realized that the door had swung inward and was hanging haphazardly on its hinges.

Just behind me Gilley squeaked, the telltale sign that he was scared witless. I reached back and took his hand with my free one. "Stick with me," I whispered.

He edged closer and when he moved, Heath did too. The three of us stepped to the door just behind Mrs. Lujan. She paused in the doorway and I could see over her shoulder. A gasp escaped me. The inside looked like a five-hundred-pound tiger had decorated it.

Furniture was smashed and broken and flung about with such violence that I could hardly believe it. There were deep gouges along all four walls and the furniture was barely recognizable as anything other than scrap.

Broken pottery also littered the floor, and when Mrs. Lujan stepped through the door into the chaotic scene, she bent down to retrieve one of the shards and a small cry escaped her.

She hugged the piece to her and pinched her eyes closed. Heath let go of my hand and went over to comfort her, his feet crunching on the debris. Gilley and I waited in tense silence just inside the door. We both looked around nervously and I could see Gil's face was as pale as when he was battling the worst of his flu. "Let's go!" he mouthed, tugging on my hand and turning his body toward the car.

I shook my head. "Not yet," I whispered.

Gil continued to eye Heath's SUV longingly. I had the feeling he was calculating how fast he could run to it.

With a sigh I let go of Gil's hand and began to move around the small space, being careful not to bump or move any of the mess. There was a plastic glove on the floor smeared with blood—probably what was left from the coroner when he came for Milton's body—and I felt my stomach turn over.

As I walked around and took in the scene, the hairs on the back of my neck rose and I became light-headed. It wasn't until I was over by the fireplace that I realized what was happening to me. "M. J.?" I heard Gilley ask, but his voice sounded very far away, as if he were calling to me from a tunnel.

I didn't answer or acknowledge him. Instead I focused on the scene around me and tried not to fight the lightness that was making my limbs tingle. And then, almost in the blink of an eye I saw it—the one-room cabin the way it had been before it was demolished.

There had been a fire crackling in the fireplace that night, and a man with long silver hair who looked remarkably like Sam was hunched over the hearth. He was putting some logs into the bin right next to me and I could smell bacon frying in a pan on the tiny stove at the other end.

The cabin was lit by the fire and two lanterns hung from the center beam. Outside, the wind howled.

Wiping his hands, the man stood up with a small grunt and I could literally hear his joints creak. He put a hand on his knees and grimaced and then he walked stiffly with a slight limp back over to the stove. I watched him crack a couple of eggs right into the pan next to the bacon, and when they were done, he scooped them onto a plate and moved over to the large stump that served as his kitchen table. Pulling up a wooden chair, the man I knew was Milton sat down and got ready to enjoy his dinner, but suddenly, from outside there was a loud *THUMP*.

I shivered. I recognized that sound.

A digging noise came from the back of the cabin and my attention went there, but there was nothing to see. I focused again on Milton, sitting very still as he looked about, alarmed and alert, the fork still clutched in his hand. Silently he stood and moved over to where I was standing. Reaching straight through me, as if I wasn't there, he pulled his hand back and I could see he had a hunting rifle.

Slowly he moved to the door, the gun held up high, and pointed it at the ceiling. He seemed to mutter something in that same tongue that Heath had spoken in.

THUMP!

I jumped. This time the noise had come from the side of the cabin, to the right of the fireplace. Whatever was out there was on the move. Milton lowered the muzzle of his gun, pointing it at the door. He muttered again in Zuni and outside, that low rumbling growl emerged. I began shaking and my heart raced in earnest. I tried to yell at him. I wanted him to hide, or fire the gun, or stay still and quiet, but my voice got stuck in my throat. Try as I might, no sound came out of me.

And then, the growling stopped. Abruptly, like a motor turning off, the low rumble quit and only the wind outside filled the background with noise. Milton lifted his head from the sight of the gun and I could tell he was listening too. Nothing but the wind came back to our ears.

Milton moved to the door, tipping the barrel to his shoulder before reaching for the handle. I shook my head. "No!" I tried. "Wait! Don't!"

But again, no sound escaped my lips, and Milton proceeded to open the door very slowly. He didn't open it far, just a crack really, and he put his eye to the crack to peer out when suddenly the entire door exploded inward, sending the poor man flying through the air to land on his back on the floor.

"M. J.!" I heard as something ancient and horrible screeched from just outside.

I could feel my chest heaving and air was coming into my lungs, but I couldn't get it to stay. Something ferocious and alien filled the doorway. Gleaming black scales and white elongated claws . . .

"M. J.!"

I squeezed my eyes shut, ducking away from the terrible scene in the doorway. I could still hear it, though, and sense the demon slithering into the room. Milton began to scream—high-pitched, the sound of absolute terror—and then I knew he was being attacked and I screamed too.

In the next moment I was on the ground, bits of glass cutting into my shins as Heath shook me again and again by the shoulders. "Come back!" he shouted. "M. J., come back!"

"S-s-s-*stop*!" I stuttered, reaching up to seize his hands. He stopped shaking me abruptly, and then he scooped me to him and clutched me in his arms. I started crying. Milton's terrified screams still echoed loudly over and over in my mind.

"Let's take her out," I heard Mrs. Lujan say.

Heath tried to get me to stand, but my legs just gave out. I was shivering so hard my teeth were rattling and I felt frozen from the inside out. Heath picked me up, even though he was still recovering from a back injury, and carried me to the car.

Somehow he managed to put me into the backseat and then he climbed right in after me, scooping me up again to hold me close. I heard the jangle of keys and Heath say, "Gil. Drive us out of here."

A moment later the engine started and the car was in motion. I sobbed through all of it, feeling like I was coming unglued. "I think she saw what happened to Milton," Mrs. Lujan said. "I think she had some kind of vision and saw who killed him."

She didn't even know the half of it.

Chapter 5

We made it to the end of the dirt road before Gilley pulled over. I'm pretty sure he would have driven us straight back to Boston if the sheriff's car hadn't blocked our exit. "We've got trouble," Gil said, and I lifted my face from Heath's chest to see red and blue strobe lights whirling.

Mrs. Lujan sniffed impatiently. "Let me handle this," she said.

"Hey," Heath whispered to me. "How you doing?"

I swallowed and worked to steady my breathing. "I'm fine."

He hugged me tightly and kissed my cheek. "I think I need to be out there with Ma. It looks like Sheriff Pena's pissed."

I cleared my throat and dabbed at my eyes with the Kleenex Mrs. Lujan had given me a minute before. "I'll come with you."

"No," Heath said quickly. "It's probably better if you stay here. You too, Gil," he added. "Stay put, okay?"

"No problem," Gil told him seriously.

I watched Heath get out and approach the patrol car. Sheriff Pena was standing next to the door, his arms crossed and a definite frown pulling at the corners of his mouth.

He wore those mirrored sunglasses that a lot of cops wear, and they made his face look alien and detached. Mrs. Lujan appeared to be doing her best to talk to him, and he just stood there, grumpily listening to her. Then, when Heath arrived, Pena pointed angrily at him and began reading him the riot act, although I couldn't make out any words.

"Someone's in trouble," Gil muttered.

Then Sheriff Pena pointed to our car and barked some more. "Yikes," I said.

Heath took all of the sheriff's anger and venom with his hands stuffed into his pockets and a contrite look on his face. Pena then wheeled on Mrs. Lujan, but after only a few words she held her hand up in a stop motion and stepped forward to point angrily at him.

"Oh, God," Gil said. "Please don't get arrested, Mrs. Lujan!"

But something remarkable happened. Sheriff Pena backed down. As in, he literally took a step back from Heath's mother, and although I could tell that he was still ticked off, his body language suggested he wasn't about to do any more yelling.

Once Mrs. Lujan had had her say, she turned and stalked back to our car, her son in tow.

When they got into the car, Mrs. Lujan said, "Okay, Gilley, we can go."

"His car's still blocking the exit," Gil said nervously.

"Just pull right up to his grille, honey," she insisted. "He'll move."

Gil hesitated just a moment before he did as he was told and eased the Durango up to Sheriff Pena's cruiser. I could see the deputy inside glaring at Gilley, but just like Mrs. Lujan had said, Sheriff Pena got into his cruiser and pulled it back and to the side so that we could pass.

Once we'd cleared the cruiser, I turned to Heath. "Why was he so mad?"

"He didn't want anyone messing around with his crime scene."

I scowled. "Then he should have put some tape and plywood up across Milton's door. Any animal or hiker could go in there and take a look."

Heath smiled. "He was just coming to do that," he said.

"A whole week after Milton's death?" That'd never fly in the city.

"We move a little slower in these parts," Heath said.

"How'd you get the sheriff to back down?" Gilley asked Mrs. Lujan.

"I reminded him that I used to babysit for him and change his diapers. Milton was my family, and as the sister of the deceased, I deserved some respect and consideration."

The car was quiet for a while as Gil worked to maneuver the car around the various potholes and rough terrain. When paved road was in sight again, Mrs. Lujan said, "Gilley, at the highway, turn left. I'll guide you to a place where M. J. can tell us what happened back there."

Gil drove while Mrs. Lujan navigated and we finally came to a place in the middle of nowhere. Or so I thought. A bright pink trailer with colorful daisy decals and a purple fence surrounding it emerged from the scrub like a mirage.

The land inside the fence was crisscrossed with laundry lines and hanging from them were herbs and dried flowers. Gil parked along the fence and I saw the sign over the doorway. "Tara's Tea Emporium."

"Cool!" said Gil.

I followed behind Heath and Mrs. Lujan when we made our way up the paved walkway to the door. I could smell the heavy overlay of burning incense and tea coming from inside. "Tara?" Mrs. Lujan called when she opened the door and stepped across the threshold.

"Serena?" came a reply from somewhere deeper inside the trailer. "Is that you?"

From the back bounded a woman who closely resembled Mrs. Lujan with long braided silver hair, a short round physique, and big apple cheeks pushed higher from her radiant smile. "You've come home!" she exclaimed.

Mrs. Lujan and Tara hugged each other, then stepped back. "You've been gone too long," chided the proprietor.

"Blame my son," Mrs. Lujan said with a wink and a nudge into Heath's side. "He goes off to be a big Hollywood star and leaves me with no house to live in!"

Heath's face flushed red. "Ma," he said. "It was supposed to be done by now! Ray promised me he'd have it finished by the time you sold your trailer, and no one thought you'd to sell it so fast."

"You expected your cousin to finish the job without you here to oversee it?" she retorted. "I told you not to hire him."

Heath sighed. "You were here," he reminded her. "And Ray usually listens to you."

"Oh, now I'm supposed to handle your business?" she clucked, but I could tell she was really only teasing. I had a feeling she'd quite enjoyed her vacation away in Phoenix with her sister-in-law and didn't mind a bit that Heath's house wasn't ready yet.

"Ah-ah!" said Tara. "No bickering in the emporium! Come, I will make you peaceful tea to soothe the mood."

"That's exactly the brew I was hoping you'd make," Serena said, and she gave me a sly wink. I realized then that bickering with her son had been a ruse to get Tara to brew the tea she had in mind for me to soothe my nerves, but she knew that asking for it directly might result in an inquiry as to why, which could embarrass me in front of a stranger.

I felt renewed warmth for Heath's mom.

"It's a beautiful day, Tara," Mrs. Lujan added. "Would you mind if we took our tea outside in the garden?"

Tara waved at us while she bustled behind her counter and began pulling out cups and pots and clear plastic bags filled with various teas. "No, of course not!" she said. "I'll bring your tea to you and some goodies along with it in a bit."

I followed behind Mrs. Lujan as she moved to the back of the mobile home and opened a sliding glass door. "This way," she coaxed.

I stepped through to the backyard and nearly came up short. It was dazzling. All kinds of sculpture and artistic accents decorated the yard, including a large water fountain made from a truly spectacular glazed clay pot. Several round plastic tables were laid out for guests to sit and take in their tea. I felt the enchantment of the place sweep over me.

I paused in front of the water fountain and marveled at the beautiful design both carved into the pottery and painted on the sides. And then I noticed a small white feather at the very bottom and the name Serena Whitefeather signed with sweeping strokes.

"Do you like it?" I heard Heath's mother ask. I turned to see her standing next to the table at the farthest corner, where we weren't likely to be overheard.

"It's beautiful," I said, leaving the fountain to join the others.

"My mom made it," Heath said proudly.

"I didn't know you were an artist," Gilley said.

Mrs. Lujan's eyebrows rose. "No?" she asked.

Heath looked chagrined. "I only mentioned it to M. J.," he admitted. "And I told her how you'd retired from it."

For a second I thought I saw a glint of sadness in Mrs. Lujan's eyes, but she quickly covered it with a smile. "Well, I haven't made anything in a very long time," she said.

"Maybe you should think about picking it up again. Maybe to make peace with the tribe you could throw a pot or two," Heath muttered, and just like that, the air seemed to fill with tension.

Gil and I exchanged a look. Yep, he sensed it too.

Mrs. Lujan, however, ignored the comment and focused on me. "If you're feeling up to it, M. J., can you tell us what happened to you at Milton's cabin?"

Immediately my mind flashed back to those final moments when something otherworldly had come through Milton's door. I shuddered. "I don't even know where to begin," I said softly.

"Start at the point where you fell into a trance," Gil said helpfully.

I tucked a loose strand of hair behind my ear and stared at the tabletop. I couldn't look at all those inquiring eyes without wanting to squirm under the pressure of telling them every terrible detail. "I remember feeling light-headed and I had the strongest sensation of being almost lifted out of my body."

"An OBE?" Gil asked, referencing the acronym for "out-of-body experience." "You've been having those a lot lately, sugar."

I'd had some experiences in recent months where I'd been asleep and really odd physical things had happened to me, but I hadn't had a waking OBE like . . . ever. "Yeah, well, maybe it happened because of the violence that took place in that cabin," I said. "The energy was pretty strong."

"I think you walked into an imprint," Heath said. When Heath's mother looked at him quizzically, he explained. "An imprint is what happens when something with a lot of emotion happens in a space and that space absorbs it like ink to a sponge. When someone like me or M. J. walks into that space, it can replay itself like it's happening right in front of our eyes."

"So it's true," Mrs. Lujan said, her eyes focused on me. "You saw what happened in the cabin when Milton was killed?"

I nodded and looked back down at the table. "I've never seen anything like it," I whispered.

"Pena thinks a mountain lion got him," Heath said, taking my hand under the table.

I laughed mirthlessly. "What I saw was no mountain lion." I then shut my eyes, trying to fight the image that kept coming to mind. Teeth, claws, and shimmering black, scaly skin. That's what I remembered most. "We were right about it looking like a dragon," I added with a shudder. "A demon dragon with black scales and fangs and claws so sharp they'd cut you in half."

"Here we are!" said a cheerful voice, and I jumped, my eyes snapping open. Looking round the table, I hadn't been the only one surprised by Tara's appearance with her tray of goodies. She paused when she caught the expressions on our faces. "You all look like you've seen a ghost!"

"We were just talking about my poor brother, Tara," said Mrs. Lujan.

Tara immediately turned contrite. "Oh, Serena, I'm so sorry! I'd nearly forgotten about that. And I hear that Bev's gone now too?"

The moment Tara mentioned Beverly, my memory shot back to the tree her minivan had hit, and those talon marks on it and the side of her car. There was now not a doubt in my mind that the same deadly beast that had attacked Milton had also been responsible for Beverly's car crash.

". . . the ceremonies will be sometime this week," Mrs. Lujan was saying, "at the Pueblo."

Tara set down the cups and teapots and two plates of small round cake balls covered in buttercream icing. "Are they open to the other tribes?" she asked.

"No," said Mrs. Lujan with a sigh. "It's family only."

Tara frowned. "You Whitefeathers," she said with a *tsk*. "So exclusive."

"Don't blame me," Heath's mother insisted. "Vernon's dictating this one, and you know Rex's going to go along with whatever he decides."

"And you don't have a vote, Serena?" Tara pressed.

Mrs. Lujan folded her hands on the tabletop and looked down at them. "Not since I left," she said. "I'm lucky to be allowed to attend the ceremonies at all."

Tara gave her friend a sympathetic pat on the shoulder and left us to our tea and conversation.

Gilley, his usual diplomatic self, said, "Family feud, Mrs. Lujan?"

She nodded soberly. "I'll tell you about it after we hear the rest of what M. J. has to say." I opened my mouth to speak when she added, "But first, drink some tea. It'll make you feel better."

To my surprise, after a few sips I did feel better, and I was able to tell them everything that I'd seen in Milton's cabin without shuddering. Much. Okay, less than I would have without the tea. The point is, when I got to the part where the creature burst through Milton's door, I didn't melt into a puddle of tears again and I was able to describe it in full detail.

Once I'd finished, I looked around the table. Gilley was stuffing himself with cake balls and staring at me with big round eyes. Heath looked sick to his stomach and his mother appeared even worse. "I believe I've heard of this thing," she said to me, her voice hollow and frightened.

"The demon?" I asked.

She nodded, and rubbed her temples. "The way you were describing it made me recall the legend, but I think Tara would know it better. Would you mind, M. J., if I brought her over and told her about what you saw?"

"Please!" I said. We needed any piece of information we could get our hands on if we were going to figure out how to fight this thing.

Mrs. Lujan called her friend over, and after about fifteen minutes of explanation and a whole lot of expressed concern from Tara, she finally told us what she knew. "Serena's right about the legend," she said. "I heard it when I was little from my aunt."

"Tara's aunt was a Whitefeather," Mrs. Lujan interrupted. "She was my father's cousin, and she married into the Picuris Pueblo."

"Which is how we all became related," Tara explained. "Anyway, getting back to the legend . . . I think you Zantos have it recorded in your histories, Serena."

Mrs. Lujan frowned. "Rex's in charge of the library," she said. "He'll give me a hard time if I ask him if I can go digging around. You know he'll want to know why."

"I already tried talking to Uncle Rex about this thing," Heath said. "He completely dismissed it."

"So tell us what you know, Tara. Please?" Mrs. Lujan said.

Tara closed her eyes and shook her head, as if she could shake out the elusive memory. "It begins with the spirit of the great hawks. The great white hawk and the great black hawk, who both wanted to claim the sky for their own.

"Even though the sky was vast, neither hawk wanted to share it, and so the two winged spirits went to war. They fought day and night, never resting, each testing the endurance and strength of the other, until one day the black hawk spirit fell to the earth, exhausted and defeated. The white hawk spirit proclaimed its victory, singing its own praises across the sky and shaming the black hawk in front of all the other spirits.

"The black hawk was humiliated and tried to hide its shame by shedding its feathers, losing its beak, and growing scales, fangs, and talons instead. It also cursed the white hawk and vowed revenge, telling its rival that it would wait for the day when the white hawk would eventually land; then it would kill the white bird, shredding it to pieces with its talons and teeth. But the white hawk spirit just laughed and rode the air currents day after day, staying up so long that it eventually became part of the great sky spirit, mingling its white feathers with the blue to become the clouds. The black hawk spirit continued to prowl the earth, waiting for the day when the white hawk might take up its old form again and come down to the ground. While the black hawk spirit waited, it feasted on the flesh of the living, leaving behind its trademark three-talon mark so all would know its power."

I raised my chin and looked to the heavens. The beautiful blue sky held just a few thin stratus clouds overhead, and I could see how the legend might've been born and how ancient tribes might've explained to one another when one of their own went missing and was never seen again.

I eyed Heath and I could tell he had never heard the legend before. "So," I said, wondering if I was just pointing out the obvious, "if I'm extrapolating correctly, you Whitefeathers were named after this white hawk spirit, am I right?"

Mrs. Lujan smiled. "In a way," she said. "But I believe the legend does play a role. When my ancestors were pushed onto the reservation territories by the whites, my great-great-grandfather fought to establish our tribe, the Zantos, on the land we still hold. There was some bad blood between my great-great-grandfather and a neigh-boring tribe, the Zitas—something about our tribe get-ting the more fertile hunting grounds—and in an effort to make peace, my ancestor agreed to marry a woman from the Zitas.

"Well, the Zitas were still bitter about the Zantos having the better land, so they sent their meekest, most sickly woman over to be the bride, hoping she might die while in my ancestor's care so that the Zitas could make the claim that he had neglected her, and the tribes would then go to war. My great-great-grandfather knew that the rival tribe had more warriors on hand, and would likely win in battle, so he took great pains to nurse and care for this woman, and because of his attentions and efforts my ancestor saw what a lovely and kind woman his new bride was, and she saw the same in him. The pair grew to love each other deeply and her health improved.

"When the new bride conceived, everyone thought the rivalry between the two tribes would come to an end and the baby would unite the Zantos and the Zitas once and for all, but during her pregnancy, my ancestor's wife suffered poor health again and she began to weaken un-der the strain of carrying a child. Then she went into la-bor too early to be good for the baby and the tribal midwife said that my ancestor's wife would likely die during childbirth along with the baby.

"My great-great-grandfather was beside himself with worry and grief and he went off into the hills to consult with the sky spirit, begging the great and powerful spirit to intervene.

"While he was praying, word came to him that his wife's condition had worsened, and that he needed to come back to his home if only to say good-bye. With a heavy heart my ancestor began his journey home, but after taking only a few steps, he saw a large white feather on the ground right in his path. He knew it was a sign from the sky spirit and he brought it back to his wife, telling her she would not die, that the sky spirit had shown favor upon her and their child.

"Sure enough, the woman, my great-great-grandmother, did live through the labor and she gave birth to a healthy baby boy with a head full of black hair and one shock of white along the temple as a symbol of his fortitude and strength, bestowed upon him by the great sky spirit. Everyone thought the white streak would go away with time, but instead, it remained and during his naming ceremony when he was two years old, my great-grandfather was named Whitefeather. This was in the mid-eighteen-hundreds, and eventually this name became the one our family took for its surname."

I thought on that a moment. "So, the white hawk *has* come to earth," I said.

Mrs. Lujan and Heath looked at me quizzically.

"Yeah," Gilley said, catching on. "According to the first legend, the black hawk was going to get its revenge as soon as the white hawk landed. The white hawk didn't land, but if a child was born and said to be of the white hawk's spirit, then the black hawk demon could just take its revenge out on you Whitefeathers."

"But why now?" Heath asked. "I mean, why would the spirit of the black hawk wait all this time to come after our family? My great-great-grandfather was born in eighteen sixty. Why would the black hawk spirit—if that really is what attacked Uncle Milton—only show up now?"

"Maybe it was asleep," Gilley suggested. "You know,

lying dormant until the time was right. Like that witch we dealt with in Scotland."

Heath shook his head. "But that still doesn't answer my question, Gil. I mean, what happened that the black hawk's spirit wanted to come after us *now*? The Whitefeathers have been around for a hundred and fifty years. What caused it to suddenly wake up and start attacking us?"

"Maybe it got tired of sleeping?" Gilley suggested.

"Or," I said, thinking back on that encounter with the witch, "maybe, someone else woke it up."

Heath, his mother, and Tara all looked at me with the same penetrating gaze. "We need to find out more about the black hawk spirit and the demon it turned into," Heath said.

"And," added his mother, "we should also tell your uncles what really happened at Milton's cabin."

"They won't listen," Heath said. "Ma, I already tried to tell them about your dad and his warning through M. J."

"Let me try," she said. "Maybe I can talk some sense into them."

"You've been trying to talk some sense into them for twenty-five years," Heath reminded her.

"What happened between you four siblings any-way?" Gil asked Mrs. Lujan.

Tara's eyes widened and she made a point of looking at her watch. "I'd better get to weeding my garden," she said, moving off quickly.

Gil poked his fork into what remained of my snack and eyed Mrs. Lujan expectantly.

"It's a long story," she told him with a sigh.

Gilley leaned forward, unperturbed by the gentle re-buff. "I'm all ears," he said. I could've swatted him.

Mrs. Lujan twisted the wedding band on her ring finger and made eye contact with Heath, as if asking him if he was okay with airing out the family's dirty laundry. I had the feeling he knew the story well, but hadn't shared it with us out of respect for his mom.

In answer to her silent question, though, Heath merely shrugged and gave her a nod of encouragement. "When Heath was very young," she began, "his father and I weren't getting along so well. Mark Whitefeather was a man of high standing in our tribe, and he was my brother Vernon's best friend."

"Hold on," Gil said, raising his hand. "Your husband's last name was Whitefeather too?"

Mrs. Lujan nodded. "Our grandfathers were twins," she said. "So we were second cousins. Second-cousin marriages are pretty common in our tribe," she added.

Gil nodded and got back to his sweets.

"Anyway, as I was saying, Mark was well respected by the leaders of the other Pueblo tribes too. Everyone thought we were the perfect couple and in public we did appear to be that, but privately, Mark was not a nice man to live with. . . ."

Mrs. Lujan's voice faded and her eyes held a faraway strained cast—as if she was remembering things she didn't want to. "I found solace in my work," she said, pointing to the fountain in the middle of the garden. "And I also found solace in the arms of another man outside of our tribe."

My eyes drifted to Heath. His body language suggested that he wasn't exactly comfortable with the story, but was doing his best not to appear judgmental toward his mother.

"Mark found out about my affair," Mrs. Lujan continued. "We argued. He punched me, broke my jaw, and I left him that very night. I got Heath out of bed, wrapped him in a blanket, took a few of our belongings, got into my truck, and I left."

"Where'd you go?" Gilley asked, pulling my plate over so that he could polish off the cake crumbs.

Mrs. Lujan fiddled with her wedding ring again. "At first I went to my brother Vernon's house. Dad and Milton were away on a hunting trip, or I probably would've ended up there. I could barely talk because my jaw was so swollen, but I managed to tell Vernon what'd happened. He told me that Mark had every right to hit me, that I had disgraced the tribe with my affair. He said that he'd been the one who'd seen me with my lover, and he'd told Mark. He said that most of the tribe knew too, and they were all going to take Mark's side. He thought I'd gotten what I deserved."

I felt my face twist with anger. That a brother would betray his own sister like that really bothered me. From the looks of the scowl on Heath's face, it seemed it hugely bothered him too.

"What'd you do?" Gilley said, his voice a little breathless.

"I gave him the finger, grabbed Heath, and walked out," Mrs. Lujan said. "Then I went to my workshop, collected all of my creations, and we came here to Tara's. I traded her that fountain for a place to stay until I got on my feet, and I never went back to the Pueblo."

"Did you report the assault, though?" I asked. I knew I was treading on thin ice here, but I don't tolerate domestic violence.

Mrs. Lujan's eyes cut to her son, and Heath turned

away. Uh-oh. "There was no need," she said to me. "Mark killed himself the day after I left."

The table fell silent. I didn't know what to say. "That sucks," Gil finally said, which wasn't exactly the sentiment I wished he'd expressed, but at least it broke the tension a little.

"My brother Vern never forgave me," Mrs. Lujan said. "Neither did the tribe. Even my father and my brother Milton stood against me for a time. It was a very dark period in my life and it only got worse when I met and married my Frank."

"Was he the man your brother caught you with?" Gilley asked. Again, I wanted to slap him.

Mrs. Lujan laughed. "No. That man was Tara's cousin. He was kind of a wild child and nothing but an escape for me. After I left the Pueblo and he learned I was living here with my son, he didn't come sniffing around much. Which was fine by me, because after Mark died, I wanted nothing to do with men. Then, a few years later, Frank came along and changed my mind."

Mrs. Lujan smiled fondly at the memory of her late husband, and I noticed Heath did too. Frank must have been a wonderful man.

"So the tribe still holds a grudge?" I asked. I couldn't believe that after so many years Mrs. Lujan's family wouldn't forgive her.

"Yes," she told me. "A lot of them go out of their way to avoid me when they can. My leaving was hard on them too," she added with more generosity than I would've had. "I was the only artist trained by my great-aunt in the way of the special firing that makes the glaze on that fountain shimmer and sparkle. It's what made her pottery so valuable, and our tribe has watched as other tribes have prospered for their artists' work. The remaining Zanto artists haven't had as much success as they could have if I'd stayed.

"Still, I did well enough on my own to support Heath and me, until Frank came along and took care of us. And then I stopped throwing pottery nearly altogether. The tribe saw that as a very selfish act on my part. Plus, they always did suspect me of taking the family urn the night I left. But I didn't. It was there on the shelf when I took all the other pieces that rightfully belonged to me."

Gil turned to me and mouthed, "Family urn?"

"Later," I whispered, and focused back on Heath's mother. "Why did you stop throwing pottery?" I asked, looking again at the beautiful fountain. "I mean, when you can create something that amazing, why would you ever want to stop?"

Mrs. Lujan's lips pressed together and she held up her hands. They were knotted with arthritis. "My hands aren't what they used to be," she admitted.

Heath frowned. "I've seen you play with some clay, though. And every time you did make something new, it always sold right away."

Mrs. Lujan sighed and there was a lot of sadness in it. "I just don't have much will to create these days," she admitted. "Not since my Frank died."

The edge of my energy suddenly tingled and my mind started to fill with an image of the Rolling Stones, but specifically the lead singer. "Does Mick Jagger mean anything to you?" I asked her curiously.

Mrs. Lujan's eyes went wide. "Yes!" she said. "Frank was a huge fan of the Stones and he won a contest once where he'd had a picture taken with Mick just before a concert. That picture hung in Frank's office right above his desk." Mrs. Lujan's eyes misted a little. "Is my Frank here?" she asked shyly.

"He is," I said with a knowing smile, before someone else entered my energy. I almost didn't mention it, but he was so insistent. "Mark's here too."

Mrs. Lujan bit her lip, but Heath lifted his eyes to me. "My dad?" he asked.

I nodded.

"He's never come through before," he said. "Are you sure it's him?"

I closed my eyes and focused on the male energy hovering in the background. I nearly smiled when another rock band image took shape in my mind. "He's showing me a Rush T-shirt," I said.

Mrs. Lujan gasped, but then she clapped her hands and gave a playful slap to Heath's shoulder. "That's all your father ever wore!" she exclaimed. "He loved that band and always had one of their T-shirts on."

"Did they come jamming in together?" Gil asked me with a sly smile.

I laughed. "You know how it goes. One spirit pushes a theme to get my attention and another one jumps on it too."

But then Heath's father showed me another series of images and I couldn't quite understand it. "What's the deal with his grave site?" I asked. "Was he moved after he was buried or something?"

Mrs. Lujan was openly crying now. "No," she said, dabbing at her eyes. "He wasn't moved, but he wasn't buried on Pueblo land. Mark committed suicide, and in doing that, he dishonored our tribe, so he was denied a burial in the Zanto burial grounds. Instead, he was laid to rest at a regular cemetery in Santa Fe."

I squinted at her. "Did you recently put flowers on his grave?"

Heath shot his mother a surprised look, but she held my gaze. "Yes. Several weeks ago, right before I went to visit Evelyn in Phoenix, I stopped by and put some flowers there. It was the first time I'd been to his grave since his funeral."

"He's thanking you," I said, adding, "And he's also apologizing. I get the feeling he's apologizing for a lot of stuff, not just the fight you two had."

Mrs. Lujan nodded, but she didn't say anything more.

I turned to Heath. "Your dad says you should check on your house. He thinks there might be a plumbing issue."

"Plumbing issue?"

My brow furrowed. "Plumbing and electrical," I said. "I keep seeing sparks and water."

Heath groaned. "That's never good. I'll call my lazy cousin and schedule a meeting at the house. He's got some explaining to do about why it's taking so long anyway."

"Never hire family," Gilley said.

With that, Mrs. Lujan got up. "Let's go, you three," she said. "I have some tough phone calls to make if I'm going to get access to the library to look up the history of this black hawk demon."

When we got back in the Durango, Mrs. Lujan called her brothers. She started with Vernon, making sure to let him know that she was coming to Milton and Beverly's funeral and that he couldn't keep her away. Their discussion quickly grew heated. I could hear his raised voice through the receiver and then the call ended so abruptly that I knew he'd hung up on her. Undaunted, Heath's mother called her other brother, and that conversation was a bit more civil.

From what I could determine, Rex was going to meet us at Heath's house along with his son, Ray, who I understood was the elusive cousin Heath was trying to pin down for the completion of the construction on the house.

I was a little anxious to see where Heath lived. He had a good eye for architecture and I wasn't disappointed when we wound our way through the hills to the west side of Santa Fe into a sparsely populated neighborhood with terrific views. Nearly at the top of one large hill Heath made a right turn into the drive and we arrived at a dark brown stucco adobe-style home with a big picture window next to the entrance and a beautiful antique-looking front door complete with large brass knocker.

"Nice!" Gil whispered, echoing my thoughts exactly.

We got out just as another vehicle pulled in behind us. I recognized Rex, but the young wiry man on the driver's side was new to me. "Cuz!" he said, clasping Heath's hand and pulling Heath toward him in that manly half hug, half handshake that guys do. "How's Hollywood, bro?"

"Wouldn't know, bro," Heath told him. "I've been in Europe for the past couple of months."

The younger man stepped back and made a gesture with his hands to indicate he was impressed. "Whoa, dude! Europe? Like with the kings and queens and shit?"

"Language, Raymond," Heath's mother said, but she added a wink to let him know she was only half serious.

"Hey, Aunt Serena," he said contritely, stepping up to give his aunt a hug. "Heard you been in Phoenix."

"I have," she said to him, stepping back to look him up and down. "But I'm back now. And while Heath is away, working on his television show, he's going to put me in charge of making this place livable. Won't that be *fun*?"

I had the distinct impression that while it would most likely be great fun for Mrs. Lujan, it was *not* going to be fun for Ray.

"Oh," Ray said, barely catching himself before saying something that would get him in trouble. "Sure, Auntie. That sounds great. Hey, Heath, why don't I show you what I've done so far?"

Heath turned to Gilley and me. We'd been left out of all the exchanges. "Want to come inside?"

"I'd love to," I said.

Ray turned to look at me and caught himself again. "Oh, man! Where are my manners?" he said, thrusting his hand at me. "Hi, I'm Ray Whitefeather. You must be the *chiquita* my cousin keeps talking about in his e-mails, eh?"

"Uh . . . ," I said, caught off guard while watching Heath's face turn red.

"Why, hello!" said Gilley, practically pushing me out of the way to take Ray's hand. "I'm sure you've guessed by now that I'm Gilley. But you can call me Gil."

Ray's eyes widened a little as he moved from attempting to shake my hand to Gilley's. "Hey, Gil," he said. "Nice to meet you. How do you know these guys?"

Gilley's face registered a bit of shock. "I'm on the cable show with your cousin," he said, as if he was trying to remind Ray of something he should already know.

"Ah," said Ray, clearly trying to let go of Gilley's palm, which was busy pumping his up and down.

"Let's go inside!" I said, if only to end the awkward moment.

Heath turned and led the way, stopping by the security panel to punch in his code. When the panel continued to beep its warning, Heath turned to Ray and said, "What'd you do to it?"

"Sorry, bro," Ray said, stepping forward quickly to punch in a series of numbers. "I had to change it 'cause I could never remember your code and I've got some tools in here I don't want to get stolen."

While Heath's and Ray's backs were turned, I grabbed Gil by the shoulder and whispered, "Behave!"

"He's cute!" Gil responded just as quietly. "Do you think he's single?"

"Hands off, Gil," I warned. I was pretty sure that Ray was as straight as they came and would only be offended, even possibly angered, by Gilley's advances.

Heath held the door open for us and we all went in. The interior was dark except for the light from the windows, but I could still tell the space held terrific promise.

Large and airy, the interior had wonderful flow, and even though it'd been gutted down to the studs, it still looked to be in great shape structurally. Heath and his cousin talked progress—or lack thereof—and Gilley and I took the opportunity to snoop around.

The home had a good-sized living room, which also flowed right into the dining room and the kitchen, with an island separating it from the eating area. Some of the appliances had been delivered but were clearly not in place yet, and Gil and I saw patches of work that had been started, but not completed. Around the corner of the kitchen was a separate bedroom that seemed large enough to be the master suite or a big spare bedroom. "I like this," I said, feeling out the energy of the place. "I think when it's done, Heath is really gonna dig it here."

"Could you see yourself living here with him?" Gil asked me quietly.

I blinked. "Huh?"

"Oh, come on, M. J.! Haven't you fantasized about you and Heath and a baby or two?"

"No!" I yelled loud enough for Heath to call out to me to see if I was all right. "Fine!" I assured him, then rounded on Gilley. "We're not *there* yet."

Gilley just cocked a skeptical eyebrow.

"We're not even close to *there* yet."

Gil folded his arms and continued with the raised eyebrow.

"I mean, we just started dating!"

Gil threw in a toe tap or two just for good measure.

"Oh!" I growled. "Whatever, Gil! Sometimes you're impossible."

I then moved out of the room to head upstairs. When Gil tried to follow me, I glared at him and he backed off. "Maybe I'll check out the backyard," he said.

I made my way to the top floor and over to the bedroom facing the front yard. Heath's mother and his uncle were out there talking, and because the window pane was fairly thin, I had no trouble hearing their conversation.

"... the girl's a medium like Heath," Mrs. Lujan was saying. "When we went to Milton's cabin, she saw what happened to him."

"Pena says it was a mountain lion," Rex said. "He's got a hunting party out looking for it."

"It wasn't a mountain lion, Rex!" Mrs. Lujan snapped. "It was a demon."

"A demon?" Rex repeated, and then he began to laugh. "What mind games have Heath and his girlfriend been playing on you, Serena?"

"No games!" she insisted. "I saw the girl with my own eyes, Rex! She went into a trance and she didn't even flinch when I pinched her! I know she saw what happened to Milton that night, and it wasn't natural."

Rex's body language suggested he didn't believe any of it. "Why would a demon attack Milton?"

"It's the enemy of the sky spirit," his sister replied. "The black hawk. It's come to take its revenge on the Whitefeathers."

"You've been filling your head with too many old Indian fairy tales," said her brother. "I talked to Cruz before we came here. He says the coroner is ruling it a cougar attack, which fits with what he says he saw at the cabin. Milt had a deer carcass hung from a tree, which he was going to clean the next morning. Cruz says it must have attracted the cougar and that's what got Milt."

"Why won't you listen to me, Rex?" Mrs. Lujan asked. "Our brother was murdered by the spirit of the black hawk and you need to warn the others! Bev could've been attacked by it too!" According to what Heath and I discovered at the accident site, Mrs. Lujan was more on target than she realized.

Rex, however, wasn't swayed, and he became visibly angry. "Oh, now Bev was killed by this spirit demon too?" he mocked. "I thought she drove off the road and hit a tree?"

"It could've been in the road, Rex. It could've caused her to lose control and hit that tree."

Rex waved an impatient hand at his sister. "Oh, stop it, Serena!" he snapped. "This is crazy talk! Bev wasn't even a Whitefeather by blood! She married into it and divorced herself away from it! You're going to tell me this demon doesn't know the difference?"

"I want access to the library, Rex," Mrs. Lujan said, folding her own arms across her chest and trying to stare her brother down. "I want to see if there's anything in the histories that can explain it."

Rex's cell phone rang and he rudely turned away from his sister to answer it. He finished the call after only three "Yeah's," then swiveled around to his sister again and stepped forward to hover menacingly over her. "That was Vernon," he said. "Beverly's body is ready for burial. The ceremonies are being held tomorrow. You and your son can come, but only until the ceremony ends. Then you need to leave the Pueblo."

"How generous of you," Mrs. Lujan snapped, her face angry and determined.

"It's your own fault, Serena. You turned your back on your husband and the rest of us twenty-five years ago. Don't act surprised that we don't want to welcome you back with open arms just because you remembered some old Indian tale."

"So, just because I got caught and you didn't, you think you can pass judgment on me?"

My eyebrows shot up. Was Mrs. Lujan referring to an affair her brother had?

"How dare you!" Rex growled, looking around as if afraid that someone would overhear. "I owned up to my responsibilities, Serena! You just wiped your hands of us, stole the family urn, and walked away."

I bit my lip. These two really knew how to sling the arrows.

I could tell that Heath's mom was about to fire off another accusation, but then she appeared to collect herself and in an instant her expression softened. "Rex—," she said, reaching out to touch his arm, but he shrugged her off.

"I'm done talking about this, Serena. Hear me? *Done.*"

"M. J.?" Heath suddenly said behind me.

I jumped. "Hey! Didn't hear you come upstairs."

Heath smiled and peered over my shoulder at his mother and his uncle. "Don't tell me," he said. "Uncle Rex isn't buying our theory that a demon killed Uncle Milt and Aunt Bev."

"He's going with mountain lion and car accident," I told him. "And he's not open to letting you or your mom into the library."

Heath wrapped his arms around my shoulders. "Figures. My uncles can all be pretty stubborn. Milton was cool, though. He would've believed us."

Abruptly we heard Rex bark something like, "I'm not listening to this anymore!" before stalking off to his truck.

I was surprised that he'd gotten so angry, but Heath didn't seem to react. "He'll go back and tell Vernon that Mom's gone crazy again," he said with a sigh.

"Again?"

"Uncle Vern and Uncle Rex both think Mom was nuts for leaving my dad. Even though he broke her jaw, they think she should have stayed with him."

"Do you remember your dad?"

Heath shook his head and his chin rubbed against my neck. "No. He died when I was only two. I did really love my stepdad, though. Frank was awesome, and I know my mom really misses him."

I could feel Frank's presence again, and there was a tightening around my heart. "He had a heart attack?"

"Yep," Heath said. "He started getting chest pains in the morning and called my mom around noon. She met him at the hospital right before he was wheeled into surgery. They got to see each other and say all the important stuff before he went under. He died on the table three hours later. The doctors said the damage was too bad to repair."

"I'm so sorry."

I felt Heath's shoulders rise and fall. "What're you gonna do?"

The smell of burning wood filled my nose. "Do you smell something burning?" I asked, pulling out of his grasp and sniffing the air.

Heath sniffed too. "No."

I lifted my chin higher and walked around the room, sniffing every corner, but the smell had all but vanished. "Weird," I said, coming to a stop in front of the alarm control panel. I remembered again why we were here in the first place. "Did you talk to your cousin about the electrical and plumbing issues?"

Heath scratched his head. "He swears the electrician was out last week and checked over all the wiring. His guy says the wiring's good. As for the plumbing, Ray says that he's waiting on a part before he can install the dishwasher, but otherwise, all the pipes are sound."

I frowned. What I'd seen in my head didn't match

what Heath was telling me. I sniffed the air again. No smoke. "Huh," I said.

"Let's check the house," Heath said, seeing that I was still nervous about the smell.

We took the next ten minutes to check every room, but neither of us could find any hint of something burning. All the light switches looked sound, and there weren't any frayed or exposed wires anywhere, so it was hard to figure out why I'd smelled what I'd smelled.

Gilley joined us just as we were checking out the garage. "Your uncle and cousin are gone," he told Heath. "And your mom's waiting in the car. She looks really hungry."

"We're coming," I told him, knowing full well that it wasn't Mrs. Lujan who was hungry—it was Gil.

Heath, however, turned irritated. "Did you say my cousin's gone?"

Gilley's eyes darted to me. "Uh . . . yeah."

Heath swore under his breath and removed his cell from his back pocket. Tapping at the screen before putting the phone to his ear, he waited a beat, then tore into his cousin. "What the hell, Ray?" he snapped. "My back's turned for ten seconds and you bounce?"

Gilley's eyes got large and he mouthed, "Yikes!" to me.

I waved him out of the room. Heath turned in a circle and faced the wall. "Ray," he said sternly. "You promised me you were gonna work on this *today*! I've given you a lot of cash to get this place cleaned up and if I have to bring in your dad or Uncle Vernon, I will, bro."

Heath's shoulders were raised and tense. I hoped for Ray's sake he didn't try and shirk out of work again. "Okay," Heath said after a minute. "Fine, drop your dad off at his house, then get back here and get to work, okay? I'm gonna check on you later, bro. Don't let me down." With that, Heath clicked off and stuffed his phone hard into his back pocket.

"He's coming back?" I asked.

Heath whirled. "Sorry," he said when he saw me still standing there. "I had to get tough with him."

"Oh, don't worry about me. It sounds like he's been taking advantage of you."

Heath shrugged. "Ray's a good guy—he's just easily distracted. He likes to start projects, but he doesn't always like to finish them. I'll come back here after dinner to make sure he's here and working."

With that, we left the house and headed to town to find some grub.

Heath took us to a lovely restaurant called Cafe Pasqual's, where Gilley ordered his way through the menu. I looked pointedly at his midsection while the waiter hurried to scribble his way through Gil's order. Gil must have taken the hint, because he canceled the appetizer.

Heath's phone rang as we were finishing up our meals and he fished it out of his back pocket again. His mother gave him a stern look. "Don't you dare answer that at the table, young man," she said.

Heath looked properly chagrined. "Okay, Mom," he said, clicking the button to ignore the call.

He'd only just managed to put it back into his pocket when Mrs. Lujan's phone went off. No one said as much, but I could see everyone at the table wondered if it was the same caller. Mrs. Lujan steadfastly ignored her ringing telephone and after four rings it stopped.

I cut into my food again when Heath's phone went off a second time. "Oh!" said his mother when he pulled it out to look at the display. "Go ahead, Heath, but keep it short, all right?"

Heath got up and turned away from the table to take the call. I followed him with my eyes. Something felt off.

"Wait, Ray, what? Dude, calm down! I can't ..." Heath's voice trailed off, but I could hear the alarm in his voice. *"WHAT?"* he shouted after a lengthy pause, and the entire restaurant fell silent as all the patrons looked round at Heath.

Mrs. Lujan got up and went to her son. "What's happened?"

"We're coming!" Heath said, clicking off the line and turning around to face us. Gone was his relaxed and easy smile, replaced by a look of shock and disbelief. I stood and our waiter came hurrying toward us.

"Is everything all right?" he asked me.

"The check," I said, barely looking at him. *"Now*, please," I urged when he just stood there and stared at me. I didn't know what'd happened, but I knew we were about to go running out of the restaurant.

"Heath!" said his mother, taking him by the arms. "Tell me! Tell me what's happened!"

He turned his wide eyes to her. "The house," he said haltingly. "Ma, it's on fire!"

Chapter 6

We got no farther than the bottom of the hill below Heath's driveway. Fire trucks and equipment blocked the road along with several firemen who were standing guard making sure no pedestrians got too close.

Heath didn't consider himself a pedestrian. "That's my house!" he shouted when he tried to push past the group and run up the hill. It took three of them to hold him back. "You need to stand over there!" one of the firemen shouted. "Sir, you can't go up there! It's too hot!"

I ran to Heath's side and took him firmly by the arm. "Come with me!" I commanded, and I think it was because he knew me that he complied. I walked him down away from the firemen to give them breathing room, but one look up the hill at the orange glow told me it was bad. Really bad.

I turned Heath to face me, away from the scene, and

hugged him tightly. I knew how much it'd meant to him to buy his first house, and I couldn't imagine losing it before even having the chance to move in.

He hugged me back fiercely and I could feel him shaking with rage and emotion.

"Heath!" I heard someone shout. I picked my head up from his chest and turned around. Ray was a bit farther down the street, sitting in the open back of an ambulance with an oxygen mask over his nose and mouth. I let go of Heath and we both ran to him.

He was barely recognizable from the youthful bouncy young man I'd met just two hours before. His face was covered in soot and he was cut and bleeding in several places along his arms and side. "What happened?" I gasped when I saw him.

But Ray directed all his comments to Heath. "It wasn't me, bro!" he said. "I swear! It wasn't me!"

Heath's lips compressed to form a very thin line and he turned to the paramedic trying to patch poor Ray up. "Is he okay?"

The paramedic shook her head. "I keep telling him he needs to let us take him to the hospital, but he wanted to wait for you guys. So now you're here, tell him to let us take him in, okay? He needs stitches for at least three of those cuts on his arms, and his lungs may have some smoke damage."

Mrs. Lujan appeared at my side. "Raymond?" she asked, her expression astonished. "My God, son, what happened to you?"

To my surprise the tough-guy persona Ray wore completely disappeared and his eyes welled with tears. "It wasn't me, Aunt Serena! You gotta believe me! I didn't do this!"

Heath's mother turned to look over her shoulder and I followed her gaze. Huge arcs of water were making their way onto the heart of the fire, but already most of the house was disintegrating into a smoky wreck.

"So what happened?" Heath said again, his tone level and barely controlled.

Ray pulled the oxygen mask off his face. "I don't know, man!" he said again. "I was inside and something freaky started happening!"

"How freaky?" I asked, my senses alert.

Ray shook his head, like he couldn't quite believe what he'd been through. "There was, like, this growl or something while I was upstairs working on your drywall, bro. I didn't know what it was. It sounded like a tiger or something!"

Mrs. Lujan's hand flew to her mouth and behind me I heard a squeak. Without looking, I knew Gilley was with us too.

"Then what?" Heath asked, and this time his voice was more patient.

Ray took a shuddering breath and coughed wetly. The paramedic shoved the mask back over his mouth and nose and told him to leave it there. It was a minute before Ray had the wind to continue. "Something hit the side of the house! Something big! With claws! It happened near the kitchen, I think, and I got, like, freaked-out, so I stayed upstairs and just waited to see if it would go away, but then something *really* freaky happened!"

"What?" we all said when Ray didn't continue, but just focused on taking big gulps of air.

His eyes were staring at the pavement as if he were seeing it all unfold again in front of him. "I heard this sound downstairs, like it had come *inside*, you know? So

I panicked and hit the button on the alarm for the fire trucks—"

"Was the house already on fire?" I interrupted, thinking I'd missed something.

Ray shook his head. "No, man, but whatever was downstairs was so freaky that I didn't want just two police guys to show up, you know? It's like that saying, you come home after a robbery, call the police, but if you're home *during* a robbery, call the fire department. They'll come with lots of trucks and noise and guys and shit."

"Language, Raymond," Mrs. Lujan said, then put a hand to her mouth. "Sorry," she said to him. "It's habit with you."

Ray nodded like he totally understood.

"So how did the fire start?" I asked.

"Well, the ALERT button for fire went off on the control panel, and it said that the fire department was on its way, and *then* all of a sudden there was this sound like a bunch of volts or something, and I heard the fuse box blow and all the electrical outlets just started crackling and burning, and then the whole house started to smoke up, you know? It was like, whatever was downstairs *was playing with me*, *yo*! Like it was saying, 'Oh, yeah? You wanna call the fire department? Well then, I'll give you a stinking fire!' Before I know it, I'm trapped on the second floor and the whole downstairs is burning up! I just stood there! I was afraid to move!"

Ray coughed and the paramedic gave us all another stern look.

Once Ray had stopped coughing, he said, "I knew I should've gotten out of there the minute I smelled smoke, but I was still afraid of the thing downstairs. I mean, what if it was still there? But the smoke got so bad and I couldn't open the window, so I had to, like, dive through it onto the roof, you know? I barely made it out *alive*, bro!"

Ray was shaking now from head to toe, and his coughing fit resumed. I put a hand on Heath's arm and he got the hint. Turning to his cousin, he said, "Ray, it's cool, really. This paramedic is going to give you a ride to the hospital, okay?"

"My ... dad!" Ray sputtered in between coughs.

"I'll call him," Mrs. Lujan promised. "You go to the hospital, Raymond. We'll be there in a little bit."

"Would you like to ride along?" the kindly paramedic asked her.

Mrs. Lujan brightened. "I would. Thank you," she said, but then seemed to think better of it. She turned to Heath, who leaned in, gave her a hug, and said, "Go, Ma. Be with Ray. We'll head over soon."

Mrs. Lujan squeezed her son tightly, then let him go and got up into the ambulance next to Ray, who'd finally stopped fighting and was lying back on the gurney, sucking in the oxygen. I felt terrible for him, and I was very glad he was alive. Once the ambulance had driven off, Heath moved back to stand near the fire trucks and watch them battle the blaze.

Gilley and I joined Heath, and I again reached for his hand. On the other side of him, so did Gilley, and I nearly smiled when I realized Heath was allowing Gilley to hold his hand too. "You were right, M. J.," Heath said to me.

I blinked. "Right about what?"

"Sparks and water," he reminded me. "Remember you said I'd have an electrical and plumbing issue?"

"Whoa," I said, realizing that sparks had caused the

blaze and now hundreds of thousands of gallons of water were being poured into Heath's ruined home. "I wish I'd been wrong."

He swallowed hard, and I could see him struggle to hold back his emotions. I felt terrible for him.

"Do you have insurance?" Gil asked.

"Not now, Gil," I said tersely.

"What? If he has insurance, it'll cover the house and he'll get to build from the slab up!"

"Yes," Heath told him, sliding his hand out of Gil's to rest an elbow on Gilley's shoulder in a more manly pose of affection. "I've got insurance. But it's still tough to watch, you know?"

"Thank God Ray's not seriously hurt," I said.

But Heath didn't seem to be listening. His focus was on the fire, which was finally showing signs of burning out. Still the flames outlined Heath's face and I could see his pain etched there. It broke my heart. He looked weary and sad, but there was also an undercurrent of anger, which I fully understood.

Finally, the fire captain motioned for Heath to come to him, and he left Gil and me at a safe distance while he talked to the firefighter. I saw the captain show Heath a small section of wood that didn't appear to have been touched by the fire except for perhaps some light scorching on one side. The captain then called over one of the cops standing nearby and the three men regarded the wood panel, talking about it while turning it over and over. The officer scratched his head as he looked at the section; then he appeared to ask the captain something, but the fireman could only shrug as if he didn't know. Heath's posture was downright rigid, and he didn't seem to contribute much to the conversation.

"I wonder what that's about," said Gil.

"Nothing good," I replied.

Sure enough, Heath came back to us with a very troubled look on his face. "We can go," he said, and began walking toward his SUV.

Gil looked at me as if to say, "Uh-oh . . ."

We got into the Durango without a word and Heath backed up carefully to avoid the hoses and other emergency vehicles. Once he'd gotten turned around, we headed over to the hospital.

Heath parked and we went into the ER. The lobby was filled with Heath's relatives, practically everyone I'd seen at Ari's house. Ari came right over to Heath and gave him a big hug. "Oh, cuz," she said. "I'm so sorry!"

"Thanks," he said stiffly. Ari backed away and eyed him quizzically. I was sure she detected the simmering anger just under the surface, but what that was about I still had no clue. I suspected that the piece of his wall was somehow involved, but I couldn't figure out what had caused the current of anger in him.

We heard that Ari's husband, Brody, was with Ray, who was getting a CT scan to check for signs of a concussion and any other internal injuries, and then he'd need to get stitched up, so it might be a little while. I was willing to wait, but Heath seemed unusually anxious to be off, and I saw him go over to his mom and whisper something in her ear that caused her to gasp and look at him with large frightened eyes.

She seemed to ask him a question and Heath nodded, patting her hand to reassure her; then he kissed her on the cheek and turned away.

Before coming back to us, he stopped to say something to Ari, pointing back to his mother. This time she nodded and he squeezed her hand before leaving her too. "We gotta go," he said quietly when he stood in front of us again.

"Okay," I said, wondering what the heck was going on. Gilley edged closer to me.

"Are we in trouble?" he asked Heath. "I mean, did we do something wrong?"

Heath's whole face changed. "No, man," he said to Gil. "Sorry. I'm just preoccupied with this demon thing. Let's get back to the car and I'll tell you what the firemen found."

We got back into Heath's vehicle and he started the engine, which was good because it was now dark and cold outside. "The fire captain showed me a section of the wall from the back of the house," Heath explained. "He said that there was an entire panel back there that had weirdly escaped the fire, and the one thing that he couldn't quite figure out was how there could be scorch marks dug so deep into the wood without it going up in flames along with the rest of the house."

"Huh?" said Gil. "Dude, I'm not following you."

Heath sighed and appeared to gather his thoughts. "At the back of the house where the kitchen sat, there was this section that Ray was working on to replace the wall because the old one had some water damage. There was no stucco on it; it was just bare wood. The section was maybe six feet by four feet, and according to the fire captain, it sustained no damage at all. It was like the wood had some sort of flame retardant on it, except for three long scorches shaped like claw marks running all the way down the side of that section. Those claw marks had been burned into the wood."

The breath caught in my throat. "*That's* what was on

the section of wood the captain showed you?" I said. "Those talon marks looked like scorch marks from where we were standing."

Heath nodded. "I've never seen anything like it," he said, and a shudder ran through his shoulders.

Gilley made another squeaking sound. "So we're absolutely positive that the fire wasn't started by faulty wiring?" he asked.

Heath shook his head. "That's the other crazy thing. The captain said it was still too early in his investigation of the cause of the fire to say for sure, but one of his guys said that the fuse box looked to be the source. The captain said that what he and his guy had seen indicated it was probably an electrical overload, but the weird thing is that you don't usually get that kind of overload unless a house gets struck by lightning."

I looked up. The night was crystal clear and all the stars were out.

"So this demon we're dealing with is capable of overloading fuse boxes and starting fires?" I asked.

Heath nodded. "We saw the same thing with the witch in Scotland."

Gilley whimpered, and I knew he was missing his personal fire extinguisher. "Gilley Gilleshpie," he whispered.

I felt a shudder trickle down my own spine as the memory of both the inn in Scotland that the witch had set ablaze and Heath's home engulfed in flames came back to me. For several minutes no one said anything; we all just looked down and stared blankly at our laps. "How do you fight something like that?" Gilley finally asked. "I mean, the witch at least had once been human. But this thing . . ." His voice trailed off while he thought about it. "How do we fight a demon that's pure evil?"

I looked up and found Heath and Gilley staring at me. Aw, hell. They wanted me to come up with the answer. "I don't know," I told them honestly. "But I think we need to start working on a plan of attack, and we need to come up with it soon."

Heath nodded. "I don't think it's a good idea for us to work it out at Teeko's place," he said, turning to the wheel and putting the car in reverse. "We should go somewhere with more people."

A sudden terrible thought occurred to me. *"Doc!"*

Heath twisted his torso to look behind him while he backed up. "I know," he said. "We'll go to the house, get him and our stuff, and find a popular hotel with all the latest in fire-safety systems. We can talk through some game plans tonight."

We found a package for Gilley on the front steps of Teeko's lodge and Doc safe and sound, half-asleep and quite cranky about being woken up. "Booger butt," he said moodily when I stuck my hand into his cage to retrieve him.

"I know, honey," I cooed. "We just need to get you packed up for a road trip, okay?"

Meanwhile Gilley alternated between being ridiculously excited that his new iPad had arrived and charging around the house like a Tasmanian devil, throwing everything he could find that was his, mine, or Heath's into an open suitcase and scuttling it to the front door. Then he found a small fire extinguisher under the sink, and continued to pack one-handed while he hugged the extinguisher tightly.

Heath went around and flipped on every single outside light he could find. I knew it likely wouldn't keep the demon away if it was in the neighborhood, but the glow did ease my nerves a little.

"We have no spikes!" Gilley complained when he took in the contents of our things. "M. J., did you pack any in your messenger bag?"

"I have two grenades," I told him, referring to the steel cases that housed the magnetic spikes we used to thwart off the nastier poltergeists.

"Two?" Gilley shrieked. "How the hell are we supposed to do anything with just *two*?"

"Hey," I said, motioning to Doc, who began fluttering on my hand. "Don't upset the birdie."

"Sorry," Gil said, lowering his voice to a hissy whisper. "How the hell are we supposed to do anything with *two*?"

I glared at him. "You were in charge of bringing our equipment, Gil."

He glared back. "You know the crew put all our stuff on the plane for L.A.," he snapped. "Gopher and his stupid inventory checks for the network accountants. We have *nothing* to fight this thing with!" His voice was back up to shrieky again and I was losing patience.

"We can make more," Heath said calmly, picking up Doc's cage to carry it to the front door.

I put Doc on my shoulder and went to Mrs. Lujan's room to pack her things too. "What're we going to do with your mom's stuff?" I asked when I'd finished and was wheeling her suitcase out to the front hallway with all the others.

I came up short at the door. Heath and Gilley were standing there with Sheriff Pena and his deputy. "M. J.," Heath said, his voice a bit stiff. "This is Sheriff Pena and Deputy Cruz from the Pueblo."

The sheriff tipped his hat. "Ma'am," he said.

"Sheriff," I replied. My eyes moved to Gilley, who was discreetly looking over the deputy, who was indeed a fine-looking man. "What brings you by?"

Doc fluffed his feathers and began to growl. He does that with strangers sometimes, and I had a feeling he didn't like the lawmen's hats.

Sheriff Pena said something, but Doc was starting to make too much noise. "Okay, okay," I told him, and hurried back down the hall, taking him out of view of the lawmen. A moment later I heard the door close and Gilley came looking for me. "Are they gone?" I asked.

"No. They just moved outside to talk to Heath."

"About what?"

"They wanted to ask him about the fire at his house," Gil said.

"Why? I mean, Heath's house is well off the Pueblo."

"According to them," Gilley informed me, "his uncle Milton's cabin also burned down tonight."

For a moment I was speechless. "Wait, what?"

"Around the time we were at dinner, Milton's cabin caught fire."

I thought of the surrounding woods and worried about the potential for a forest fire. "Is it out?"

"Yeah," Gil said. "But they still want to talk to Heath about it. And get a look at the inside of his SUV."

"Why's that?"

Gilley shrugged. "Probably to see if he has any accelerant or anything incriminating like that."

"Wait a minute," I said. "They think *he* might be responsible?"

Gilley gave me a level look. "My guess is that they think one of us did it."

"But we have an alibi, right?" I figured our waitress was bound to remember us after I'd barked at her to give us the check. Plus, Heath's outburst when he'd learned his house was on fire had to be pretty memorable to all the patrons there.

"Oh, I'm pretty sure they're going to make the rounds tonight, M. J., and check out our alibi, but I got the impression that they don't like Heath or his mom so much, and that they like you and me even less."

Gil and I heard the door again and we both walked out of the hallway to find Heath with a moody glint to his eye. "How'd it go?" Gil and I asked at the same time.

He scowled. "Pena can be a real asshole," he snapped. "And Cruz is like his mini-me."

"Cruz could mini-me anytime," Gil cracked.

I couldn't help it—I let out a laugh, but sobered quickly when Heath's eyes cut to me. I cleared my throat and said, "Sorry."

"Birdie go night-night?" Doc asked, fluffing his feathers again.

"Come on," said Heath. "Let's get the car packed and find a hotel."

It took us an hour to drop off Mrs. Lujan's luggage with Ari, who was taking her aunt in for the time being, and then to find a good hotel well away from the thick trees that could hide an eight-foot-tall, red-eyed, scaly-skinned demon. I wondered if AAA had a rating for that.

Heath picked the place; it was called the St. Francis, and the minute we pulled up to it, I knew why he liked it—the thing was clearly haunted. "We'll be hiding amongst the spooks," I said to him. "Nice."

"If anything nasty comes close to us, we'll feel a spike

in the paranormal activity around us and that should give us time to protect ourselves," he said reasonably.

"Good thinking."

"No!" Gilley said from the backseat. "*Bad* thinking, Heath! Very *bad* thinking!"

I sighed. "I'm sure nothing here will be too scary."

Gilley continued to pout. "I miss my van!" he moaned, still hugging the fire extinguisher from Teeko's lodge, which he'd "borrowed."

I undid my seat belt and got out of the car. I didn't have the energy to argue with him.

We got our two rooms and I let Gilley have Doc to help calm both their nerves. He took my bird into his room, got him settled, then came back into ours because, according to Gil, it was still early. (The clock read ten p.m.) He then promptly used our phone to order up some room service. I didn't utter a single protest because we did still need to think through a plan, and the food would give us at least ten whole minutes of peace while Gil stuffed his piehole.

Once his burger, fries, and milk shake arrived, the three of us got down to talking through our options. First, we looked at our arsenal, which was woefully lacking. We had only one working electromagnetic meter—we'd lost all the other ones in Europe—and we had only my two magnetic spikes, the others having been taken by our production staff with them when they went back to L.A.

"We're pathetically low on good ghostbusting equipment," Gilley grumbled in between fries, while he also connected a wireless keyboard to his new iPad.

"Can we put you in charge of making more, Gil?" Heath asked.

Gil shrugged noncommittally. "I guess," he said. "But who's going to pay for it?"

Heath blanched, I knew he was thinking of all the expenses he'd incurred coming here, and now with his house up in flames, he was out some serious cash until the insurance check came in.

My finances weren't much better. I'd used much of my paycheck to pay a bunch of bills and I knew I had to be conservative until we got back to a regular shooting schedule.

Still, Heath said, "I'll pay. Gil, can you get us any equipment you think we absolutely must have on this bust? But try to keep it reasonable."

Gilley set down his milk shake and began typing. "Here's a night-vision camera for a grand," he said. "And I think I can get some electrostatic meters for about four hundred a piece. Then there's the monitoring equipment," he added, typing even more furiously.

"We don't need a night-vision camera," I said quickly. Left to his own devices, Gilley was likely to order an entire Best Buy. "And we'll only need one electrostatic meter and some more spikes. The monitoring equipment we can also go without. Bare bones, Gil."

My best friend frowned but tapped away anyway. "Here's a used electrostatic meter for three hundred," he said, turning up his lip in distaste at having to buy used.

"Sold," I told him, offering him my credit card, which he waved away.

"I know the numbers by heart," he said, typing in the sequence with amazing speed.

Heath reached out and squeezed my hand. "Thanks, babe," he said, "but this is my problem, and I should pay for it." Reaching into his own pocket, he pulled out his credit card and handed that to Gil.

Gilley's brow rose, but he took the card and typed in the digits, then hit ENTER with a flourish and said, "Let's hope it works when it gets here."

Once Gil had ordered an entire box of powerful magnets and aluminum tubes to carry our spikes in, Heath said, "Now, let's get down to brass tacks about this demon."

I leaned forward. "Other than the story your mom told us this morning, Heath, do you know anything else that might help us figure out what we're dealing with?"

He rubbed his chin before answering. "I heard the legend as a kid," he said. "My grandfather told it to us, but we all thought it was a story invented to keep us little kids from wandering around at night and getting into trouble. After about the age of eight I outgrew any thought that the legend was true."

"Well, now we know it's definitely true, and it's specifically targeting you, just like your grandfather told me in my dream the night Ari called you about Milton."

"Why do you think the demon went back to Milton's cabin to burn it down, though?" Gilley asked us, looking up from his list.

"I have no idea," I admitted. "Heath?"

He shook his head. "No clue. It seems like overkill, though, doesn't it? I mean, the damage was already done and I can't think of anyone in the family who would want to go hang out at Milton's cabin when they knew he'd died there."

"You mean besides we fools," Gilley said.

"Yes," said Heath with a hint of a smile. "Besides us."

"But that seems too coincidental, doesn't it?" I asked.

"I mean, we go to Milton's cabin and later that same day it burns down and then your house also burns down? It almost feels like this demon is trying to hide something and kill off anyone who might be getting too nosy by burning them to a crisp."

"But that would mean that it's got something to hide," said Heath. "What could a demon possibly want to keep secret?"

"The identity of the person who helped wake it up?" I asked, throwing the idea out there.

"That poor bastard's probably dead," Heath said. "I mean, something as big and powerful as this demon would likely be hungry, and I'll bet its first meal was whoever had the bad luck to wake it up."

I drummed my fingers on the tabletop. I wasn't so sure that was true, but we couldn't overlook the obvious. Turning to Gilley, I said, "Can you hack into the Pueblo sheriff's system and get us a list of missing or recently deceased people in the area?"

"Child's play," Gilley assured us.

"Look for anything unusual to go along with any of the recently deceased," I added. "We're looking for unusual markings on the body, similar to Milton's, that were also deemed an animal attack like a mountain lion. But narrow the search to within a week or two of the attack on Heath's uncle. I doubt this demon waited long to strike once it'd woken up."

Gilley typed some notes to himself. "You'll have it by tomorrow."

I focused next on Heath. "We'll need to get a look at the Pueblo histories. I overheard Rex shutting out your mom, but do you think there's any way you might be able to sneak into the library and take a look at it?"

"I'm not an active member of the Pueblo," Heath reminded me. "Since my mom left, I've got no rights without an elder's express permission. If Mom was shut out, then I'm not gonna have any luck either, and my hanging around the library would definitely get noticed."

"Okay. Then maybe you should ask Rex directly? I mean, in light of what happened to his son tonight, maybe he'll be more open to our black hawk spirit demon theory."

Heath sighed and pulled out his cell. He checked the time before dialing. I knew it was late and hoped that Rex was still up with Ray at the hospital. "Hey, Uncle," he said after a moment. "It's Heath. I was calling to check on Ray and ask you—" And that's as far as he got. Rex began yelling so loud both Gilley and I could hear him through the phone. I didn't catch the entire tirade, but I heard enough to know that Rex was blaming Heath for Ray's brush with death.

I couldn't fathom how he'd managed to point the finger at Heath, but he was loud enough and angry enough to feel justified doing so.

For his part, Heath didn't say a word. He just listened with his eyes on the tabletop. Abruptly the tirade ended, and Heath pulled the phone from his ear. Setting it on the table, he got up and said, "I need some air."

Gil and I watched him walk out of the room and neither of us thought it was a good idea to follow him.

"Sheesh!" Gil said once the door closed behind Heath. "The Whitefeathers sure put the fun in dysfunction."

I smirked. For the record, I hadn't spoken to my father or brother in well over three years, and Gilley's dad abandoned him and his mother the moment Gilley began showing signs of preferring Barbie dolls to G.I. Joes. (Mrs. Gillespie claims that Gilley practically pranced out of the womb.)

Gil yawned while we waited for Heath to come back in. "Now what?" he asked me when twenty minutes had passed and Heath still hadn't come back to the room.

"You can go to bed," I told him, having trouble keeping my own eyes open. "We'll tackle this in the morning."

Gil got up and gathered his iPad and the keyboard; then he came around behind me and gave me an impromptu hug. "I'm glad you're my family, M. J."

And that's the thing I really love about Gilley. Oh, sure, he'll say the most inappropriate thing at the most inappropriate moment ninety-nine percent of the time, but that one time when it counts, Gil will nail it with just the right words.

"I'm glad you're my family too, Gil."

With that, he left me alone to ponder what to do next.

Chapter 7

Heath came back to the hotel room sometime later that night. I was fast asleep by then, but that doesn't mean that I wasn't still working. Sam came to me somewhere in the middle of my slumber. It was good to see him, but hard not to notice the troubled expression he wore. "Hello, M. J.," he said, sitting down next to me on a bench in the middle of a park that reminded me so much of home I could actually smell the gardenia and peach tree blossoms.

"Hi, Sam," I replied. "You here about the demon?"

Sam nodded. "I'm very worried," he admitted. "Ray barely escaped his death today. The spirit of the black hawk has powers beyond even what we elders had guessed."

"Can you tell me anything that will help us fight it?" I asked.

Sam shrugged. "What have you done to fight against it so far?"

"Not a lot."

"I'd do a little more," he said, the corners of his mouth quirking up.

"I'm serious, Sam. We need help here."

"There's a book," he replied, all pretense of humor gone now. "It's in the Pueblo library, and it details the legend of the black hawk. You should look there for some clues."

"That's what we were thinking, but we're having trouble getting access to the library."

"Rex?"

"Yep. He and Vernon have pretty much told us we're full of it."

Sam sighed. "You know, I love all my sons, but those two were born with a stick up their butts."

I barely managed to hold in a laugh. "Any ideas how to get around him?"

"The funerals will be tomorrow. They'll have Beverly's body cremated in the morning, and they'll hold the ceremonies tomorrow night."

"Okay," I said, not really knowing where this was going.

Sam seemed to sense my confusion, because he got to the point. "The whole tribe will go, of course. And not even Rex and Vernon would dare keep Serena and Heath from the ceremonies. No matter how the tribe feels about what Serena did twenty-five years ago, to keep her from Milton's funeral would make my sons look bad. So, when the tribe moves to the burial grounds, that'll be your opportunity to sneak into the library. You may have to break in, but this is more important than petty larceny. Find the histories, read the legend, and get out before anyone notices."

"Can't you just tell me what the legend says?" I asked. That seemed like a lot of work and a lot of risk to take.

Sam held the fingertips of both his hands up to his temples. "A lot of memory gets left behind when you come here," he said to me. "I can't remember the legend specifically, but I do think it might be important to go have a look at it, so that you'll know exactly what you're up against."

"We've already had that demo," I told him soberly. "And it was no carnival ride, let me tell you."

Sam leaned back and squinted up at the cloudless blue sky. "Well, maybe there'll be something within the legend that tells you how to defeat the demon, or at least tells you how it was contained the first time around."

"Okay," I said. "I get it. Go to the library and look up *D* for demon. Anything else?"

Sam stood and held his hand out to me. I took it and he waited until I was on my feet to say, "My ancestors have always been a powerful group, M. J. When the time is right, call on us and we'll do whatever we can to help you vanquish this evil."

"Good to know, my friend," I said. I then looked at the far edge of the park. A figure was standing there, waving to us. "Anyone I know?" I asked, pointing over Sam's shoulder.

He turned. "One of the ancestors," he said. "And I have to get back to Beverly."

"She made it across to your side?"

Sam nodded. "Yes, but she's quite traumatized. You've figured out that the demon killed her too, right?"

"That's been my theory ever since I saw the talon marks on the side of her car."

"Yes. It appeared in the road in front of her and she panicked, losing control of the car and plowing right into that tree. She was here an instant later, but she's very upset, not making much sense, and she still needs our help to adjust to her new surroundings."

I'd heard that sometimes people who died very suddenly and found themselves on the other side went through a period of intense anxiety before they made peace with the fact that they could no longer interact with their earthbound loved ones. I wondered if that was a rare thing or quite common.

"It's quite common," Sam said.

I smiled. "As is mind reading, huh?"

"It's the preferred method of communication here, M. J. Forming actual words with our mouths is an ability we all lose over time around here."

The figure at the edge of the park waved to Sam again. "I think you better go," I said.

He nodded but seemed reluctant to leave me. "Milton hasn't come over yet," he said. "If you find him, please send him home."

I winced. "Of course, Sam," I promised. "Just as soon as we figure out what's going on and how to fight this thing, we'll work on finding Milton and helping him over. I promise you."

Sam took the sides of my head in both his hands and regarded me. "Tell Heath that none of this is his fault and he will always be a member of my tribe, no matter what his uncles say, all right?"

"Uh . . . okay."

"You be careful, M. J. This demon isn't after just my

bloodline. It's after all the Whitefeathers, actual and ceremonial, which is why I think Beverly ended up here.
I'm still trying to get her to tell me what she saw and
exactly what happened to her, but she's too traumatized.
I can hardly get a rational word out of her. If she tells me
anything that I think you'll find useful, I'll come visit you
again. But I may be away from you while I deal with this
from my side, all right?"

"Sounds like a plan, Sam," I said with a smile.

He smiled too, kissed me on the cheek, and vanished
into thin air.

I woke up a bit later only to find Heath's muscular frame
wrapped around me. I ran my fingers over his skin, trac-
ing a lazy trail down from his shoulder over his bicep to
his forearm. He was naturally lean and very fit, so his
muscles stood out a little more than those of most men
I'd dated. But he wasn't a muscle head; no, he was de-
fined and beautifully sculpted.

Under my touch his skin was smooth, soft, and warm.
He tended to run hot under the covers, both literally and
figuratively, and right about then I wanted him in the
more figurative sense. Literally.

"Mmmm," he hummed when my fingers found their
way under the sheets. "What'cha doin'?"

"Playing," I said, turning around to face him.

"Playing?" he repeated drowsily, but a smile tugged
at his lips.

"Yep. Your body's like an amusement park for my
fingers."

Heath chuckled and the sound was low and throaty.
"Well," he said, moving his own hand to rest on the top
of my head. "You're in luck, pretty lady, because you

have to be exactly this height to ride my merry-go-round."

"Here's my ticket," I said, kissing him.

"Oh, babe," he replied, pulling back to eye me with smoldering intention, "for you, this ride's free."

We didn't do a lot of talking after that.

Well, that is until Gilley began pounding on our door loud enough to wake the dead. Heath groaned and got up to answer it, holding a pillow over his privates to open the door and look out. "What's up?" he asked tersely.

I'd pulled the covers to my chest and was peering at Gil from the bed. "I just wanted to . . . ," Gil began, but then he took in the state of our nakedness and his voice trailed off. "Uh . . . ," he said, a hint of red coloring his cheeks as he looked from Heath's pillow to me and back to Heath's pillow. "Jeez, you guys! Get a room!"

I stared levelly at him. "We *did*!"

"Oh!" Gilley said. Then he began to giggle nervously and he couldn't stop himself. "I guess you did!" He doubled over with laughter and began whooping and hooting and making an ass of himself.

Heath turned back to me as if to ask, "What the hell?"

I rolled my eyes.

Heath let go of the door and it shut in Gilley's face. He dropped the pillow then and took two leaps back to the bed, where he tackled me and pinned me to the mattress. "Now," he said. "Where were we?"

"The amusement park."

"Ah, yes," he said. "And I think we were just about to set off on the love canal. . . ."

BAM, BAM, BAM, BAM, BAM! came the pounding on the door again.

Heath and I sighed in unison. "We really need to find him a boyfriend," Heath growled.

"Hey!" Gilley's muffled voice called through the door. "Guys, come on! I'm hungry, and I have news to report!"

Heath rolled off me and I got right up, grabbing my sweatshirt and jeans to quickly shrug into them and then yank open the door. "If mood killings were a crime, you'd get *serious* jail time!" I snapped.

"Oh, please," he said, completely unfazed. "I was working my fingers to the bone while you two had all night to bone each other."

I narrowed my eyes at him.

He stood there meeting my gaze with a mocking grin. "So can we get some breakfast?"

I let go of the door, but Gil was faster and he blocked it with his foot. "Play nice," he said, waltzing past me into the room.

Heath's beautiful bare derriere was just disappearing into the bathroom. Gilley's jaw fell open right before that door closed in his face again. "You're getting a lot of that," I told him.

"Because you are both a couple of killjoys," he said.

I offered him my hand. "Pot, meet Kettle!"

He slapped it away. "Do you want to hear what I found?"

"Yes, but I would've preferred to hear it twenty minutes from now." I shuffled over to my suitcase, and began to rummage around for some clean clothes.

Gilley rocked back on his heels. "Twenty minutes, hmm? My, he's not quite the *stallion* I thought he was."

I threw my sweatshirt at him. "What'd you find out, Gil?"

"I think I located the guy who woke up your demon."

My head snapped up from the suitcase just as the door to the bathroom opened. "What?" Heath and I said in unison.

Gil moseyed over to the chair by the window. "I came across an unusual report in the Pueblo sheriff's system," he said, taking a seat and leaning back to look smugly at us. "A dead body was found in the hills not far from your Pueblo, Heath, about ten days ago."

"Just a dead body?" Heath said.

"Well, not exactly," Gil told him. "They only found a few pieces. Only what was left of him."

"Ewww!" I said. "Gil!"

"You asked," he said without a hint of apology. "Anyway, the report curiously states that the cause of death was likely from a mountain lion."

I eyed Heath. "Seems like there's a lot of mountain lion attacks around here."

Heath nodded, then focused on Gilley again. "Did they mention any cougar sightings or evidence to back up their theory, like paw prints or animal droppings in the area?"

"Nope," Gil said. "Well, aside from some claw marks in the dirt, that is."

My brow furrowed. "What kind of cougar leaves claw marks in the dirt but no paw prints?"

"An imaginary one," said Heath. "That's our demon, Gil. Good work."

Gilley blushed. "Thank you," he said, looking pointedly at me. "It's about time *someone* appreciated my efforts."

I rolled my eyes. "Did you get a location for the body's discovery?"

Gil pulled out his iPhone and tapped at the display. "Not an exact location, but from what I gather, it was found near this stretch of road, right . . . here," he said, swiveling the display around so we could see.

Heath and I approached Gil's outstretched arm together and eyed the screen. "Huh," said Heath when he took a good look at where the body had been discovered.

"What's 'huh'?" I asked.

Heath lifted the phone away from Gilley to scrutinize the screen. "That's not far from where my aunt Bev crashed into the tree."

My eyes widened. "Whoa, really?"

Heath nodded.

"So, wait a second," I said, trying to sort through the order of the events. "Someone woke this thing up by trespassing on your tribal lands?"

Heath nodded, but he appeared clearly troubled. "It's also not far away from our burial grounds."

I remembered that Vernon and Rex had thought that Bev was going to check out Milton's planned grave site when her truck went off the road. "Do you think there's a connection between this demon and those burial grounds?" I asked. When Heath looked at me curiously, I added, "I mean, could someone have put it there to protect the dead, and an outside trespasser woke it up and angered it into taking action?"

Heath shook his head. "The burial grounds are sacred, but I've never heard of anyone putting a demon out there to stand as a lookout. I mean, it'd be far too risky to future generations if the thing woke up by accident and started attacking the people it was meant to protect."

"Like it's doing right now?" I said.

"Exactly," he agreed.

"Isn't the funeral of your aunt and uncle today?" Gilley asked.

Heath went a little pale. "Yeah."

I felt a chill go down my own spine. "Will they be buried in that area?" I asked, pointing to the phone, which still displayed the red dot for the road leading to where the unidentified man was found.

"They will."

"That could be bad," I told him.

Heath nodded again. "It really could."

"We've got to warn your family," Gilley said. "Even if your mom and your cousin Ari are the only ones to listen, they should know."

Heath pulled out his own cell phone and walked out into the hallway without another word.

While he was out talking to his family, I took a very quick shower, returning from the bathroom to find Heath sitting moodily in a chair while Gilley played a game on his phone. "I take it the Whitefeathers didn't take the warning well," I said the moment I saw his face.

"Not so much."

"Who'd you talk to?" I pressed.

Heath sighed and ran a hand through his hair. "My cousin, my mom, then my uncles."

"Your *mom* didn't believe you?" I was surprised that Mrs. Lujan wasn't supportive.

"Oh, no, she believed me, but both she and Ari are still going to the funerals today."

I went over to sit on the bed across from Heath's chair. "So where do we go from here?"

He leaned forward to rest his elbows on his knees

and stared at the floor. "I'm going to the funerals to look out for my mom and my cousin. I think, since the whole tribe's going to attend, there might be safety in numbers. If anything looks off, I'll haul my mom and Ari the hell outta there. You guys should stay here where it's safe, and wait for me to get back."

I looked at Gilley. He seemed to really like the last part of that idea. "Actually . . . ," I began.

"Oh, here we go," muttered Gil.

". . . what I didn't have a chance to tell you yet, Heath, was that your grandfather came to visit me last night."

Heath looked up from the floor. "What'd he say?"

"He said what you just said, that the whole tribe was going to be at the funerals today, which includes the sheriff and his deputy, right?"

Heath squinted at me. "Probably."

"And how long do your tribal funeral ceremonies last?"

"All afternoon and into the night," he told me. "They'll start around three with the actual burials taking place around five and then there'll be a feast and ceremonial dances in honor of Milton and Bev. It'll probably finish after midnight."

"Sooooo . . . ," I said, drawing out the word while I gathered the courage to propose Sam's idea, "what Sam had suggested was that while the whole tribe attends the funeral, we could sneak into the library and read the histories."

"Uh," said Gilley, "who's this 'we' you're talking about?"

"You and me."

"I was afraid that's who you meant."

"M. J.," Heath said patiently. "I can't let you onto

Pueblo land. It's against our laws to allow a nontribal member onto the property during sacred ceremonies. I'd get into major trouble if you two got caught."

"Okay," I said. "Then don't let us onto the property."

Heath frowned. "That felt too easy."

I shrugged. "I respect your position and your tribal laws, Heath."

"Really?"

"Yes," I told him with a firm nod. "Now, how about we grab some grub?"

Heath and Gilley exchanged a worried look but didn't comment further, and after I'd had a chance to check on Doc, we all went out to get something to eat.

Later that afternoon Heath left, telling us he wouldn't be back until very late, and the moment he was out the door and safely down the hall, I pulled out my phone and began searching for a rental car agency.

"What're you up to?" Gil asked.

I held a finger to my lips. "Hold on."

Gilley folded his arms across his chest and stared disapprovingly at me until I was finished reserving the rental car and turned to explain my plan to him. "Why do I think I'm not going to like what you're about to say?"

"Because you won't." I then got right to the point. "We have to break into that library."

Gilley's jaw fell open. "Are you *crazy*? Or do you just plan to drive *me* completely nuts?"

"Do you have a better idea for finding out what the heck we're dealing with?"

"I have *fifty* better ideas!" Gil practically shouted.

I folded my arms across my chest. "I'm listening."

Gilley's lids blinked rapidly. "We could wait for Mrs. Lujan to go to the library for us!"

I shook my head. "Rex told her last night before Heath's house burned down that he wasn't granting her access to anything but the funerals."

"Well, then we'll just have to wait until he changes his mind."

"Gil," I said evenly. "We can't wait. We have to go and figure out what the heck is out there *today*."

"But you heard Heath!" Gil protested, digging his heels in. "He said it'd be a violation of tribal law to allow us onto the Pueblo during the funerals!"

"Yes," I agreed. "That's why we'll be the ones totally responsible for trespassing, and not involve Heath or his mother."

Gilley narrowed his eyes at me. "Oh, well, if that's *all* we'll be doing, then of course, let's drive right over there!"

"I'm ignoring your sarcasm," I told him, turning to dump the contents of my messenger bag out onto the bed and sighing again at how little we had in the way of protective ghostbusting equipment. None of the stuff Gil had ordered to arm us had arrived yet.

"I'm not going," Gilley snapped when I'd turned my back to him.

"Fine. I'll go alone."

"I mean it, M. J. I'm not going."

"I heard you."

"I'm serious."

"I'm sure you are." I had two spikes, two flashlights, and nothing else useful in my bag. I repacked those and moved over to my suitcase to get out some warm clothing.

"You can't talk me into it," Gilley snapped.

"I'm not trying to," I said, checking my watch. I'd have

to pick up the car, head to the hardware store, and hope I found some more metal spikes and a good magnet to magnetize them with before heading to the Pueblo.

Behind me I could feel Gilley's eyes boring holes into my back. Without looking at him, I moved to the door. "Watch Doc for me, okay, Gil? I'll be back around seven."

With that, I walked out into the hallway and headed down the corridor. No sooner had I gone ten steps than the door opened up behind me and Gilley shouted, "*Fine*, okay? I'll come! Just stop with all this pressure!"

I smiled slyly and waited for him to catch up. Wrapping my arm around his shoulders when he came abreast of me, I said, "Thanks, Gil."

"Whatever," he grumbled. "If we get caught, I'm going to say you kidnapped me."

I stopped the car in front of a row of orange cones at the entrance to the Pueblo. There was a sign strung across the cones that read:

ZANTO PUEBLO CLOSED TO TOURISTS TODAY.

I pulled the car over to the shoulder and hid it behind a large sagebrush. Beside me, Gilley looked nervous and bulky in his magnetized sweatshirt, which sagged comically all about him. "How many extra magnets did you glue onto that thing?" I asked. We'd hit pay dirt at the hardware store on both magnets and spikes.

"Just a few," he said.

I eyed him skeptically.

"Twenty."

I chuckled. "Pretty soon it'll be too heavy to wear."

"It's fine," Gilley assured me.

I made a point to sniff the air. "Maybe it's time to trade that thing in for a less fragrant version?"

"It smells?" Gil asked, sniffing at the material.

"Big-time."

"Well, I can't wash it."

"I know, which is why I suggested a new one."

"No way," he said. "This is my lucky sweatshirt."

I decided to stop arguing about it, grateful that he was along for the ride. I hadn't wanted to face trespassing and breaking and entering alone.

"Come on, buddy," I said, getting out of the car with my messenger bag.

After locking up, I pocketed the keys and Gilley and I began to make our way along the road toward the Pueblo. After we'd walked quite a way, he asked, "Jeez, how far is it?"

"About two miles from the road," I told him, lying through my teeth. It was closer to four miles.

Gilley stopped walking. "Uphill?"

I stopped too and turned back to him. "Naw," I lied again. "Just around that ridge it levels out."

"Oh, okay," he said, and began walking again.

Twenty minutes later Gilley was reading me the riot act. "Two miles my sore ass!" he complained. "We've been walking for hours! Uphill!"

"Will you please keep your voice down?" I warned.

"I'm not walking another foot!" he suddenly said, planting himself in the middle of the road like a five-year-old.

I kept going, waving good-bye to him over my shoulder. "Fine, Gil. I'll pick you up on the way back. After dark. When the demon is most likely to be out and about."

He was next to me in a hot second and we continued on for another thirty minutes when the Pueblo finally came into sight.

By this time Gilley was wheezing and sweating profusely in his already well-scented sweatshirt. "There," I said, pointing. "You see? We made it."

Gilley glared sideways at me. He was panting too hard to comment.

Once onto the main living area, which felt eerie because it was deserted, I edged Gil over to the left, behind where most of the public buildings were located. The library was clearly marked and stood right next to the sheriff's station. "Be really quiet," I told him as we crept along the side of the building. "This is the sheriff's station."

Gil placed a hand on my arm. "You're sure Pena and his deputy are at the burial ground?"

"Kind of but not entirely sure," I whispered. "Which is why I'm asking you to be quiet."

Gilley nearly growled at me. "Of all the harebrained, stupid ideas you've had, M. J. . . ."

"This is your favorite?" I asked with a winning smile

Gilley's glare became downright murderous.

I decided to quit while I was ahead. "Over there," I said, dropping the grin and pointing to the side of the building. "That looks like a side entrance."

"How're you planning to get in if it's locked?"

I shrugged. "I thought I'd figure that out when we got there."

"Oh, perfect!" Gilley snarled. "What a *great* plan that is!"

I moved over to the side door and tested the handle. It was locked. I looked back to see Gilley still huddling next to the sheriff's station. I pointed to the front of the library to tell him I was going to try the front door. He crossed his arms, scowled hard, and shook his head. Encouraging.

I edged to the front of the library and peeked around the corner. All was quiet. Even the dog that I'd heard barking from a few days ago was quiet. I didn't like it, but I moved to the front door anyway. I tested the handle. Locked.

"Crap," I muttered, glancing around. And that's when I noticed that a window along the front was cracked open. "Eureka!" I mouthed, moving over to it. Carefully I pushed on the pane and it lifted with only a slight creak.

I stopped again and eyed the area. Still quiet. I shoved hard on the rim to make the opening big enough to let me in, then hoisted myself up and slid over the sill into the dim interior, which was musty and cluttered.

I blinked several times until my eyes adjusted, then made my way through the tightly packed volumes of books, pottery, scrolls, etc., to the side entrance.

I opened it with a big old "Ta-da!" smile only to find that the spot where I'd left Gilley was completely empty. "What the . . . ?" I said, looking right and left but seeing no sign of him.

I leaned out of the entrance and craned my neck around, trying to spot him, but he was nowhere in sight, and the longer I looked, the more panicked I got. "Gilley!" I called in a harsh whisper.

"What?" came his reply right behind me.

"Eeeeeeeek!" I screamed, and let go of the doorframe, only to land hard on the top step.

Gilley leaned over and placed a hand over my mouth. "Shhh!" he said.

I slapped his hand away. "Don't you *ever* do that again!"

Gilley helped me up. "It's your own fault for insisting that I come with you."

It took a bit of effort, but I resisted the urge to argue with him. Instead, I closed the door quickly and shooed him deeper inside.

Once we were in the main room, Gil put hands to his hips and declared, "This place is a mess!"

"I know," I said.

"How're we supposed to find this tribal-histories book in all this?"

I looked at Gilley expectantly. "Isn't that *your* area of expertise? I mean, you're the guy who knows how to find the needle in the haystack."

Gil grinned. "I am good, aren't I?"

"The best," I said. Sometimes, the only way to get Gil to do what you want is to pile on the flattery.

Gil surveyed the area with renewed interest. "Well, there's not a computer in sight," he said. "Which means all my normal methods for locating the book are out."

"Then what would you suggest?" I asked.

Gil pointed to an area off to the left. "I'll take that section," he said, before moving his finger all the way over to his right. "You take that section and we'll meet in the middle."

"Awesome," I said, already moving off.

Gil caught me by the arm. "Do we know what this book is called?"

"We've got no clue."

"Awesome," Gil mimicked, but with far less enthusiasm.

He let me go and we got to our tasks. My section began over near the open window and I could see from outside that the sun was sinking fast. It'd taken us a little longer than I'd anticipated to get here and I also hadn't factored in that the library would be this cluttered and disorganized. Locating the histories book would take some time, and time was something we weren't in large supply of.

I felt a small tingle of fear when I thought about the long trek back to the car without any protection save my spikes and Gilley's sweatshirt. And I didn't know exactly how long it would be before members of the tribe came back from the burial grounds. What if only the White-feathers stayed until midnight, but other families came back earlier? All I could do was dig through the piles of stuff and hope we'd get lucky sooner rather than later.

After forty-five minutes, I knew we weren't going to get lucky anytime soon. The sun began to disappear into the early-evening sky and the already dim interior quickly grew dark. I was about to dig out my flashlight when all the lights came on.

I froze. Had someone come in?

My eyes darted around the room, and I saw Gilley walking away from the light switch in the corner. "Turn that off!"

"I can't see!" he told me.

I marched over to the panel myself and flicked it off. Then I dug through my messenger bag and came up with two flashlights. I handed one to Gil. "Keep the beam low," I told him.

"What's the big deal, M. J.? Everybody's still at the burial grounds."

"We don't know that, Gil. What if some people come back early?"

He frowned, still grumbling, "They can take as long as next week and we'll still be here looking for that stupid book."

I gave him a pat on the back. "That's the spirit."

We got back to work and I found myself constantly checking my watch as my nerves began to get the better of me. It was nearly seven thirty and I had a feeling some people would be back any minute. Plus, it was now completely dark out and the persistent nagging thought about walking the four miles back to the car kept tugging at me.

I noticed that I started to skim the titles of the books in boxes, on the floors, and along the shelves more quickly and I had to mentally check myself a few times to make sure I hadn't skipped right over the volume we were looking for. I also berated myself for not asking Mrs. Lujan or Heath what the name of the book was, or even what it looked like, but there was no hope for it now.

And then, just like a lightbulb going off, I had an idea. I sat down on the floor, closed my eyes, and whispered, "Sam! I need your help! Where is this tribal-histories book we're looking for?"

I felt a tugging sensation in my solar plexus and I opened my eyes, got back to my feet, and followed the tug.

It led me to the left side of the room, where Gilley was working with his back to me. In fact, it led me right to Gilley. I walked to him and sure enough, I saw a regular-sized volume in his hand. He was hovering his flashlight over the cover and in the next moment I saw him lift his head slightly and say, "M. J.!"

"I'm right here."

"Eeeeeek!"

"Shhhhhhh!"

Gil clutched a hand to his heart. "Don't *do* that!"

"Not so fun when the shoe's on the other foot, is it, Gil?"

He glowered at me.

"What'cha got there?" I asked, pointing to the volume.

He glared harder.

I sighed. "Sorry," I said. "I didn't mean to scare you."

Satisfied with my apology, he held up the text and read, "*History of the Zanto Pueblo Tribe*, volume one."

"Thank—God," I said, breathing a huge sigh of relief and reaching for the book, but Gil held it away from me.

"I got it," he said, flipping to the back.

"See if there's anything about the black hawk demon in the index."

Gil stopped and eyed me with irritation. "Will you please?"

"We're running out of time, Gil!" I said, out of patience myself. "Seriously, look it up and read it to me."

Gil handed me his flashlight so that he could hold the book more easily, and I was about to shine some light for him onto the page when outside something slapped against the side of the building hard and the sound was eerily similar to what we'd heard at Teeko's lodge the night the demon paid us a visit.

Gilley and I immediately squatted down behind a stack of boxes and froze.

All was quiet.

I clicked both the flashlights off and listened.

Nothing.

"*What* was *that*?" Gil whispered in my ear.

I was about to tell him that I wasn't sure when a growling sound rumbled along the wall.

Gilley made his usual scared-witless squeaking sound. I shook my head at him and squeezed his hand. I could feel him trembling next to me. Then, a slow grating sound began from the outside wall of the library, originating from the far right corner all the way along the wood.

I followed the sound with my eyes, holding my breath as it grated, and grated, along the wood.

Gilley crouched even lower and scooted behind me, shivering so badly that I could practically feel the floor vibrate next to him.

I released his hand and dug into my messenger bag. Careful not to make a sound, I pulled up a fistful of new spikes and held them close to my chest.

We were near the center of the room, tucked behind a pile of boxes and directly opposite the window I'd climbed in through. I peeked up over the boxes as the clawing continued to gouge its way along the side of the library, and in the next moment a giant black shadow emerged in the window, blocking out the faint twilight from outside.

I felt myself tense, and I held perfectly still, waiting for the shadow to pass, but only the grating sound stopped while the shadow hovered there.

Behind me and very faintly I heard Gilley whisper, *"Please, God, please, God, please, God!"*

I reached back and tapped him very gently with the flashlights I was still holding. He stopped whispering immediately.

The demon continued to hover there, as if listening for any sounds of life from inside the library, and I waited for it to start moving again. And then, it did move on, the grating sound against the wood picking up where it'd left off to travel down the length of the building. My fight-or-flight impulse took over, and I scooped my arm under Gilley's armpit, lifting him to his feet. Then I tugged him away from the boxes and mouthed, *"Move!"*

Gil grabbed my wrist and we darted around the piles of books and clutter. I nearly went down when my foot caught on something, but Gil managed to keep me upright.

Behind us the growling started up again, and there was another slap against the side of the building so hard that it made the walls shake. I didn't stop, though; I kept pushing us on tiptoe to the opposite side of the building, near the side door. I had no idea if the demon knew we were inside the library. I hoped that it was only trying to scare us into making a sound and reveal ourselves, because if it came inside, we'd be toast.

"Where do we go?" Gil said, his whisper high and pitched with fear.

I spotted what I was looking for and pushed him inside the restroom; following him in, I whirled around, closed the door softly, and locked it from the inside.

The space was somewhat cramped with a single toilet and only a small window at the top of the wall. Gil and I pressed ourselves against the door while we listened for any sound from the demon, but all was once again quiet. Well, save for Gilley's wheezy panting.

After ten minutes of silence I finally nudged him and said, "Easy there, Gil. You're going to give yourself a heart attack."

He stared at me incredulously. "I'm not going to give myself a heart attack! That *thing* is going to give me one!"

"I think it's gone."

"Yeah, well, you can stick your neck outside and see, 'cause I'm not moving."

I looked around the restroom. "We can't stay here, Gil. We have to get out of here before the tribe comes back."

Gil's jaw dropped. "And *where* exactly do you want to go, M. J.? I mean, there's no way in hell I'm walking outside in the open tonight with that thing out there!"

"Maybe we can go to Ari's," I suggested. "She might've kept a door unlocked and we can get inside and hide there."

"How is that going to be any better than hiding here?"

I stared at the door nervously. "The demon may know we're in here," I said. "And if it does know we're in here, Gil, it'll kill us for sure. We've got to go someplace else and try to hide out until the tribe comes back."

"Don't you think Ari and Brody are gonna be a little ticked off when they find out that we've burglarized our way into their home?"

"Better than someone from the tribe discovering that we've burglarized our way in here," I told him.

"Yeah, well, I'm not leaving," Gil insisted. "It's too risky, M. J.! What if that thing sees us!"

I sighed. "Okay. I'll go and make sure it's safe."

"You're leaving me?" he whined.

"Yes," I told him bluntly. Handing over two of the four spikes I held, I added, "You should be safe enough here with your sweatshirt and the spikes."

Gil stared at me like I'd gone insane. "It'll kill you!"

I cupped his face and looked directly into his eyes. "Stay here. I'll be back soon. I promise."

"Don't go!" he whispered.

I kissed the top of his head and left before I changed my mind. Making my way out of the restroom and over to the side door, I hesitated with my hand on the doorknob for a full minute before I worked up the courage to open it a crack.

The cool night air seeped in through the opening, tickling my skin. I listened carefully but heard nothing.

I took a deep breath and opened the door a little more. Gripping my spikes tightly, I leaned out and swiveled my head right and left. Nothing disturbed the night air.

Still, my heart was racing a mile a minute and I wondered if this demon could sense my fear.

I knew from personal experience that most demon-like creatures patrol the lower realms—those realms closest to our plane of existence—but they all need a portal of some kind to emerge into our territory.

This beastly creature, however, was far bigger and deadlier than anything I'd ever encountered. And I couldn't imagine what size portal it'd come through, or, for that matter, how the hell we were ever going to find its portal and lock the demon back inside the lower realms again.

I remembered Sam's words from my dream . . . what? A week ago? He'd said I'd need to kill the person who controlled the demon. "Well, that's not happening," I muttered. I wasn't going to murder anyone, that's for sure.

"What's not happening?" said a voice right behind me.

"Eeeeeeek!" I jumped a foot and whipped around.

"Shhhhh!" Gilley said.

I grabbed him by the sweatshirt and pulled him close to me. "*Stop* doing that!"

"I will if you will."

I let go of him and turned around to survey the area. If my squeal hadn't brought the demon into view, then it had likely moved on . . . for the moment at least.

I turned my attention back to Gilley. "I told you to stay in the bathroom!"

"I got scared," he said meekly.

I inhaled and let my breath out slowly. "Come on. We've got to get to Ari's."

I then grabbed Gil's wrist and pulled him along with me. It took me a minute to get my bearings, but eventually I located the cul-de-sac where Ari and Brody lived, surrounded on all sides by their relatives. As we neared the house, I could see Heath's Durango in the driveway. They must've taken Ari's car to the burial grounds.

"Thank God," I said. We approached the house slowly and slightly crouched. Gil stuck to my side like glue, and I saw that he was gripping a spike in each hand. Once we got up next to Heath's car, I happened to glance inside and to my surprise I saw Heath's keys sitting in the cup holder. "Eureka!" I said, pointing them out to Gilley, who pointed his flashlight inside and nodded.

"We can drive this back to our rental and leave Heath a message that his car's at the entrance of the Pueblo!" he said, reading my mind.

I tried the handle and gave a slight tug. It opened and just when I thought we were home free, the car alarm went off and it was so loud that I had to back away several steps and cover my ears.

"Make it stop!" Gilley yelled.

I looked around in a panic. There still didn't appear to be anyone around, so I relaxed a little. Still, I was very worried the noise would alert the demon before I had a chance to grab the keys and make it stop.

Fortunately, the alarm didn't alert the demon.

Unfortunately, it did alert the sheriff.

The moment I was reaching for Heath's keys, a patrol car zoomed down the street and a strobe light clicked on, temporarily blinding both Gilley and me. "Put your hands in the air and step away from the car!" came a booming voice over the loudspeaker.

Gilley shot both hands in the air. I followed suit.

"Drop your weapons!"

"Aw, crap!" I muttered. I'd completely forgotten about the spikes. I dropped those to the ground and Gil did too.

"And your bag and backpack!" he ordered. "But move slowly!"

Gil shrugged out of his backpack and I slowly lifted the leather strap of my messenger bag over my head to let it plop to the earth.

The strobe light stayed on and the driver got out. I squinted into the brightness and made out a man with a gun pointed right at us. I've had a gun or two pointed at me before. For the record, it's not something you really get used to, or wish to have repeated.

"On the ground!" the lawman shouted. "Facedown with your hands behind your head!"

I got down and lay flat on the cold dirt and did as he said. I heard his footsteps approach and I held very still, even though a rock poked into the side of my rib cage.

"Don't you move!" he shouted at us.

"We won't!" I told him. Jeez, for a sheriff, this guy was really flinchy. But then I figured that he had caught us standing next to a car with the alarm going off while we were holding flashlights and metal spikes in our hands. Of course we looked like we were trying to steal it.

I turned my head slightly so that I could face Gilley, who looked at me with big, round, frightened eyes. "Just do as he says," I told him.

A boot landed on Gil's back and he grunted. Then the sheriff bent and pulled Gil's hand down off his head, twisting his arm at the elbow to cuff one wrist, then the other, before patting him down.

A moment later I felt his full weight press on my back too. I winced as the rock bit deeper into my side, but I didn't protest because I knew it was going to be much worse if I did.

I felt the cold metal of the handcuffs on my wrists when they were locked tightly behind me, and the guy gave me the same pat down. Then the lawman's weight lifted off me when he'd made sure I wasn't hiding a weapon, and I was grabbed roughly by the arm and yanked to my feet. I was then spun around to face him and I realized why he'd been so flinchy. It wasn't Sheriff Pena; it was his deputy, whose name currently escaped my panicked mind.

Without a word he marched Gil and me over to the side of his squad car, pushing us one at a time into the interior; then he slammed the door and for a few seconds we were left alone. "Say nothing," I told Gil. "Let me do all the talking, okay?"

"A time to worry," Gil said.

"I'm serious."

"So am I."

Chapter 8

An hour later my patience was wearing thin. The deputy had left us in the squad car while he went inside the station and didn't appear to be coming back out. "This blows," Gilley said.

"Are your cuffs supertight?" I asked him, leaning forward to try to find a comfortable position, but why I bothered I couldn't really say, because when your hands are restrained behind your back while you're in a sitting position for longer than ten minutes, there is no comfortable position.

"They're not as bad as yours," Gil said, and I noticed he was looking down at my hands. "Your fingers are turning blue."

I glanced out the window again. "The son of a bitch cut off my circulation." I sat back up again and planted my feet on the floor, arching my back for a moment to angle my hands under me. I squirmed and wiggled and contorted myself until I managed to get my butt through the loop of my arms. "If a life of crime doesn't work out for you, M. J., might I suggest Cirque du Soleil?"

I grunted, shimmying my wrists forward to just behind my knees, then had to sit there and pant for a second before craning my neck all the way to the side to mash my face against the back of the seat so I could get my boots through the loop.

With a sigh I sat back and held up my hands. "Ahhhh," I said. "That's better."

"Now what?" Gil asked.

I tried the door handle. It was locked and there was a cage separating the front seat from the back. I eyed the window. "With a few good kicks I could break us out of here."

"Oh, please *do*!" Gil said with mock enthusiasm. "By all means make a bad situation worse by breaking out of the squad car!"

"We're already in trouble," I reasoned.

"Yes, but we're not necessarily facing jail time. Once Heath shows up and vouches for us, I'm pretty sure they'll let us go with only a fine for trespassing."

I laid my head back on the seat and closed my eyes. I'd almost rather risk escaping police custody than face my boyfriend after this. "Do you think he'll break up with me?"

"Who, Heath?"

"Yes."

Gilley was quiet for a minute. "Maybe," he said. "I mean, what you did was pretty bad for a girlfriend, and if I were a straight guy, I'd probably break up with you."

"Gee, thanks."

"On the bright side, maybe you and Steven could get back together?"

I shook my head. "That ship has sailed," I told him. "He's dating some new girl."

"How do you know?"

"Teeko."

"Ah," Gil said. "Well, then maybe you should leave all the talking to *me* when Heath shows up."

I smiled. "What would you say?"

"That it was my idea to come here," he said simply.

I lifted my head and stared at him. "You'd do that for me?"

He seemed surprised that I'd even ask. "Well, duh, M. J. It is my job, isn't it?"

"Your job?"

"Yeah. Don't you remember what your mom told us? That it was my job to watch out for you?"

My eyes widened. "You remember that?"

"Of course I remember it," he said. "We were playing on my back porch and your mom came over and told me to look after you. That was right before she died, wasn't it?"

I smiled. Gilley's mind had reshaped the events of that morning so that the memory wouldn't frighten him. "Yes," I said, not seeing any point in correcting him.

"Well, see?" he said. "I've been doing that ever since."

I nudged him with my shoulder. For all the bickering and petty arguing we did, Gilley was still the best friend I could ask for. I saw his eyes flicker to somewhere behind me. "Here comes the law," he said.

I turned and saw the deputy approaching the squad car. Opening my door, he said, "Out."

I scooted forward and exited the car, noting that he

was looking pointedly at my hands, which were now in front of me. The deputy didn't say anything or recuff me, which I was grateful for. Gil struggled out and nearly fell when his legs got tangled under him. I reached out and caught him because the deputy seemed just fine with letting him take a tumble.

Jerk, I thought.

"Inside," he ordered.

We headed in and waited for him to get the door. "Down the hall and to the right," he instructed.

We followed his every command without a word between us, moving along the well-lit corridor to a doorway that led into a large room with two desks, rows of filing cabinets, and a single jail cell.

The smell of pizza still lingered and I noticed a mostly eaten microwave pizza on one of the desks. Ah, so he'd decided to catch his dinner before dealing with us. My own stomach grumbled and I could hardly say that I blamed him.

"Sit," he commanded, pointing to two chairs in front of the desk with the pizza.

Gil sat in the chair on the right and I took the one on the left. The deputy then went behind his desk, which was oddly placed in the center of the room, with his back to the jail cell.

Putting his fingers to a keyboard, the deputy said, "Names?"

I glanced sideways at Gilley. He stared at me as if he didn't know what to say.

"Names?" the deputy repeated, and this time his tone said, "Right the freak now!"

Gil and I spoke at the same time, so the words came

out in a tumble. The deputy eyed me. "You first," he said before those eyes swiveled to Gil. "Then you."

We relayed all our information to him, and in front of us he took out all the contents of our bags one at a time, laying them out on the desk to catalog them. He'd already confiscated our cell phones, which both Gil and I had had in our back pockets, and thrown them into his desk drawer.

After he'd cataloged all the contents of Gilley's backpack (he'd brought his tablet and keyboard along—why I didn't know), the deputy put the items back, then moved on to the contents of my messenger bag.

He looked over the magnetic spikes curiously, but didn't ask me about them. Instead he wrote them down, then put them back and tossed my bag and Gilley's backpack onto a nearby chair.

By the time he was done, my hands, which had been throbbing, were now completely numb. I eyed them and became concerned. They were both swollen and blue. I held them up to show the deputy. "Can you do something about this, please?"

He ignored me and continued to type at his keyboard.

"We know the Whitefeathers," I said. "Heath and his mom are friends of ours."

That got the deputy's attention, but maybe not in quite the way I'd hoped for. "You were the other two with them at Milton Whitefeather's cabin, right?"

"Yes. Heath and Gilley and I are in a television series together."

The deputy leaned back in his chair and considered us. "Did he bring you here tonight?"

I shook my head vigorously. "No!"

"Then how'd you get here?"

"We drove," I told him.

He looked at me skeptically. "Where's your car?"

"At the entrance to the Pueblo," I admitted.

"We had car trouble," Gilley piped in. "Our car died on the side of the road and we thought we'd come find Heath to see if we could get a ride back to the hotel."

I took up Gilley's story with ease. "That's right," I said, nodding my head. "We had car trouble and we came looking for Heath."

"Entering the Pueblo on sacred ceremonial days is a crime," the deputy said.

"We're so sorry," I told him, doing my best to sound contrite. "We were just looking for our friend and we didn't realize we were doing anything wrong."

The deputy squinted at me. I could tell he didn't buy it. "You can't read?" he asked.

I knew he was referring to the sign posted at the entrance of the Pueblo. I smiled tightly. "Technically, we're not tourists," I said. "I've been here before, so I just figured the invitation extended to tonight."

"Heath has no authority to invite you onto tribal land," the deputy said. "He doesn't live on the Pueblo, so he couldn't legally invite you here."

"He didn't," I told him.

"Then who did?"

"Ari Whitefeather." I knew I was in quicksand, but I couldn't seem to stop myself from offering up names.

"Ari invited you here tonight?"

I shook my head again. We were going in circles, and I had a feeling the deputy was trying to find the holes in our story. "No. The day her aunt Beverly died. She invited me into Molly's house. At least I think it was Molly's house.

It's the one at the top of the cul-de-sac, three down from Ari's. Oh! *And* we were invited here just yesterday to drop off Serena Whitefeather at Ari's house! So, technically, we've been invited onto the Pueblo twice now."

The deputy's fingers drummed on the desk, but he didn't ask any more questions. Instead he checked his watch, rubbing the back of his head, before getting up and coming around to grab Gilley by the arm and escort him over to the jail cell. He placed Gilley inside before ordering him to turn around and put his wrists against the bars. Gilley did as he was told and the cuffs came off.

The deputy then moved over to retrieve me and do the same, and with immense relief I felt the pressure subside from the cuffs, even though I couldn't really feel my hands.

"The ceremony will go on until after midnight," the deputy said. "I'm going to run my patrols and find your car, then head home. You two behave until tomorrow morning when I ask Ari to vouch for you."

"Can we have something to eat?" Gil asked him.

The deputy walked over to the pizza, which was now cold and congealed. He folded two pieces and handed them to Gilley with two plastic plates and got us two cups of water, for which I was very grateful. By now I was both really thirsty and hungry.

"I'll be back at six a.m.," he told us. And then we were left alone, most of the lights shut off, save the one desk lamp next to his computer.

Gil chowed down and I had to wait until the feeling returned to my hands before I could join him. The pizza was pretty bad, cold, hard, and rubbery; it took most of the water in my cup to get it down, but it was definitely better than nothing.

About a half hour after finishing the meager meal, I was regretting drinking the water. Gilley seemed to be in the same boat, because we both eyed the one open toilet in the cell nervously.

"I need to pee," he said from the bunk on the opposite side of the cell from mine.

"Right there with you."

"No, I'm serious, M. J. I gotta go."

I closed my eyes, plugged my ears, and rolled away from him. "I won't peek or listen if you promise to do the same." I then began to sing.

A few minutes later, just when I thought that Gilley was taking the longest pee in history, I felt a tap on my shoulder. I jumped a little and twisted around. Gilley stood there with a big old grin on his face and the earphones to his new iPad in his ears.

"Your turn!"

I looked at him curiously. "Where'd that come from?"

"My backpack," he said, his grin broadening.

I sat up. "Huh?"

Gil pointed to his bunk. Sitting in the middle of it was his backpack.

"How'd you manage that?"

Gil pointed to his belt. "Do you remember that episode of *The Brady Bunch* where the family got locked in the jail of that ghost town and they had to use their belts to get the keys?"

"Vaguely."

"Well, that method works!" he said triumphantly.

My messenger bag was still on the chair next to the deputy's desk, however. "You couldn't get mine too?"

"I figured you'd want to do your business. Then we could work on your bag."

I jumped up from the bunk. "Turn the music up, Gil." I had to go so bad I was about to pee in a cup and I didn't care who watched.

When I was done, Gilley and I worked on getting my messenger bag. It took us seventeen tries, but eventually, we managed it.

Once we had our bags with us, I felt a little better about being cooped up. "Maybe I'll call Teeks in the morning and she can look for a good lawyer in the area in case things get sticky for us tomorrow."

Gilley, however, was busy rummaging around in his pack again, searching for something. At last he pulled up a small pair of binoculars with a satisfied, "Ha!"

I looked around the room, which was mostly windowless, and all the blinds were closed anyway. "What're you gonna do with those?"

Gil ignored me while he fiddled with the focus. He seemed to be looking through them at the deputy's desk. "Crap," he said. "Too close."

He then got off the bed and moved to the very back of the cell, fiddling again with the glasses before saying, "Okay, I should be able to read the type on the computer."

I looked over at the computer on the deputy's desk. The screen saver was on, displaying a running message with the words *Zanto Pueblo PD*. "What the hell are you talking about?" I demanded.

Gil lowered the lenses and moved back to his backpack to pull out his wireless keyboard. "This has an amazing range," he said. "And it's the same model as the one the deputy uses. So, all we have to do is . . ." Gilley clicked the space bar and suddenly the screen saver was gone. "That."

"Whoa!" I said, thoroughly impressed. The screen displayed the e-mail window, but I couldn't read any of the type. It was too far away. "Now what?"

Gil fumbled around inside his backpack again until he'd pulled out his wireless track pad too. He then scooted to the back of the cell and offered me the binoculars. "Will you hold them for me?"

"Sure," I said, moving over to hold them while Gil got comfortable, placing the keyboard in his lap and the track pad at his side. When he was ready, I held the lenses over his eyes and marveled at how quickly his fingers flew over the keys.

I had to switch hands after a while, and Gil continued to type. After another fifteen minutes without him uttering a single word, I said, "Can you give me a status report?"

Gil backed away from the glasses and blinked his eyes a few times. Then he told me to put the binoculars away and got up from the floor. I watched him retrieve his iPad from the backpack and bring it back to our corner. He whipped his finger around the display for a minute, then turned the tablet toward me so I could see. "Whoa!" I said again when I scrolled through all the new e-mails from Deputy Cruz. Oh, yeah, that was his name . . . Cruz.

"So, what's in these e-mails?" I asked absently, scrolling down the subject headers.

"I pulled every e-mail that had to do with any mysterious deaths on the Pueblo, including the remains of that John Doe, who's not so much a John Doe anymore."

"Huh?" I looked up at Gilley.

"The coroner was able to pull a print off the lone finger they found."

I swallowed hard. "Ick."

Gilley smirked. "Ick aside, the identity came back as Daryl West of Los Alamos. And if you'll scroll down to that e-mail from the Los Alamos PD, you'll see that the attachment is Daryl's rap sheet, which, among the many offenses listed, has on there eight charges of grave robbing, and defiling a corpse."

I swallowed again. "Ick squared."

"Yeah, yeah," Gil agreed. "But there's a pretty long exchange between Cruz and the deputy in Los Alamos who booked West for the grave-robbing crimes."

"So?"

"*So*, there must be a reason Cruz is so interested in West's past, and who the hell robs graves in the twenty-first century anyway?"

"Someone looking for gold," I said easily. "Seriously, Gil, the price of gold is ridiculous these days. And people get buried with their jewelry all the time."

"Yeah, but, M. J., even if they recovered a ring or a bracelet or a necklace, that's an awful lot of work and even more risk for a few hundred bucks."

"To you," I said. "But maybe not to West."

Gilley nodded but held his ground. "I say there's something there."

"Okay," I agreed, knowing that Gil had pretty good instincts when it came to information. "I trust you. When we get outta here, we'll check on it."

Gil shifted sideways and pulled up his sweatshirt. "In the meantime," he said, lifting out a book from his waistband, "I figure we can read up on the history of our demon spirit."

My jaw dropped. "*Please* tell me you did not steal that from the library!"

"I did not steal this from the library."

I glared at him.

"I didn't!" he insisted. "I *borrowed* it. That's what you do at a library, M. J. You *borrow* the books and promise to bring them back."

I leaned against the wall and stared up at the ceiling. "Heath is gonna break up with me for sure."

"No, he won't," Gil said, but there wasn't a lot of conviction in his voice.

I glanced at my watch. It was nearly ten o'clock. "Do you think they're back from the burial grounds yet?"

Gilley shrugged. "Maybe."

I sighed. I didn't know if Cruz was going to tell Heath we were locked up here, and if he decided not to—which was what I suspected—then Heath was going to return to an empty hotel room and wonder where I was. I looked longingly at the desk drawer where Cruz had put our phones. Then I eyed Gilley's tablet with interest.

"Don't," Gil said.

I looked up. "What?"

"You're getting ready to ask me if you can e-mail Heath."

"He'll be worried if he goes back to the hotel and sees that I'm not there, and I don't think Deputy Dog is going to tell him where we are until morning." And then I thought about Doc and my heart skipped a beat. "What about the birdie?"

Gil sighed, and set the book down to pick up his tablet, where he then opened up a blank e-mail. Without letting me look, he typed very fast, then punched the ENTER button with emphasis.

"What'd you do?"

"I sent Heath an e-mail."

"Oh, God. What'd you say?"

"That you were hanging out with me tonight at a club and we'd catch up with him in the morning, and could he please put the bird to bed because we were bound to be very late getting in."

"He should know the truth about where we are, Gil."

But my best friend only shook his head. "He's at a funeral, M. J. He's upset enough for one night."

I suddenly felt ten times worse. "What the hell was I thinking?"

"You weren't. Which is why we're stuck in this jail cell."

"Thanks, Gil," I said woodenly.

"You asked."

I reached over and took the book from his side. Flipping to the back, I looked for an index, found one, and then read through the list for the legend of the black and white hawk spirits.

It was on page 229 and began exactly the way Mrs. Lujan had described. I read aloud to Gilley from the part where the battle ended and the black hawk fell to earth.

"The great White Hawk circled the whole of the sky, claiming it all for itself and boasting its victory to all the world. The Black Hawk was so angry at its rival that it plotted its revenge by shedding its feathers for scales, and losing its beak to grow fangs, but it kept its talons and grew two more sets. 'One day you will land, White Hawk,' it shouted up to the sky. 'And on that day, I will kill you!'

"But the White Hawk only laughed, planning to

*ride the currents forever. It stayed in the sky for so
many moons that it eventually lost its bird form,
turning into mist and becoming the clouds. On days
when the clouds are absent, the White Hawk travels
to the edge of the sky, where it can rest without
needing to land.*

*"Sometimes, however, it misses the land and the
White Hawk grows dark and moody, shedding tears
from the sky, mourning the touch of the earth below. But once it has shed its tears, it remembers the
glory of the sky and again rides the currents with
great happiness."*

I looked up to see Gilley gazing at me. "I kinda dig
that story," he admitted.

I folded the book closed over my thumb to look at
the cover again. "Yeah, me too."

"Okay, so find the part about the Whitefeathers."

I opened the book back up and skimmed the next
page, but the story seemed to end there without anything more about the white hawk spirits. Flipping to the
back again, I moved my finger down the list to the *W*s
and found the pages for "Whitefeather."

I then skimmed the story of Whitefeather's father,
finding the white feather on the ground. "Did you know
that Whitefeather's father was named White Wolf?" I
said to Gil.

"No. Did Heath's mom mention his name?"

"I don't think so," I said, still reading the passage.
"Hey, Gil, listen to this.

*"On the night of the naming ceremony for the son
of White Wolf a great darkness enveloped the land*

of the Zantos. The moon hid from the tribe and the stars hid too. A mist of smoke spread over the land so thick, no one could see, and a terrible rumble sent fear into even the bravest hearts.

"All but White Wolf, who was not afraid. He knew what the mist hid and he summoned all the warriors of the tribe together. 'The Black Hawk has come,' he told them. 'It has come to claim my son, Whitefeather of the White Hawk Spirit. We must not let the Black Hawk kill my child. He was born in the spirit of the White Hawk, and if he dies, the White Hawk who favors us with his clouds and his tears will disappear from the sky. We must destroy the Black Hawk, and protect my son.'

"All the warriors agreed and armed themselves for battle. They kept watch in large groups over little Whitefeather, but the demon spirit was crafty and one by one the warriors were abducted in the night and torn to pieces by the demon Black Hawk.

"For thirty days the Black Hawk preyed upon the tribe, and each night one of them was taken by the Black Hawk and killed. When the full moon arrived again, only fifty Zantos were left. 'We must hand over the Whitefeather!' one elder declared. 'Only when it has killed the boy will it be satisfied and leave our tribe alone!'

"Cries from the tribe rose up, supporting the elder's idea and White Wolf and Hummingbird were afraid for their child."

"Who's Hummingbird?" Gil interrupted.

"She must be White Wolf's wife."

Gil nodded and I got back to the story.

"White Wolf wanted to fight the elder who had suggested the tribe hand over his son, but Hummingbird stood and addressed the tribe. 'The Black Hawk is too clever to battle us all together,' she said. 'It relies on the darkness to catch us alone and unaware, and I do not think the spirit of the Black Hawk can be killed, even if it were set upon by all of our brave warriors.'

"A murmur rose up from the Zantos, angry that Hummingbird would say such things, but she merely raised her hand and begged the tribe's permission to speak again. 'I don't think that the spirit of the Black Hawk can be slain, but I do believe it can be captured,' she said. 'We must lay a trap for it and lure it without placing any of us in danger.'

"'And how do you propose we do that?' asked Running Water, the tribe's most revered elder.

"'With this,' said Hummingbird, holding up the belly root from her son, Whitefeather—"

"Belly root?" Gilley asked.

I thought for a moment. "It must be the stub of his umbilical cord."

"Ahh," said Gil. "Yeah, you're probably right."

I went back and reread part of that sentence again.

"... holding up the belly root from her son, Whitefeather. 'It still has the scent of my child on it, and it will easily lure the Black Hawk.'

"'And what kind of trap would you lay?' asked Half-Moon. 'If we dig a pit, it will claw its way out. If we lure it to a cave, it will kill us before we have a chance to lock it inside.'

"At this time the medicine man stood and said that the previous night he'd dreamt about the spirit of the White Hawk, who had come to him in his slumber and given him powerful words which would create a trap for its enemy. He said all he needed was a vessel to inscribe the words on, and it would work.

"Hummingbird rose before the tribe and announced that she would make the vessel. The next day Hummingbird gathered clay from the river, and grass from the meadow, and wood from the forest, and set to work. By nightfall she appeared once again before the elders and proudly presented the medicine man with a beautiful pot painted all in black with a white wolf's paw crushing a black feather etched on the side. The medicine man declared it perfect, and with a brush he dipped it into the black paint and began to write the powerful words the White Hawk had given him on the side of the pot. The words were invisible against the black paint on the pot, making it the perfect trap to catch the Black Hawk Spirit.

"When the medicine man was through, he placed inside the pot Whitefeather's belly root and held the vessel aloft, declaring, 'This will capture and keep the spirit of the Black Hawk, and the Zantos will forever be one with the spirit of the White Hawk.' The medicine man then asked for an escort to the highest cave overlooking the Zantos' land. Ten warriors volunteered and walked him to the cave. They were willing to stay with him and wait for the Black Hawk Spirit, but the medicine man insisted he be left alone to face the demon.

"*The warriors returned to the tribe and everyone gathered around the fires to wait for the spirit of the Black Hawk to come or go up to the cave where the medicine man was.*

"*Late that night when the fires were low, the tribe heard a terrible scream, and they knew that the powerful words had not worked. The ten warriors raced to the cave and found the medicine man grievously injured, still clutching Hummingbird's vessel. 'Kill me,' the medicine man begged them. Thinking he'd gone mad, the warriors lifted the elder and returned him to the tribe.*

"*Once there the medicine man pleaded with the tribal elders to kill him, but of course they refused, asking him instead what happened in the encounter with the Black Hawk.*

"*The medicine man confessed that his plan had been flawed; the Black Hawk had suspected a trick, but could not refuse the magic of the words on the clay vessel. In an effort to escape entrapment, it had entered the medicine man's body, and was doing terrible harm to him inside.*

"*Again the elder begged to be given the mercy of death. He knew it was only a matter of time before the power of the Black Hawk's spirit inside him would devour his own spirit and once again roam free. 'You must kill me quickly,' he said, 'before I begin killing you. You must then immediately burn my body and place my ashes inside this vessel. It is the only way to trap the spirit of the Black Hawk.'*

"*But the tribe hesitated and none of the elders would vote to kill their medicine man. As dawn emerged on the horizon, the medicine man sud-*

*denly jumped to his feet, reached for his knife, and
ran straight at Hummingbird, who was holding
Whitefeather.*

"*At the last moment, White Wolf stepped in front
of the medicine man and took the knife in the chest,
saving his wife and child. It took five warriors to
restrain the medicine man, and when they had, the
elders knew his soul was lost to the spirit of the
Black Hawk.*

"*Hummingbird drew the knife that had killed
her husband and plunged it into the medicine man,
killing him in turn. The tribe did not banish her,
however; instead, they knew that her justice was
well served and they threw the body of the medicine
man onto the flames of the largest fire.*

"*All the next day and night the fire burned, because the medicine man's body fought the flames. It
is thought that the spirit of the Black Hawk used all
of its power to thwart being turned into dust, but finally, with careful attention to the fire, the medicine
man's body was reduced to ash and all of it was
placed inside the vessel, which was then sealed and
buried in a secret place with the body of White Wolf,
so that his spirit could watch over the vessel for as
long as the Zantos and the sons of Whitefeather
walk the land.*"

I finished the tale and closed the book and for a time,
Gilley and I sat in silence, absorbing all that I'd read
aloud. "Huh," said Gil after a bit. "So this thing was
stored in some sort of clay pot?"

I remembered what Sam had shown me that day at
Ari's home, the urn with the beautiful design on it, which

held some of the ashes of every Whitefeather since the son of White Wolf. I told Gil about it and he asked, "So where is *that* clay pot?"

"No one knows," I said. "It disappeared the night Heath's mom left the Pueblo, remember?"

"Oh yeah," Gil said. "But she swears she didn't take it, right?"

"Right, but that doesn't mean people believe her. Even her own brothers think she took it."

"Man," Gil said, "am I glad that my family is only made up of you, me, and my ma."

I was so touched by Gilley's statement that it took me a minute to say something. "Yeah," I agreed at last. "Me too."

Gilley yawned and looked at his watch. "It's after eleven. You feel like turning in?"

"Might as well get some sleep," I said. "Cruz said he'd be back at six."

Gil got up and crossed the cell to his bunk, while I rolled onto mine. The mattress was nothing but a thin layer of foam encased in plastic, and the pillow and blanket left a lot to be desired, but it was better than nothing.

I turned my back to Gil to help block off the light from the lamp on Cruz's desk and closed my eyes, trying not to think about the next day or how fast it might take Heath to break up with me.

"Night," Gil said with a yawn.

"Night," I said with a sigh. No sooner had I closed my eyes than the sound of glass breaking somewhere at the front of the station caused me to turn and face Gilley. Given his wide-eyed expression, I knew he'd heard it too.

"What was that?" he whispered.

I focused on the hallway leading into the large office space. "Hello?" I called.

No one answered.

I sat up and stared at the front of the room as the hairs on the back of my neck stood up on end. "Hello?!" I called more loudly.

A loud crashing sound echoed down the hallway. Gilley was at my side in a hot second. "*What* was *that*?" he squeaked.

I looked around the cell for some kind of a weapon. Something had entered the station, and I didn't think it was anything good.

Another loud crashing sounded from the front of the building, and then, that awful and now familiar grating sound along one of the walls. "Oh, shit, shit, shit!" Gilley cried.

We both looked desperately around the cell for somewhere to hide. There was nothing other than our bunks, and those were clearly bolted to the floor. We were in a large cage at the back of the room—completely exposed.

"Where's your sweatshirt?" I asked Gil, who was hanging on my arm and shivering head to toe.

"On my bunk!"

I got up and pulled Gilley with me. Crossing the ten-foot space, I recovered his sweatshirt and passed it to him. "Put it on," I told him, dragging him over to the very back of the cell next to the toilet before shoving him down next to it.

Gilley fumbled with the sweatshirt while I grabbed my messenger bag and his backpack and was once again by his side. Another crash—this one closer and more violent—vibrated the floor. Gilley gave a small shriek and looked at me with huge frightened eyes. "It's gonna kill us!"

I wanted to tell him that it wouldn't, but I didn't know that for certain. The bars might be strong enough to thwart the demon, but what if it could slip through the bars like smoke?

I sat down in front of Gilley, using my body to block him, and got out every spike I'd brought along, placing them in a semicircle around us. I also kept two clutched in my hands. I then braced myself and fought down the mounting panic filling my chest.

No sooner had I gotten a tentative grip on my nerves than something invisible but incredibly powerful burst into the room, toppling chairs, filing cabinets, and shelving in one terrible swoop.

Behind me Gilley screamed when a pair of chairs came flying through the air to crash against the front of the jail cell, and any grip I'd had on my own fear went right out the window.

Chapter 9

As the assault on the room continued, I shook so hard that I could barely hold on to the spikes. I knew I had to get up, but all I wanted to do was curl up into a ball and pray.

At that moment, the sheriff's desk scraped along the floor for several feet before it lifted into the air and slammed against the side of the cell. The noise was deafening and Gilley and I both launched ourselves sideways, flattening our bodies against the floor. Gilley wouldn't stop screaming, and one of the spikes fell away from my hand when I covered my head with my arms.

I could feel myself joining Gilley in a chorus of screams. I couldn't help it; I tend to panic when furniture starts flying around a room by an unseen poltergeist. And it didn't stop with the sheriff's desk—no, a second after Gil and I had flattened ourselves, one of the computers crashed into the jail cell door, smashing with terrible force as plastic, wires, and small bits of metal rained down all over us.

Gilley's screaming reached new heights and I was afraid that the terrifying scene would send him insane. Of course, I was more worried that the demon might kill him before he went cuckoo.

I tried to locate the demon, but I couldn't see it anywhere. And then, as if it'd sensed me trying to find it, two glowing red eyes appeared on the far left-hand side of the jail.

I reacted without thinking: I thrust my hand up and threw my lone spike like a dart right at those glowing red orbs.

My aim was true for once. The spike hit the demon between the eyes, clinking against one of the bars before it buried itself right into the evil spirit.

The black hawk demon screeched; then it hissed at me, and I felt the wind of its breath on my arms. It made me shudder that this thing could have such power in the land of the living. The victory of the spike hitting its mark bolstered me a little and I got to my knees and grabbed another spike, ready to throw it too. *"Get back!"* I roared, throwing the second spike.

That one, however, hit the metal bars and bounced off back into the cell.

The demon eyes disappeared and only the whirl of papers along the side of the cell revealed that it was still in the room.

Gilley finally stopped screaming and huddled into a ball on the floor with his sweatshirt pulled up over his head. His form was so pathetic that it brought out the warrior in me. I grabbed two more spikes and approached the front of the cell. *"Get out!"* I screamed.

The demon answered by launching the other computer right at me.

I dived to the floor just before plastic and metal exploded against the metal bars. But I wasn't going to back down so easily. I got up again and threw one of the spikes at a trail of paper. I heard this odd noise, like a *thwack*, and for an instant my spike hovered in the air like it was stuck in something.

That something revealed itself in the next second as a monster right out of a nightmare. It looked like a cross between a giant crocodile and a cobra. Its body was long and bulky with a wicked-looking tail. Four-footed and talon-toed, it stood at least eight feet tall, with black scales that appeared liquid when it moved.

The demon turned around slowly and considered me with its glowing red eyes, and I will admit that if I hadn't previously emptied my bladder, I would've right there and then. I'd *never* been that scared in my whole life, and I've dealt with some *truly* terrifying stuff.

In the next second the demon came at the front of the cell so fast I barely caught the movement in time to throw myself backward.

It hit the bars with tremendous force and raked its talons across my arm in the process. I swiped at the burning sensation along my forearm and managed to stick a stake into the demon's shoulder. It shrieked and tried to reach its big claws through the bars to tear me to shreds.

And then, something extraordinary happened. Gilley, my sweet, often irritating, scared-of-his-own-shadow, but always loyal best friend, was next to me, a fistful of spikes in each hand. He began pounding them into the demon, striking it as fast as he could raise and lower his arm through the bars.

He also started shrieking in a key no human should be capable of reaching—somewhere between howler monkey and Harpy.

Whether it was the spikes or Gilley's high note, the demon shrank back and with a final loud bang of its tail on the jail cell, it vanished from the room, leaving nothing but a swirl of fluttering paper and a roomful of destruction.

Gil and I dropped down to our knees, both of us panting heavily and eyeing the area in disbelief.

"You . . . okay?" I asked him between gulps of air.

"Gilley Gilleshpie!" he gasped. "Gilley Gilleshpie, Gilley Gilleshpie!"

I lifted my arm limply and managed to pat him on the shoulder. "You're not having a stroke at least."

"Are you sure?" he demanded, staring at me with an expression full of *what-the-freak?* "I feel a little tingly."

I sat back on my heels. "You're fine," I assured him. "And thanks to you, so am I."

"I don't know what came over me!" he exclaimed. "Normally I leave the hero stuff up to you fools."

I wrapped an arm around him. "That thing was going to fillet me like a tomato against a set of Ginsu knives, so whatever moved you, buddy, I for one am really grateful."

"Don't get used to it," Gilley warned. "That thing could scare the gay right out of me."

I giggled, then I started to laugh, and then I couldn't stop. I was just so relieved to have survived the demon attack that Gil's humorous remark was like someone turning a relief valve in me. He chuckled along too, and before long we were lying on the ground, giggling and slapping each other on the shoulders.

After a bit we settled down, but neither one of us moved off the floor back to our bunks. "What do we do now?" Gil asked.

I shrugged. "Wait for the sheriff or Deputy Cruz to come back, I guess."

Gil propped himself up on his elbows and stared at the room. "How're we going to explain *that*?"

I propped myself up too and took in the mess. The lamp was still giving off some light from where it'd landed on the floor, and as I took in all the damage done, I could hardly believe it myself, and I'd witnessed the rampage.

"We'll tell Pena and Cruz the truth," I said.

"They'll never believe it."

"Well, *we* couldn't have done all this, now, could we, Gil?"

Gilley sat all the way up. "You have a point." He then seemed to notice something on my arm and lifted it up to inspect. "You're bleeding, sugar."

I glanced at it, only now realizing that it was throbbing like crazy. "Got any first aid in that pack of yours?"

Gilley stood up, his shoes crunching on the bits of plastic from the smashed computers as he walked to his backpack. After rooting around, he came back with some antibacterial ointment and a cotton ball. He cleaned up the wound and I hissed, winced, and complained all the way through it. "You might want to get that looked at tomorrow," he suggested. "I mean, for all we know, demons might carry some terrible disease, like . . . demon *rabies*."

I rolled my eyes and rotated my wrist to inspect the wound. "I've been slashed by a demon before," I reminded him. "And I survived it just fine."

"M. J.," Gilley said. "This wound is much deeper than the last time. I really think you need stitches."

I surveyed the cut, which did look pretty deep. "There's not much I can do about it now, Gil."

He frowned and went over to the john to retrieve the roll of toilet paper, which he then proceeded to wrap round and round my arm. The end result was comical, but at least it was better than nothing. "Put your free hand over the wound to keep pressure on it," he advised me. "First thing in the morning, after they let us out of here, we're hitting the emergency room."

I yawned, got to my feet, and shuffled back over to my bunk. "Better get some sleep," I told him. "I have a feeling tomorrow's gonna be a long day."

"What if it comes back?" Gilley asked as I slid onto the plastic surface and rolled away from the light again.

"I don't think it will, Gil."

"Why don't you think it will?"

I sighed and sat up, looking pointedly around the room. "Because it came here to kill us, but it obviously can't work its way past the bars. We're in the safest place we can be."

"That's not very comforting," he said with a frown.

I shrugged. "It's all I got, buddy." I then turned away again, hoping he'd eventually do the same. Before long, I was actually asleep.

Six a.m. felt like it arrived about sixty seconds later and our wake-up call was a long stream of profanity that be-

gan with "What in the . . ." and several seconds later
ended with ". . . here?!"

My eyes flew open and I sat up sorely, my hand still
clamped over the wound on my arm. The makeshift bandage of toilet paper was dark red with blood, but at least
it seemed to have stanched the flow.

Gilley was out of his bunk and over to the door of the
cell in a flash. "Let us out of here!" he demanded in a
deep tone completely uncharacteristic of him.

Cruz, who was standing in the middle of the chaotic
scene, stared at him with wide disbelieving eyes. "What'd
you two . . . ?" he asked, pointing around at the mess.

"We'll explain after you let us out of here and M. J.
gets some medical attention."

Cruz's eyes drifted to me and more pointedly to my
wounded arm. More expletives followed. Then he pulled
out his cell and hit a button. "Sheriff?" he said. "You
gotta come to the station right away. We got a situation
on our hands."

Cruz made no move to let us out of the jail cell, even
though Gilley was doing his level best to insist that he
unlock the door immediately. "Cool your jets," Cruz
barked at him, sifting through the contacts on his phone
to make another call.

With a frustrated sigh I lay back down on the bunk. I
was a little light-headed all of a sudden and even more
exhausted than when I'd first turned in just a few hours
earlier.

I didn't have a chance to recline for long. Within five
minutes Sheriff Pena had entered the station and his reaction was identical to Cruz's right down to the string of
expletives. He then turned to his deputy and demanded

to know what'd happened. "I got no idea, Nick," Cruz said. "I locked those two up last night around eight and left 'em here for the night. When I walked in this morning, this place looked like a bomb went off."

Pena stepped carefully over the debris to the front of our cell, where Gilley and I were both sitting on our bunks staring moodily out at the two lawmen. "What happened?"

Gilley and I exchanged a look and I nodded to him. He could take the lead. "We'll tell you exactly what happened the moment you let us out of here and have someone look at M. J.'s wound."

"Did someone call for a doctor?" asked a voice from the hallway just as the figure of Ari's husband, Brody, entered. "Whoa!" he said when he took in the condition of the station. "What the hell happened here?"

"We know but we're not talking till the sheriff lets us out," Gil said, glaring at Pena and Cruz. I half expected him to stick his tongue out at them for good measure.

"Hi, Brody," I said, getting up from the bunk to come to the front of the cell. "Can you call Heath for me and let him know I'm here?"

Brody blinked as if he didn't quite know what to say. "Uh, sure," he said. "But maybe I could take a look at that arm of yours first?"

"She's got a terrible cut," Gil told him. "Might've hit an artery, but these guys won't let us out so we can go to the hospital."

Brody stepped over a pile of files and asked Cruz to open the door. He did, but instead of letting us come out, the deputy motioned the doctor in. Gil glared harder at him, but Cruz wasn't backing down. Instead he turned his attention to what was left of his desk and the demolished computer on the floor.

"Let's see what we've got here," Brody said, coming over to kneel in front of me and gently tugging on the thick layer of toilet paper. "Whoa," he said again when he caught sight of the mean-looking wound. "How'd you get this?"

"Shark bite," I deadpanned.

Brody grinned but sobered quickly. "Really, M. J., how'd this happen?"

My eyes drifted to Gilley; I knew that by answering Brody we'd be giving up the one bargaining chip we had to get us out of the cell. He nodded reluctantly. It wasn't like Cruz and Pena were chomping at the bit to let us out anyway. "It was the same demon that got Heath's aunt and uncle," I told him. "The spirit of the black hawk."

Brody sat back on his heels. "The one Heath and his mom have been going on about?"

I nodded, and swept my good arm around in an arc. "It did all this too."

Brody's eyes followed my hand, but came back to meet those of Sheriff Pena. "I told you," he said to him. "I told you when I checked on Ray at the hospital that he wasn't delusional. This thing is real, Pena."

I focused on the lawmen. I'd had no idea that there were discussions going on between Pena, Brody, and other members of the tribe about the veracity of the demon hunting Heath's family.

Pena stepped forward and motioned to Cruz to open the cell door. He then came inside, bringing with him one of the only chairs left intact. He turned the chair around to straddle it and stared pointedly at me before speaking. I did my best not to wither under his glare. "Tell me what happened, *exactly* as it occurred."

"Starting from when?" I asked, wincing when Brody got back to work on my arm.

"Starting from when you ignored the sign posted at the entrance to the Pueblo, and you and your friend here thought it was a good idea to trespass on sacred ground."

I swallowed. I'd sorta been hoping they'd forgotten about that. "Gil and I rented a car and decided to search for signs of this demon," I said, making up relevant parts as I went along. "As it happened, our car died right at the entrance to the Pueblo."

"Spectral activity can have that effect," Gilley said, helping my story along. "As the technician expert on all of the *Ghoul Getters* episodes, I can tell you that we've had many a camera, gadget, and car battery drained of power when we were out hunting ghosts."

Pena showed no sign of either believing or disbelieving Gilley. He just continued to level his cool gaze at me. So, after an awkward pause, I got on with it. "*Any*way, we couldn't get the car started again, so we decided to come here for help, but the place was deserted."

"What time was this?"

"Yeee-ouch!" I cried, jumping when Brody put some antiseptic on my wound.

"Sorry," he said, swiveling his head to look at Pena. "She's got a set of three marks just like the patterns we found all over Milton's body, Nick. And I don't think a mountain lion got in here and caused all this."

Pena said nothing; he just continued to eye Brody and me with his steely gaze. Finally, though, he asked me again what time Gilley and I had arrived at the Pueblo.

"It was early evening," Gilley said quickly. "Around seven p.m."

I thanked God he'd spoken first, because I was so fuzzy-headed that I'd been about to tell Pena the truth, which would then have required me to explain what Gilley and I had done between about five and seven. I couldn't very well have mentioned the library. We'd never get out of here if I did.

"Yeah, around seven," I said, like I was just remembering the time. "But it took us a while to walk here from the entrance."

"I rolled on them a little after eight, Nick," Cruz said from his place outside the cell.

"Then what?" Pena asked.

The rest of the story Gilley and I took turns telling, leaving out the part where Gil had managed to snag our packs and then raided Cruz's e-mail with his wireless keyboard and track pad, of course.

Pena seemed to notice the bags, however, because he pointed to Gilley's backpack and said to his deputy, "You let them keep those?"

Cruz's brown eyes focused on the backpack and my messenger bag. "No," he said, and there was an undercurrent of anger in his voice. "I left those on a chair next to my desk."

"The demon knocked them on the floor and we were able to reach through the bars and grab them," Gil said. "And good thing too, because you didn't come back to check on us and M. J. could have bled to death if I hadn't had my first aid kit handy!"

Pena and Cruz let the subject go after that, but I couldn't help thinking that Pena was seriously pissed about something.

By now, Brody had finished stitching up my arm (it'd taken over fifty to close the wounds!) and he got up to head to the sink and remove his gloves so he could wash his hands again. "I'll call Heath," he said from the sink. "He'll confirm that he knows these two and that they weren't trying to steal his car."

"They're still guilty of trespassing," Cruz was quick to say.

Pena got up from his chair and swung it around in front of him to carry it back outside the cell. "They had car trouble, Jimmy," he growled. "Let 'em go."

Cruz's face flashed to anger for a moment and he pointed to the disaster all around him. "But what about *this*, Nick! You *know* they had something to do with it!"

Pena was unfazed by Cruz's outburst. "How'd they pull that off, Jimmy?" he asked calmly. "Locked inside a cell and all. How'd they tear this place to shreds and get a wound like that in the process?"

"Oh, come on, Nick! You can't actually *believe* this black hawk crap!"

Pena rounded on the younger officer, and it was clear that to him Cruz had just spoken out of turn. "It's not a question of what I believe, Jimmy. It's a question of what I've *seen*. And I've seen enough to realize we're dealing with some serious shit right now. I had my doubts about that coroner's report on Milton when it came back as a mountain lion attack. You and I didn't catch one track or paw print out at the cabin, and then there was the side of Bev's minivan. Remember *that*?"

I knew that Pena was referring to the talon marks on the side of Beverly's vehicle, and there was a huge part of me that felt totally relieved that Pena at least was taking this seriously.

His deputy, however, was a different story. "Well, I think it's bullshit!" he snapped. "It's some kind of hoax or something, and I think Heath and his mom and these guys are all in on it. I mean, who's ever heard of a ghost murdering people or tearing up homes and public buildings?"

Gilley and I both shot our hands in the air. "We've heard of it," Gil said eagerly. "And we've encountered it firsthand. If you don't believe me, I can e-mail you some footage from our last ghostbust that'll curl your hair."

Cruz ignored him. "I say we hold these two until we get the truth out of 'em."

Pena moved to the cell door and pulled it open, motioning to Gil and me. "Get your gear. I'll drive you to your car and see if we can't get it started."

Gil moved with lightning speed, gathering up all our belongings and the few stakes we had left. As he was shoveling those into his backpack, however, Pena took notice of them. "Hold on," he said, pointing to the spikes. "What's that?"

Gilley placed one of the spikes next to a bar on the cell, where it pulled free of Gilley's fingers and clinked against the metal. "It's magnetic," he explained. "We use them to fight the nastier spooks."

Pena pulled the spike off the bar to examine it. "How?" he asked.

I answered him. "Either by putting it close to the spook to drive it back, or by driving it into the spook's portal—the gateway it uses to enter or exit our realm for one of the lower ones."

I expected Pena to ask me a few more questions about the spike and our methods. He didn't. Instead, he surprised me by asking, "Can I keep this?"

I looked at Gil and he shrugged. "Sure," I said.

Brody came back over to me then and handed me a slip of paper with some writing on it. "That's a prescription for some antibiotics," he explained. "And when was the last time you had a tetanus shot?"

"Three years ago."

"You're sure?"

"Positive."

Brody nodded. "Okay. Change that bandage once a day and keep your arm away from water for the next ten days. You can have the stitches removed by me or your own doctor after that."

I thanked Brody and got stiffly to my feet. The woozy feeling I'd been having became overwhelming then and I sank like a stone to my knees. "Whoa!" Brody said, barely catching me.

"I'm a little dizzy," I told him.

"She hasn't had anything to eat since yesterday morning except one small, cold, pathetic piece of pizza last night, which was all Deputy Cruz let us have," Gil said, looking pointedly at the lawman, who had the decency to duck his chin when Pena glared at him.

"We'll take you back to your car so you can get something to eat," the sheriff said kindly, coming into the cell to take me easily from both Brody and Gil—neither of whom were nearly as tall or brawny as the large, muscular Pena. Gilley left my side to root around in the wreckage outside the cell, coming up with our phones and ID. "We'll be taking these back," he said to Cruz, who merely glowered darkly at him.

With the sheriff's help I was soon loaded into his cruiser and we were headed down the long and winding road to our car. When we got to the entrance of the Pueblo, however, we discovered that our car was gone.

"Where'd it go?!" Gilley practically screeched upon seeing that our rental was missing.

"You're sure you left it here?" Pena asked, parking the cruiser right next to the large sage bush where we'd left the rental.

"Positive," I moaned. Had I gotten the added insurance for the car if it was stolen? I couldn't remember.

Pena popped the locks and Gilley got out fast, running over to where our car had been parked to stare in astonishment at the ground as if he could blink it back into place. "Where'd you rent it from?"

"The Enterprise on St. Michaels," I said.

"Seriously?" Gilley screeched. "Someone *stole* our friggin' car?!"

"Was it locked?" Pena asked, reaching for his clipboard.

"Yes," I said.

Pena began scribbling on his clipboard. "Well then, someone either broke in and got it started, or they towed it."

"You think someone had it towed?" I asked hopefully, remembering that I'd said no to the extra insurance.

"No," Pena said. "I'd have a report on it if they did."

I sank back in the seat. "Crap," I said moodily. I was right. This was gonna be a long day.

Two hours later Gilley and I were finally sitting down to a meal when Heath burst into the diner we'd found near our hotel. I slapped my forehead. In all the hassle of dealing with the rental car theft, I'd completely forgotten about my boyfriend.

"I texted him," Gil said, looking up when he heard my name called from the doorway.

I set down the forkful of pancakes and got up just as Heath swept me into his arms. "Are you okay?" he asked, hugging me tight.

"Fine," I assured him.

"The demon attacked her," Gilley said, most unhelpfully.

Heath stepped back but held me at arm's length. "Brody told me." He then looked down at my arm, lines of concern etched into his face. "He said he put fifty-two stitches into you."

"They were really little sutures," I told him, holding my bandaged arm up so he could see I was okay.

Heath hugged me again, but all I could think about was how hungry and light-headed I still was.

"Heath," Gilley said to him. "M. J.'s a little fuzzy from blood loss and low blood sugar. Let her sit down so she can eat, will ya?"

Heath immediately let me go and helped me into my chair, then came around and sat down next to me. I took up the fork again, so happy to finally get to eat uninterrupted.

"So what the hell were you two thinking, anyway?" Heath demanded.

I sighed and set the fork back down. But Gilley held up his hand to Heath and said, "We'll eat first, explain second, okay?"

Once I'd plowed my way through nearly the entire stack of flapjacks, Gil and I confessed everything to Heath, including the part about the stolen volume of Pueblo histories, which Gilley had tucked back into the bottom of his backpack without anyone seeing it. To my surprise, Heath didn't appear nearly as mad as I thought he'd be. He merely nodded and let us get on with the story.

When we were finally finished, he said, "I think you two should fly back to Boston today."

"Hallelujah!" Gilley said, his eyes lighting up with the idea.

"Are you crazy?" I snapped, knowing exactly what Heath was thinking. "You want us to go away *now*?"

Heath put his hand gently on the side of my face. "This isn't your fight, babe. It's mine and my family's."

"Oh, and so far, you Whitefeathers are doing such a great job of defending yourselves," I said, angry that he wanted to send me away.

Heath winced. "We'll do better now that Pena's on our side," he vowed. "Hell, even my uncles are starting to come around. We all went over to the station and took a look at the damage. I don't even want to think about what would've happened if you two hadn't been safe inside that cell."

"We'd have been safe inside our hotel room," Gil muttered, earning a glare from me.

"We're not leaving," I told Heath, and I didn't even bother asking Gil to stay. I just assumed he would. Or, should I say, I just hoped he wouldn't throw a major hairy and have one of his epic meltdowns at the suggestion of staying.

Which is why he secretly shocked me when he sighed dramatically and said, "M. J.'s right. We have to stay. There's no way you guys can handle this thing without us."

Heath's eyes moved to Gilley. "There's no guarantee that we'll be able to handle this thing *with* you two here either," he reasoned. "But at least I won't be distracted every minute worrying about you guys. Do you know I didn't sleep a wink last night, I was so worried about you, Em? I didn't think to check my e-mail till around four a.m."

"Sorry," I said, looking down at my lap. "I would've sent you a text or left a voice mail, but Cruz took our phones."

"He can be a real prick," Heath said, moving his hand to cover mine. "But the point is that you two need to go home and let me deal with this thing. It's my family and my business."

"Um . . . ow," I said, pulling my hand away.

Heath sighed and reached for my hand again. "Em, you just don't get it. If this demon attacks my family again and you're in the room, I'm gonna have to make a choice between trying to defend you or one of them, and I can't make that choice. I'd lose either way."

"I *can* take care of myself, you know," I told him.

Heath ran his fingers lightly across the outside of my bandaged arm. "Yeah, I can see that."

I pulled my arm away from him again. "Heath, you have *no* idea how dangerous and ferocious this thing is! You can't handle it alone!"

"Oh, trust me," he replied. "I *do* know how dangerous it is, and I won't be alone. I've got my mom and my family to help fight it."

"But no one believes you!" I countered. "Your uncles think it's a freaking mountain lion, for Christ's sake!"

"Pena's talking to Vernon and Rex right now," Heath assured me. "I think after what happened last night at the station, there's no way they can deny this thing exists or that this demon is out for blood."

"Cruz thought it was a stunt *we* pulled," Gilley reminded him.

Heath shook his head. "Cruz isn't the smartest guy in the tribe, Gil. No one's going to listen to him. They'll listen to Pena."

"We're not leaving," I said, digging in my heels.

Heath opened his mouth to protest, but at that moment we heard someone call his name and we all turned to look at the door. None other than Sheriff Pena himself was coming into the diner. He nodded to Gilley and me when he got to our table and said, "I see you took my recommendation on where to go for breakfast."

I smiled. "It was just what the doctor ordered," I told him.

He pointed to my arm. "How's the wound?"

"Sore, but I've been assured it's not fatal."

Pena's serious face softened and the edges of his mouth lifted. "Glad to hear it," he said. He then pulled over a nearby chair and turned it around to straddle it like he'd done when he'd asked Gil and me about our night in jail.

"I've had a long talk with Vernon and Rex," he began, "along with your mom, Heath, and a couple of the other elders, and we all agree that some sort of evil spirit is out for Whitefeather blood."

Even though the conversation was very serious, I felt my shoulders relax. Finally the tribe believed us! "We're calling a tribal council," he continued, "and we'll be consulting with a few other Pueblos to see if they've ever dealt with anything like this."

Pena paused long enough to reach into his pocket and pull out a plastic-wrapped toothpick, which he unwrapped and stuck in his mouth to chew. We waited in silence for him to continue. "My guess," he said next, "is that none of the other tribes have ever encountered *anything* like what we're dealing with at Zanto. I've also spent a lot of the past hour combing the library for a copy of the histories to see if there's anything in there about this evil spirit . . . but it's odd. I can't seem to find the book anywhere." Pena didn't exactly come right out and accuse us, but the implication was there in his voice.

I cleared my throat and motioned with my head for Gilley to cough up the volume.

Gilley narrowed his eyes hard at me and looked like he wasn't about to confess for all of ten seconds, and we had ourselves a little silent argument with plenty of glares, stares, head motions, shakes, chin thrusts, and finally a kick under the table. That was from me, of course, and Gil finally, reluctantly, and with plenty of grumbling reached into his backpack and pulled out the missing volume.

"We . . . uh . . . found this in the grass outside the library," he said. "It must've fallen out the window or something."

Pena curled his large hand around the volume and pulled it close. "You know books," he said. "Always leaping off shelves and running out the door, trying to flee the confinement of their libraries."

I chuckled, and was a little relieved that Pena actually had a sense of humor.

I then took the opportunity to fill him in on what we'd read in the histories. Pena listened without comment, and when I was done, he said, "If you're right and it's the black hawk that's after the Whitefeathers, then this would be some serious shit we'd be dealing with. I'm no medicine man, but I do know that the older the spirit, the more powerful it is. The legend of the black and white hawks dates back centuries to the very first stories our people told."

"What're you going to do?" Gilley asked him.

"Officially?"

Gil nodded.

"Host a bunch of meetings, consult the elders in our communities, and probably hold a few ceremonies, which likely won't do a damn bit of good, and in the interim this thing'll continue to try and pick off your family, Heath, one by one."

Gilley audibly gulped, but I saw the small glint in Pena's eye and I knew there was more.

"Unofficially," he said after rolling the toothpick around on his tongue, "we'd like to hire you three."

I shook my head. Had he just said what I thought he said? "Wait . . . what?" I asked.

Pena pointed to the three of us at the table. "You guys are professional ghostbusters, right?"

Gilley, Heath, and I looked around at one another. "Uh . . . ," said Gil.

"Er . . . ," said Heath.

"We are," I told him.

Pena reached to the belt around his waist and pulled out the spike we'd given him. "I'm not sure if you can kill this thing, but seeing how you defended yourselves against it last night convinced me to give you three a shot. I can't pay you much—I've only got about two thousand earmarked for discretionary spending in our budget—but it's yours if you'll take the job."

"We'll take it," I told him.

"Hold on," Heath said abruptly. "Last time I checked, we were a team, and as a team I think we should vote on this."

Uh-oh. "We don't need a vote," I said, directing my comment to Sheriff Pena. "We're in."

"Not without a vote," Heath insisted, and the way he was eyeing Gilley, I knew what he was doing. He was going to try and get Gil to vote no and send the two of us packing.

I glared at Heath, then turned steely eyes on Gilley, silently warning him to vote with me or there'd be trouble. "I vote we take the job," I said with emphasis while I continued to stare hard at Gil.

"I vote we don't," said Heath. "Gilley? Would you rather take this very dangerous job where you will probably die a really painful death, or go home to the safety of Boston for a few days of R and R?"

I redirected the steely-eyed look to Heath. "Do we *really* need the theatrics? He's not likely to *die*, Heath!"

But he refused to look at me. Instead he kept his eyes on Gilley and reached for my bandaged arm. Lifting it before I could pull it away, he said, "No theatrics necessary. Just imagine if this had been *your* arm, Gil. Or your chest. Or your face!"

Gilley visibly paled and touched all three places on his body as if checking to make sure they were unmarred.

It was then that I decided to throw off the gloves. "Gilley," I said sharply, pulling his attention from Heath. "If you want to go, you can go. I won't stop you. But I'm going to stay here and work this case with or without you, and with or without Heath for that matter. You can head home, but you'll be going back on the promise you made to my mom to always stand by me. If you can live with that, then fine. I'm sure Mama's spirit will get over it . . . eventually."

Gil folded his arms across his chest and frowned at

me. "Really, M. J.? You're going to throw your dead mother into this?"

I shrugged. "I'm just stating facts, Gil. You have to make a decision you can live with."

"*If* you live," Heath countered. It was clear he was banking on me backing down if Gil wouldn't commit.

Gilley sighed and muttered something under his breath, which didn't sound very flattering to either Heath or me, but in the end he sided with me. "Sheriff Pena," he said. "We're in. But we'll need the check up front. There's some equipment we need to buy."

Pena nodded and motioned with his chin to Heath. "You in, Whitefeather?"

Heath looked as angry as I'd ever seen him, but I didn't much care. He needed my help and for that matter he needed Gilley's help too, so he'd just have to get over it. "I was always in," he said levelly.

"Good," said the sheriff. "Then we'll need to set a few ground rules so these two don't ruffle too many feathers."

I couldn't imagine ruffling any more feathers than we already had, but I didn't say anything—I just let Pena talk. "The first rule of the Pueblo—"

"Is that there is no Pueblo!" Gilley said quickly, giggling at his inside joke. I kicked him again under the table and that wiped the grin off his face. "Sorry," he said. "I'll be good."

Pena continued without missing a beat, ". . . is that you three are guests of the tribe. In other words, you're one notch above tourists, but not much above them, understand?"

"We can't go into any unauthorized places or public buildings like the library without permission," I said.

Pena nodded. "No more of this leaving your car at the entrance to the Pueblo during sacred ceremonies and walking on tribal ground, okay?"

"Understood," I told him.

"Also," he continued, "the Pueblo is normally closed to outsiders after eight p.m., but I'm going to grant you three special access until two a.m. Again, you won't be able to enter any homes or buildings unless you've been given special permission, but you may patrol the Pueblo and the highlands as you see fit. The only area completely off-limits to you is the burial grounds. No outsiders are allowed there under any circumstances."

"Can we have a map of the Pueblo, Sheriff?" I asked, worried that we might wander onto some off-limits territory without realizing it.

Pena got up and swiveled the chair around to tuck it back under the table. "No," he said without explanation, which surprised me. "You two just stick with Whitefeather here, and he'll keep you out of trouble, right, Heath?"

"Yes, sir," Heath promised, keeping his eyes on the table.

The sheriff nodded and wished us luck with a tip of his hat, and then he left us alone to hash out a plan.

Gil brought up the story of the black hawk legend again and how the medicine man had taken the spirit of the demon into his body, and it had turned him into an evil person who killed White Wolf. "They're all buried in some secret location," Gil said.

"And that must be where the black hawk escaped from," I reasoned. "My thinking is that someone—"

"Daryl West," Gil cut in, reminding me of the remains that were found on the Pueblo.

"Yeah, Daryl West," I said. "He must've stumbled onto the secret burial place and somehow freed the demon, who then tore him to shreds."

Heath made a T with his hands. "Time out," he said. "Who's this Daryl West dude?"

Gil explained how he'd managed to break into Deputy Cruz's e-mails and found the identity of the remains of Daryl, who'd been declared by the coroner as having been the victim of a mountain lion attack.

"He comes from Los Alamos," Gilley said, retrieving his tablet and scrolling through the e-mails. "And he had a few run-ins with the law over grave robbing, if you can believe it."

Heath sat up straighter and leaned across the table to squint at Gilley's screen. "Hold on," he said. "Did you say grave robbing?"

Gil turned the tablet toward Heath so he could read it. "Yeah," he said. "See?"

Heath took the gadget and studied the e-mail. "What is it?" I asked him.

"The reason Pena was reluctant to give you a map of our lands isn't just because our burial grounds are sacred, but because there's a pretty good black market that's cropped up in recent years trading in ancient American Indian artifacts."

My eyes widened. "You think West was robbing Native American burial grounds?"

"I'd bet on it," he said.

"So then he really could've stumbled onto the vessel that held the black hawk," I said, tapping my finger on the tabletop while I thought on that. "We need to find that vessel, guys."

"Wouldn't the demon have destroyed it?" Gil said. "I

mean, if it escaped because West uncorked it, or did whatever to free the demon, it's probably in a thousand pieces by now."

I nodded. "You know, you're right, Gil. Okay, so the place to start is where West's remains were found. That's got to be close to where the demon was hidden away all those years ago. Can you find us that locale, Gil?"

He nodded. "Yep," he said, pulling out his wireless keyboard and clicking his fingers across it.

"And we'll need to get some proper equipment," I added while Gilley typed. "Now that we have some funds, we can get that night-vision camera and a couple more meters. When's that used meter you already purchased going to get here?"

Gilley eyed his watch. "Today," he said. "Should be dropped off at the front desk anytime before noon."

We then hashed out a plan for the next hour, at the end of which Heath and I were once again on good terms.

Chapter 10

"That's weird," Heath said, staring at Gilley's iPad later that day when we'd gone back to the hotel for a bit of rest before tackling the demon again.

"What's weird?" I asked, peeking over his shoulder as he looked at the image of where Gil had pinpointed the exact location that the remains of Daryl West had been found.

"This isn't as close to our burial grounds as I'd thought," he said.

I squinted at the aerial snapshot. All I saw was scrub and rocky terrain. "Where is it, then?"

"No-man's-land," he said. "It's on the other side of the foothills that surround the Zanto burial grounds."

"Maybe Daryl went over the foothills to reach them?" I suggested.

Heath shook his head. "That'd be really stupid," he

said. "The foothills are steep and filled with loose rock and tricky terrain. Going over them would take four times as long as traveling by road, and you'd have to go in by foot, which would make for a really slow getaway. Unless of course you had a three-wheeler, which would only get you as far as the foothills and you'd still have to climb over them. Naw, if you were going to head to our burial grounds, you'd take the same road Bev took before she crashed."

I studied the dot on the screen. "What the heck was he doing way out in no-man's-land, then?"

"Probably running for his life," Gil grumbled drowsily while he reclined back on his bed.

I ignored him and directed my next question at Heath. "How long will it take us to drive there?"

Heath poked at the screen to move the map around. "We can drive up the main road and get close, then hike in. It should only take us about an hour."

"Well, we'd better go now, then," I suggested. "I don't want to get caught out there after dark."

"We're not even sure it's safe during the day," Heath said.

"Yeah, but at least the humidity will be at its lowest point now in the afternoon, which means that even if the demon did rear its ugly head, it'd be weaker than during the hours between midnight and dawn."

Heath eyed me skeptically. "How many spikes you got?"

"Ten or so," I said. "Five each should be enough."

"Okay," he relented. "And let's see if Gil will let us borrow his sweatshirt."

I eyed the bed where Gilley was lying back with his eyes closed. "Gil?"

No answer.

"Gilley?" I said a little louder.

He replied with a long nasal snore.

"He says we can take it," I whispered.

Heath grinned at me and offered his hand. "Come on. Let's get out there and see what we see."

The trip to the site where Daryl's remains were found took exactly one hour and we traveled the same road we'd come down when we went to check out the site where Beverly had crashed her car.

In fact, we parked very near the tree she'd hit, which was still scarred with the evidence of the crash and the talon marks of the demon. "Why doesn't this feel like just a coincidence?" I said when we got out of the car.

Heath pulled out two of the spikes from the loops in his belt. "The demon must like this area," he said, motioning for me to get my spikes out too.

I did and we set off on foot through the scrub and mostly bare earth. This wasn't quite the desert, but it was certainly close.

I could see the foothills weren't too far away, but the going was a little rough, that is, until Heath found some three-wheeler tracks.

"Who do you think made these?" I asked as he and I bent low to inspect them.

"I don't know," Heath said, and I could tell he was a little bothered by them.

"One of your younger cousins coming out here for a little joyride, maybe?" I asked.

Heath stood up and wiped his hands together to get the dust off. "Maybe. There were two ATVs along here," he said. "One following the other."

The tracks headed right for the foothills and as we walked along them, ever closer to the red dot on the screen of Heath's iPhone, I gave up my theory that the ATV tracks belonged to someone from the tribe.

Especially when Heath pointed to yet a third set that had intersected the pair of tracks we were navigating almost exactly at the point where the satellite pinpointed the location where Daryl's remains had been found.

There wasn't much to this intersection except for a confusion of tire tracks and some wooden stakes planted in the ground with orange tags on them to mark the site for the coroner.

The energy around all this was bad, though. As in BAD.

"Something very violent happened here," I said, holding my arms out to really feel the area around the wooden stakes.

Heath nodded. "You ain't kidding," he said. Then his eyes drifted to the tracks again, which carried on toward the foothills. "I want to see where they were coming from, Em."

"Lead the way," I told him, and we began walking again.

It didn't take long; the foothills were only about two hundred yards away from where Daryl had died, and when we got to the base of the steep slope in front of us, it was clear that Daryl and his companion had either stopped here and hiked up or stopped here to rest for a while, because the ATVs had sunk into the loose dirt, which clearly indicated that they'd been parked there for a period of time.

"Do you think they went up there?" I asked, squinting toward the top of the hill.

Heath approached the slope. "I do," he said, already starting up.

I didn't question him, but tucked in right behind as we hoofed it up the slope.

About three-quarters of the way to the top, Heath suddenly stopped and pointed to the ground. In front of him was a long metal rod with a wooden handle. "What's that?" I asked.

Heath moved over to it and picked it up, anger clouding his features. "They *were* after our burial grounds," he said, showing me the rod like I might understand what he meant.

"I don't get it," I said. "Heath, what is that thing?"

He came back down the slope a few feet to me and punched the rod into the earth. "It's how these bastards locate a grave," he explained. "They jam this into the ground and if they feel it give way, they start digging."

I eyed the rod closely. It was covered in dirt midway up the shaft. "Looks like they found something."

Heath looked up the slope again. "Sons of bitches," he muttered.

I surveyed our location, a bit confused. "But these aren't your burial grounds, right? Why would they bring that out here?"

Heath suddenly pointed to the ridge at the top of the slope. "There!" he said. "See that, Em?"

I squinted to where he was pointing, spotting a set of five caves along the ridge. I then eyed my watch. It was going on four p.m. "How long would it take to get up there?"

"Half hour."

"When does the sun set again?"

"Around six thirty."

I squeezed Heath's hand. I knew he really wanted to see what was at the top of that ridge, but once we got up there, we'd have precious little time to check it out if we didn't want to get caught out here after sunset. Then again, the demon was on the loose and there was another night ahead where it could terrorize one of Heath's relatives. I made up my mind quickly, because we didn't have another minute to spare. "Race you to the top," I said, and let go of his hand to sprint up several yards of the slope.

Heath kept pace with me and we didn't speak as we pushed our way up the hill. Huffing and puffing, we made it in twenty minutes, which gave us a little more wiggle room.

Still breathing hard, we began to inspect the caves. There were six of them—only five were visible from the slope—and what was interesting was that I could see right away that the second one had been enlarged by human hands. There were chisel marks in the rock on the cave's ceiling and I pointed those out to Heath. "The Anasazi Indians used to inhabit these lands, didn't they?" I asked, remembering the literature from a pamphlet in our hotel room.

"Yeah," Heath said. "But I didn't know there was a settlement up here. I wonder if my uncles know about this place."

Heath and I left that cave and entered the third, which was barren and cold. The fourth cave along the row was the one where we hit pay dirt. "There!" I said, rushing forward to pick up another rod identical to the one Heath found on the slope and still carried. I held it up so he could see, and he made a grim face. "That confirms it," he said. "There were definitely two of them up here, looking for graves."

I walked into the cave and came up short. My sixth sense was on high alert with the demon lurking around, so when I walked into the cave and felt it buzzing and nearly crackling with energy, it was a moment before I could even process it. "Whoa!" I said, looking over my shoulder at Heath. "Honey, come in and feel this!"

Heath eyed me curiously but came into the cave, and I smiled when he too came up short. "Whoa, is right," he said, turning in a circle with his arms outstretched. "There is some pretty amazing energy here."

"It feels almost like a vortex, doesn't it?" I was referring to the energy of certain geographic locations known to contain extra-high quantities of electromagnetic currents.

"I think you're right," Heath said. "It does feel like a vortex, but not a big one."

"It's still pretty powerful, though," I said, feeling a tingling sensation all along my limbs. I'd need to watch myself in here, because it was easy to lose track of time and one's surroundings within a vortex.

And then something odd caught my eye. In particular, something peculiar about the ground. Instead of being mostly packed earth like in the other caves, it appeared to be layered with loose rock and dirt and also littered with pockmarks. I placed the rod into one of those small depressions and it fit perfectly. "Hey, look at *this*!" I said to Heath.

He came forward and surveyed the cave floor, then pointed to a three-by-three section of dirt that had clearly been disturbed. "Looks like our grave robbers found what they were looking for," he said, walking over to inspect it.

I took a step to follow after him, but I felt a tug in my solar plexus that pulled me up short. Something felt off. I moved in the direction of the tug, letting the rod tap the ground as I walked, and at the back of the cave, the resistance against the tip gave a little and it sank into the earth a good three inches.

The sensation of being pulled intensified for one quick instant; then it vanished and I knew I was standing over something very important. "Heath?"

"Yeah?" he said, without looking up.

"I think I found something."

This time he did lift his chin, and the expression on my face must have been enough to convince him to come over. I held still, with the rod still sunk into the ground, because I wanted him to see it.

"What is it?" he asked.

"I'm not sure. But when I tapped the ground right here, the rod sank in a couple of inches."

Heath poked his own rod over the ground. It bounced up off the hard surface several times, except when it got to within about six inches of my rod, and then it too sank into the earth. Heath got down on both knees and used a rock to scratch at the loose dirt. I got down too and helped him, and before long we could see a two-by-two-foot hole had been previously dug out of the hard-packed earth and inside that hole was something man-made. "What is it?" I asked, staring at the top of the thing, which had an odd shape.

"It's a clay pot," Heath said.

I felt a chill down my spine. "The vessel?" I asked.

Heath continued to scrub away the loose dirt with his hands. "Em," he said as he worked.

"Yes?"

"Get out Gilley's sweatshirt and put it on."

I hesitated only a second before I pulled out all my magnetic spikes and laid them out in a semicircle around

Heath; then I dug Gil's sweatshirt out of Heath's back-pack and put it on.

Meanwhile, he'd managed to remove enough of the dirt around the pot to pull it carefully free of its enclosure. Wiping away the dust on the outside, he gasped when the exterior design appeared. "What the . . . ?" he said.

"What is it?" I peered at the clay pot, which was fairly large and looked kind of heavy. The outside was tinted all in black, but on the side a white feather was etched into the clay.

Before Heath could answer me, however, I realized I'd seen that pot before. Sam had shown it to me in Molly's house the day Heath's aunt had been killed. "That's the missing urn that holds your family's ashes!"

Heath stared at the artifact as if he couldn't quite believe it. "Everyone thought my mom took this," he said. "And it's been here all along."

"So someone took it, hid it here, and framed your mom?"

"Looks that way."

"Well," I reasoned, "at least now you can prove that it wasn't her."

But Heath shook his head. "Em, if I show up with this, the tribe's just gonna accuse me of trying to cover up my mom's crime. They'll say that she's had it all this time and only now that my uncle Milton has died did she feel guilty enough to bring it out in the open again."

"So . . . ," I began, not knowing where he was going with that line of reasoning. "You're *not* going to give it back to the tribe?"

Heath lifted the pot carefully onto his lap and wiped at the dirt some more. "I didn't say that," he told me. "I just need to think about how to show up with it. And I don't think I should do that right now. I mean, while we're dealing with this demon, it's just going to look too suspicious."

"Are you gonna tell your mom at least?"

Heath sighed. "No," he said softly. "It'll only upset her to know that someone took it and hid it here, letting her take all the blame. I'll wait until after we've dealt with the black hawk. Then she and I can have a sit-down and figure out how to explain its sudden appearance to the tribe."

"Okay," I said, wanting to fully support his decision, but knowing I'd do it differently.

"We better leave," Heath said, nervously looking at the dwindling light from outside.

"You carrying that thing down?" I asked, motioning to the urn in his lap.

He nodded, grunting as he got up with it. It was clearly heavy. I eyed him skeptically and he said, "I'll be careful."

I got up too and turned to the exit when my vision sort of clouded over and I heard a buzzing sound in both ears.

The feeling was so intense and so swift that I nearly fell over onto my side, and I had to sink back down to the ground again.

"Em?" I heard Heath say, but his voice sounded like he was calling me from far away.

I fought the light-headed and dizzy feeling coming over me and tried to get to my feet again, but my limbs turned to jelly and I plopped right onto my butt.

"M. J.?" Heath said again, his tone more insistent. "Babe, are you okay?"

I opened my mouth to tell him that something was

happening to me, but no sound came out. Instead, the air around me seemed to shimmer and all of a sudden the cave brightened, like the sun was shining into it instead of where I knew it was setting on the other side of the hill. Against the wall where the slightly raised mound of dirt had been, I saw two figures with short shovels, digging at the earth and moving it to the side, their movements quick and excited. When I focused on the figures, I could see that they were both men, in their early-to-mid thirties. One was slim and short—scrawny even. The other was about four inches taller and built to move the dirt aside at a much faster pace.

They didn't talk, but I could hear their shovels striking the earth and then the shorter man waved his hand and stopped digging. In unison they both tossed their shovels aside and the short one knelt eagerly and said, "You got something, Wyatt?"

"Yeah!" said his companion. "Right there! See it, D.?"

D. bent and wiped at something below my sight line. "Ho-ho!" he said triumphantly, reaching into the hole with both hands to wiggle something back and forth.

"Easy!" Wyatt yelled. "Don't break it!"

"I got, I got it," D. told him, and a moment later he pulled out a clay pot so similar to the one Heath and I had just brought up that at first I thought it was the same one. But then when the stranger wiped away the dirt to reveal the surface of the artifact, I happened to catch a glimpse of the white marking on the side, which clearly showed a white wolf's paw crushing down on the faint outline of a black feather, and I knew deep in my bones these two had just pulled up the vessel that contained the spirit of the black hawk, and I then knew that "D." was Daryl West.

"Whoa!" West exclaimed, holding it up so his partner could have a look. "This is gonna fetch us some serious cash, dude!" He then handed it to Wyatt, who seemed to take stock of the pot's weight. "It's heavier than it looks," he said.

"It feels like something's inside," Daryl told him, climbing out of the hole and reaching for the vessel again.

"Should we take out the plug and see what's inside?" Wyatt asked, pointing to the narrow opening, which had a clay stopper in it, held in place by what looked like layers of thin leather strips.

"Naw," said Daryl, holding the vessel away from Wyatt protectively. "It's worth more if we don't mess with it. We can show it to the professor and he can tell us what's in it. Hell, he might even put a bid on it!"

Wyatt's attention was suddenly pulled back to the hole his partner had just climbed out of. "Hey, D.!" he said, pointing to it. "See that?"

Daryl looked. "It's a skeleton!" he said, nearly whooping with excitement. "Aw, man! Dude, we hit the jackpot here!"

"Should we dig it up now?" Wyatt asked.

"Naw," said Daryl. "Let's get down the slope with this jug and come back later. It's gettin' pretty light out and we don't want no one to see us."

In the next moment I felt a firm squeeze to my shoulders. *"M. J.!"* Heath shouted so loud that I flinched. And just like that, the lighting inside the cave changed back to dusk and I found myself staring into Heath's very worried face.

"Daryl had a partner named Wyatt," I blurted out.

Heath didn't let go of my shoulders, but he did dip his

chin and mutter a "Thank God," before looking me in
the eye again. "Where'd you go, babe?"

I shook my head. "Into another imprint," I told him,
pushing off the ground to my feet, but I was still really
wobbly and had to steady myself against Heath. "It must
be the vortex that caused it, but that's not the important
part. Honey, I saw Daryl and Wyatt! They were here digging, just like we suspected, and they found the vessel. It
looked exactly like that one," I told him, pointing to the
one in his arms, "except that the design on the side was
different. It showed a wolf's paw crushing a black feather."

"Sounds like the symbol Hummingbird painted on
the side of the vessel that was supposed to trap the black
hawk," Heath said.

I nodded. "The hole also held a skeleton. I'm guessing they were the remains of White Wolf."

Heath's lips pressed together, his anger barely held in
check. "Did they dig him up too?" he asked, looking at
the raised mound of earth near the back of the cave.

"No," I told him. "At least, not on that visit. The imprint ended before I could see if there was a time when
they might've come back."

Heath moved over to the loose dirt of the grave. "We'll
have to hope they didn't come back," he said softly. Then
he looked at the top of the clay pot cradled in the crook
of his arm and asked, "Did they open the vessel?"

I shook my head. "No, and that's what's so weird. Wyatt wanted to, but Daryl said that it was worth more if
they didn't. They also mentioned taking it to a professor."

"Professor?" Heath repeated. "Professor who?"

I shrugged. "Don't know. You pulled me out before I
could get much else."

Heath's expression became chagrined. "Sorry," he said. "You were just staring off into space for so long that I started to get worried."

I realized then that the light inside the cave was quickly fading. "What time is it?" I asked, and before Heath could even answer, I was staring at my watch. "We've gotta go!"

"You okay to walk?" he asked me.

"I'll be fine as soon as I get away from this vortex," I said, taking a few unsteady steps, refusing to stay here a minute longer.

I followed Heath out of the cave and we started down the steep slope. I was a little weak and tired and wondered if it was my experience in the cave mixed with a heavy dose of jet lag that was making me stumble and head clumsily down the side of the hill. We were just about at the bottom when Heath called out, "Careful!" to me as I slipped rather inelegantly and nearly went down on my butt.

"You just worry about that heirloom," I told him, embarrassed that I was having such a difficult time. And no sooner did I say that than I slipped again and cut my hand on something sharp. "Son of a bitch!" I yelled, pulling my hand up and seeing my palm immediately turn red.

"What?" Heath said, rushing over to my side.

I closed my fist and gritted my teeth. "It's nothing," I told him, realizing that dusk was quickly fading. "I just hurt my hand a little."

"Let me see," he insisted, already turning to set aside the heirloom.

"No! We don't have time, Heath. We've got to get back to your car before we're completely out of daylight."

Heath looked as if he wanted to argue with me, so I got up and took a slight leap down the slope to level ground. I managed not to trip this time and turned back to him. "Can you jog with that thing?" I asked when he came up next to me.

"You set the pace and I'll keep up," he promised.

I started off, feeling a slick wetness slip through my fingers and I made sure to keep to Heath's left so that he couldn't see my hand. I knew that if he realized I was bleeding pretty bad, he'd stop and want to do something stupid like take care of me.

Within fifteen minutes we were nearly to the SUV, but twilight had come fully onto the landscape and I could feel a chill run down my spine. I hated being out here, exposed like this, so I turned on a little extra speed and was glad when Heath did too.

We reached Heath's Durango in no time, and although I was winded, I felt very glad for the safety it offered. That is, until I rounded the car to my side and happened to pass by the flat tire on the rear passenger side.

"Shit!" Heath growled after I'd pointed it out to him.

I eyed the area around us nervously. "How fast can you fix it?"

After settling the urn in the backseat, Heath lifted the rear lid to the SUV and began to rummage around for his jack and the spare tire. "Quick," he assured me.

I offered to help, but he insisted it would go faster if he did it himself. I knew he was right, especially since my hand was a mess, but I still felt a little helpless as I watched him work.

Because I was still wearing Gilley's sweatshirt, I decided to make sure I stuck close to Heath and kept my eyes and ears peeled for any hint of an approaching menace.

The landscape was quiet—not even the crickets had started up yet—which made it even creepier. I kept feeling like we were being watched, but I couldn't manage to locate the source, so I just kept my eyes on the road and shifted nervously from foot to foot.

Meanwhile, Heath was really struggling with the lug nuts. He would place the wrench on one and have to jump on it several times before it would move. I was worried he'd knock the car off the jack, but luckily, that didn't happen. Still, I gave him and the car a little room until he'd managed to get all four of them off.

As the darkness around us deepened, the air turned decidedly chillier and I shivered and wrapped my arms around myself, while Gilley's sweatshirt sagged around me like a potato sack. "How's it coming?" I asked, looking up and down the road.

"It's coming," he said, and I could detect more than a hint of irritation in his voice. I walked a little bit away from the car, determined to give him some space until he'd gotten the tire back on, and that's when I felt something I can only describe as a terrible evil headed straight for us.

"Heath!" I whispered, feeling that evil approaching from the road. "Come here!"

"I'm a little busy right now, Em," Heath grunted as he worked to tighten the bolts on the spare.

"I think we need to get in the car," I told him, inching backward.

"Hang on," he said.

I turned around and grabbed him by the arm, pulling on it hard. He dropped the wrench. "Hey!"

I ignored that. *"Get in the car!"*

Heath's eyes finally lit with understanding and his attention also went to the road. Without a word he reached out to me and pulled me toward the passenger-side door, shoving me inside before running around to the driver's side and sliding inside.

The SUV was still on the jack and we were pitched slightly forward while we sat still for a minute, waiting for something to happen. "We need to move!" I told Heath, knowing we were about to be in deep, deep trouble.

Heath's hand shook while he inserted his key, but after rolling the engine over, he hesitated putting the gearshift into drive. "I gotta let the jack down!" he said, his hand moving to the door handle almost at the exact moment a tremendous *WHACK* sounded against the rear quarter panel.

The car jostled and there was a grinding sound before the rear tire plopped down hard to the ground.

Accompanying all of that was a low, terrifying rumble, vibrating through the steel of the car and rippling the hairs along the back of my neck.

Heath and I were both pinned to the seat by fear, not daring to move or utter a sound. Very slowly I moved my head to look at Heath, but caught a glimpse of his window instead. Something glistened in the dark before a red eye emerged; glowing and demonic, it glared at me with pure hatred.

I screamed at the top of my lungs and that seemed to set Heath into motion. He gripped the gearshift and shoved it back two notches while pressing down hard on the gas. The SUV rocketed forward and Heath spun the wheel hard.

We fishtailed, half on the pavement of the road, half off, and all I could think about was that Heath hadn't gotten all the bolts on the spare.

If he had the same thought, he didn't let it interfere with getting us the hell out of there. We whipped around in a circle, moving off onto the opposite shoulder, and then sped down the road, gaining speed with every passing yard.

We got about a mile or two before the rear end of Heath's car began to wobble, and I knew the spare was about to come off. "You've got to slow down!" I shouted. "Heath! If you lose that back tire, we'll roll!"

His hands were white on the steering wheel and his face was just as pale, but I felt him ease off the gas and focus on maintaining control of the car.

My eyes darted again and again to the side mirror—I was terrified that the demon would chase us down, but if it was coming after us, it was impossible to tell. And just as I had convinced myself that maybe we'd lost it, we literally lost it. The spare tire, that is.

I cried out as the car jostled, then began to fishtail in earnest before spinning around in a 360. Then I felt it tilt and my body slammed into the door just as I felt Heath's side of the car leave the ground. The road ahead tipped. I shut my eyes, and just prayed.

Chapter 11

By some miracle we didn't tip over, but it was several seconds before either of us could get ahold of our breathing.

Heath was the first to recover himself, pulling out his cell and calling Brody. When he hung up, I asked, "Is he coming?"

Heath nodded. "He's on his way. He's working the midnight shift, so he's got a little time before he has to be at the hospital, and he's the only one I could call who wouldn't ask me a lot of questions."

"We couldn't call Pena?"

Heath shook his head. "He'd want to know why I took you up into the foothills close to the burial grounds."

"Will Brody get here quick, do you think?" I stared

nervously out the windshield at the road. We'd spun fully around to face the way we'd just come.

"I told him to get here as fast as he could," Heath said. "Don't worry, he will."

I didn't speak the thought that came into my mind, namely, that I hoped Brody arrived before the demon did, because I was pretty sure that thing was once again on the prowl after us. "How far away from it do you think we got?"

Heath looked at the dashboard. "Four and a half . . . five miles," he said.

I gulped. Not far enough.

Thankfully, Brody arrived about five minutes later and drove us back to the Pueblo. It was on the ride back that the kind doctor noticed my hand. "What'd you do now?" he asked, reaching out to lift my wrist.

From the backseat I heard Heath shift forward. "Em!" he said. "When did you do that?"

My hand was locked in a fist and I knew it was still bleeding a little. "It's nothing," I said, trying to shrug it off. "Nothing that a little peroxide and a few Band-Aids can't handle."

Brody's eyes darted from the road to my hand and back again. "Oh, that looks way more serious than a little peroxide and a few Band-Aids," he said. "Heath, how about I drop you at Rocky's garage so you can get a tow for your SUV and I'll take your girlfriend to the hospital and have a look at her hand?"

"Sounds good, cuz, thanks."

"I love how the two of you decide what to do with me without even consulting me," I said.

Heath leaned over the seat and kissed my cheek. "Honey?" he said.

"Yeah?"

"How about you go with Brody to the hospital while I get my car towed?"

"Was that so hard?" I asked.

"It was a little," he said with a chuckle.

"Men," I grumbled. Still, I was very troubled by the fact that Heath was going back out on that road to get his Durango. "Heath?"

"Yeah?"

"Maybe you should wait until tomorrow to get your car towed."

Heath sighed. "It's in the middle of the road, Em. I can't leave it there."

"But—"

"How about if I call Pena and ask him to meet me there too? There'll be three of us then, with an extra car in case we need to get away fast."

I didn't like it, but what could I do? Heath was right; he couldn't leave his car in the middle of the road. What if someone hit it?

A few minutes later, I thought of something else. "Heath? What about Gilley? The note we left him said that we'd be back before dark, and it's way after dark now. He'll be worried."

"I'll call him and explain," he assured me just as we arrived at Rocky's garage.

"He'll be hungry," I reminded him.

"He can order room service on me," Heath said easily, leaning in to kiss me again before getting out of the car and waving good-bye to us.

I thought that once Heath got a look at his bill, that'd be the last time he gave Gil that option, but I didn't push it because I was too tired and my hand hurt.

When Brody and I were under way again, he asked me, "What'd you cut your hand on, anyway?"

"I don't know. Maybe a rock or a piece of glass. It's tough terrain out in the badlands."

"So, what were you guys doing out there, anyway?"

"Pena hired us to bust the demon that killed Milton and Beverly."

I felt Brody's eyes on me. "He did?"

"Yep."

"Huh," Brody said. "That's big for Pena. This thing must've really gotten to him."

"You saw the condition of his station, Brody," I reminded him. "After encountering that thing firsthand, I can safely say that it'd get to anybody." Heath had suggested we not give too many details about what we were up to—or the demon attack on Heath's car—lest it get back to Pena that we were in a place we shouldn't have been.

Brody was quiet for a bit before he shifted in his seat and said, "You think it'll come after anybody else?"

"I do."

"Like who?"

"Like any and all Whitefeathers," I said. "By birth or by marriage, that thing's out for blood."

Brody was quiet for a minute before he asked his next question. "Do you think it'll come after Ari?"

I cleared my throat, wondering if I should be straight with him or cushion it a little. I decided that cushioning it might get the nice couple killed, so I told him the honest truth. "Yes," I said. "I think it'll come after her, you, Heath, Heath's mom, his uncles, cousins, and even me."

Brody sighed heavily. "I've been telling Ari that we

need to move closer to town," he said softly. "I mean, it's not like we can't afford it now that I'm a senior resident at the hospital."

"Then why don't you?"

Brody shook his head, clearly frustrated by the situation. "It's Ari's dad," he said quietly. "He's got this pull over her that no one can break. We have a great marriage except when it comes to her dad."

"Oh?" I said, remembering how cold Ari had been to her father, Vernon, at Molly's house. "I didn't think that Ari and Vern got along."

"They do and they don't," he said, a note of bitterness in his tone. "I mean, Ari does whatever Vern tells her to do, but she's motivated more out of fear than love. Which is why I want her to move with me into town, so we can get out from under his thumb and she can figure out how she really feels about her dad."

"Why won't Vern let her move?"

"It isn't that he won't let her go," Brody said. "It's more like every time she brings it up, he brings up Serena, and how she betrayed the tribe by leaving her husband and the Pueblo. Ari knows that if she goes, her dad's gonna turn the tribe against her just like he did with his own sister."

"We found the Whitefeather urn," I said, the words leaving my mouth before I could really catch them. I knew that Heath wouldn't approve of my saying anything to Brody, but he seemed like a genuinely good guy, and maybe he could give us some advice about how to handle the discovery.

Brody turned surprised eyes on me. "*The* urn?" he said. "The one that disappeared over twenty years ago?"

"Yes."

"Where?"

"In a cave up in the foothills. That's where Heath and I were coming from when we lost the tire."

"You knew where the urn was this whole time?" Brody asked, his tone sharp.

"No," I said quickly. "We went looking for another urn of sorts."

"Another urn?"

I leaned my head back against the seat and closed my eyes. I was starting to feel the exhaustion I'd been fighting the past few days creep over me again. Still, I managed to explain to Brody all the events that had led to the discovery of the Whitefeather family urn.

"So, who hid the Whitefeather urn in a cave up in the hills?" he asked me when I'd finished.

"That's the big question, isn't it? But not quite as big as what happened to the vessel that housed the spirit of the black hawk."

"It's either been destroyed, or someone's got it hidden," he told me.

"That's exactly what we were thinking," I said, right before I started to have second thoughts about revealing so much to him. "Hey, Brody, would you mind keeping all of this to yourself for the time being? We don't know who from the tribe took the Whitefeather urn and until we figure out how to handle it, we don't want anybody to know we have it."

Brody turned left into the hospital parking area. "Sure, M. J.," he said easily. "I'll be discreet." He then used his key card to get us into a section reserved for hospital staff. "I'll take you in with me and get you patched up before the official start of my shift," he said, finding a slot to slide his truck into. "That way you won't have to wait for me to get a free minute. You'll have to fill out paperwork afterward, but at least this way it'll be quicker."

I thanked him and we headed in.

As it turned out, I did have to wait. Heath didn't come to collect me until nearly nine o'clock, and by then I was so hungry I could've wolfed down a crusty old pizza and been quite happy about it.

When my S.O. finally did come through the double doors, he brought Gilley along, and I was so relieved to finally see them that my irritation ebbed a bit.

"How's your hand?" Heath asked the moment he found me in the waiting room.

I held up my palm, now covered in gauze. "They tell me it's not fatal."

He grinned. "Good to know."

"You spend too much time in hospitals," Gil said, handing me a bag with a club sandwich, fries, and a chocolate cupcake in it.

After peeking inside, I sighed happily. "God love you, Gilley Gillespie."

"Come on," Heath said, wrapping an arm around my shoulders. "You can eat in the car. We've got some news to share."

I ate rather ravenously while Heath drove us back to the hotel. "I see you got your car fixed," I said diving into the sandwich the moment my butt landed in the front seat.

"Rocky's fast," Heath said. "Too bad he doesn't do construction," he added.

That reminded me of his house and I asked, "Have you heard from the insurance company?"

"Not yet, but they said it could take a week before the fire department sends them their final report."

"Let's just hope there's no clause in your insurance policy excluding damage caused by paranormal activity," Gilley said from the backseat.

Heath eyed Gil soberly in the rearview mirror. "No kidding. I'm just glad that no sparks flew when you and M. J. were in that jail cell."

I felt a small jolt go through me (no pun intended). "Oh," I said, "that *would've* been bad!"

Gil fished around in his backpack and held up an orange canister. "I was prepared," he said proudly.

"What's that?" I asked him, squinting in the dark.

"It's a travel fire extinguisher," he explained. "I'm thinking of making it part of our standard ghostbusting equipment from now on."

"Good thinking," I told him, and thought how funny it was that even three months ago I would've made fun of him for buying such a thing.

"Did Pena say anything about your car being in the middle of the road with a flat spare?" I asked Heath.

Heath glanced sideways at me. "Naw. I think he and Cruz got into another fight about the existence of the demon. He was in a really bad mood and didn't talk much."

We arrived at the hotel shortly after I polished off the last of my sandwich, and Gil brought Doc into our room so that my birdie could get a little one-on-one time with us while we discussed what to do next.

Once Gil had handed over Doc to me and I'd placed him on the arm of my chair, he surprised me by thrusting out his left foot and yelling, "Drumstick!" He then set that one down and stuck out his right foot, looking down at it he repeated "Drumstick!" Then he went back and forth from right foot to left in a little birdie cancan, calling out "Drumstick, drumstick!" While I sat there both stunned and horrified, my sweet, sweet birdie finished his chorus by ruffling his wings, singing, "And buffalo wings!"

For the next several minutes Gilley and Heath were lost in a fit of laughter. Doc felt encouraged by this, and began a long litany of fart noises, interspersed with the occasional repetition of the birdie cancan.

Meanwhile I concentrated a stern glare at Gilley, but he didn't notice for several rounds of drumstick. "What?" he asked innocently when he finally saw my furious face.

"Why?" I roared.

Gil gave a half shrug. "You leave me alone with your bird all day, darlin', and you know I'm gonna think up something new to teach him."

I sighed and offered Doc a peanut. He stopped with the farty noises and cancan almost immediately and dug into the shell.

"Can we please focus here?" I grumbled when Gil and Heath continued to rib each other and chuckle. Only to a couple of guys would that disturbing feathered comedy routine be funny.

They both cleared their throats and mumbled apologies. "So!" Gil said, setting his iPad on its kickstand and getting out his keyboard. "Heath tells me you walked right into another imprint today."

"I did," I confirmed. "We found a small vortex in a cave up in the foothills, and that amplified the energy enough to toss me right into one. I was able to see Daryl on the day he found the vessel which held the black hawk spirit, and I also caught a glimpse of what the sacred pot looks like."

"I hear Daryl wasn't alone," Gil added as his fingers began to fly over the keys.

"He had a partner. Some guy named Wyatt."

"Did you get a last name?"

"Nope."

Gil frowned. "That's going to make it a little trickier," he said.

"I can describe him," I told him.

Gil looked up from his tablet screen. "Shoot."

"Tall," I said. "About Heath's height with strawberry blond hair and blue eyes."

"How old?"

"Uh . . ." I had to think about it for a second. "I think around our age, maybe a little older. Early-to-mid thirties."

Gil typed away and I wondered if he was hacking into law enforcement records as we spoke. "There's nothing about a guy named Wyatt in Cruz's e-mails," Gilley said, which let me know exactly where he was getting his info.

"Yeah, but aren't you only looking in the e-mails you sent from Cruz's computer to yours?" I asked. "I mean, there could be mention of him in one of the older e-mails."

Gil gave me the patronizing look that someone who considers himself a mental giant might reserve for someone exiting the short school bus. "I'm *in* Cruz's e-mail, M. J."

I felt a small burst of alarm. "How did you get into his e-mail from here?"

"I reset his password, and put a tracer on his e-mail so that when he reset it again, I'd get a text and voilà! I can root around in here at will."

"Gil!" I snapped. "Don't you think he's gonna *notice* that?"

Gilley remained unfazed. "Oh, relax!" he told me. "He's never going to notice unless we're both in his e-mail at the same . . . uh-oh."

Gilley sat forward and his typing took on some urgency. "What's happening?" Heath asked into the prolonged silence that followed.

"Gilley just tipped his hand," I said, crossing my arms and shaking my head at him.

"It's fine," Gil said, and a few keystrokes later he sat back and wiped his brow. "Phew!"

Gil smiled winningly at us then and found us looking expectantly back at him. "Right," he said, hunching over the keyboard again. "Wyatt something . . ."

"Why don't you start with Daryl and see if that leads us to Wyatt?" I suggested.

"I'm already on it," Gil said, like he didn't need me to remind him.

And then I remembered that the two grave robbers had mentioned something about a professor. "Hey, Gil?"

"Busy," he said, his fingers still flying over his keyboard.

I ignored him and continued with, "While you're looking into Daryl, see if he was enrolled in any of the local colleges or universities."

Gil stopped typing and looked up at me. "Why?"

"In the imprint, they mentioned taking the vessel to someone they called 'the professor.' I'm thinking that maybe they were enrolled in some sort of class with someone who might've been an expert on Native American artifacts."

I didn't think it was possible, but Gilley's fingers actually typed faster. After several minutes he finally said, "Aha!"

"You found Wyatt?" I asked.

"Uh, no."

"Did you find the professor?" Heath offered.

"Er . . . no to that too."

"Then what did you find?" I said impatiently.

"An address for Daryl," Gil said.

I stared at him. "How does *that* help us?"

"Maybe you can ask some of his neighbors if they know this guy Wyatt," Gil suggested.

I leaned back in my seat and Doc fluttered on the arm of the chair, sensing my irritation. "A lot of legwork was something I was hoping to avoid, Gil. I mean, isn't there anything else out there in cyberspace on Daryl or his buddy Wyatt?"

"Not according to public records," Gil replied. "I mean, I've got some charges levied against Daryl for grave robbing and a DUI a few years ago, but nothing traceable to any other involved party."

"Crap," I said, realizing this was going to be harder than I thought. "Okay," I conceded. "Heath and I will go root around Daryl's place tomorrow and see if we can't come up with a little more information."

Gilley stretched lazily in his chair. "While you two are off doing that, I'm gonna call Gopher and see if I can't bum some equipment from him."

"I thought we were buying it with the two grand Pena was giving us?" Heath said.

Gilley did the short-school-bus look again and said, "Why pay for what we can borrow?"

"Take a temperature check with him too, will you, Gil?" I asked. I was worried that our producer was going to start getting impatient with the amount of time we were taking off. "Make sure we still have jobs to come back to once we finish up here."

Gil tapped his lip. "Good thinking. Make sure we're all still employed before we ask to borrow expensive equipment."

After that, we all turned in.

Chapter 12

"What a dump!" I whispered when Heath pulled to a stop in front of a run-down mobile home at the very back of a trailer park in a rather seedy section of Los Alamos.

The trailer was weatherworn and in a bit of a shambles, with paint peeling off battered siding and decaying wood. The windows had paper taped over them and the door looked ready to fall off its hinges.

The yard was littered with beer cans and trash all in various stages of decay. An old milk box held up one side of a set of wooden steps leading to the door, and I wondered who'd be brave enough to step onto those going either in or out.

"I don't want to get out of the car," I admitted.

The door to the trailer suddenly popped open, and an elderly woman with curlers in her hair and a cigarette hanging from her wrinkled lips eyed us with suspicion.

"Looks like we'll have to get out and talk to her," Heath said.

"Yippee," I said woodenly.

We hopped out and approached the trailer, being careful where we walked. The whole place smelled of smoke and mold, and the combo caused my stomach to bunch. Still, Heath and I both pressed forward on our mission to find out more about Daryl West and hopefully his buddy Wyatt. "Hi there!" Heath said, all friendly-like.

"What you want?" the woman snapped.

I held back the urge to correct her English.

"We're here about Daryl," Heath told her, getting right to the point.

The woman's suspicious eyes turned downright hostile. "He ain't here."

Her answer surprised me somewhat, as, by the looks of her, she'd be the type to tell us he was dead and to go away and leave her alone. I wondered suddenly if she'd been told about Daryl's fate. I also wondered if she was related to him. Either way, she didn't seem like someone willing to tolerate a lot of questions. Whatever we asked about Daryl, we'd have to ask carefully. "Actually," I said as nonchalantly as I could, "we're really trying to find Daryl's friend Wyatt."

The old lady continued to scrutinize us, and puff on her cigarette, which was in serious need of having its ashes knocked off, lest they dribble onto her housecoat.... Oops. Too late. "What you want with Wyatt?" the old lady asked, swiping at the ashes now dirtying her clothing.

Heath and I exchanged a look and he nodded to me to take the lead. "We need the expertise of a friend of his," I said.

"Expertise?" she said, mocking my word choice.

I was careful to hold my distaste for her and her mocking tone in check. "Yes, ma'am. Wyatt told us that if we ever found anything that needed to be ... uh ... appraised, then we should go see this guy he knows. A guy he calls the professor."

The old lady cocked her head, pulled the cigarette butt out of her mouth to tap it on the side of the trailer before flicking it with two fingers onto the dirt a few feet from where we were standing. I refused to flinch. "Why don't you just go to Wyatt's?" she asked next.

"We couldn't find it," I said quickly. "I mean, I've only been there once, and I'm having a hell of a time finding it again."

"Why don't you call him?"

I held up my phone and wiggled it. "My old phone got stolen last week, and I never backed up the contact list. I had to start from scratch all over again."

"So how'd you find us?" she asked, and I assumed that the "us" included Daryl.

"Information," I said. "He's listed at this address."

I had no idea if that was true or not, but I hoped that she wouldn't check before she helped us. *If* she helped us, that is.

The old lady rolled her tongue around for a few moments—and I wondered if she was playing with some ill-fitting dentures. Finally, she said, "I ain't seen either Wyatt or Daryl in a week."

I nodded like that didn't surprise me.

"They go off sometimes together when they come into a little money, and then Daryl don't come home for a few days and when he does, he's usually drunk off his ass and not a penny to help me pay the bills."

I nodded again, encouraging her to keep talking.

With a sigh, she finally gave us what we came to find out. "Wyatt lives in the apartments behind the Wal-Mart. I don't know what unit, but maybe someone over there'll know. If you see Daryl, you tell him to get his ass home before I throw his stuff into the street. And he better come home with some rent money!"

I pumped my head up and down enthusiastically. "Yes ma'am," I said. "You got it. If we see him, we'll tell him exactly what you said."

I turned to Heath and took his hand, ready to go back to the car, but he resisted. I looked at him then and was surprised to find his eyes unfocused. I knew that expression, well. I'd seen it reflected on his face during several ghost hunts before. "You okay?" I whispered.

"She's in trouble," he said, motioning with his chin to the old lady, who was still eyeing us warily.

I hesitated and gave him my full attention. "Who's talking?" I knew he was communicating with someone on the other side just by his expression and the cast to his eyes.

"I . . . I think it's Daryl," he whispered.

That surprised me. "Has he crossed?"

"No," Heath said, and pointed to a withered and dying tree. "He's over there."

I swiveled my head and detected the faintest disturbance in the ether near the trunk.

"Is he talking?" I asked.

"What are you two whispering about?" snapped the old woman.

"That's his grandmother," Heath said softly, still unwilling to have the woman overhear. "She's his only living relative and he's convinced someone's out to kill her."

"Who?"

"Don't know," he said, closing his eyes so he could concentrate.

I turned my attention back to Daryl's grandmother. I'd so wanted to leave without being the one to tell her Daryl was dead. "You say you haven't seen Daryl for a week?"

"Yeah. Maybe a little longer."

I swallowed hard. "Should we tell her what we know?" I whispered to Heath.

He frowned and opened his eyes. "No. She won't believe us and she might think we had something to do with it. We should send her to Sheriff Pena, though. I don't know what's taking them so long to notify next of kin."

"Has anyone from the Zanto Pueblo been out here to see you?" Heath suddenly asked her.

The elderly woman—clearly not Native American— actually laughed. "Why would anyone from a Pueblo come to see me?"

Heath didn't answer; instead he pressed his point. "Has anyone from the sheriff's department come to see you . . . Trudy?"

Her eyes narrowed again suspiciously. "Why don't you cut the crap and let me know what this is about?"

Heath turned back to his Durango and rooted around inside his glove compartment. Finally, he came up with a pen and a piece of paper and he scribbled down something on it before walking up to her. Handing the paper to her, he said, "That's the number to the sheriff's department on the Zanto Pueblo. Ask to speak to Sheriff Pena. You need to call him, Trudy. Tell him you're Daryl's next of kin. Then, if there's anyone you can stay with for a couple of days, you'll need to do that too, okay?"

Trudy looked at the paper in her hands and then back at Heath as if he were talking crazy. "Are you high?" she asked him, quite seriously.

Heath didn't answer her. Instead he turned and walked purposefully back to me. "Let's go," he said, taking my hand.

Before he got into the car, I noticed that he gave the tree one more long look while Daryl's grandmother remained on the top step of her crappy trailer, still moodily eyeing us.

When we'd cleared the exit of the trailer park, I said, "Feel like talking?"

"She wasn't going to listen," he said—a bit defensively, I thought.

"You're probably right."

"And Daryl wasn't giving me much to go on," Heath added, as if I hadn't already agreed with him. "I mean, you could see how suspicious she was. I start talking about her grandson who's speaking to me from beyond the grave and she doesn't even know he's dead yet? She would've laughed us off the property."

"Hey," I said, laying a hand on his arm. "You're preaching to the choir here, darlin'. I would've done the same thing."

Heath sighed and leaned back from the hunched-over position he'd assumed when he started driving. "Daryl's in a really bad state," he said. "He thinks he got away from whatever attacked him, but he was insisting that it was right behind him. I'm thinking that the death-blow came from behind while he was trying to run."

"The black hawk demon spirit," I said knowingly.

"Had to be," Heath said. "Daryl wouldn't tell me much about what happened. He was too busy trying to convince me to help get his grandma out of the house. He kept saying that they knew where he lived."

"They?"

"Yeah, weird, huh?"

"Did he say anything about Wyatt?"

"I asked and that's when Daryl disappeared. It was like he'd just remembered he was with Wyatt when he was attacked. He said something about needing to warn him too, and poof! He was gone."

"So, Wyatt's still alive?"

Heath shrugged. "If he is, then we have to assume either he or this professor guy has been taken over by the demon. It just depends on who opened the urn."

I thought about where we were heading. "Do you think Wyatt's at his place?"

"Only one way to find out," Heath said, then pointed to his backpack, which was tucked next to my messenger bag by my left foot. "We'd better be ready for anything. Make sure you've got a few spikes handy, okay?"

I considered the attack that Gilley and I had sustained while we'd been locked in the jail cell. The magnetic spikes had finally proved to be too much for the demon, but it'd taken a whole lot of stabs on Gil's part to get it to back off.

"I think we should've brought a few more," I told him.

We cruised into the parking lot of a low-budget apartment complex, which had three floors and a catwalk that spanned the perimeter of each level. It looked like an old hotel that'd been converted to cheap apartments and likely had paper-thin walls and residents who paid their rent in cash . . . *when* they paid.

"Homey," I said after Heath cut the engine.

"Can't be any worse than Trudy's trailer," he reasoned.

"True dat," I told him, and dug into my messenger bag to get out as many spikes as I could carry. Still, it wasn't a lot, only five apiece for me and Heath.

He looked at the spikes with disappointment. "Man, I feel so unprepared for this, you know, Em?"

I stuffed all my spikes into the inside pockets of my jacket. "I do."

We got out and surveyed the front of the apartments. It wasn't a very big complex, only eighteen units in total by my count. "How do we find Wyatt?" I asked when we began walking toward the front.

"We can check the mailboxes," Heath proposed. I thought that a very good idea.

When we approached the mailboxes, a woman with a bag of groceries hanging on her arm was just sticking her key into the keyhole. "Hi," Heath said to her, offering a smile too.

The woman turned her attention to him, and her whole face lit up. I wondered if I beamed like that when he looked at me. Probably.

"Hi," she said shyly, a blush coloring her cheeks.

"Can I ask you for some help?" he said.

"Sure!" she replied, a bit rushed. She must have realized it too, because her blush deepened. "You lost or something?"

"A little," he said. "We're looking for a buddy of mine who lives here, but I can't remember which apartment he's in. Do you know a guy named Wyatt?"

"Wyatt Benoit?"

"Yeah!" he said. "You know him?"

Her smile widened. "He lives in three F. It's up those stairs and to the left. But I don't think he's home," she added. "I live two doors down from him, and I haven't seen him the last couple of days."

"Oh, yeah?" he asked. "But you saw him this week, right?"

She considered that. "I think I saw him Sunday night," she said.

Heath eyed me discreetly to see if I'd caught that. We knew that Daryl's remains had been discovered ten days previous, which was likely the last time his grandmother had seen him alive. I nodded to Heath and let him continue. "Okay, I'll try him anyway and leave him a note," he told the girl. "But if he's not home, would you happen to know another friend of his—"

"Daryl?" she interrupted.

Heath tripped over that a little. "Uh . . . actually, I was referring to his buddy the professor."

"The professor?" she laughed, like Heath had just said something really funny. "No. I don't think Wyatt knows anybody called that."

Heath shrugged and thanked her for the help, letting her get back to her mail. I noticed as we walked away that she didn't hurry to open her mailbox—she was too busy watching his ass as we climbed the stairs.

"Having a hot boyfriend has its perks," I chuckled.

Heath flashed me that brilliant smile and I found my own heart racing. It felt like I hadn't seen him do that in forever, but really, it'd only been since his uncle died. "There's the face I miss," I told him, leaning in for a kiss.

For an instant, he seemed surprised, but he went with

it and pulled me closer. His lips were soft and hungry and for a minute, I forgot completely where we were and what we were supposed to be doing until someone nearby called, "Get a room!"

I backed away from him, but he caught the side of my face and leaned in again to whisper, "Remind me later to get us back to that room, okay?"

"Will do," I told him.

We continued our way up the stairs and paused at the landing. The catwalk had some dingy carpet on it that had definitely seen brighter days . . . with far less wear, tear, and duct tape. Probably it had smelled better too. "Sweet Jesus," I whispered, covering my nose. "It smells like a urinal up here."

Heath covered his nose too. "That's one way to attract tenants," he said. "Come on, let's see if Wyatt's home."

We approached apartment 3F cautiously. I let Heath knock while I got out a few spikes, gripping them tightly, and ready to plunge them into whatever horror show might appear.

The seconds passed with nary a sound coming from inside the apartment, and after several more seconds, Heath knocked again, but this time he called Wyatt's name.

I could feel my pulse pounding in my ears, and sweat broke out at the small of my back, but nothing happened. Heath leaned in and put his ear to the door, listening intently. After a few moments he pulled his ear away and said, "It's quiet inside. No TV or radio on that I can hear."

"He's not home," I concluded, tucking the spikes back into my leather jacket.

"Nope."

"So now what?"

"Well," he said, "we've got a last name at least. We can give that to Gilley and see if he can come up with something on Wyatt Benoit."

"Maybe he can find Wyatt's place of employment and we can go there to see if he's around?" I suggested.

Heath wrapped an arm around my shoulders. "Great idea," he said.

As we were walking down the steps, we encountered the same helpful neighbor. "He wasn't home, huh?" she asked.

Heath shook his head. "No. We thought maybe we could run by his work, though."

Again the woman laughed like he'd said something funny. "Wyatt's not working much, these days. Not after he dropped that statue."

Heath cocked his head. "He dropped a statue?"

The lady nodded. "Yeah. I guess it was crazy expensive too. Like, twenty thousand bucks or something. Can you believe anybody would pay twenty thousand for a statue?"

"How big was the statue?" Heath asked, fishing for details.

The woman said, "Wyatt said it was only like eighteen inches tall!"

"How could an eighteen-inch-tall statue be worth twenty thousand bucks?" I asked.

She shrugged. "I guess it was some old Native American antique or something. Wyatt said it came from one of the Anasazi caves and this guy bought it for twenty grand. Wyatt was the guy who was supposed to deliver it, but he admitted to me that he got high before he went and tripped on the way up the stairs. He said he couldn't even glue it back together 'cause it got smashed, even though it was packed in Bubble Wrap."

"Wyatt just can't catch a break, can he?" Heath said with a laugh.

The girl laughed too. "I know, right? Anyway, his boss was crazy mad, and stopped scheduling him except for when he's really hard up for some help."

"I remember Wyatt said his boss was a real prick," Heath said, to keep her talking. "What was his name again?"

The woman shrugged, shifting the bag of groceries from one arm to the other. "Brad, I think," she said. "He came here once looking for Wyatt 'cause he'd overslept, and the guy tore him a new one right on these stairs! I'd never work for a guy like that!"

"Brad," Heath said, as if he were just remembering it. "Yeah, that was it. . . . What was his last name again?"

That seemed to be just one question too many, because the woman's whole demeanor suddenly changed and she cocked her head at Heath and said, "You know, I've never seen you around here before. How do you know Wyatt?"

"He used to work for my brother before he went to work for Brad," I said quickly, trying to take the heat off Heath a little. "That's why we're here, actually. My brother's looking for some hired hands and wants to try and get Wyatt to come back."

I didn't think the woman believed me, but she didn't question us further. Instead she hugged her bag of groceries and said that she had to go.

When we got back to the car, I called Gilley and told him what we'd learned about Wyatt. "His last name is

Benoit, and he used to work for a guy named Brad
something, but we have no idea who Brad is or where he
works."

"Why is it important that we find out?" Gil asked me.

"Because Brad has something to do with ancient Native American art," I said, seeing Heath nod beside me.
I had a feeling that Wyatt had learned about the value of
ancient American Indian artifacts from his job working
for Brad, and I further wondered if maybe Brad had
some sort of connection to this "professor" person, or
maybe *he* was the professor.

Gilley, however, seemed less than enthused, at least
by the sound of his big old sigh. "Fine," he said. "I'll see
what I can come up with."

"Quickly," I told him, knowing that Gilley could pro-
crastinate with the best of them.

"Yes, yes," he grumbled, clearly annoyed.

Once I'd hung up with Gil, Heath and I decided to
check in on his mother, who was still staying with Ari.
But when we got to the Pueblo, we found Mrs. Lujan
looking very sad. As we sat and talked with her, it was
apparent that the loss of her brother and sister-in-law,
and all the added stress from the presence of the demon,
were taking their toll on her.

"What can I do, Ma?" Heath asked her, wrapping an
arm around her.

"She wants to go to the workshop," Ari said from the
doorway of the kitchen.

Heath pulled his head back to look at his mother in
surprise. "You do?"

She gave a meek nod. "I think it'll be good if my
hands have something to do. And maybe it'll help mend
old wounds. Maybe if I replace the urn that went miss-

ing, Rex and Vernon will finally get over the fact that it's gone?"

Heath wrapped his arms around his mother and said, "I think that's a great idea, Mom."

His response disappointed me—I mean, when was there going to be a better opportunity to tell his mom what we found buried up in the caves? Still, it wasn't my place to say anything, so I held my tongue, but grudgingly.

We drove Heath's mother over to the Pueblo art center, which was a small building with one window. She had to get permission from one of her brothers to enter it and set to work, of course, and Rex surprised me with his enthusiasm to allow her to create something to replace the urn. I figured he might think it would finally settle the feud if a replacement urn was made.

I also discovered that since the disappearance of the old urn, small portions of Whitefeathers' ashes had been meticulously collected and were being stored in a coffee can. Yes. You read that right. A coffee can. Rex even showed it to us, so no wonder he was happy to let his sister create a more appropriate container.

Heath and I hung out with Mrs. Lujan while she set to work. Heath didn't want to leave her alone, and neither did I. We hadn't told anyone what we encountered out in the foothills—well, except Brody, but it didn't look like he'd blabbed either.

I knew that our tale of being chased out of there by the demon would've fallen on deaf ears anyway—and could've even gotten us kicked off the Pueblo for good. Still, it irked me that everyone seemed content to walk around like there was no danger. It was a situation ripe for disaster, and the reason why Heath and I discreetly kept Mrs. Lujan company all afternoon.

Heath wanted her to come back to the hotel with us, but Mrs. Lujan said she was too tired to make the trip and just wanted to crash out at Ari's place. Heath didn't seem happy about it, but he didn't argue. Instead, we left all our spikes with Ari and made sure to let her know to call us at the first sign of trouble.

Heath seemed reluctant to leave the Pueblo, and I didn't blame him, but Ari's house was nestled in a row of six other homes, and a tall stone fence bordered the house, so it felt more protected than most. Rex's house at the end of the row appeared the most exposed, and Heath and I talked about that on the way out to the road.

"Can I ask you something?" I said while we cruised out of the Pueblo.

"Anything."

"How come you didn't tell your mom about finding the original urn?"

He glanced at me. "Because if she knew we'd found it, she'd want to let everyone know."

"Is that really such a bad thing, Heath?"

He grunted. "You don't know my family, M. J. They'd accuse her of stealing it and getting me to pretend that I found it. It wouldn't clear her name and it'd only add to the suspicion around us."

"Okay, so what if you made her promise not to tell? I mean, did you see how upset she was when she mentioned the lost urn? I think it still really bothers her to know that it's unaccounted for."

"I know," Heath said, and I could hear the guilt in his voice. "But if she knew that we'd found the original urn, then she might not make a new one."

"My point exactly," I said to him. "Why encourage her to create something that's never going to be used?"

"Because throwing pottery makes her happy," Heath told me. "My mom's been sad for so long, Em. I think sometimes it's the reason she's in such bad shape physically. And if I told her about finding the original urn, she might've skipped making anything at all."

My brow rose. I hadn't considered that. "When will she be done with it?" I'd seen the new urn, which had a lovely shape, but was still dark gray with no glaze yet. Mrs. Lujan had left it on a shelf to dry when we left the workroom.

"She should be finished with it the day after tomorrow or the day after that—depending on what kind of design she wants to put on it."

I stared out the windshield at the road. "So, do we just come back tomorrow and babysit your mom again?" I was anxious because a whole day had passed and we were still no closer to finding out how to deal with the demon.

Heath inhaled deeply and let it out slow. "No," he said grudgingly. "Tomorrow we'll need to focus on finding this professor and figuring out how to deal with this demon. We can't wait for it to hit another Whitefeather and for everyone to wake up to the fact that this thing is real."

"At least we've got Sheriff Pena on our side."

Heath was quiet for a moment while he considered that. "Pena's our one saving grace," he said. "But he's not one of the elders like my uncles are. If they find out Pena's paying us to investigate this demon, they could do something drastic, like fire him."

"Why would they fire him for hiring us?"

"Because that discretionary money he's paying us with is really for things like office equipment and the ammo he and Cruz use for gun practice and stuff. It could look really bad for him if it got out that he'd hired two ghostbusters—especially now when so much at the station house needs to be replaced."

"But I still don't understand how anyone who saw that station could think anything other than a demon destroyed it!" I protested. "How can they argue with the evidence that's right in front of them?"

"The rumor is that it was you, me, and Gilley trying to make it look like an evil spirit did it," Heath said. I opened my mouth to protest again (really loud), but Heath cut me off by saying, "And if we didn't do it, then they think you guys might be covering for some vandals who broke into the station when they found the Pueblo abandoned that night."

I gave Heath a look that said, "You have *got* to be kidding," and he simply shook his head. "What can I say? They're only willing to believe what they see with their own eyes."

"Let's hope it doesn't come down to that," I grumbled.

"You said it, sister."

Later that night, Heath was moody and withdrawn. He was too worried about his family to be much in the way for small talk, and try as we might, he and I couldn't really come up with a good plan to find and defeat the demon. I'd tried to talk him into going to dinner with Gilley and me, but he said he just wanted to order a pizza and stay in.

So, we ordered pizza, and after giving Heath his half, I took mine to Gil's room to hang with him and Doc. "Trouble in paradise?" Gilley asked when he saw me bearing pizza and a six-pack on his doorstep.

I sighed. "Yes and no."

Gil waved me inside and made room on the table for the pizza. "Is it more yes than no?"

"Hard to say," I told him, opening the lid to the pizza and getting right to a warm gooey piece. "I mean, I know he's got all this family drama to deal with, not to mention the fact that the poor guy's just lost his favorite aunt and uncle, so if he's a little distant and moody, I can hardly fault him."

Gil picked up his slice and sat down in the chair opposite me. "And yet," he said knowingly, "I feel like you are."

I sighed again. "It's just hard, Gil," I said, picking at the pineapple on my pizza. "I mean, I want to be this totally supportive, understanding girlfriend. . . ."

Gilley laughed. "Oh, sugar," he said, eyeing me knowingly. "That just ain't your gig."

I was a little injured by that. "What does *that* mean?"

Gil leaned in and looked me dead in the eyes. "It means that, in so many ways, you're still the little eleven-year-old girl that lost her mom to cancer, and I'm still the four-year-old boy who lost his dad to homophobia. You can't suffer that kind of loss and not clam up a little around people going through something similar."

I felt my eyes well; inexplicably and irretrievably he had set off the waterworks. "I'm so ready to grow up, Gil," I told him.

Gilley set down his slice of pizza, and took my hand. "What you're ready for, M. J., is to let go of all the pain associated with losing your mama. And that ain't likely in this lifetime. Some wounds just don't heal. But you do learn to cope. It's like someone who loses an arm or a leg. You figure out how to get around and get by, and pretty soon, no one else notices."

I sniffled and squeezed his hand, realizing with a burst of clarity that Gil got me like no one else ever would. "Thanks, honey," I told him.

"Now eat," he said, taking back his hand. "And then we'll talk about Wyatt."

Gil and I finished up our dinner and I huddled behind him while he typed fast and furious on his computer. I tried following along as he whizzed in and out of screens, but it was incredibly dizzying. Although soon enough he opened up a somewhat familiar e-mail and clicked the COMPOSE button.

"Hey!" I said over his shoulder. "Isn't that Pena's e-mail?"

"It is," Gil said a little smugly. "I decided to hack into his account rather than continue to look through Cruz's e-mail because our favorite deputy uses his e-mail a little too much and might notice our snooping around."

"You mean *your* snooping around," I corrected. "I had nothing to do with this illegal activity."

"Shhh!" he replied. "I have to be super quick just in case Pena logs on and sees this."

I read the e-mail while he typed, and was surprised to learn that Gil was writing to the same sheriff in Los Alamos who'd sent Cruz the info on Daryl West.

Gil wrote as if he were Pena, and asked the sheriff if he had any information on Wyatt Benoit, who might have been with Daryl at the time he was attacked by the mountain lion, and could possibly shed some light on what'd happened.

Gilley ended the e-mail by asking the sheriff to reply to a different e-mail address, as the one he'd been using had been compromised and he now needed to change it for security reasons. He then left him the new address at the bottom of the e-mail, hit SEND, then clicked over to the sent file and deleted the copy. Once he'd done that, he clicked out of Pena's account altogether.

Gil then peered at me over his shoulder to get my reaction. "Ballsy," I told him.

He flashed me a big smug smile and got back to work. After another hour, Gil gave up, but not without a few grumbles. "Don't these people own computers?" he asked. He'd been searching for any electronic signature of Wyatt and couldn't find a thing.

I thought back to Wyatt's shabby apartment. "I don't think the guy owned much of anything," I told him.

Gil rubbed his eyes tiredly. "There's no trace of him," he said. "If he was employed by a guy named Brad, then it was under the table, because his last known employer was a McDonald's and that was three years ago."

I scowled. "I had the impression that Brad had something to do with selling Native American art," I said. "Maybe coming at it from that angle will help?"

"You mean like an art dealer?"

I shrugged. "Possibly."

Gilley got back to work, typing and pulling up screens and Internet sites as he went along. "There's nothing here," he said after another hour of fruitless searching. "No Brad, Bradley, or first initial *B* listed in the Santa Fe or Los Alamos area connected to art dealing."

"Crap," I said, eyeing the clock. It read eleven p.m. "Is there any word from your sheriff friend in Los Alamos?"

Gil switched windows. "Nope," he said, then hacked into Pena's e-mail one last time. "And he hasn't replied to Pena directly either."

"Will you stop hacking into that account?!" I snapped, fatigue and frustration catching up with me.

"Chill," Gil said, still snooping into the e-mail. "It's only a problem if the other sheriff doesn't follow directions and replies directly back to Pena."

"Gil," I warned. I had a bad feeling we were going to get caught, and I didn't want our antics getting back to the sheriff when he'd gone out on a limb to hire us in the first place.

"I'll be careful," Gil promised, holding up his hand like he was taking a solemn vow.

"All right," I said, giving up and moving to give Doc a good-night kiss before I turned in. "We'll wait to hear from your sheriff, and in the meantime, Heath and I'll head back to Wyatt's apartment and maybe ask his neighbor if she's seen him since we last talked to her."

With that, I headed back to my own room.

Chapter 13

The next morning, after discovering that Gil hadn't gotten an e-mail reply back from the Los Alamos sheriff yet, Heath and I took off to try Wyatt's apartment again. Like the day before, he wasn't home, so Heath tried the door of the friendly neighbor we'd met at the mailboxes. "Hey there!" he said when she opened the door to him.

I stood just down the way, out of sight but not out of hearing range, because I was pretty sure he'd have better luck on his own. "Remember me?" he asked.

"Oh, hi!" she replied. "I do remember you. Did you find Wyatt?"

"No, and it's so weird that he's not returning my texts or voice mails."

"Yeah, well, that's Wyatt for ya."

"Do you think maybe Brad would know where he is?" Heath pressed.

"Like I said, Wyatt's not doing much for Brad these days."

"Do you have Brad's number, so I can call, just to check? I mean, I don't want to say that I think anything bad has happened to Wyatt, but it's weird for him not to call me back."

There was a hesitation and then the woman said, "I don't know Brad's number. But he knocked on my door once looking for Wyatt and he left me his card. Hang on a sec and I'll see if I still got it."

I leaned out from my hiding place and saw Heath looking in my direction. He managed to give me a discreet thumbs-up before his attention turned back to the door and I ducked back out of sight.

"Here," she said. "I found it."

"Aw, man, you rock!" Heath told her.

"My number's on the back of the card," she said.

Uh-oh. I peeked around the corner and saw the woman leaning seductively against the doorframe.

Heath turned the card over. "Thanks, Holly," he said, leaning in to give her a peck on the cheek. I think she blushed down to her toes. "Later!" he said, and took his leave. She watched him walk away until she spotted me looking at her and her expression changed in an instant.

I smiled.

She snarled.

We understood each other perfectly.

Heath reached me at that moment. "I got it," he said, showing me the card.

"Art Treasure Movers," I said. "What kind of a name is that?"

"They move art," Heath told me, obviously getting the subtext better than I did. "They're probably hooked into the art dealers around Santa Fe, and whenever one of the locals purchases a large work of art, or something fragile, these guys move it from the gallery and install it for the buyer."

"Huh," I said, never even considering that there could be a need for something like that until Heath talked about it. "Now we know how Wyatt came by a twenty-thousand-dollar statue. He was probably delivering it from one of the dealers when he dropped it."

Heath nodded and we went back to his car, hopped in, and drove mostly in silence to the address listed on the top of the card. It led us to a grungy-looking office space next to a car wash. The signage out front matched the logo on the card, and we went in to find a young blonde with pigtails manning the front desk. "Hi," she said cordially. "What can I do for you?"

"We're here about one of your employees," I said to her, deciding to take the lead. "Wyatt Benoit."

The girl appeared taken aback by the mention of Wyatt's name. "Did he damage something?" she asked quickly.

I swiveled slightly on my heel to discreetly make eye contact with Heath, who seemed to read my mind. "Actually, yes," he said. "He did."

Pigtails became gushingly apologetic. "Ohmigod! I am so, so, *so* sorry! Wyatt's usually pretty good, but sometimes he's not, you know?"

Heath and I nodded like we knew perfectly.

Turning to her computer, the woman said, "What was the name on the account?"

"Uh . . . ," said Heath.

"John Dodge," I told her quickly, giving her Teeko's fiancé's name. "Although it could also be under Karen

O'Neil." I turned to Heath and flashed him a smile. "I can never remember, honey, if I put things under my name or yours."

After typing on the keyboard, Pigtails nodded and said, "Here it is. You put it under Dodge." I breathed a huge sigh of relief while she dug into a drawer rummaging around for something. She came up with an entire folder of forms. "Mr. Windsor will need you to fill out and sign these, and he'll probably need you to take some photos, if you don't mind. Then we'll have our appraiser come out and take a look. If the artwork can be salvaged or repaired, he'll be able to tell on the spot. He'll also be able to give us an idea of the current market value of your artwork given the damage, and then, as long as everything checks out, we'll give you a check for the difference between the damaged value and the original appraised value. Or, if you'd rather, we can buy it from you for a negotiated price."

"An appraiser's coming out to look at it?" I asked. This was suddenly becoming a little bigger lie than I'd anticipated.

Pigtails, however, misread my apprehension. "Oh, he's wonderful!" she assured me. "He used to teach art history at Santa Fe University and he knows his stuff, believe me!"

I felt a little buzz of excitement. "He was a professor of art history?" I said, taking the forms and swiveling them around as if I'd like nothing better than to fill them out.

Pigtails nodded. "For, like, twenty years or something."

"I was an art history minor at SFU," Heath said. "I probably had him. What's his name?"

"Dr. Richard Bissell," she said.

"Professor Bissell?" Heath said, as if he knew the man well. "No way! I loved him!"

Pigtails looked relieved, and I had the strange feeling that she'd had to calm down upset clients before—perhaps more than a few times.

Heath turned to me. "We can trust Professor Bissell, Karen."

I worked to look relieved too. "Awesome," I said. "Let's take these forms home and fill them out there so we can take some pictures and come back with everything at one time."

And then Heath and I made a hasty exit.

Once we were safely back in Heath's car, I made the call to Gilley. "We found out where Wyatt and Daryl worked," I told him. "Some place called Art Treasure Movers. They move art from the local galleries to the buyer's home. Anyway, they have an appraiser on the payroll who assesses any damage caused from the move or the mounting."

"I know you're going to land that plane and make your point soon, M. J.," Gilley said smartly, "but if you don't mind, I've already put up my tray and my seat, so could you get there faster?"

I refrained from growling back something mean and got to the point. "The appraiser is a former professor of art history at Santa Fe University. His name is Dr. Richard Bissell. We think he's this professor character Wyatt was talking about."

I could hear Gilley scribbling himself a note. "... Bissell," he said. "Got it. Give me twenty minutes and I'll get back to you."

I hung up with Gil and told Heath that he'd call us in

a bit, but Heath didn't look like he was listening. "Hey," I said. "You okay?"

Heath's expression was serious, and although he was obeying all traffic signals, I couldn't help but feel he wasn't really focused on the road. "Yo!" I said loudly. "Earth to Heath."

"Something's wrong," he told me.

"What?" I sat up and looked around nervously. "Is it the demon?"

Heath shook his head. "I don't know," he admitted, making a left at the next light.

"Where're we going?"

"I have a hunch."

"What kind of hunch?"

"A bad hunch," he said. "One that I hope I'm wrong about."

"Okay," I said, deciding against pressing him for details. Either I'd figure it out when we arrived at our destination, or he'd tell me sooner or later.

Unfortunately, it turned out to be a little of both. The longer Heath drove, the more I recognized the area around me. "We're heading back to Daryl's grandmother Trudy's?"

Heath nodded, and in that moment, I too had a sense of dread. No sooner did we pull into the front entrance of the trailer park than our fears were confirmed. There was a patrol car by the side of the road leading to Trudy's trailer about a half mile down with its lights on and obviously there to intercept traffic. Heath pulled to the side of the road and looked at me. "They'll never let us through."

"What do you think happened?"

Heath eyed the road. "Nothing good."

We sat there for another minute or two, and the county sheriff's officer watched us suspiciously. "I don't think he likes it that we're here watching him," Heath whispered.

And just as he'd said that, the officer approached our car and waved us forward.

"Uh-oh," I said.

Heath pulled up to the patrolman and rolled down his window. "Morning," I said, leaning over so that the man could hear me. "We came to see Trudy. Is she okay?"

The officer eyed first me, then Heath, and I couldn't help but notice his gaze stayed on Heath for a minute. "You two family?"

I shook my head. "No, just friends. We came out to visit her yesterday and thought we'd drop in again today."

Heath discreetly gave me a look that said to stop giving the man so much information, but I couldn't help it—cops make me nervous.

"You Pueblo?" the sheriff asked suddenly, indicating Heath.

"Yes, sir," Heath told him.

"Zanto?"

"Uh . . . yes, sir," Heath confirmed in a way that suggested he was surprised the guy guessed the right tribe.

The officer turned away then and spoke into the mic Velcroed to his shoulder. "You two pull over there by that cone, and wait for Sheriff Dunlap."

"Keep cool," Heath said as he slid to a stop where the deputy had pointed.

"Do you think we're in trouble?"

"Do you think we're not?"

I could tell by Heath's tone that he thought I might've

been the one to put us in this particular predicament, but I wanted to know what'd happened to Trudy, and if we left, we weren't going to find out until the news later that night, if they even reported it.

A large man with a barrel chest and egg-shaped head with one of those marine-type buzz cuts walked toward us wearing mirrored sunglasses. I knew he'd wear them through our conversation, which made me even more nervous. "Mornin'," he said, tipping his hat to us, when he stopped at Heath's window. "I understand you were friends with Trudy West?"

"Yes, but we didn't know her very well," Heath said.

"When did you meet Trudy?" the sheriff asked next.

Heath hesitated and I jumped in, going for the truth, as it was likely the quickest way to get us out of there. "We met Trudy yesterday, Sheriff," I said. "We were looking for an old acquaintance of her grandson's and thought she might be able to help us find him."

The sheriff took out his pen and small notebook and began to scribble into it. "Who were you looking for?"

"A guy named Wyatt Benoit," I said, watching the sheriff closely. The sunglasses hid a lot of his expression, but I swore he stopped writing for a moment as if I'd surprised him.

"What did you want with Wyatt?" he asked, lifting his chin to look into the cab of Heath's car at me.

"That's our business," I told him boldly. I already knew by the way he'd called Wyatt by his first name that he and the sheriff had a history together.

"I see," he said, shifting slightly. He was used to asking a question and getting it answered, and he didn't seem to like that I'd dodged him. "What time did you say you two were here talking to Trudy?"

We told him and answered a few more, somewhat mundane questions when the sheriff surprised us by reaching into his pocket and pulling up a small evidence bag with a crumpled and bloodstained piece of paper in it. "You two recognize the handwriting on this?" he asked.

I pressed my lips together so that I wouldn't answer, and let Heath take the lead. "No," he said, shaking his head. "I don't."

The sheriff pushed the plastic bag into the window toward me. "How about you?"

I stared at the small bit of scrap paper where Heath had scribbled the name of Sheriff Pena and written the Pueblo sheriff's phone number under it, trying not to let my face show that I recognized it. I pretended to study it, though, then shook my head as well. "It's not Trudy's?" I asked innocently.

"No," said the sheriff. "It ain't."

"Is she okay?" I asked next.

The sheriff just looked at me and I pointed to the blood on the note. "No," he repeated. "She ain't. We found this clutched in one hand and her phone in the other."

That was all he would tell us before asking us for our cell numbers and snapping his notebook shut, shoving it back into his pocket. "You two stay close to town for the next few days in case I need to reach you, you hear?"

"We hear," Heath muttered, and pulled back on the gearshift to move his Durango into reverse. As he backed up and turned the car around, I saw another patrol car drive on down the road and get waved over to the side.

Heath moved his vehicle to the far left side of a large

tree and waited until the driver of the other car had gotten out and turned his back to us; then Heath sped on down the road and got us the hell out of there.

"Do you think he saw us?" I asked, twisting around to look back in the direction Sheriff Pena had parked his car.

"I hope not," Heath said, his face grim. "I can't deal with Pena right now. He'll have way more questions than Dunlap, and I'm not sure how to answer him in light of what I think happened to Trudy."

I was silent for a moment. Then the image of that bloody slip of paper Dunlap had tucked into an evidence bag came to my mind. "Trudy must've tried to call for help when the demon showed up," I said. The way the sheriff had told us Trudy wasn't all right and that they'd found the paper and her phone clutched in her hands led me to believe they'd also found her dead.

Heath's shoulders slumped. "Do you think we led it to her, Em?" he asked me.

"The demon?"

"Yeah."

I turned toward the side window, hating to admit that there might be a possibility that we'd done just that. "It's impossible to know," I told him. "It could've just as easily been that the demon finally tracked down Daryl's next of kin."

"But why kill Trudy?" Heath asked. "I mean, what'd she have to do with any of this? The woman wasn't even Pueblo."

I shook my head. I had no idea.

Heath opened his mouth to say something else, but at that moment his cell rang. He answered it and the noise from the receiver was loud enough to reach my ears. Immediately I knew something terrible had happened. *"Whose house?"* Heath practically shouted. And then, most upsetting of all, he said not another word; he simply tossed aside his cell and floored the accelerator.

The Durango surged forward and I held on tight. Heath drove at crazy speeds, weaving in and out of traffic, and I didn't dare ask him to slow down or even distract him with a question like, "What happened?" I figured I'd find out soon enough.

We reached the Pueblo within fifteen minutes and Heath barely slowed down enough to make the turn into the drive without tipping us over. I kept my eyes closed and my hand gripped on to the overhead assist handle for most of the rest of the drive.

Finally we arrived at the center of town, and Heath bypassed the row of Whitefeather houses and aimed his car farther down the street toward the end, where one lone house stood and a crowd had gathered.

He and I both saw the ambulance at the same time. "Who is it?" I gasped. "Who's been hurt, Heath?"

"Rex," he replied through gritted teeth.

He punched hard on the brakes and we skidded to a stop. Heath was out the door faster than I thought possible, and as I hurried to catch up, I saw him weaving through the onlookers like he'd done through the traffic to get here. I knew whom he was searching for, and my eyes darted every which way too, looking for Mrs. Lujan.

I didn't see her, and apparently neither did Heath. Meanwhile, Cruz hovered in Rex's doorway arguing with Vernon, while Ari stood nearby, hugging herself as tears streamed down her cheeks. No one seemed to notice me; all eyes were looking forward to the house and to the ambulance, which was just starting to pull away. In the window I caught a glimpse of Brody's profile while he hovered over his patient. At this point, I didn't know if it was Rex or someone else who might've been in the house with him.

Anxious for details and knowing I wasn't likely to get them hanging around with the tribe, I moved away from the throng and over to the side of the house, slipping easily through the back gate and moving into the back-yard.

There was a high fence surrounding Rex's backyard— no one was likely to see me. I heard a noise from the corner of the scrubby lawn and spotted something moving inside a large doghouse. I eased over slowly and carefully, and found a quivering old hound curled up in the corner. "Oh, man," I said, squatting down so I could be level with it. "You poor thing! You must've been scared to death!"

The hound eyed me with droopy eyes and a patheti-cally frightened face. I looked at its dog bowls—both food and water were empty.

Picking them up, I headed toward the house. I saw the talon marks well before I got to the torn screen on the back door. The demon had entered easily here. And judging by the interior of the place, it'd had one hell of a party.

As I surveyed the interior, I admit that I braced my-self for any sign of blood. With some relief I registered that there didn't appear to be any. I followed the trail of the carnage, and it led me across the living room to the stairs, then up to the landing and down a short hallway to a door, which had been partially opened.

The exterior of the door seemed to be down to splinters and it hung loosely on its hinges. Inside the bedroom, I could see that the door had been barricaded from the inside, as if all the bedroom furniture, including the bed frame, had been shoved up against it.

How the paramedics had gotten past the barrier to reach Rex was a mystery. I was still in the hallway, clutching the dog bowls, when I heard voices down below. I held perfectly still until the voices approached the stairs. Being careful not to make a sound, I squeezed in through the opening to the bedroom, and cast around with my eyes for a place to hide. Meanwhile, the voices grew closer and at the last second I darted into the adjoining bathroom and hid behind the shower curtain in the bathtub.

Barely daring to breathe, I waited while the two voices that I'd identified as Pena's and Cruz's came up the stairs, down the hall, and into the bedroom. Pena gave a long low whistle from just ten feet away. "What the hell was he up against in here, Jimmy?"

"It's got to be the same punks that attacked the station, Nick."

There was a pause. "You really believe that?" Pena asked.

"What?"

"That all this was done by a bunch of punks?"

"What other explanation is there, Sheriff? I mean, I know you got a soft spot for Heath Whitefeather and that girlfriend of his, but come on, no ghost did this!"

"What about what happened at Milton's lodge?"

"Well, if it was the same punks, then that was murder, Nick. Which is what I been telling you. Something don't add up about that hunting lodge, and I ain't talking about ghosts and goblins. I think some*one* killed Milton. Not some*thing*."

Pena sighed audibly. "You don't believe the legend of the black hawk turning into a demon and wanting revenge against the sky spirit?"

Cruz's mocking laughter echoed against the walls of the bathroom. "Oh, come on, Nick! Do *you* really believe it?"

Another pause, then, "You know, Jimmy, I don't know what to believe anymore."

Cruz snorted. "Well, if you'd listened to me, we could've held those two trespassers and gotten the truth out of them sooner or later. They're holding something back, Nick. I swear they are. They know more than they're saying about all this."

"They couldn't have had anything to do with Milton's death, Jimmy," Pena argued. "I checked. They were all out of the country when he died."

"Well, we'll ask old Rex about all this when he wakes up. If he makes it, that is."

I grimaced. I didn't much care for the deputy.

"What'd Brody say?" Pena asked.

"He said that Rex must've had a heart attack brought on by either pushing the furniture around or from fright—maybe both. He looked pretty bad when we found him. Brody thinks he'll make it to the hospital, and he'll probably need surgery, so it still could go either way."

"Who called you?"

"Brody. Said his wife couldn't reach her uncle on the phone after Rex was late for breakfast, so she sent the doc over to make sure he was okay. When he walked in the front door, he saw the place was a wreck and came and got me. I called you as soon as we got to Rex. Where were you anyway?"

"Had a dentist appointment in town," Pena said. My brows shot up at the bald-faced lie. I'd just seen him at Trudy's trailer park.

"That tooth still giving you trouble?"

"It is," Pena said, and there were some shuffling noises as the two moved their conversation out of the bedroom. Their voices quickly became muffled and I couldn't make out a thing they said next, but I sat there for a while, really troubled about why Pena had lied to Cruz. I was sure that Dunlap had filled Pena in on what'd taken place at Trudy's trailer—why not tell Cruz and offer it as further proof about what they were really up against?

Still, I reasoned, maybe Pena had had enough of his deputy's derision. I know I certainly had. I waited a bit longer, huddled in the bathtub, until I was certain Cruz and Pena were back outside, and then I slowly and carefully got up and headed back out into the hallway, careful not to touch a single thing.

Making my way quickly downstairs, I ducked into the kitchen, filled the dog bowls up with food I found under the cabinet and water from the sink, then hurried back outside and left them for the poor hound still huddled in its doghouse.

I wanted to stay and try to comfort the old coot, but decided that as a stranger I might be making the dog even more anxious, so I left it alone and moved out of the yard.

Slipping back out the gate, I managed to spot Ari, Heath, and thankfully Heath's mother all hovering together away from the others. Ari was still crying and

Mrs. Lujan looked terribly worried. I moved over to slide into the space next to Heath and he looked at me with some surprise. "Where'd you go?"

"I heard a dog barking in back," I said, pointing to the fence. "I thought it might be hurt."

"Hank?" Ari said, her head snapping in the direction of the gate. "Oh, God! I forgot all about Rex's dog! My uncle loves that hound. Is he hurt?"

"He's fine physically," I told her. "But I do think he's pretty freaked-out. Maybe he could stay with you until your uncle feels better?"

I knew that Ari probably needed something to comfort and be comforted by right about then, and I was very relieved when she nodded and moved away from us to go in search of the hound.

When she'd gone, I leaned in and whispered in Heath's ear, "I have lots to share."

He eyed his mother, who hadn't noticed our exchange— her gaze was still fixed on her brother's house. Then he whispered back to me, "Later."

"I have something for you," Mrs. Lujan said suddenly, turning to us as if she'd just thought of something important. I'm sure I appeared puzzled, because she added quickly, "I was in the workshop when all this was happening. Wait here. I'll be back in a minute."

The moment she left, I pulled Heath even farther away from anyone who might overhear, and quickly told him what I'd heard upstairs in Rex's house. "Pena lied?" he said.

I nodded. "Said he had a dentist appointment."

Heath's brow was furrowed. "None of this makes sense, Em."

"Here!" said a voice right behind me, and I jumped at least a foot at the sound. Whirling around, I saw that Mrs. Lujan was holding a beautiful urn in her hands, colored black on black with an arrow stenciled in gray. The shaft was tipped in white feathers, and the arrow was impaling a large black bird. There was no mistaking the subtext there.

As I took the rather heavy object, Mrs. Lujan explained, "Late last night I had the most vivid dream," she began. "My father came to me and he brought along another man, telling me only that he was an ancestor and that I needed to listen carefully to what he said.

"The ancestor told me that the moment I woke up, I needed to go back to my workshop and paint this urn. He said that I would need to paint it all in black, and that I was to write some very specific words on the urn — please don't ask me what they were, because they were all in Zuni, and I'd be hard-pressed to give you the full translation."

"No worries," I said, trusting that the words didn't need my understanding to work.

"The ancestor then told me that when the urn was finished, I had to give it to you. He named you specifically, M. J. And then my dad stepped forward again, and told me that after delivering this to you, I'd need to get my butt back to Phoenix."

Heath and I exchanged a look of total surprise. "You're leaving?" Heath said.

His mother nodded. "The minute I'm sure Rex is all right, I'm going back to Evelyn's." I had to hand it to the woman — she firmly believed that her brother would be all right.

Ari appeared then with Rex's hound, and I was relieved to see the bits of dog food around his wet muzzle, which meant that Ari had coaxed him into eating a little. At that moment Ari's phone rang. "It's Brody," she said when she looked at the display. I held Hank's leash while Ari answered the phone and after a few minutes I could read the relief on her face. "Thank God," she said into the receiver. "Okay, sweetie, keep me posted."

"How's Rex?" Mrs. Lujan asked even before Ari had hung up.

"He's stable. They're going to get him into surgery in the next hour or so, but the heart attack doesn't seem to be as bad as they first thought. They think they can get by with just a stent and avoid a bypass this time."

Mrs. Lujan closed her eyes and whispered something to herself. Then she looped her arm through Ari's and said, "Come on. I have to pack my things and then we'll head to the hospital and wait out the surgery. You can take me to the airport as soon as Rex is in the clear."

"I can take you to the airport, Ma," Heath said, turning to go with the women.

Mrs. Lujan stopped in her tacks and eyed her son. "No," she told him. "You and M. J. need to stop this thing. That's what both the ancestor and your grandfather said. It's up to you two. And as long as I'm here, you'll be distracted. That's why I'm going, son. You two need to stay here, find that demon, and kill it once and for all."

Heath's expression was inscrutable, but his mother's was crystal clear. It said, "Do as I say . . . or else!"

I took Heath by the hand. "We'll do our best, Mrs. Lujan. You go back to Phoenix. Stay safe and we'll tell you when the job is done."

She flashed me a grateful smile, and hurried off with her niece. Heath stood there looking after her for a good long while, but he finally turned to me, took the urn from my arms, and said, "Let's go kick some demon butt."

Chapter 14

"I found your professor," Gilley said the moment Heath and I walked into his room.

"Bissell?" I asked, wearily taking the chair at the desk and holding out my fingers so that Doc could climb onto my hand.

"Yep."

"Drumstick!" Doc crowed, sticking out his right foot.

I glared at Gil. "I'm gonna kill you for teaching him that."

"Hooters has buffalo wings!" Doc added, fluttering his wings for effect.

I sucked in a breath and had I not been holding my bird, I would have flown at Gilley and thumped him on the head. *"Gilley!"*

Heath snickered, ducked his chin, and laughed into his hand. He quickly stopped and cleared his throat when I turned my evil eye on him. "Sorry," he said, working hard to suppress a grin. "You're right, it's not funny."

"Babalooooooooooo! Order up!" Doc sang, again sticking out his right foot. "Drumstick! Side of wings! To go!"

I closed my eyes for a moment, opened them back up, and placed Doc back onto his perch. Then I got up, took three steps around the table, and swatted the top of Gil's head. "Ow!" he cried. "Hey! No hitting!"

"Stop teaching my bird to say such inappropriate things!" I shrieked. I was on my last nerve with Gilley at the moment.

"I couldn't help it!" he protested, rubbing his head. "I was bored and a Hooters commercial came on."

"Hooters!" Doc mimicked, dancing around in a circle on his perch. "Hoot-hoot-hooooters!"

I moved menacingly toward Gilley again, but Heath interceded. "Okay, then!" he said, putting his arm across my shoulders and gently pulling me back. "How about if everybody takes a second to calm down?"

I let Heath maneuver me back toward my seat, but I narrowed my eyes at Gil and made a slashing motion across my neck.

Gil stuck his tongue out at me, but I knew he'd at least think before he taught Doc anything else. Of course, then he'd think again and teach Doc something awful anyway, but at least he'd likely give it a rest for a while.

Once I was safely back in my seat, Heath turned to Gil and said, "You found the professor?"

Gil nodded enthusiastically. I figured he was trying to keep Heath, at least, on his good side.

"Do you have an address?" Heath asked next.

Gilley handed him a slip of paper, eyed me, and wisely said, "I'll wait here while you guys go check it out."

Heath and I loaded back into his Durango and I navigated while he drove back toward town. When we entered a neighborhood near Santa Fe University, I pointed to a small gray adobe house with tinted windows. "That's it," I said.

Heath pulled into the driveway and we got out, noticing only as we crested the top step of the porch that it was littered with newspapers. "Uh-oh," I whispered.

Heath rang the doorbell and knocked on the door. No one answered. I moved over to peer in through a window, bracing myself for what I might see, but the interior seemed to be in order.

"Let's go around back," I told him.

We moved to the back door and Heath tried the knob. No surprise it was locked tight. I cupped my hands and looked in through the kitchen window to view a fairly orderly kitchen, except for the table, which was cluttered with papers and files.

"Hey," Heath whispered.

I turned and was surprised to find him holding open the door. "There was a key in here," he said, holding up one of those fake rocks with a hidden compartment that hides a key.

"Dude! We can't go in there!"

"You're right," he said. "I'll go in. You stay here."

My jaw dropped. "Don't!" I told him. "Heath! That's breaking and entering!"

He looked at me steadily. "Em, if we don't start getting some answers here, more of my family members are going to end up dead or in the hospital. I'm taking the risk, okay?"

With that, he disappeared inside the house. I wavered maybe ten seconds before I swore under my breath and followed after him.

I found him sitting at the table sifting through a small pile of papers. Looking up, he said, "Nice of you to join me, Bonnie."

"Yeah, well, I figure if you get caught, I'm still gonna go down as an accessory, Clyde."

Heath winked at me and focused again on the pile of papers.

"What'cha got there?" I asked, stepping close.

"Not sure," he muttered, handing me a few of them to look over.

I eyed the papers curiously. They seemed to be appraisals for various pieces of art that had incurred some damage, because printed on the page was a photo of an object and a detail of the damage, then a figure below that labeled *Purchase Price*.

The odd thing was that written in red pen below *that* was another figure, substantially higher than the purchase price.

"What do you think it means?" I asked, showing Heath one of the slips and pointing to the higher figure in red.

"All of these are Native American pieces," Heath said, barely glancing up from the stack he was sorting through. "And they all have minimal damage, according to Bissell."

I looked again at the paper in front of me, which did indeed detail that an Anasazi figurine had sustained only a nick on the bottom. It even had a "repair" esti-

mate figure quoted beside the photo, which was only
twenty dollars. But the new value that had been assigned
the figurine was substantially less than the number in
red. And a note on the page suggested that the figurine
had been purchased for well below the value at the bottom of the page.

I looked up from the paper and started to put the
pieces together. "Heath," I said.

"Yeah?" he replied, his voice distracted as he continued to sort through the sheets he was holding.

"What if this Professor Bissell was running some sort
of racket with Wyatt and Daryl?"

Heath lowered the papers, giving me his full attention. "You mean like getting them to slightly damage
some of the artwork they moved in order for the owners
to submit a claim to Art Treasure's so that after they collected the insurance money, Bissell could offer them a
chance to sell the damaged goods at a reduced market
rate, repair it, and resell it as undamaged on the black
market?"

I grinned. "Yeah. Pretty much exactly that. But what
if Bissell also encouraged Wyatt and Daryl to go hunting
for buried treasure too?"

"Then he'd have quite a racket going, wouldn't he?"
Heath said, glaring at the surroundings before handing
me another one of the papers.

I gasped when I saw it. "The black hawk vessel!" I
said, seeing the photo match perfectly the image of it I'd
seen in the imprint I'd been sucked into back at the cave.
"So it wasn't destroyed when the demon escaped!"

"I don't know how he got his hands on it," Heath said
angrily. "But from the picture you can tell that the top of
the pot has been broken off."

I squinted at the photo. Sure enough, the lid of the clay pot appeared to have been broken off. Bissell's notes indicated the pot sustained only minimal damage, and he estimated its price tag in the thirty- to fifty-thousand-dollar range. "Whoa!" I exclaimed. "Is he kidding with this figure?"

"He's not," Heath said. "Relics like that go for a lot of money. It's why we keep the location of our burial grounds a closely guarded secret and send out regular patrols along our back roads, but as you can tell, we're not always successful stopping the grave robbers."

Something clicked in my head when Heath said that, but with so many synapses firing at once, I found it hard to focus on the thought, especially when I watched Heath get up and move into the other rooms. I'd sort of hoped we'd be going soon. I badly wanted to get out of there, afraid that Heath's SUV in the driveway would call attention to us if we lingered and Bissell's neighbors knew he wasn't home.

"I think we should go," I said loudly when Heath disappeared down a hallway.

"In one sec," I heard him say from the interior. "If the vessel's here, I want to find it."

I followed after him, preparing to talk him into leaving quickly, but came up short when I found him in what was obviously Bissell's bedroom. "Whoa," I said.

Heath stood just inside the doorway, allowing me a good view of the interior. Dresser drawers were pulled open and some of the clothing was spilling over the sides. The closet door was also open and several empty hangers hung on the rod and also cluttered the floor. On the bed was a small suitcase, which was open and empty.

"Somebody left in a hurry," I said.

Heath walked over to an answering machine with a blinking red light on the nightstand. I would've made fun of it if the situation weren't so tense; I mean, who still has an answering machine?

Heath hit the PLAY button and we both listened to the first message. "Bissell?" said an anxious male voice. "Dude! Where the hell are you? I'm at the storage unit, man. You gotta get here soon, okay? I'm freaking out! I think he knows we have the pot, Professor! I think he was at my apartment!"

The time stamp indicated that the message had been left the same day Heath, Gilley, and I had flown into Santa Fe.

Another message began, and again that same anxious male voice came through the recorder. "You son of a bitch!" he began. "I been waiting for you for three hours! I know you fuckin' left me out here to hang, so you know what I'm gonna do? I'm gonna call that cop and tell him what I know and then I'm gonna point the finger at you! I'll have him meet me right here at this storage unit, and I ain't leaving till he gets a load a what you been up to!" With that, the line went dead.

There were a few more messages after that: one from Brad, the owner of the moving company, asking Bissell to return his call, and one from a girl who identified herself as Jenny, asking him to call her back because they hadn't heard from him on a few of their appraisals and the clients were getting anxious.

"That sounds like Pigtails," I said, pointing to the machine.

Heath grunted and hit the END button. With a sigh he said, "I don't think the vessel's here."

"That's my guess too," I said. "I bet he either took it

or hid it in the storage unit Wyatt was talking about."
There was no doubt in my mind the caller was Wyatt.
His partner Daryl would have already been dead, and
really, who else could it have been?

"So, where *is* Wyatt?" Heath wondered.

I shook my head. I had no idea what'd become of
him. I almost asked Heath to play the message again,
because there was something on the message that was
wiggling around in my mind, but Heath was already focused on something else and he had his cell out, motioning for me to follow him out of the room.

A second later, I overheard him say, "Hey Gil, I need
for you to find a storage unit registered to Professor Bissell." There was a pause, then, "Yeah, I know that's gonna
be hard . . . but next to impossible? If there's anyone that
can do it, buddy, you can. . . ."

I grinned. Heath knew exactly how to get Gilley to
work on something: Ply him with flattery. "What's that?"
he asked, reaching the back door and holding it open for
me. "You already got it?"

I took the key from his hand and relocked the door
while Heath tapped the address into his phone. "Thanks,
bud," Heath said. "I owe you one."

We arrived at the U-Haul storage facility just five
minutes later. Bissell had chosen something close to
home at least.

Heath led the way to the unit Gil had pegged as Bissell's, and we were a little surprised to find it unlocked.
Heath pulled at the latch on the bottom of the door, and
it rose easily, revealing an empty room, save for a few
remnants of packing paper.

It was my turn to call Gilley. "Did you find it?" he
asked the moment he answered my call.

"Yes. But it's empty."

"Figures," Gil said. "What do you think was in it?"

"A whole lot of valuables," I said. "But that's not why I'm calling. Can you maybe get a trace on Professor Bissell? We're pretty sure he's left town, and when we go to the police, we'd like to point them in the right direction."

I heard Gilley's fingers flying across the keyboard again. "I've already run his credit report," Gil said. "He has a credit card with Santa Fe University Credit Union."

I stared at the floor. "And you're telling me this because . . . ?"

"Credit union systems are easier to hack into than the big banks," Gil told me. "I can run a trace on his credit card and see where he's gone."

I stifled a chuckle. "It is a really good thing you aren't a criminal, Gil."

"For everybody," he agreed. "Here it is. Bissell purchased a ticket through American Airlines ten days ago. That was the last purchase he made with that credit card."

"Does it say where he went?"

"Hang on," Gilley said impatiently. "I have to hack a different system for that."

I waited and in a moment Gil said, "He left two days after he purchased the ticket, headed for Buenos Aires."

My brow furrowed. "What day was that?"

"The seventeenth," Gil said.

I thought back to Bissell's answering machine. The time stamp on Wyatt's message had been the eighteenth. Something wasn't adding up. "Gil, can you hang on a minute?"

"Sure."

I put the phone to my chest and said to Heath, "Gil says Bissell left the country on the seventeenth."

"Son of a bitch," Heath swore. "He probably took the art with him. Did Gil find out where?"

Heath was missing the point. "Argentina. But that's not what's bugging me. There's something off here."

"What do you mean?"

I walked over to the storage unit and closed the door. I stared at the latch, which was missing any form of a lock. "If Bissell left in a hurry, do you really think he'd risk trying to smuggle the black market artifacts out of the country too?"

Heath shrugged. "Maybe. I mean, I know I'd probably give it a shot if the pieces were valuable enough."

"Okay," I said, pointing to the bare latch. "So, you mean to tell me that Wyatt comes here and waits for three hours for Bissell to show up, which we already know he doesn't, because he's left the country the day before, and in the three hours Wyatt's waiting for him, he doesn't notice the lock is gone from the storage unit and that all he has to do is pull the door up and take a look inside to figure out that Bissell has ditched him?"

Heath squinted at the latch. "What if it was still locked when Wyatt was here?" he suggested. "Maybe Wyatt managed to break into it and steal the contents himself?"

I pointed to the somewhat crowded facility. There were lots of students around and security cameras everywhere. We'd been able to enter the building because we'd come between the hours of eight and five, but after that, the sign out front said you'd need a key card to enter. "So he somehow manages to break into this unit without anyone noticing? I don't think so."

"What's your point, M. J.?" Heath finally asked.

"If Wyatt didn't take the art, then who did? I mean, we know that Daryl's dead, and Wyatt somehow survived the demon escaping from the vessel, but someone's got to be controlling the demon right now, and it sure doesn't seem like it's the professor—we know he's flown the coop—and from that voice message, it sure as hell doesn't sound like the demon has control over Wyatt."

"Who does that leave, then?" Heath asked.

I closed my eyes and thought back to something that I'd heard on Bissell's answering machine. "He said that someone knew he had the vessel," I said softly.

"What?"

I opened my eyes. "Wyatt. On the voice message, he said that someone knew he had the vessel and was after him."

"The person controlling the demon," Heath supplied.

I nodded. "And then you said something, Heath. . . ." I closed my eyes again, because I knew that the biggest clue was lying right there in the puddle of facts we'd just sifted through. But the more I tried to find it, the more the clutter seemed to get in the way. My mind flipped back to that slip of paper found in Trudy's hand, and then shot forward again to an image of Heath sitting at Bissell's table, sifting through the photos and appraisals. And then, in an instant, I had it! My eyes flew open and I stared at Heath in shock. "Holy *shit*!" I exclaimed, putting the phone back to my ear so that Gilley could hear too. "Guys! I said excitedly. "I think I know who controls the demon and who murdered Milton and Beverly!"

Chapter 15

Heath gently eased his shovel underneath something long and thick buried in the same cave where we'd discovered the Whitefeather urn. Gilley shifted nervously next to me, his eyes continually darting to the front of the cave entrance. I knew he didn't want to be here, and I'd even offered to have him stay behind, but in an odd moment of bravery he'd opted to come. I could tell by his expression that he was seriously regretting that decision.

Heath tilted the handle of the shovel and something truly foul smelling crept up through the soil. "Bach!" I exclaimed, covering my nose with my arm.

Gilley hurried to the mouth of the cave, his hand covering his own mouth while he pinched his nose. For a minute, I really thought he was going to lose his lunch.

Heath had backed away too, and he pulled out a bandanna from his back pocket, wrapping it around his face before he began to pile the small amount of dirt he'd excavated back over the dead body he'd just disturbed.

I tried not to breathe more than I had to until he was done, and then the pair of us wordlessly moved to the mouth of the cave and motioned Gil down the slope.

"That was the worst thing I've ever smelled!" Gilley exclaimed, taking long leaps down the side of the hill.

I said nothing, lost in thought because now that I'd confirmed where Wyatt was, the rest of my plan felt far too flimsy. "How'd you know he'd be there?" Heath asked when we were partially down the slope.

"I couldn't figure out why Beverly had been killed," I said. "I mean, I know she married a Whitefeather, but the only reason to attack her specifically was if she saw something. Since no one ever heard from Wyatt again after he left that voice message for Professor Bissell, I figured he was probably killed right after he called Pena. Pena then took his body here to bury it, and Beverly— who was on her way to check out the spot where Milton was going to be buried—must have seen something she shouldn't have."

"I'd like to rip Pena apart," Heath said angrily.

I put a hand on his shoulder. "It's not Pena calling the shots, Heath. It's the demon."

I had already figured out that Trudy had in fact called Pena, and that's what triggered the demon showing up at her trailer. I'd also figured out why Pena had "hired" us. He'd wanted to keep tabs on us and our investigation, especially after he and the demon hadn't managed to kill Gilley or me at the station. He'd known we were there on the reservation—the demon must have sensed us near the library—but he'd kept his cool and waited for Cruz to depart the area; Cruz, after all, wasn't a Whitefeather, and maybe there was a residual part of Pena that still cared about his deputy.

And I knew that the demon would want to take care of the Whitefeathers one at a time, picking them off one by one, but I'd been pretty convinced it would go after the Whitefeathers in order. Milton was obviously the firstborn; then it'd been about to get to Mrs. Lujan when we were at John's lodge, but what flummoxed me was Ray. Why had it bothered with Rex's son before going after Rex—and for that matter, why had it skipped over Vernon to go after Sam's youngest son?

I'd concluded that it'd been nothing more than opportunity. Pena was obviously trailing us, looking for said opportunity, and when he and the demon saw Ray Whitefeather alone and vulnerable in that shell of a house, well, he and it had moved in for the kill. It was sheer luck that Ray had survived.

We arrived at the bottom of the slope and made our way back to Heath's Durango, parked not far away. Gilley edged over to a patch of sagebrush where we'd hidden the rental car in case things went south. I got out Mrs. Lujan's urn from the front seat of the Durango and set it down nearby and then I remembered something and opened the rear door to get out the original Whitefeather urn, carefully carrying it to the rental car and tucking it into the front seat. I didn't want Pena anywhere near that precious urn. "Here he comes," Heath said, and I closed the door of the rental and hurried to his side to face the approaching cloud of dust making its way toward us. And then I saw something else and my heart sank.

"Dammit!" I swore. "Why the hell is he bringing Cruz?"

"We told him to come alone!" Gilley squeaked. I glanced to my side and Gil was wringing the hem of his trusty sweatshirt.

We didn't even have time to come up with an alternate plan—Pena and Cruz were closing in. "We'll have to do the best that we can," I told them. "Just get Pena into Heath's car, and Gil, you hit that switch to lock him in, okay? The magnets should do the trick and we'll deal with the consequences."

The plan I'd come up with was to trick Pena into getting into Heath's SUV, which we'd padded with about three hundred pounds of magnets from stem to stern. It'd taken us all day to tack the magnets in place, but if we could get Pena into the Durango and lock him in, then we might be able to generate a break in the hold the demon had on him.

After that, it was just a matter of holding up Mrs. Lujan's new vessel and begging Sam for some help, because I had no idea how to get the demon genie back in its bottle.

"Maybe we should abort," Heath said, his knuckles white as he gripped the shovel.

But it was too late. In the next few seconds Cruz and Pena had come to a stop in front of us and they each got off their three-wheelers and came to stand in front of us. "What's this about a dead body?" Pena asked, getting right to the point.

None of us spoke for a minute—I think we were all still wondering how this would go—so Pena took off his mirrored sunglasses and squinted at me. "M. J.?" he said. "You okay? You look a little pale."

I found my voice, but it was anything but steady. "I'm fine," I said. "The body's in the back of Heath's SUV."

I looked at Heath to lead the way and for a second I didn't know if he was going to play along, or swing that shovel up and pummel the sheriff. Finally, he pivoted on his foot and moved over to the back of his SUV, where we'd put some pillows under a thick blanket as a prop and positioned it in the very back of the Durango.

While I walked with Heath and Pena over to the rear of the SUV, a quick-thinking Gilley was doing his best to distract Cruz away from his efforts to follow. And one glance over my shoulder suggested he was succeeding.

Cruz didn't like Gilley; that much was obvious. Maybe the guy was a homophobe or maybe he just found Gil annoying, but he backed up several feet as Gil pretended to take a shine to his physique, even asking if he could feel the deputy's biceps, which allowed us the chance to maneuver Pena over to the rear door of the Durango without trouble.

"He's in there," Heath said, opening the door wide so that Pena could look in. Without hesitation, Pena moved into the backseat and propped his elbows on the headrest.

"You covered him," Pena remarked, leaning over the seat to pull at the blanket. Heath and I made our move.

In one swift action I reached in and, unlatching the small leather catch, jerked Pena's gun out of its holster, while Heath dropped the shovel, grabbed Pena by the legs, and pushed him all the way into the car. The moment Heath was out of the way, I slammed the door shut, leaned against it, and shouted, "Gilley!"

An instant later Pena couldn't do anything more than yell in protest; all five locks on the Durango clicked home.

Gilley then dashed away from Cruz to stand with us,

while Pena straightened himself in the backseat and
tried the handle. "Hey!" he shouted through the glass.
"Unlock this door!"

Heath and I ignored him, swiveling around to try to
talk to Cruz. "What the hell's going on?" the deputy
roared, stepping quickly forward, with his hand on his
own gun.

"Wait a second, Deputy!" I said, dropping Pena's
weapon into the dirt and holding up my hands to show
him that I meant him no harm. "Please, just give us one
second to explain!"

"Whitefeather!" Pena roared behind us. "Open this
goddamn door!"

"Jimmy," Heath said to the deputy, his back still to
Pena. "Seriously, give us just a few seconds to explain."

Cruz's eyes darted back and forth between Heath
and me. I could tell he was trying to assess the scene.
"What's going on?" he said.

I exhaled. He was going to let us explain! "I know you
don't believe in this whole black hawk demon thing," I
told him in a rush. "But I'm here to tell you, the demon
isn't just a legend—it's real. And like most demons, it
needs a human host to help it accomplish its goals. Pena
is that human host. It's possessed Pena and it's controlling him. Tonight, as soon as dusk hits, it'll emerge from
Pena's body and go on the hunt looking for more vic-
tims. It got to Daryl and Trudy West, Milton and Beverly,
and Wyatt Benoit, who's buried up that slope in one of
those caves."

Cruz, who'd been holding a slightly crouched position
while he listened to me, did something unexpected at
the end of my speech. He stood straight again, took his
hand off his gun, and laughed.

"Why's he laughing?" Gilley said, coming over to stand next to me again.

I couldn't even fathom it. Meanwhile Pena continued to pound on the glass and we continued to ignore him.

Cruz removed his mirrored shades, and as he did so, a tiny spark of red flashed from their dark depths. "Oh . . . *shit*!" I cried, reaching out to grab Heath by the shirt.

"What?" Gilley shrieked, moving in to huddle next to me. "What is it?"

"It wasn't Pena!" I gasped, pointing to Cruz. "It was *you*!"

A growl rumbled along the ground from somewhere nearby and I felt the hairs on the back of my neck stand straight up on end. I remembered something at that moment—a key piece of the puzzle that I'd never put together. When Heath had given Trudy the slip of paper, he'd said, "This is the number to the Zanto Pueblo sheriff's station. Ask for Sheriff Pena." He hadn't given Trudy Pena's number. He'd given her the *station's* number.

I knew, deep in my bones, that Cruz had taken that call. It was Cruz who'd intercepted the two grave robbers. That's why Trudy hadn't been notified that her grandson was dead. Cruz was trying to find Wyatt without Pena knowing about it. He'd probably held back on the details of the remains found in the desert belonging to Daryl, and I wondered if that's why Pena had lied about being at the dentist's office when Cruz asked him where he'd been when Rex was found. He was probably wondering how much to trust Cruz once he'd talked to Dunlap about a mysterious e-mail exchange. An e-mail sparked by Gilley the night before when he'd asked the county sheriff to e-mail him any info he had on Wyatt.

"Jimmy!" Pena suddenly cried from inside the Durango. "Don't!"

But it was too late. Cruz's face changed into something barely recognizable as human. His eyes narrowed, his lips pulled back into a fearsome snarl, and his nostrils flared, giving him a most terrifying countenance.

"Ahhhhhhhhhh!" Gilley cried, and ran straight for Heath's car, which was closest. But when he got to the door, of course he couldn't open it; it was locked by his own remote control gadget.

"Keys!" I yelled to Heath, who was still standing in front of Cruz, dumbstruck and momentarily frozen. *"Heath! Keys!"* I shouted, turning my attention back to Gil, who was now patting himself down frantically, looking for the remote, which he'd obviously put away, or dropped.

Meanwhile, Pena was kicking at the window with his feet. The window cracked, but it didn't shatter. And then, from the road I saw it coming. A giant, black, slithering thing with fangs and claws and glowing red eyes. It moved toward us with lightning speed, and I barely had time to grab Heath by the elbow and whirl him away from Cruz, whose face continued to take on a more and more monstrous look. He no longer looked human—and no doubt he no longer was.

From his lips came a deep and terrible growl. I'd never heard anything anywhere, living or dead, make that kind of noise. "The car!" I shouted, still tugging on Heath's arm. "Open your car!"

Heath jammed his hand into his jacket pocket and pulled out his key ring, but he was shaking so hard that he dropped it. He bent to retrieve it and as he did so, I saw something move so fast through the air where

Heath's torso had just been that I didn't quite catch it—
but I swear it looked like a giant claw.

I screamed and fell to the earth, crawling backward
away from the black gleaming monstrosity swirling the
dirt around us. Gilley screamed too, and I swear to God
so did Pena.

Heath was the only one who kept his focus—well, besides Cruz, whose eyes blazed red now like something
straight out of Amityville. While I shuffled backward,
Heath clenched his keys and pressed the button to release the locks; then he rolled to the side as the dragon-
like demon nearly pounced right on top of him.

"Get to the car!" Heath cried, crawling to his feet and
trying to lure the monster away from me.

Like an idiot, I didn't do as he said. Instead I grappled
with the canisters at my belt, which each held a magnetic
spike. *Why hadn't I gotten a few out earlier?* I wondered
in the split second before I yanked off the top and tipped
out a spike, getting to my feet.

Heath managed to weave and bob away from the demon for all of three seconds before it swatted at him hard
enough to send him flying back into the dirt. *"Heath!"* I
screamed, and darted straight at the demon, my hand
held high.

As I got close, I could feel the air all around me buzz
with electrostatic energy. The thing was crazy powerful,
and I felt my hair stick out straight on the back of my
neck and along my arms like I'd just walked into a room
crackling with static electricity.

The demon must have heard my cry; it whirled and
raised its giant clawed hand. I got my own arm up in the
nick of time; otherwise, I swear it would have decapi-
tated me. The spike I was holding did exactly what it was

supposed to—it stuck right into the beast's palm and the horrible creature whirled away from me.

That allowed the two seconds I needed to get to Heath and pull him to his feet. He had a terrible wound on his shoulder and across his collarbone and he seemed dazed and barely conscious. *"Up! Up!"* I commanded.

"Throw me the keys!" I heard Pena shout.

I got Heath's arm across my shoulders and began to drag him toward his car, craning my neck to look for the keys in his hands and finding both of them empty. "Shit!" I swore, wrapping my arm around his waist. I'd get him to the car first and worry about getting us out of there second. I moved him maybe five feet when Cruz stepped in front of us. "There's nowhere to run," he said, his voice vibrating and gravelly—just the way you'd expect the devil himself to sound.

I stared at him, my chest heaving as panic filled me head to toe. The demon was somewhere behind me, and I knew that at any moment we were going to be slashed to ribbons.

And I realized that Cruz was right—there was nowhere to run. I couldn't get us to Heath's car in time, and I couldn't fight the demon alone. I could even feel it hovering there behind me, and see its shadow pass over Cruz. I braced for the deathblow, but to my surprise, the action actually happened in front of me.

Someone rushed Cruz, and tackled him to the ground. Reflexively I pulled to the side to avoid them as Cruz and his attacker rolled in the dirt. That terrible growl went up again, and the demon moved away from Heath and me to hover over the pair fighting to the death in the dirt.

"Move!" Gilley shouted, coming to my side and taking up Heath's free arm. It was all the encouragement I

needed. Racing to the Durango, I realized that the brave soul who'd tackled Cruz had to be Pena, as he was no longer stuck inside Heath's car.

"We have to help him!" I shouted as we arrived at the SUV.

"Give me the keys and I'll run that thing and Cruz over!" Gilley offered.

But the only keys I had were to the rental. And that gave me an idea. "Stay with Heath!" I told Gil, ducking under Heath's arm and racing to the sage bush ten yards away. I rounded the bush and came up short. There stood Sam!

"Use the urn!" he commanded.

Behind me I heard a terrible scream—the cry of someone caught in the jaws of a hideous monster.

"The urn!" Sam repeated. "Quickly, M. J.! You have to use it!"

I flew into action, turning back for the new urn that Mrs. Lujan had created, which was closer to the Durango. *"No!"* yelled Sam, stopping me. "The other one!"

I didn't have time to ask him what the hell he meant, so I turned again, pulled open the door, and grabbed the other clay pot. For good measure, I darted to the new urn too. With effort I held both bulky urns tightly to my chest. Pena's bloodcurdling screams seemed to go on and on. "How?" I shouted at Sam when I realized I didn't know what to do next.

"Go!" Sam said, pointing back toward the others.

It was the only direction he gave me, and I didn't hang around to ask for more. Instead, I flew back to Heath and Gilley's side. Gil was trying to get Heath inside the Durango, but he was shaking so hard and had gone so pale that I knew he was close to fainting.

I looked next at the source of the screams. Pena was writhing on the ground while the demon slashed and tore at him. He was covered in blood, and Cruz looked on as if he was truly enjoying the show.

I held both urns and screamed at the top of my lungs, *"STOP!"*

Of course, no one did, but Cruz cast me a casual glance over his shoulder. His laughter turned my blood to ice. "Throw down the urn!" I heard from right behind me. It was Sam's voice. "Go on, M. J.! Throw it!"

I didn't know which one he meant, and I hesitated. Sam seemed to read my mind. "Throw the old one!"

Without hesitation I set the new urn down, lifted the Whitefeather family urn up high, then threw it hard onto the ground, where it smashed into a gazillion pieces.

While I watched, something seemed to be rising from the wreckage of the broken pottery in front of me. And in the next instant, I realized that it was white smoke, curling and swirling in separate but distinct columns, and with it came voices.

Time seemed to stand still as I watched the smoke curl and weave and form itself into shapes that looked strangely human. Before I knew it, I realized that the shapes *were* human! Where there had been only dirt and scrub now stood at least two dozen souls! At the head of the throng was a tall, muscular man with bronze skin, a gorgeous face, and a long flowing mane of jet-black hair intertwined with an array of white feathers and one long lock of white hair at his temple.

He looked so much like Heath that for a moment I thought I might be hallucinating. I had no time to think on it, however, because out of his mouth rose a war cry that filled my chest with hope and courage. He raised his fist as he cried, and every other soul with him did the same.

And in the next instant, I knew exactly what to do. I reached to my belt and pulled at the lid of another grenade. Tipping it out, I raised my hand too and joined the chorus of cries.

The effect was electrifying. The air buzzed and crackled with energy, and the demon whirled away from Pena and turned to face the gathering mob. The warrior at the front, who had to be Whitefeather himself, stepped forward and rushed at the demon, never losing pitch as his cry went on and on. His descendants joined him and to my total shock, so did Heath! Bleeding and pale, he'd somehow found the strength to join his ancestors, and as one the crowd charged straight for Cruz and the demon black hawk spirit.

Cruz turned away from the approaching mob just as I joined the spirits, fist held high and moving straight for my target. I felt a sense of invincibility as I ran, surrounded by warriors and brave women alike, all charging with unyielding courage straight at the demon who may very well have taken a few of their lives.

We fell upon the demon, I moved to the side of the monster, and Heath aimed right at the center, raising his own spike before bringing it down into the heart of the beast. But of course, this beast had no heart. It had only darkness, and this poured out of the thing like sludge. I drove my own spike down into the side of the demon, and another thick gush of sludge poured out, coating my hands and turning my stomach. In the back of my mind I knew the substance had to be ectoplasm, and it left my hands sticky and smelled distinctly like sulfur.

We all attacked without mercy, Heath being the most

ferocious as he drove his spike again and again into the demon, who writhed and clawed at everyone around him, trying in vain to throw us all off. But Whitefeather and his tribe had gained the advantage. At one point I glanced up to see that the warrior had wrapped his powerful arms around the neck of the beast, pulling and tugging it and the rest of us closer and closer to the urn I'd set down just yards away.

Heath seemed to realize what his ancestor was trying to do, because he looked up, met Whitefeather's eye, then left his position at the center of the beast to join him at the demon's head and help pull the monster closer to the vessel.

All this I took in as I brought down my spike again and again, feeling the demon's energy slowly draining from it—but it was a powerful creature and it would not give in so easily.

We fought, all of us, with as much vigor and commitment as we had, each one of us taking up the war cry over and over, and slowly, painfully, we moved the demon inch by inch closer to the urn that would ensnare it.

And we almost made it too. It was as we were within feet of the urn that I began to see the black gleaming scales of the thing flake off and move into the neck of the urn. I never stopped stabbing it with my spike, willing the beast to die either at my hand or within the urn, but just as victory seemed imminent, I saw the vessel being lifted off the ground.

Distracted, I paused in my attack to see that Cruz had gone for the urn, and had hoisted it above his head, ready to dash it to the ground. The demon must have sensed that Cruz had done this, because it struggled with a renewed energy that quickly turned the tide against us.

I was flung to the side with a blow to my cheek that had me seeing stars, and even the powerful team of Whitefeather and Heath were losing their grip. The demon freed one of its arms and swiped at the ancient warrior, and to my horror I saw that the demon actually drew blood!

Heath snarled and fought to hold on to the beast's head, but it was writhing with furious intensity, and I knew he couldn't hold on to it much longer.

And then, out of nowhere came three explosions so loud that they made my ears ring. I saw Cruz's twisted demonic face go slack as three large red blossoms of color stained his uniform, and for an instant there was nothing but surprise in his eyes and possibly a bit of the former man reflected in them, and then he sank to his knees, the urn still held high above his head.

As his eyes rolled up and his body began to fall backward, Gilley dashed forward, caught the urn, and slid out of the way.

Heath then did something extraordinary. He said something to his ancestor in Zuni, and when White-feather nodded, Heath let go, came around to the front of the demon, held his spike high, then brought it down one final time with a primal cry so true and pure that I felt it reverberate right through me.

As Heath plunged the spike into the demon's head, right between its eyes, it gave one final horrible shriek and melted underneath Heath, curling into its own column of black smoke and winding its way into the urn that Gilley still held clutched to his chest.

All around me every one of the tribal members seemed to evaporate into white smoke and was carried away by the wind into the mouth of the urn too. The last to go was Whitefeather, who stood for a moment in front of Heath, laid a hand on his shoulder, and spoke to him. I didn't know what he said, but he punctuated the words by putting a fist to his heart, then tapped his finger to the white lock at his temple before flashing Heath a brilliant smile and vanishing into white smoke.

"Heath!" I cried when the spirits had all disappeared. Getting to my feet, I raced over to him as his strength finally gave out and he sagged against me, bleeding and barely conscious.

Still, he managed to grin at me and say, "That was *intense*!"

Chapter 16

Heath and I waited outside the central Pueblo courthouse for the verdict. He and I had both testified before the tribal judge and jury as to what'd happened out in the foothills, and my stomach twisted with the thought of Sheriff Pena being sent to jail for shooting his deputy three times in the chest.

I thought it a miracle that Pena had lived through the demon's attack, and the poor man would have scars on his face, chest, arms, and hands for the rest of his life, but the true miracle was that he'd been physically able to shoot Cruz at all. And thank God he had, or it was quite likely that we all would have been killed.

We'd been encouraged by Pena's tribal lawyer to simply present our separate stories about the events of that day in their entirety, and not edit or delete certain details because we were worried that we wouldn't be believed. "Understanding of the way the spirits work runs deep in the Pueblo culture," he'd advised. "Your white man's jury would listen to what happened and think you two were a bunch of Froot Loops, but here, we know these evil spirits exist, and given the right circumstances, they can possess even the most honest man."

So, we'd gone in there one at a time, me first, then Gilley, and finally Heath, and we'd told the courtroom everything that'd occurred, even how Gil and I had snuck into the Zanto library and stolen their histories book.

I'd gotten a few disapproving glares from the jury, but I didn't think it would do Pena any favors to withhold how it was that we had learned so much about the black hawk spirit.

As nontribal members, Gil and I weren't allowed to sit in on the trial as it proceeded, but Heath did and he'd come out at every recess to report what was going on.

We'd learned a lot we didn't know about Cruz as the facts came out. The biggest surprise was that Jimmy Cruz was the illegitimate son of one Rex Whitefeather.

Rex had gotten a white woman pregnant when he was seventeen. He'd hidden this fact from almost everyone, including most members of his family (save his sister), until Jimmy was about fifteen and started getting into trouble. Rex offered to bring him to the Pueblo and put him to work and it was right around the time that Jimmy first showed up that the original Whitefeather urn went missing.

I had a feeling that Jimmy resented the fact that his own father wouldn't claim him as a Whitefeather, and stole the urn out of spite. I also believed he buried it up in the caves, and one day when he saw two grave robbers carrying something that looked like that urn, he chased them down, and in the ensuing struggle, the urn was broken and the demon released.

Jimmy was the perfect host for the demon, as it was clear he resented the Whitefeathers and knew all about their comings and goings. With him as a guide, the demon could track them down, wait until they were isolated and vulnerable, and kill them one by one.

Jimmy could also work to keep a lid on the two grave robbers. He let the demon tear one to pieces, and the other—Wyatt, who'd managed to escape—did make that call just like he'd threatened to on Bissell's answering machine. Cruz met him at the storage facility, killed him, and took his body back to the cave, burying it in the hole where the old urn had been kept.

On his way back he'd seen Beverly, who must've wondered what Cruz was doing up in the hills and maybe why he had blood on him. (The coroner had found Wyatt's throat slashed.)

Jimmy had called up the demon that night, and it'd chased her right into that tree.

And we also knew that Trudy had made that call to the Zanto sheriff's station. Her phone records showed that she'd placed the call about two hours before she'd been attacked. I knew she had the great misfortune to reach Cruz instead of Pena, and trusting the deputy, she'd probably told him she was calling about her grandson, Daryl, believing the department might know where he was. We figured Cruz had wanted her dead for two reasons: First, he probably figured she knew about her grandson's grave robbing, and second, she might call back another time, get Pena instead of Cruz, and inform him about Wyatt and Daryl. Pena testified that until he spoke to Sheriff Dunlap, he'd had no clue about the remains found in the foothills. Cruz had handled that investigation all on his own, and he'd worked to keep it quiet so that Pena wouldn't get suspicious.

The hard part was that Heath and I knew we'd inadvertently led Cruz and the demon right to her. Letting go of the guilt was difficult for both of us.

I looked over at my sweetheart while we waited, and my eyes lingered on his face. He'd noticeably changed in the time since he and his ancestor had battled the black hawk demon. For starters, Heath was now sporting a shock of white hair right at his temple. I'd asked him what Whitefeather had said to him out in the foothills. "My ancestor called me brother," he'd told me, the pride leaking into the smile he wore when he recalled the memory. "He said I was the brother of his heart, and true son of his tribe."

I couldn't think of more powerful words for Heath, who'd always felt like he and his mom were outcasts from the tribe. I think Whitefeather had done quite a bit to heal old wounds for my sweetie, and for that, I'd always be grateful.

Beyond that, though, Heath had changed in more subtle ways. He walked differently—with more purpose and confidence. He spoke differently—also with more purpose and confidence. And his eyes had changed. They were less haunted, more ... alert, focused, and wise.

He'd always been a gorgeous man—but now he was striking, breathtaking even. It was hard to put into words, but he wasn't the same guy six years my junior I'd met a year and a half ago. Now he had this air of supreme confidence about him, a man other men would readily listen to, and I had to admit I was seriously digging it. I'd loved him before, of course, but this renewed sense of belonging to the tribe had awakened the true Heath, I think. A guy I could seriously get serious about.

"You're doing it again," Heath said without looking at me.

"What?"

"Staring at me like you've never seen me before."

I smiled. "What if I was staring at you because I had seen you before, and wanted to see more of you all the time?"

Heath cut smoldering eyes to me and my pulse quickened. "That could be arranged," he said.

I grinned. "When?"

Heath looked at his watch and sighed. "After the verdict if it gets announced today," he promised.

Then I remembered another promise. "But we're supposed to go to what's left of Milton's cabin today." Sam had come to me in a dream the night before and told me that he'd managed to find Milton sifting through the wreckage of his cabin, but he'd been unable to convince his son that he'd been murdered. Sam had told me to show up at the cabin around dusk, because he was predicting rain in the forecast and knew the atmosphere would be perfect for us to find Milton and talk him over to the other side.

After that, Heath and I were going to head to Trudy's trailer and make sure both she and Daryl had gotten across too. And, I thought, while we were at it, we might as well work to make sure Wyatt wasn't left out either.

"So," Heath said, tucking a lock of my hair behind my ear, "after we're done dealing with ghosties, you and I will put out the do-not-disturb sign on the door and finally get some one-on-one time together."

My grin widened. That was exactly what I was hoping he'd say.

"A little help, please!" we heard from down the street. Heath and I swiveled to see Gil carrying a large paper sack while balancing three soft drinks in a cup holder. I moved to get up, but Heath beat me to it, and just as they arrived back at our spot under a large tree, the courthouse doors opened and Mrs. Lujan stepped out. "The jury's back!" she said, waving her son inside.

Heath handed me his soft drink, gave me a kiss, and said, "I'll be back soon. You two go ahead and eat."

I watched him disappear into the building with his mother and sighed contentedly. "Uh-oh," Gil said.

I swiveled my eyes to him. "What?"

"You've got it bad, girl."

I ignored his comment and asked, "Have you noticed a change in Heath recently?"

Gilley handed me my sandwich and began to unwrap his. "You mean, like how he's suddenly gone from just pretty sexy to crazy hot, hot, *hot*?"

I nodded. "So it's not just me?"

"No, it's not just you."

I felt my lips quirk into a smile. And then Gilley said something really unusual for him. "I had a dream about your mom last night," he told me.

I'd been about to bite into my sandwich, but I was so surprised by his statement that I held very still and just waited for him to continue.

"I was dreaming about visiting that old house we used to live in—you remember the one on Cypress Street with that big back porch?"

I nodded eagerly and set the sandwich aside. "What'd Mama say?"

"Well," Gilley said, picking at the crust on his sandwich, "she told me that she really liked how I'd grown up, and that she was really, really happy you and I were still best friends."

I swallowed past the lump in my throat and tried not to well up too much. Gil hated it when I got soppy. "Anything else?"

Gilley met my eyes then. "She said, 'Thank you for looking after my Mary Jane and please tell her that I approve of that young Mr. Whitefeather.'"

I barked out a laugh and tears formed in my eyes anyway. Wiping them quickly, I patted Gil on the back and said, "Thanks for sharing, Gil."

After that, we ate in companionable silence for a while until the doors opened again and people began to pour out. Most of them were talking excitedly, and it was hard to tell if that was because there was a guilty or an innocent verdict given, or maybe there'd been a hung jury.

Finally, however, Heath emerged and just by his expression I knew the verdict. "Innocent?" I said, putting aside my sandwich and jumping to my feet.

Heath nodded, broke into a wide smile, and held out his arms. I raced into them and for the first time in what felt like forever, all was right with the world.

Read ahead for a sneak peek at the next
Ghost Hunter Mystery,

WHAT A GHOUL WANTS

Coming in January 2013 from Obsidian.

My best friend, Gilley, has this list. It's not necessarily a long list, but it's definitely growing. The list is best described as:

Things That Give Gilley the Weirds.

Once an item gets listed, it's never removed. If you make it onto the list, you're there for life.

It's probably good then that there's only one actual named person on Gilley's list—Dakota Fanning. Why her? Well, in Gilley's words, "No one that young should be that talented and that smart. It's just weird."

Other notable items include: mice—but not rats or bugs; lady parts—for obvious reasons (or, if it's not so obvious, Gil plays for the boys' team); baby corn ("It's not corn but it *looks* like corn and that *can't* be okay!"); leggings worn as pants; people who give an uncommon spelling to an otherwise common name, like Jyan, Mykel, or Dyafdd; and Cirque de Soleil acrobats ("*No* one should be able to bend like that!").

Animated talking animals are near the top of the list,

and if you combine these with Dakota Fanning—say in the movie *Charlotte's Web*, for example—you're liable to send Gil right over the edge.

Last on Gilley's list, but certainly not least, are ghosts.

Yes, you read that right. Ghosts give Gilley the weirds. Which can be super problematic due to the fact that Gil is also the technical adviser on our ghost-hunting cable TV show, *Ghoul Getters*.

In fact, the ghost thing was proving more than a little problematic on this particular late night—or early morning according to my watch, now set to Greenwich Mean Time—as I squatted next to Gil in the middle of the aisle of the British Airway's jet that had brought us back to England.

"Gil," I said for the eleventieth time. "Please. For the love of God, let go of the armrest and come off the plane."

"Sir, ma'am, we really must insist," said the most unhelpful flight attendant ever. "You *must* deplane immediately."

Gil ignored him and focused his fearful gaze on me. "Please don't make me, M. J.," he begged. "I can't do it."

I rubbed his arm. "Sweetie," I said, fighting to keep my lids open. I was so exhausted I felt punch-drunk. "Come off the plane and we'll talk about it, okay?"

"Talking about it means you'll talk me into it," he countered. He knew me too well.

My eyes flickered nervously to the front of the plane, where Gopher, our TV producer, stood watching us with an impatient and irritated look on his face. "Gil," I said (eleventy times plus one if you're counting), "I swear to you, I'm not going to try and talk you into anything other than coming off the plane and heading to bed. I know you gotta be exhausted, right?"

Gil bit his lip. "I want to go back," he whispered.

"Ma'am," said the flight attendant. "If he doesn't de-plane, I'll have no choice but to alert security."

I turned my head and glared so hard at the attendant that he frowned and took two steps back. I then refocused on Gilley. "Honey," I said gently. "This plane is parked for the night right here. It's not going anywhere for the next six hours at least. You don't want to sit here for six straight hours, do you?"

"If it means going back home, I'll stay put," Gil said stubbornly.

"But you won't be able to sleep," I told him.

"I can sleep okay," he replied, and I knew he was right. Gil could sleep standing up.

"There'll be no food," I tried next.

I heard a tiny gurgle from Gil's stomach. "I'll be fine."

I sighed and thought for a second. Then I had it. "Well," I said, "you won't be able to use the restroom, Gil. And I saw you down a bottled water and a couple of Cokes on the way here. That's gonna be hard to hold for the next six hours."

Gil shifted in his seat.

"I mean, don't you have to go even right now?" I asked, standing up like I didn't care anymore if he refused to get off the plane.

Gil squirmed again and crossed his legs.

"I know *I* really have to use the restroom," I lied. I'd hit the head right before our final approach. "Yep. Has to be a pretty uncomfortable feeling knowing you'll have to hold it for the next six . . . long . . . hours."

Gil gripped the armrests tightly and set his jaw with determination. "I can do it," he said.

I nodded like I totally believed him. "Sure you can.

While you're holding it I'm gonna hit the ladies' room. Then I'm gonna head to the hotel and drink a nice big glass of water. Then I'm gonna take a nice long shower. You know the kind where you just turn the water on and stand under it forever? It's like standing in the rain. Water just streaming down and down . . ."

With an irritated grunt Gil unfastened his seat belt and bolted to his feet. Tearing down the aisle he nearly took out Gopher as he passed him on his way off the plane.

I bent down and grabbed Gilley's gear before hurrying after him, making sure to send the flight attendant one final glare before the exit.

By the time I made it to the top of the Jetway, Gil wasn't in sight. My boyfriend and fellow ghostbuster, Heath, was there in the seating area, though, waiting for me. "He ran into the men's room," he told me when I sidled up next to him and looked all around for any sign of Gil.

"Phew," I said. "I thought I'd never get him off the plane."

"What's gotten into him?" Heath asked me.

I rolled my eyes, and made a face at Gopher, who'd also just appeared at the top of the Jetway. "Gopher just *had* to tell Gilley all about the moors."

"I told you not to let them sit next to each other," Heath reminded me.

I shook my head and sighed. "It's not like I could've done anything to stop Gil from sitting next to Gopher once our oh so helpful producer announced he had a two-pound bag of M&M's for the flight."

Heath smirked. "How many of those two pounds do you think went into Gil?"

"At least one and a half, which of course gave Gil a

really good sugar high, and he soaked up everything Gopher had to tell him about the moors."

The moors I was referring to were located in northern Wales in a place called Penbigh, and by the looks of our research, it appeared to be one of the most haunted places in Britain. There were literally scores of ghost stories, legends, and myths about things that went bump in the night to choose from.

It was exactly the type of location we needed after shooting our last episode in Dunkirk, which had been a complete bust. The most we'd managed to record were some faint disembodied footsteps and the sound of a horse whinnying in an abandoned stable. Otherwise, it'd been a whole lotta footage of Heath and me looking for spooks and finding nothing. And that shoot had unfortunately come immediately after a particularly harrowing haunting that had involved Heath's tribe and the Pueblo he once lived on. But we had no footage of that ghost-bust because it'd involved a death in Heath's family and our crew hadn't been with us at the time.

Now that *Ghoul Getters* had switched networks, I knew the pressure to produce something good was heaped on all of our shoulders. We needed to score a good episode and do it quick, before the new network execs canceled us.

As we were wrapping up the shoot in Dunkirk, our two production assistants had alerted Heath, Gopher, and me to the terrifically haunted location in northern Wales. We'd all thought that the moors held such promise, which was why we'd all agreed that we should come here and investigate it next—well, except Gilley. None of us had told him about the moors and all the ghosties haunting them. And the reason we hadn't told him was that for the past few weeks, he'd been acting crazy. I'm talking crazier than normal, which for Gil meant *crazy*!

He's always been afraid of the spooks, but as long as we give him a nice, safe place to work out of, like a van parked somewhere outside the haunted zone, and keep him relatively in the dark about what we might encounter, he's usually more than willing to provide his considerable technical expertise to our shoots.

But in Dunkirk something happened, and I still didn't quite know what. Gil stopped showing up for our morning meetings and every time he thought he saw something creepy on one of his monitors, he flipped out. I'd been called off the location a couple of times to try to talk some sense into Gil, and my calm reasoning had worked well enough to finish the shoot and load him onto a plane, but I hadn't counted on Gopher spilling the beans about how haunted the Penbigh moors were. And I had a feeling Gopher had even highlighted the fact that we'd be focusing our investigation on one particular section of the moors where the ghost of a woman was said to lure young unsuspecting men to their deaths by drowning them in one of the boggy marshes or the surrounding lake.

It seemed that was Gil's breaking point. Right before landing, he'd convinced himself that the ghostly woman was going to come after him specifically, because that's what all the other ghosts have always done. Pick on Gilley.

The sad thing is . . . he's mostly right. Gil makes a nice target for a spook. It must be something about the electromagnetic frequency he puts out, because ghosties just love him. Or, more to the point, they love to torture and terrorize him. I've never actually told him this, but I've been in enough haunted locales to understand that Gilley is a magnet for spectral activity. It's like he's wearing Hai Karate for spooks or something, but I also couldn't think about doing a ghostbust without him. Gil's my best friend, and he's been my best friend since I was in grade school. For most of my life, in fact, it's been me and Gilley, facing down every challenge the world had to offer. We'd always managed okay, and I had no reason to doubt that this little episode was just another challenge to work through together.

So, after ten minutes of waiting near the men's room door with no sign of him, I sent Heath in to check on Gil. He was back in a minute to tell me that Gilley had locked himself in one of the stalls and wasn't coming out until morning.

I turned to Gopher at that point and shouted, *"Why?"*

"I didn't know he didn't know!" our producer exclaimed. "You guys gotta tell me what's safe to tell Gil and what isn't!"

"Nothing," I growled. "*Nothing* is safe to tell him, Goph! You got that?"

Gopher shifted the strap of his duffle to his other shoulder. "I do now, M. J.," he said contritely.

I then looked about for the rest of our production crew, spotting John, Meg, and Kim. I waved them over. "I'm sure you can tell we have a situation," I began.

"Gilley?" John said.

"Yep."

"What do you need?" he asked. I liked John. He was a good guy and he was always ready to do what I asked.

"I need for you three"—I said, pointing to him, Heath, and Gopher—"to go in there and get Gil out of that stall. Then, we've somehow got to get him through customs without causing an international incident, and take him to the hotel. He just needs a good night's sleep. He'll be okay by morning."

Heath, John, and Gopher all exchanged uncomfortable looks. They knew how big of a challenge it was gonna be to get Gilley to go anywhere he didn't want to.

Still, without a word they marched into the men's room, and me, Kim, and Meg all stood outside, where we heard a pretty good commotion erupt.

At last the four of them appeared, Gilley's torso slung between Heath and John while Gopher carried his legs, and all the while Gil put up a really good fight, kicking and struggling for all he was worth. I looked around at the alarmed passengers and sure enough, two security guards began to trot over. "I guess avoiding an international incident was a little much to hope for," I grumbled, moving to intercept the guards.

Six hours later we were still being detained by those same guards in a stuffy detention room at the Manchester Airport. By this time, Gilley was asleep on my shoulder, having thrown his hissy fit and exhausted himself, but managing to get us into deep doo-doo in the process. He was lucky I loved him and had known him all my life.

Still, I was pretty angry at him. Shifting in my seat I pulled my shoulder out from under his cheek, and his head lolled forward. He snorted himself awake. Looking about blearily, he asked, "What's happening?"

"Nothing," I said through gritted teeth. "We're still being detained."

Gil yawned and took in all the angry faces of our crew glaring back at him. "You guys shoulda just let me get back on that plane and go home," he groused.

"Trust me," I told him, "the six of us are currently unanimously in favor of voting you off the island."

Gil looked down at his hands and sighed. "I can't help it," he said. "I'm really scared this time, M. J."

I frowned as I felt my irritation ebb. Darn it. Why'd he have to sound so sad and pathetic? "What's so different about this time?" I asked gently. "Seriously, Gil. We've faced some super-crazy stuff before and you've come out of it okay. What's got you so spooked this time?"

Gil leaned his head back against the wall, and I could see that his eyes had gotten moist and he was trying to hold back the tears. That took me aback. Sure, Gil was emotional and flamboyant, but he didn't usually cry unless he was really shaken up. "It's just . . ." he began, without adding anything more.

"Just what, honey?" I encouraged. "Come on, Gil. Tell me. What's got you so freaked out?"

Gil wiped his eyes and cleared his throat. He wouldn't look at me, which troubled me even more. "At some point," he finally said, "I think my luck's gonna run out. Someday on one of these busts, either you or me or Heath or one of our crew is gonna end up dead, M. J."

"Oh, Gil," I whispered, laying a hand on his arm.

I wanted to throw my arms around him and hug him until he wasn't afraid anymore, but at that point Gilley looked up at me with big liquid eyes and said, "And this time, I really, really feel that it's gonna be me."

Gilley then dissolved into real tears and I hardly knew what to do. I'd never seen him so undone before, so I threw my arms around him and hugged him as tight as I could. When Heath's concerned eyes met mine across the room, I shook my head. I found I couldn't talk. And deep in my heart I noticed for the first time my own sense of foreboding. It was like a small dark hole began to form in the center of my chest, and try as I might, I couldn't ignore the feeling that maybe, this time, Gilley's intuition might be right.